The Clockwork Century novels

Boneshaker
Dreadnought
Ganymede
The Inexplicables

The Inexplicables

Cherie Priest

TOR

First published 2012 in the US by Tom Doherty Associates, LLC

This edition published 2012 by Tor
an imprint of Pan Macmillan, a division of Macmillan Publishers Limited
Pan Macmillan, 20 New Wharf Road, London N1 9RR
Basingstoke and Oxford
Associated companies throughout the world
www.panmacmillan.com

ISBN 978-1-4472-2559-1

Copyright © Cherie Priest 2012

Map by Jennifer Hanover

The right of Cherie Priest to be identified as the
author of this work has been asserted by her in accordance
with the Copyright, Designs and Patents Act 1988.

3 5 7 9 8 6 4 2

A CIP catalogue record for this book is available from
the British Library.

Printed and bound by CPI Group (UK) Ltd, Croydon, CR0 4YY

Visit **www.panmacmillan.com** to read more about all our books
and to buy them. You will also find features, author interviews and
news of any author events, and you can sign up for e-newsletters
so that you're always first to hear about our new releases.

For Angeline and her father

For Seattle

Acknowledgments

It feels strange knowing that *The Inexplicables* will probably be the last book I write in Seattle. I won't say "absolutely the last" because one never knows, and it's not like I'm planning to run away and never look back; but as you may or may not know, my husband and I bought a house in Tennessee . . . and by the time you read this, we will be living in Chattanooga (once again).

We lived in Seattle for six years, and in many ways, the city was very, very kind to me. It gave me *Boneshaker*, after all—as well as the subsequent books in the Clockwork Century series. None of these stories would've ever happened if I hadn't come out West in 2006, so I will always be grateful for my time here.

Thank you, Seattle. You gave me more than I deserved, and I was not always gracious about it. I hope I've done you proud with these stories. They are a song of appreciation.

So. Yes.

When it comes to more specific thanks, I scarcely know where to begin. But this time, I'll save the usual suspects for the end and start with the local crew.

Thanks of the highest order go to the bookstore folks: Duane Wilkins, plus Caitlin and Art, and everyone else at the University Book Store; Steve Winter and Vlad Verano at Third Place Books; and all the kind people at the Seattle Mystery Book Store, who have carried a torch for my Eden books (much to my continued delight).

Thanks of a matching caliber go to my wonderful friends of the writing and non-writing variety. To the Cap Hill Crew— Ellen Milne, Suezie Hagy, and Nova Barlow; to Jillian and Pete Venters—two lovely and loving grown-up Goths who I simply can't recommend enough; Richelle Mead and Mark Henry for being cornerstones in my first actual group of Writer Buddies; and to Kat Richardson, another cornerstone—who has become one of my very dearest friends in the last couple of years. Also, I must note the amazing Mary Robinette Kowal, who, it must be mentioned with some small measure of irony, hails from Chattanooga. But I did not know her—or come to adore her—until we met on the West Coast.

Further thanks to the following folks for their outstanding support in a personal and professional nature, though they aren't Northwest locals: George R. R. Martin, for teaching me more about writing in six months than a four-year B.A. and three years of grad school ever did; Sam Sykes, a damn fine convention pal and all-round great correspondent; John Scalzi, for good guesses and secret-keeping; William Schafer, for his persistent waving of pom-poms in my general direction, even though I'm a horrible person who hasn't written that next novella for him yet; Mike Lee, for talking me off the ledge repeatedly re: THINGS THAT ARE SECRET and might be secret forever; Wil Wheaton, for his effervescent enthusiasm and unwavering positivity; Warren Ellis, a man I can't help but idolize and constantly want to hug, so it's just as well (for his sake) that he's overseas; Jess Nevins, the kindest, most brilliant archivist in Texas and well beyond; and to everyone else in the clubhouse that serves the world—you people know who you are, and why I love you.

And now to the publishing team—the people who prop me up, urge me on, keep me moving, and make all the magic happen.

A million and one thanks to my editor, the inimitable Liz Go-rinsky, who saves me every damn day; my amazing agent, Jennifer Jackson, because, dear God, I don't know how I'd ever survive this business without her on my side; my publicist, Aisha Cloud, who sends me on the road and takes care of me while I'm there; Irene Gallo in the art department for all the beautiful covers; and everyone else at Tor who helps these books find their way into the world.

Lifesavers, each and every one of them.

And finally, thanks to my husband, Jaymes Aric Annear—who loves me enough to come home with me. I couldn't do it without him.

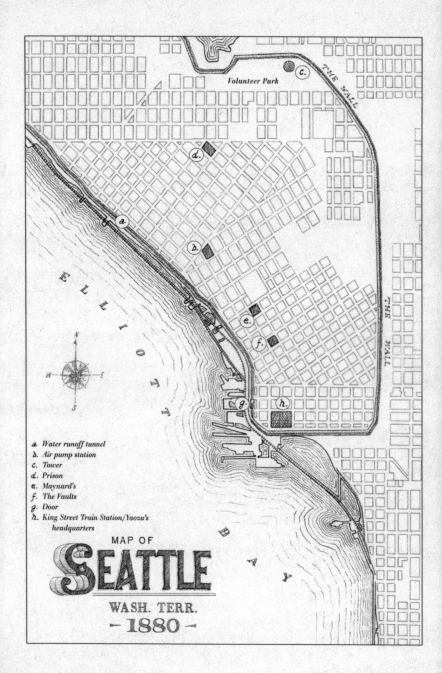

Volunteer Park

THE WALL

THE WALL

ELLIOTT

BAY

N
W E
S

a. Water runoff tunnel
b. Air pump station
c. Tower
d. Prison
e. Maynard's
f. The Vaults
g. Door
h. King Street Train Station/Yaozu's
   headquarters

MAP OF

SEATTLE

WASH. TERR.
~ 1880 ~

So I became a dreamer, and acquired an indisposition to all bodily activity; and I was fretful and inordinately passionate, and as I could not play at anything, and was slothful, I was despised and hated by the boys.

—SAMUEL TAYLOR COLERIDGE,
in a letter to his friend Thomas Poole

The Inexplicables

 *One*

Rector "Wreck'em" Sherman was delivered to the Sisters of Loving Grace Home for Orphans the week it opened, on February 9, 1864. His precise age was undetermined, but estimated at approximately two years. He was filthy, hungry, and shoeless, wearing nothing on his feet except a pair of wool socks someone, somewhere, had lovingly knitted for him before the city went to hell. Whether she had been mother or nursemaid, governess or grandmother, no one knew and no one ever learned; but the child's vivid red hair, pearl white skin, and early suggestions of freckles implied rather strongly that he was no relation to the Duwamish woman who brought him to the shelter. She'd carried him there, along with another child who did not survive the month. Her own name was lost to history, or it was lost to incomplete records only sometimes kept in the wake of the Boneshaker catastrophe.

The little boy who lived, the one with hair the color of freshly cut carrots, was handed over to a nun with eyes too sad for someone so young and a habit too large for someone so small. The native woman who toted Rector told her only his name, and that "There is no one left to love him. I do not know this other boy, or what he is called. I found him in the bricks."

For a long time, Rector did not talk.

He did not babble or gesture or make any sound at all, except to cry. When he did, it was a strange cry—all the nuns agreed, and nodded their accord sadly, as though something ought to be done about it—a soft, hooting sob like the desolate summons of a baby owl. And when the dark-haired boy who'd been his circumstantial companion passed away from Blight poisoning, or typhoid, or cholera, or whatever else ravaged the surviving population that week . . . Rector stopped crying as well.

He grew into a pallid, gangly thing, skinny like most of the refugees. At first, people in the Outskirts had bartered for what they could and took ships and airships out into the Sound to fish; but within six months, Blight-poisoned rainwater meant that little would grow near the abandoned city. And many of the children—the ones like Rector, lost and recovered—were stunted by the taint of what had happened. They were halted, slowed, or twisted by the very air they'd breathed when they were still young enough to be shaped by such things.

All in all, Rector's teenage condition could've been worse.

He could've had legs of uneven lengths, or eyes without whites—only yellows. He might've become a young man without any hair, even eyebrows or lashes. He might've had far too many teeth, or none at all. His spine might have turned as his height overtook him, leaving him lame and coiled, walking with tremendous difficulty and sitting in pain.

But there was nothing wrong with him on the outside.

And therefore, able-bodied and quick-minded (if sometimes mean, and sometimes accused of petty criminal acts), he was expected to become a man and support himself. Either he could join the church and take up the ministry—which no one expected, or even, frankly, wanted—or he could trudge across the mud flats and take up a job in the new sawmill (if he was lucky) or at the waterworks plant (if he was not). Regardless, time had run out on Rector Sherman, specific age unknown, but certainly—by now—at least eighteen years.

And that meant he had to go.

Today.

Sometime after midnight and long before breakfast—the time at which he would be required to vacate the premises—Rector awoke as he usually did: confused and cold, and with an aching head, and absolutely everything hurting.

Everything often hurt, so he had taken to soothing the pain with the aid of sap, which would bring on another pain and call for a stronger dose. And when it had all cycled through him, when his blood was thick and sluggish, when there was nothing else to stimulate or sedate or propel him through his nightmares . . . he woke up. And he wanted more.

It was all he could think about, usurping even the astonishing fact that he had no idea where he was going to sleep the next night, or how he was going to feed himself after breakfast.

He lay still for a full minute, listening to his heart surge, bang, slam, and settle.

This loop, this perpetual rolling hiccup of discomfort, was an old friend. His hours stuttered. They stammered, repeated themselves, and left him at the same place as always, back at the beginning. Reaching for more, even when there wasn't any.

Downstairs in the common room the great grandfather clock chimed two—so that was one mystery solved without lifting his head off the pillow. A minor victory, but one worth counting. It was two o'clock in the morning, so he had five hours left before the nuns would feed him and send him on his way.

Rector's thoughts moved as if they struggled through glue, but they gradually churned at a more ordinary pace as his body reluctantly pulled itself together. He listened over the thudding, dull bang of his heart and detected two sets of snores, one slumbering mumble, and the low, steady breaths of a deep, silent sleeper.

Five boys to a room. He was the oldest.

And he was the last one present who'd been orphaned by the

Blight. Everyone else from that poisoned generation had grown up and moved on to something else by now—everyone but Rector, who had done his noble best to refuse adulthood or die before meeting it, whichever was easier.

He whispered to the ceiling, "One more thing I failed at for sure." Because, goddammit, he was still alive.

In the back of his mind, a shadow shook. It wavered across his vision, a flash of darkness shaped like someone familiar, someone gone. He blinked to banish it, but failed at that, too.

It hovered at the far edge of what he could see, as opposed to what he couldn't.

He breathed, "No," knowing that the word had no power. He added, "I know you're not really here." But that was a lie, and it was meaningless. He didn't know. He wasn't sure. Even with his eyes smashed shut like they were welded that way, he could see the figure outlined against the inside of his lids. It was skinny like him, and a little younger. Not much, but enough to make a difference in size. It moved with the furtive unhappiness of something that has often been mocked or kicked.

It shifted on featherlight feet between the boys' beds, like a feral cat ready to dodge a hurled shoe.

Rector huddled beneath his insufficient blankets and drew his feet against himself, knees up, panting under the covers and smelling his own stale breath. "Go away," he commanded aloud. "I don't know why you keep coming here."

Because you're here.

"I didn't hurt you."

You sent me someplace where you knew I'd get hurt.

"No, I only told you how to get there. Everything else was *you*. It was all your own doing. You're just looking for someone to blame. You're just mad about being dead."

You murdered me. The least you could do is bury me.

The ghost of Ezekiel Wilkes quivered. It came forward, moth-like, to the candle of Rector's guilt.

You left me there.

"And I told you, I'll come find you. I'll come fix it, if I can."

He waited until his heart had calmed, and he heard only the farts, sniffles, and sighs that made up the nighttime music of the orphans' home. He moved his legs slowly beneath the blanket until his feet dangled off the edge of the flat straw mattress.

The air on the other side of the blanket was cold, but no colder than usual; it seeped through the holes in his socks and stabbed at the soft places between his toes. He flexed them and shivered. His boots were positioned just right, so he could drop down into them without even looking. He did so, wriggling his ankles until he'd wedged his feet securely into the worn brown leather, and he did not bother to reach down and tie their laces. The boots flopped quietly against the floor as he extracted himself from the bedding and reached for the jacket he'd left over the footboard. He put it on and stood there shaking in the frigid morning darkness. He blew on his hands to briefly warm them, then took a deep breath that he held inside to stretch his chest and urge himself more fully awake.

He was already wearing gray wool pants and a dull flannel shirt. He slept in them, more often than not. It was entirely too cold in the orphan's home to sleep in more civilized, sleep-specific attire—even in what was considered summer almost anywhere else in the country.

In the Northwest, they called this time of year the June Gloom.

Until the end of July, the clouds always hung low and close and cold. Everything stayed damp even if it wasn't raining, and usually, it *was.* Most of the time it wasn't a hard rain, but a slow, persistent patter that never dried or went away. The days didn't warm, and at least once a week there was frost in the morning. People grumbled about how *It's never usually like this,* but as far as Rector could recall, it was never usually any different. So on the third of June in 1880, Rector's teeth chattered and he wished for something warmer to take with him.

Cobwebs stirred in the corners of Rector's mind, reminding him that something dead was prone to walking there. It kept its distance for now—maybe this was one of the benefits to being unwillingly sober and alert, but Rector didn't want to count on it. He knew too well how the thing came and went, how it hovered and accused, whether he was waking or sleeping.

And it was getting stronger.

Why was that? He had his theories.

The way Rector saw it, he was dying—killing himself slowly and nastily with sap, the potent, terrible drug made from the poisoned air inside the city walls. No one used it more than a year or two and lived, or lived in any condition worth calling that. Rector had no illusions. He didn't even mind. If anything, his death would factor nicely into his plan to evade responsibility in the long term, even if he was being forced to address it in the short term.

Dead was easier than alive. But the closer he got to being dead, the nearer his dead old chums were able to get to him. It wasn't fair, really—it was hard to fight with a ghost when he wasn't yet a ghost himself. He suspected it'd be a much simpler interaction when he and Zeke were both in a position to scare the bejeezus out of each other, or however that worked.

He exhaled hard, and was dimly glad to note that he could not see his breath. This morning was not as cold as some.

And, dammit all, he was almost out of sap.

In the bottom of his left coat pocket, Rector had constructed a secret corner pocket, between the two threadbare layers that made up his only outerwear. Down there, nestled in a crinkly piece of waxed wrapper, a folded slip held a very small amount of the perilous yellow dust.

Rector resisted the urge to seize it, lest the added noise from the paper summon someone's half-asleep attention. Instead, he comforted himself with the knowledge that it (still, barely) existed, and he jammed a black knit hat down over his ears.

He surveyed the room.

It was too dark to see anything clearly. But he knew the layout, knew the beds.

Seizing his own blanket by the corner, he folded it in half and laid out his few personal effects: One extra pair of socks, in no better shape than the ones he wore already. One additional shirt, neither smelling fresher nor appearing newer than what he had on. A box of matches. An old gas mask, soft from years of being worn by somebody else, but still working fine. Rector didn't have any extra filters, but the ones in the mask were new. He'd stolen them last week, just like he stole everything else he'd ever owned: on a whim, or so he'd thought at the time. In retrospect, the idea might've already been brewing, bubbling on a back burner where he hadn't noticed it yet.

He reached underneath the mattress, to a spot where the fabric covering had rubbed itself threadbare against the slats that held it above the floor. Feeling around with his left hand, he retrieved a small bag he'd stitched together from strips of a burlap bag that once held horse feed. Now it held other things, things he didn't particularly want found, or taken away.

He added this pouch to the stash on the bed and tied up the corners of the blanket. The blanket wasn't really his to commandeer, but that wouldn't stop him. The Home was throwing him out, wasn't it? He figured that meant that the muttering nuns and the cadaverous priest practically owed him. How could they expect a young man to make his way through life with nothing but the clothes on his back? The least they could do is give him a blanket.

Slipping his hand inside the makeshift bag's loops, he lifted it off the bed and slung it over one shoulder. It wasn't heavy.

He stopped in the doorway and glared for the last time into the room he'd called "home" for more than fifteen years. He saw nothing, and he felt little more than that. Possibly a twinge, some tweak of memory or sentiment that should've been burned out of operation ages ago.

More likely, it was a tiny jolt of worry. Not that Rector liked the idea of worrying any better than he liked the idea of nostalgia, but the last of his sap would take care of it. All he needed was a safe, quiet place to fire up the last of the precious powder, and then he'd be free again for . . . *Another few hours at most,* he thought sadly. *Need to go see Harry. This won't be enough.*

But first things first.

Into the hall he crept, pausing by the stairs to loosely, hastily tie his boots so they wouldn't flap against the floor. Down the stairs he climbed, listening with every step for the sound of swishing nun robes or insomniac priest grumblings. Hearing nothing, he descended to the first floor.

A candle stub squatted invitingly on the end table near Father Harris's favorite reading chair beside the fireplace in the main room. Rector collected the stub and rifled through his makeshift bag to find his matches. He lit the candle and carried it with him, guarding the little flame with the cup of his hand as he went.

Tiptoeing into the kitchen, he gently pushed the swinging door aside. He wondered if there was any soup, dried up for boiling and mixing. Even if it wasn't anything he wanted to eat, he might be able to barter with it later. And honestly, he wasn't picky. When food was around, he ate it. Whatever it was.

The pantry wasn't much to write home about. It was never stocked to overflowing, but it never went empty, either. Someone in some big church far away saw to it that the little outposts and Homes and sanctuaries like these were kept in the bare essentials of food and medicine. It wasn't a lot—any fool could see this was no prosperous private hospital or sanatorium for rich people—but it was enough to make Rector understand why so many folks took up places in the church, regardless. Daily bread was daily bread, and hardly anybody leftover from the city that used to be Seattle had enough to go around.

"They owe me," he murmured as he scanned the pantry's contents.

They owed him that loaf of bread wrapped in a dish towel. It hadn't even hardened into a stone-crusted brick yet, so this was a lucky find indeed. They owed him a bag of raisins, too, and jar of pickles, and some oatmeal. They might've owed him more, but a half-heard noise from upstairs startled Rector into cutting short his plunder.

Were those footsteps? Or merely the ordinary creaks and groans of the rickety wood building? Rector blew out the candle, closed his eyes, and prayed that it was only a small earthquake shaking the Sound.

But nothing moved, and whatever he'd heard upstairs went silent as well, so it didn't matter much what it'd been. Some niggling accusation in the back of his drug-singed mind suggested that he was dawdling, wasting time, delaying the inevitable; he argued back that he was scavenging in one of the choicest spots in the Outskirts, and not merely standing stock-still in front of an open pantry, wondering where the nuns kept the sugar locked up.

Sugar could be traded for some *serious* sap. It was more valuable than tobacco, even, and the gluttonous, sick part of his brain that always wanted *more* gave a little shudder of joy at the prospect of presenting such an item to his favorite chemist.

He remained frozen a moment more, suspended between his greed and his fear.

The fear won, but not by much.

Rector retied his blanket-bag and was pleased to note that it was now considerably heavier. He didn't feel wealthy by any means, but he no longer felt empty-handed.

Leaving the kitchen and passing through the dining area, he kept his eyes peeled against the Home's gloomy interior and scanned the walls for more candle stubs. Three more had been left behind, so into his bag they went. To his delight, he also found a second box of matches. He felt his way back to the kitchen, and onward to the rear door. Then with a fumbled turning of the lock and a nervous heave, he stumbled into the open air behind the Home.

Outside wasn't much colder than inside, where all the fires had died down and all the sleeping children were as snug as they could expect to get. Out here, the temperature was barely brittle enough to show Rector a thin stream of his own white-cloud breath gusting weakly before him, and even this chill would probably evaporate with dawn, whenever that came.

What time was it again?

He listened for the clock and heard nothing. He couldn't quite remember, but he thought the last number he'd heard it chime was two. Yes, that was right. It'd been two when he awoke, and now it was sometime before three, he had to assume. Not quite three o'clock, on what had been deemed his "official" eighteenth birthday, and the year was off to one hell of a start. Cold and uncomfortable. Toting stolen goods. Looking for a quiet place to cook up some sap.

So far, eighteen wasn't looking terribly different from seventeen.

Rector let his eyes adjust to the moonlight and the oil lamp glow from one of the few street posts the Outskirts could boast. Between the sky and the smoking flicker of the civic illumination, he could just make out the faint, unsettling lean of the three-story building he'd lived in all his life. A jagged crack ran from one foundation corner up to the second floor, terminating in a hairline fracture that would undoubtedly stretch with time, or split violently in the next big quake.

Before the Boneshaker and before the Blight, the Home had been housing for workers at Seattle's first sawmill. Rector figured that if the next big quake took its time coming, the Home would house something or somebody else entirely someday. Everything got repurposed out there, after all. No one tore anything down, or threw anything away. Nobody could spare the waste.

He sighed. A sickly cloud haloed his head, and was gone.

Better make myself scarce, he thought. *Before they find out what all I took.*

Inertia fought him, and he fought it back—stamping one foot down in front of the other and leaving, walking away with ponderous, sullen footsteps. "Good-bye, then," he said without looking over his shoulder. He made for the edge of the flats, where the tide had not come in all the way and the shorebirds were sleeping, their heads tucked under their wings on ledges, sills, and rocky outcroppings all along the edge of Puget Sound.

 *Two*

Past the burned-out husk of the first sawmill and over the rocks, Rector found a familiar fissure in the ground. He hopped over the great crack as easily as crossing a creek, though it unnerved him. It unnerved everyone, ever since it was opened by the last earthquake of the previous year—the same quake that had collapsed the brick water-runoff tunnels that led into the city. It was too much a memento, this scar in the earth. It whispered warnings from the Boneshaker, and reminded the Outskirts how the world's foundation could be rattled apart.

Rector glared at the crevice. He sniffed, but it was not a gesture of disdain, just curiosity. No, nothing suspicious. The odor of Blight was no stronger here at this unsettling cranny than anywhere else on the mudflats outside the wall.

"They still ought to fill you in," he told the crack. "Shouldn't leave it to chance."

Because what would happen then, if the Blight escaped? Everyone quietly knew that it was bound to overflow the wall someday, but it would be far worse if it didn't need to—if the fumes found their way up other passages, like this one. It'd poison the whole earth, given time enough to leak.

He shuddered and clutched his shoulders, then looked around to make sure no one had seen him act like a chicken. No, he was alone as far as he could tell. No lights, no commotion. No footsteps. Not even the quivering scuttles of wharf rats rustling through the grass.

Beyond the crack and past the clot of dead trees—which Rector always thought looked like monsters, though he wouldn't have told anyone—he started following a narrow path. He knew it by heart and needed no light. Before long he reached a small ring of five shacks. They were run-down and rotting, propped up by half-hearted measures and patched together with afterthoughts that kept them upright, but did nothing to improve their appearance.

This was a logging camp, abandoned in 1879 like so many other things near the ruined city. Once there'd been eight buildings, then none, but a combination of dangerous, illegal work and the need for privacy had revived three of the uninspiring structures. In time, convenience had restored two more to something like their former glory.

Dim, half-shuttered lights burned in four of the occupied shacks, but a vivid light shot out from the cracks of the largest. This near-blinding whiteness streaked past broken slats in the old shutters, speared through the weatherworn splits in the walls, and shot out from around the door.

Rector winced. His eyes weren't ready for the light, not quite yet, but here he was at Harry's place, and he was almost out of sap. He felt woefully ill-prepared to begin this whole adulthood thing without it, and that meant it was time to beg, borrow, or steal.

Christ knew he didn't have a dime to call his own.

Steeling himself against the inevitable wash of light, he put one hand on the door and gave it a gentle push. Its hinges let out a small squeak, and the damp-swollen wood scraped against the doorjamb, then scooted inward, revealing a jumble of tall stills, jars, boxes, tubes, and funnels. And light, always the light . . . so much light that Rector wondered how anyone could see anything at all.

He shielded his eyes and stepped inside, calling out, "Harry? It's just me."

Harry Sharpe, chemist or alchemist or something between the two, was hunched over a table of delicate equipment, measuring spoons, and beakers. He did not immediately look up from his work, but he stopped what he was doing. "Stay where you are, Rector. I won't have you jostling me now, boy—you hear?"

"Sure, Harry. Whatever you say."

He closed the door behind himself and leaned against it, fully prepared to do as he'd been told. Harry was cooking, and cooking was dangerous. One ill-timed interruption or misplaced hand, one extra drop of the wrong ingredient in the wrong decanter, and the resulting explosion could level the old lumber camp like a meteor. Even Rector knew better than to interfere, so he stayed where he was. He watched Harry's wide back, and the resumed motion of his shoulders, and the back of the man's salt-and-pepper hair, which had gone flat with perspiration.

"You shouldn't show up without warning like this. If I hadn't been cooking, I might've had a gun in my hand."

"Sorry," Rector mumbled.

Harry made a finishing gesture—adding a final dose of something sizzling and bleak—and stood up straighter than before, though he did not yet turn around. He watched the chemical reaction before him, waiting to see if anything needed adjustment before deciding all was well.

Still keeping his back to the boy, he said, "I don't suppose there's a chance in hell you're here with a fistful of money, is there?"

Rector shifted his weight from one foot to the other and scratched idly at his elbow. "Well, you see, Harry, it's been a strange week."

"Nothing strange at all about you coming by empty-handed."

"Aw, don't be like that. It's my birthday."

"Birthdays aren't strange either."

"But this is my *eighteenth* birthday," he insisted, not sure the approach would work, but not yet ready to abandon it. "I been kicked out of the Home."

Harry did not immediately respond. He waited for some faint smoldering sound to level off, then turned his head. A large, multi-lensed set of spectacles was fastened around his face, and each round slip of glass was polarized. The apparatus looked heavy, and indeed, the straps had worn grooves into Harry's fleshy pink jowls. He pushed the glasses up onto his forehead, then farther up onto his skull. He wiped at one sweaty cheek with the back of his hand.

"That day was bound to come."

"Yep. So now I'm ready to—"

Harry interrupted. "You're a man now, Rector, in every way that counts. And I've been treating you like a boy for all this time." Finally too annoyed with the spectacles, he pulled them away. The strap snapped off his head with a humid *pop*. "I haven't really done you any favors."

"You done me plenty of favors, Harry."

"Not the good kind. I felt sorry for you, but it wasn't very help-ful."

Rector sensed a shift in the conversation and didn't like it, but he wasn't sure how to play it. "You've helped me out for years, and I appreciate it like a good Christian orphan ought to. Now I'm here to earn a proper living, and get myself a proper job."

Harry laughed, maybe at the "Christian" part. "Selling ain't no trade. And you've been using more than you've been selling."

Rector mustered a smattering of false dignity. "I do not believe that's a fair assessment."

"Goes to show how much you've smoked then, don't it? Look, kid," he said more kindly, but not by any great measure. "I've always let you slide, haven't I?"

"And that's my favorite thing about you."

"Boys get room to slide, Rector. *Men* have to make their own way."

Rector was being dismissed. He could see it coming, as surely as he'd seen his birthday looming. And now the fateful day had clicked, and here he was, more desperate than he'd realized even five minutes ago for a good, solid dose of his favorite habit.

Hastily, trying to get ahead of the inevitable shutdown, he said, "Then Harry, teach me how to cook. Teach me a trade, like the one you got. I'm smart enough to learn it."

"Smart enough, I reckon. But not careful enough." He took another swipe at his glowing, overheated face, then wiped his own body's grease on the brown canvas overcoat he wore to keep his clothes covered. "You'd send yourself sky high with your first batch."

"No, I wouldn't. Harry, I'm begging you, I don't have noplace to go, and I don't have anyone waiting for me, or looking out for me. I need for you to teach me." Nervously, his eyes skittered across the apparatuses and gloves, the tables, the charts, and the supply boxes. Something jumped out at him—something he should've noticed sooner, but hadn't. "You're expanding shop here, aren't you? This is more sap than I've ever seen you work."

Harry's eyes darkened. Rector couldn't imagine what he'd said to make things worse than they already were.

"Yes, I've been busy. There's a war going on, remember? It's all I can do to keep up with demand back East."

"And that's all the more reason you need a . . . an apprentice. Or a helper, or something. Harry, *please.*"

"If I liked you any less or trusted you any better, I might consider it. But neither of them things are true, so I've got to tell you no. You don't want to be part of this right now, Wreck. Things are getting hot back East, and . . ." He faltered and stopped, like there was something else he meant to say, but he couldn't figure out how to add it.

"That stupid war's been happening longer than I been alive. It'll peter out one of these days, don't you think?"

Harry shook his head. "It might. But right now, let's pray it's not replaced with something even worse."

"What's worse than war? And why would we have a war out here, on this coast? That don't make any sense."

With a grim chuckle, the older man stood up straighter, and quickly checked a simmering beaker. "It's a shame you have to ask. Maybe you'll go inside the wall sometime, and you won't wonder anymore."

He stepped away from the cluttered table, revealing a still much larger than his old system. A vast network of tubes, tubs, and valves stretched almost to the ceiling. Another foot, and it'd jut up through the tinplate roof.

"Maybe I'll do that. Maybe I'll go inside the wall," Rector said as if he hadn't been planning it anyway. "But it looks to me like you need help. That's a mighty big kit you've got there."

"I don't need help, and you don't know what you're asking. You want to stay here with me, maybe sleep out in one of the side houses? You want to take up a place in the war that's coming? I don't think you do, boy."

"What are you talking about? The war stops at the river, don't it?"

"That's not what I mean," Harry said. "Things are getting uncomfortable for fellows like me, you understand?"

"No, I don't."

"There are plenty of men out here, much closer to home, who want a piece of what we're doing. Especially since business has boomed so big." Rector wanted to jump in and ask again, *Why?* but Harry was too fast for him. "Yaozu's no dummy, but he's only one man. Half the dealers and distributors on the West Coast are thinking about coming up here and taking the operation away from him."

"You think that could happen?"

Halfway under his breath, he said, "It's happening already." Then he bent over a wooden crate stacked on the floor with others of its kind, looking for something. "They're already coming, already circling like sharks. It won't be long before I have to head inside the wall myself, much as I don't like the prospect of it. I'm not defenseless, but I'll be outdone by the kind of men coming up from Mexico, California, and the Oregon Territory."

"How do you know they're coming, Harry? Who tells you anything, except me and maybe Bishop? And he's inside the wall. He don't know nothing."

Harry looked back at Rector with a chilly, unhappy frown clamped down on his face. "I hear things. I heard the thunder last week—did you? It wasn't natural."

"You're going 'round the bend, old man."

"Maybe, but soon the last of us here—the last of us original makers, I mean—will need a fortress."

"You could do worse than Seattle," Rector noted.

"I agree, but the thought of a life spent in a gas mask doesn't agree with me much. I may have to find some other line of work."

"You could go east, if that's where the demand is."

Harry found whatever he was fishing for. His knees popped when he stood back up to his full height. "True. Inside the wall with the rotters and gas, or back East into the war. If it weren't for shitty options, I'd have no options at all. Anyway, here," he said, offering up a very small packet.

Rector tried to keep his eyes from lighting up. He tried to stop himself from gliding across the rough-hewn floors and snatching the small fold of waxed paper right out of Harry's outstretched hands. But there he was, eager as a dog at the prospect of a bone. Some small part of him had the grace to be embarrassed.

"What's this?" he asked coolly. "A birthday present?"

"It's what you came here for, and the only thing you want. You don't want to learn anything, and you don't want to work if you can help it. I've watched you run and burn for what now . . . a couple of years?"

"Something like that," Rector muttered, taking the packet and stuffing it into his pocket while pretending not to care.

"I was dealing with a child before, and today you're a man. So from here on out, you pay your own debts. I won't protect you if you don't."

"Never asked you to," Rector snapped before he could stop himself. That small, embarrassed corner of his soul grew a size or two. He felt himself blushing, and he wasn't entirely sure why. "But thanks for the birthday present. I'll use it wisely."

"Nobody uses sap wisely."

Rector turned on his heels and grabbed the door, pushing it open and launching himself out into the night, where the trees were too thick and the sky too dark to show him anything but a bright stain in his vision from the brilliant lights of the chemist's shack.

When he could see again, he looked toward the wall.

"Wait for me," he told it. "I'll deal with you soon enough." And he headed off toward the water instead.

 **Three**

The beach was deserted.

It was also shiny with a glaze of moonlight and the intermittent sweep and flash of a powerful lamp scanning the water a few miles away. The lighthouse wasn't for boats, not mostly. Not anymore. These days it guided the airships and their crews coming and going from Bainbridge Island, serving as a beacon for the kind of madmen who didn't mind flying at night—or the kind of ships that had no choice in the matter. The distant beam came and went, blinking in and out, grazing the tops of the subtle waves and glinting off the edge of the Outskirts.

Rector picked a large, flat rock that looked more dry than not and sat on it. For a moment he thought about staying and watching the sun rise, and then he realized what a dumb idea that was, considering he was facing west. But it might be pretty anyway, seeing the sky go from black to smoky foam gray.

The last time he'd sat on this strip of coastline, the sky had gone the other way—from an overcast panorama of sickly white clouds to a deep, rolling, ominous shade of dark. A storm had crashed in from the north, coming over the ocean like it did only once in a great blue moon. One week before, he'd watched the sky change above him without caring. When the rain came down, pelting him so hard the droplets stung, he didn't care about that, either. But when the thunder had begun, he'd gathered his things and headed inside.

He almost hadn't. He'd waited a few minutes in the downpour to see the lightning that always came with thunder—he thought those brilliant gold lines cracking across the waves might look like God on a bender. But there wasn't any lightning, and he didn't know why. He'd asked around, but no one could tell him. What did Northwesterners know about weather? Practically nothing, unless they were the sort who sailed. And the old mariners told him there hadn't been any thunder at all—they said he'd only imagined it.

But Harry'd heard it, too, and so did a bunch of other people. Rector might make things up and hear or see things once in a while, but he wasn't wrong about the thunder.

He untied a corner of his blanket pouch and shoved his hand down inside it, withdrawing a box of matches and the burlap pouch. Then he reached for the packet Harry had handed him on the way out the door, his birthday present. He deserved this one, and deserved it *richly*.

But when he unfolded the little package, he found only another folded piece of paper stuffed inside it. The paper was blank and empty.

"Goddammit, Harry! Some lousy goddamn birthday present from you. Goddammit! I thought we were friends, you old horse's ass!" He shouted louder than someone who wished to remain inconspicuous ought to, but it was dark and he was mad. He crushed the waxed paper and the blank paper up into a ball and chucked it toward the ocean.

If it hit the waves or just made it to the beach, he didn't know. He didn't hear it land.

"All that talk about doing me a favor," he growled. "Maybe I could do him the favor of burning down that stupid shack. Save him the trouble of deciding where to go, yeah. How would he like *that* favor?"

Shaking now with rage as well as the symptoms of withdrawal, he retrieved the last dregs of his personal stash from his jacket pocket. With quivering hands he tapped the bottom edge against his palm to settle the contents, and he assembled his tools.

The pouch held scraps of tinfoil, a tiny teaspoon, a wooden napkin ring, and a broken glass pipe. He wouldn't need the spoon; there wasn't enough sap left to measure. He left the glass pipe's bowl wrapped in the old handkerchief he'd found someplace, since he couldn't use it and he didn't want to cut himself.

He extracted a square of foil and held it firmly between his fingers, suddenly second-guessing his decision to do this out on the beach. But the wind wasn't strong; if anything, it was almost curiously absent. The birds were still sleeping, the world was still dark, and no one was watching.

No one saw as he bent the foil around the napkin ring so that it made a shiny little surface like the top of a drum.

No one saw him dump the last few precious grains of yellow dust onto the foil, or strike the first match to cook the stuff into fumes. Not even the birds yawned and peeked, and not even the most curious tide-pool residents winked up at him as he bent his head down low over the foil, held it firmly but gently in his fingers, closed his eyes, and lowered the glass stem.

In a rush of concentrated, sulfurous fog, the cobwebs in his head were blasted clean.

Urine-colored fire washed over his brain; brimstone and brine simmered and smoked, and in the wake of that first astonishing explosion (which never became less astonishing with time, or less painful, or less needful and joyful), a placid, pale nothingness dawned.

Rector privately suspected that this was what it felt like to die. First there'd be shock, an outburst of fear and sensation. Then would come this calm, this warmth and smoothness, and the pleasant apathy drawn from an ironclad knowledge that the world no longer mattered.

Given time for the powder to cool and the residue to blow away . . . given scorched fingertips and a nose that ran with pink and yellow mucus, blood, and Blight in a biological slime . . . this harmonious eggshell of bliss would . . . crack.

And shortly after that, Rector's eyes also cracked.

All the light, all the darkness, all the rustling sounds of nearby water, the scuttling clicks of crabs and the tiny splurts of spitting clams half buried in the soggy sand . . . every soft noise scraped against the inside of his skull—loudly, but not quite unpleasantly, rather like a headache made of candy.

He was lying on his back, and he didn't remember how he'd gotten that way—if he'd fallen over, or opted to lie down. An odd-shaped rock or starfish was wedged against one of his lower vertebrae, so he shifted his weight and clenched his fists, flexing his fingers and remembering that he needed to breathe even as he realized that his nose was too stuffy to help with the task. It was clogged with the flavor of copper (his own blood) and tin (from the foil) and whatever other salty gunk saw fit to occupy the great sloshing space behind his eyes.

Still high enough to not mind any pain very much, Rector struggled to a seated position. His few worldly possessions remained right where he left them, and the incoming tide was within a few yards of soaking the lot.

Shakily at first, and then stronger as the drug was given more room to move, more blood flow to carry it through his system, he grabbed his supplies and packed them back up. Foil and pipe stem and matches into the pouch. Empty waxed packet tossed into the oncoming waves. Blanket tied back up at its corners. Everything over his shoulder, bouncing against his back as he left the beach.

He'd already forgotten that he was angry at Harry.

Just for now, for this stretch of minutes—hours, if he was lucky—he did not worry about where he'd sleep or what he'd eat, or whether or not Zeke's phantom was coming for him. He didn't even worry about how he was going to get past the Seattle wall, or what would happen once he got inside. For these moments, everything was clear. The path was as straight and illuminated as if it'd been painted onto the ground at his feet. And not only would there be no deviation from this course, but he could see no peril whatsoever attached to following it.

First, up onto the mudflats. Then, into the Outskirts and around their edge.

Next, up to the wall at the far southeast side of its expanse.

And then, through it. Into the lost, poisoned, abandoned city of Seattle.

It used to be that there were only two ways into Seattle: under the wall, or over it. Going over could be trouble, because it meant finding an air captain who was bribable enough to bring you into the roiling cauldron of thick, ugly air inside the wall. By and large this meant pirates, and pirates were, by definition, not the most trustworthy sort.

Rector did not like pirates.

He didn't care so much for scrabbling around through soft, wet, smelly underground tunnels, either, but that was the better option up until six months ago, when an earthquake had collapsed the last easy access point—a water-runoff tube made of brick, part of the old sewer system from back when the city was alive. There were other ways to get underneath; Rector was positive of that. But he didn't know any off the top of his head, and he didn't want to ask the kind of people who could've told him. He owed them all money.

Anyway, these days he knew a third means into the city. A very recent one, still under construction: a gate cut into the wall about forty feet up. He'd seen men working on it by the water's edge where the old piers rotted in the tidal muck. They'd picked a spot where no one was likely to see them working, and with King Street Station just on the other side of the barrier.

As a professional delinquent and occasional trafficker in illicit substances, Rector had access to a great deal of information that wasn't strictly common knowledge—including the often disbelieved truth that people still lived inside the city . . . and the fact that most of them weren't very nice.

Some of the city's least nice residents lived and worked in King Street Station, which was ruled like a small, wicked kingdom by a mysterious Chinaman named Yaozu. Rector had never personally set eyes on Yaozu, but his imagination suggested an enormous, evil-looking man in billowy black clothing and a gas mask set with spikes. He might have tattoos on his face, or fingernails filed to points, or a terrible voice that sounded like it came from the chest of the devil himself.

No man who rules by the power of his name could be anything less than fearsome.

Rector knew roughly how the world worked, and he had no interest in meeting the monstrous Chinaman or his army of minions. Even if his empire *had* been built on sap, and even if his Station *was* where most of Rector's drug of choice was presently made. But somewhere in the back of Rector's head—bouncing feebly among the parts of his brain that still worked the best—he was prepared to admit that he had considered asking Yaozu for a job.

Of course, this would only come up if he survived his little quest, which he didn't expect to. Which was fine by him. And even if he did survive, there was always the chance that Yaozu wouldn't be in charge very long anyway. Nobody in the Outskirts except the chemists cared whether or not Yaozu managed the flow of sap that oozed out of the walled-up city. If some newcomer came along, up from Tacoma or Portland, or even from as far away as San Francisco, or wherever Harry was talking about . . .

Rector cared only insomuch as it might affect the supply chain, but he didn't give two small shits if the operation was run by a Chinaman named Yaozu, or an Irishman named Hark O'Reilly, or a New Yorker named Louis Melville, or a Californian named Otis Caplan. Let them fight over it all they liked. Just let the best man win, and let the sap flow.

Let the whole world burn, for all Rector Sherman cared. After all, it had no place for him.

 *Four*

Rector's quest was fuzzy, but it was not altogether ridiculous: If he could find his way into the city, locate his deceased friend's corpse, and treat it with a smidge of dignity, he could perhaps be freed from the nagging phantom that dogged his waking dreams.

It was not the worst plan he'd ever had. It didn't rank among the finest, either, but the end of Rector's rope was dangling near, and it was this or nothing. It might even redeem him a little bit if his last act on earth was an attempt at recompense, in case of pearly gates or skeptical angels.

A short, sparkling pang of guilt poked through the muffling layers of sap and jabbed him in the chest. "Zeke, I'm coming, goddammit. Isn't that enough?" he said under his breath. "Christ, that's all I can do now, ain't it?" He trudged through darkness over the mudflats, to the wall looming blacker than any starless midnight—a false horizon created from something thicker and worse than the mere absence of illumination.

He could see the wall best when he did not look at it directly. It was most apparent from the corner of his eyes, from a sideways gaze as he hiked past ramshackle clusters of houses and businesses.

Over at the waterworks plant a steam whistle blew and something heavy clanked, like a large clock's gears tipping together. One shift was ending, and another would soon begin. The plant ran day and night because there'd never be enough clean water if it didn't—and without clean water, the Blight truly would have wiped out the Sound.

Rector remembered a stray, sharp fact in an uninvited flash: Briar Wilkes, Zeke's mother, used to work there. She'd gone inside the wall after her son. She'd never come out, and, like her son, she was almost certainly dead. It weighed on Rector somewhat less than Zeke's untimely passing, as he hadn't liked Briar at all: the last time he'd seen her, she'd threatened him with bodily and spiritual harm, so if she was gone, well, that didn't keep him up at night—and neither did her ghost.

The churning cranks and hisses of steam from the waterworks plant faded as he hiked farther away from the Sound, higher up the ungroomed hills, and along the worn dirt roads that had settled into uncomfortable ruts. He left the ruts and took to the grassy spots between the houses and sheds and barns. As these buildings thinned out, the open spaces became wider, more open, and almost more frightening because they gave him nowhere to hide.

Standing out in the wet scrub with mossy rocks and trees that rotted where they'd fallen, Rector felt small and conspicuous as he approached the looming monolith of the Seattle city wall.

Flat and plain, the wall was made of unevenly sized stones, mortared swiftly together. The overall color was gray with a hint of sickly green, for even the ever-present mold and mildew took its cues from the Blight-tainted air. It was inscrutable and blank. It appeared unbreachable by all but the most foolhardy daredevils, given the slippery flora, wet slime, and treacherous patches of fickle moss that would slough away without remorse even under the desperate fingers of a fervently praying climber.

But once he got up close, Rector could see that it harbored secrets and promises.

He tiptoed, moving his legs more carefully through the vegetation and keeping his eyes peeled against the heavy darkness that kept him guessing about his progress. He did not want to light a candle, not yet. Besides the fact that he had so few, he did not wish to draw attention to himself. Not until he figured out exactly where he meant to go, and exactly whose attention he needed.

This next part would be tricky.

He listened for all he was worth and, around the swirling fuzz of the sap still sparkling between his ears, he heard the gruff, intermittent chatter of men who were bored and not very happy. Rector turned himself sideways and walked along the tall stone barrier, its shadow made thicker still by the wee morning hours and a moon smudged over by clouds.

The men were somewhere above him and ahead of him. He followed their voices.

His footsteps ground into wet grass and against slippery pebbles, leaving streaked prints along the groove at the wall's base. The path was uneven, broken by tree roots and fallen pieces of rock; it was clotted with the detritus of leaves, dead grass, and human trash blown by ocean winds to collect against the stones like snowdrifts.

At times, he sank to his calves in rotting mulch, the compost of things lost, forgotten, and turned damp by the climate.

Rector muttered a sour curse and wished out loud that, just this once, the June Gloom would take it up a notch and freeze. Frozen mud would be easier to navigate, and ice was no slicker than the vitreous slime that squished down the grade.

The conversation above him grew louder.

Both participants were wearing gas masks. Rector could hear it from the muffled hum to their words, and the way their consonants were rubbed off around the edges, but as he came closer, he could pick out the gossip more clearly.

"I just don't want to hear about it later, that's all. If Yaozu tries to cuss me about it, I'll . . . I won't be real happy. But if we're late, that's what he gets for putting a kid in charge. That ain't right."

"Can you install the gears?"

"No."

"Then you aren't right for the job. Me either," the other man added quickly, possibly in response to some threat Rector couldn't see. "If Houjin knows how, let him. He mess it up, it's not our fault. He do it right, we look good for helping. See?"

"Yeah, I see," came the grudging response. "That don't mean I like it."

A crackling snap of pleasure or pain—Rector couldn't tell which—zipped across his vision and was gone, leaving a comet trail of contentment in its wake. He smiled and listened a little longer, until he was absolutely confident that these were workmen and not guards. Almost certainly an older white man and a somewhat younger Chinese man.

Rector took a deep breath and flinched as a pang of tomorrow's hangover made itself known in the soft spot just behind his ear. He shook it off and stepped away from the wall, but not far enough out to be easily seen or shot at.

"Hey, you fellas up there?" he called, not in a big shout, but loud enough to make it clear that he wasn't sneaking up on anybody.

The two men above went silent, then the Chinaman called back, "Who is there? What do you want?"

"Rector Sherman here. I want to get inside the city." It sounded grandiose when he put it that way, but he decided he was all right with that, so he let it stand. "I don't want any trouble, and I don't want to bother nobody. I got business inside, that's all."

"Business? What kind of business you got in the city? Did Yaozu send for you?"

"No sir," he said—fast, so the two words ran together in his mouth. "I'm looking for work."

"How old are you, son?" the white man asked.

"Not sure what that's got to do with anything. I've been selling for a couple of years already."

After a pause, the other man concluded, "So you want to come on up."

"That I do, sir. That I do." He took this opportunity to step out of the wall's shadow and into the lesser dark of the cloud-covered evening, which left him somewhat less invisible but still quite fuzzy to anyone that far overhead.

A brilliant white shaft of light flared to life. It swiped at the night, curving back and forth as someone up there adjusted a focus-beam lantern. The beam settled on Rector without mercy, blinding him outright and forcing him to close his eyes against the sudden, painful attention. He crooked his elbow and tried to shield his face without hiding it. The last thing on earth he wanted was for these men to think he was up to something . . . which he was, but it wouldn't do for them to suspect it.

"You're a regular ghost of a thing, ain't you?"

"What?"

"Whitest man I ever see," observed the Chinaman dispassionately. "His hair . . . what color you call that?"

"Ginger. Hey, I think I heard about you, boy."

Rector forced a smile. "Is that right?"

"You've been dealing from the orphanage, haven't you? I heard about a boy so white you could see right through him, with hair the color of rust, besides. Is that you?"

"I reckon it must be," he confessed.

The Chinaman asked, "You know this boy?"

"I know about him," the white man said. "He uses Harry, don't he?" he asked down at Rector, who still cringed against the light. "Harry's your chemist, ain't he?"

"That's right, sir. I buy offa Harry." *Or at least I used to.* "And Harry gets all his stuff right here, through Yaozu. He don't truck with Caplan or O'Reilly, so you can trust I'm one of yours."

The white man snorted as if trust wasn't something he handed out quite so easily, but Rector knew the lingo and he'd dropped enough names to prove himself.

"Caplan and O'Reilly . . . Either one of them ever approach you?"

"No sir." But that wasn't quite true. He'd met Caplan once in passing, through one of Harry's rival chemists. Harry'd been laid up with consumption and hadn't been able to cook, so Rector'd been forced to look up another source. "And if I did, I wouldn't work with 'em. I know which side my bread is buttered on."

"All right, then. Hold on. We'll throw down the ladder. Be careful hoisting yourself up. We don't care to scrape anybody's bits and pieces off the rocks, you hear me?"

He unrolled a long ladder; it unfurled like a flag, in a great lurching arc that hit the ground mere inches from Rector's toes. He jumped back with a start.

"You see it?" the Chinaman prompted.

"Sure enough, I do. Say, could you maybe aim that light somewhere else? I can't see with it shining down in my face. You said you don't want to scrape me off the rocks, and well, I'd rather not require that service, either."

The light wobbled, wavered, and the beam shifted a few feet to the right.

Once Rector's eyes stopped swimming with bold white orbs that obscured all the evening's details, the remaining glare was enough to see by—so long as he didn't need to see anything directly in front of him. But the glowing white ghosts seared into his vision refused to disperse entirely, so he held out his arms and relied on his peripheral vision until he could swat the rope ladder into his hands.

He climbed its loose dowel footholds by feel, bracing himself against the wobble of the unsecured steps; one hand over the other, and then one foot following the next, he scaled it slowly, uncertainly, and suddenly quite glad that the light was off his face but pointed too far away for him to see anything if he were dumb enough to look down.

He looked down.

As predicted, he saw nothing, except for a big circle of vivid brilliance cast by the lantern above. It hit the ground someplace below, illuminating only grass, gravel, and the edge of a fire pit that hadn't seen any cooking action in years.

His stomach did a quick lurch, but there was nothing inside it to slosh or heave, so he didn't even burp at the sudden realization of how high up he'd come, and how quickly. Was he climbing so fast? It was hard to tell. His hands and feet guided themselves, or maybe what was left of the sap churning around in his head was shielding him from the facts of the matter.

Forty feet or more. Straight up. A gate into someplace like hell.

He was half that distance before the Chinaman called down, "You got a mask?"

"Yes, I got a mask," he panted.

"You put it on. The seal here not so good."

"I will. Put it on. When I get. Closer." He puffed out the words in time to his climbing.

"You put it on *now*. There gas up here. You smell it?"

"Sure, I can smell it," Rector admitted. You could almost always smell the gas if you were within five miles of the city and if the wind was canted just right. It was easy to forget the low-level stink because you never smelled anything else.

But this was worse.

There was a leak, as though someone had drilled a hole in a barrel and the contents were oozing free. It came from above, from the gate. It drooled down onto his head and up his nose, the yellow-fire stench of Blight slipping through the compromised wall.

Briefly Rector wondered who'd ever thought it'd be a good idea, this gate cut into the place where poison billowed and spilled day in and day out.

"Three cheers for bad ideas," he wheezed, knocking his forearm against the next rung and wincing hard as the closest rope dragged a thick red mark along his wrist. He seized the knots, got a better grip, and kept climbing. His palms ached from the squeezing, the dragging, and the slivers of hemp and twine wedging themselves into the small wrinkles and cracks of his hands.

But he was almost there.

Maybe another dozen feet. That's all he needed. He braced himself with one knee locked and crooked around the rope and one arm twisted and holding likewise, and he withdrew his mask from the blanket-bag. One-handed and gracelessly, he yanked it over his head and kept on climbing.

The light swung back around and caught him in the eyes once more. He yelped and cried out, "What are you doing, man? I can't see when you point that thing right at me! You trying to make me fall?"

"Naw, sorry. Just looking at your progress. You're almost here."

Before Rector could wonder about the particulars of "almost," a hand jutted down into his face, smacking him between the eyes.

"Here, come on. Get up here, would you?"

"Yes sir," he said, flailing about until he'd successfully snared the hand. A combination of his own wobbly inertia and the man's help got him up onto a wood platform that felt rickety, looked rickety, and sounded rickety when it groaned under the added weight of Rector's body. He stayed on his hands and knees until he shook off enough of the vertigo to stand. When he did, he was very, very careful to make eye contact with the gatekeepers. It was better than looking down at the ground.

He was right: Both of them were wearing gas masks—the slim-fitting kind that hugged the face without a lot of unnecessary valves, cogs, filters, and levers. These were lightweight, practical devices that wouldn't help anyone survive long inside the city—the filters would clog in a couple of hours down at street level—but up high and half outside, they'd suffice.

Rector had heard enough from the chemists about how people rationed their filters and planned their masks. There was a science to it—a science everyone learned eventually, or else they joined the ranks of the shambling rotters down on the roads below. As this thought flickered through his head, he adjusted his own mask so it fit him better and seemed less likely to leak.

"Watch your wiggling," the white man urged. He was precisely what Rector had expected: average height and size, with ratty brown hair and clothing that had been tied up tight at the wrists and ankles to keep the gas off his skin. The Chinaman was likewise no great shock, except that he was wearing almost the same exact outfit. In Rector's experience, the Chinese population tended to dress differently, in outfits that had odd, chopped-off-looking collars and lines that white men more commonly wore to bed than out for business.

"I can see that, sir. And I will absolutely watch my step. And my wiggling." Planting his feet on one board each, he balanced against the slight tilt of the platform and then took note of the gate itself. "So this is it, huh? This is how people are going to get inside and out?"

"Someday, but right now it's not even halfway sorted. Turned out to be a bigger job than anybody'd expected."

"How much longer 'til it's open for business?"

"Two or three weeks, if we're lucky. Longer than that, if we ain't."

The hole was shaped as if it ought to host a drawbridge. It was arched and somewhat unsteady despite the braces of timber and pulleys that held the hole open and clear. Rector imagined he could hear the posts straining against the wall's weight, another hundred and fifty feet above it—and when he thought about it that way, he went weak. How many tons of rock was that, anyhow? How many thousands of pounds, held up by timbers and stones and the calculations of a despot?

At present, the hole was shielded by a set of curtains fastened behind the buttressing timbers. Rector reached out past the boards and felt for one of the dangling swaths of fabric, rubbing it between his bare fingers.

"You got gloves?" asked the Chinaman. "You need gloves."

He lied, "I got some. I'll put 'em on in a minute."

"Gas burns skin."

"I know that." The curtain was several layers of burlap fused with wax, or pitch, or something else to keep it water- and gastight. It felt waxy and unpleasant, like the flesh of a cooled corpse. "Pretty good way to hide your work," he observed.

"It does all right," the white man said. As if the reference to hiding had prompted him, he adjusted the lantern, shuttering the bulk of its light and turning down the wick so that it gave the weird little way station a dim glow instead of a brilliant beacon. "Nobody much comes around to this side of the wall. Not yet, anyhow."

Rector had questions, but none of them were very pressing except the obvious: "So, I just go through this hole . . . and then what? Is there a staircase or something over there?"

The Chinaman laughed, and the white man shook his head. "Not yet. You'll walk along the temporary steps. They're not very wide, and it gets a little slick from the gas and the wet—you know how it goes—so watch your step. Go either way you like, left or

· · · · · · · · · · · · 53

right. Both of them stop at a set of ladders and rooftops. Go right, and you'll wind up closer to the Station. Take the left, and you'll be aimed toward the Doornails' territory."

"Is that good or bad?"

"Depends. They got themselves some law, and they don't much care for the sap. Mostly they leave us alone and we leave them alone, and that works all right, but we stay off each other's blocks. You never been inside before, have you?"

"No sir, I ain't ever been inside."

"You know about the rotters though, don't you?"

"I do."

"You got a gun, or anything?"

He lied some more. "Yes sir, in my bag. I'll fetch it out once I'm in, and I don't need both hands for climbing." As he said this, he considered retying the bag so it could sling across his chest. The jar of pickles weighed heavily against his kidneys, and the loaf of bread felt like a stone between his shoulder blades. None of it sat comfortably, but it sat, and he didn't have to hold it.

If either of the two men noticed that he hadn't pulled out any gloves, neither of them said anything.

"I reckon I'm as ready as I'm gonna get," Rector said. He was still high enough to believe it, and to not worry about it half so much as he should have. "Left is toward the Doornails, and right is toward the Station, yes? And I follow the ledge until it dead-ends, regardless."

"You've got it."

With a small salute that was meant to look brave, Rector pushed the curtain aside—opening a slit to the deadly, stinking world within.

Gas billowed up and out, swirling around his face so thickly that its tendrils ghosted smokelike on either side of his visor. The visor itself was wide and clean—it gave him a good view with only a little detriment to the fringes of his sight—but it soon felt dirty from the greasy, ghastly Blight.

Rector wiped at the visor with the back of his sleeve, flashed the two men a smile they couldn't see behind his mask, and, with a deep breath that hurt to take, ducked inside.

 *Five*

At first, without even the shuttered glow of a leaky lantern to guide him, Rector saw nothing at all behind the burlap-and-wax curtain that lurked on the other side of the timber scaffolding. He blinked repeatedly, wondering if he ought to drag out one of his candles and light it. Then he realized that the sun was coming up—just barely and vaguely, as if it wasn't sure about this whole rising business—so maybe he wouldn't need the extra light after all.

The runny gray haze that passed for dawn showed him only the faintest outlines of the ruined city, but the view stunned him all the same.

He'd heard stories. *Everyone* had heard stories, about how the city rotted inside its wall, dissolving and decaying in the heavy, poisonous gas that billowed out from the fissure at the city's heart. *It's just a skeleton now,* the chemists would say. *The buildings remain, most of them—the ones the earthquakes didn't take after the Boneshaker disaster. But everything that still lives, lives underground.*

He blinked furiously, trying to clear his vision. Shapes emerged slowly from the gloom, coming into semifocus in clumps. They sharpened and wavered in cycles, in response to the drafts of sludge-thick air that moved, parted, and collected in currents of toxin.

Seattle sprawled before him and below him, drowning and dead.

As the ghostly, ghastly clouds of yellowish air gave way, Rector detected outlines and right angles. He spied windows, mostly broken, and balconies and drawbridges that connected those windows over alleys. These things appeared in a flash and were gone in a smear, only to reappear, dreamlike and hazy. The whole world inside the wall was uncertain like this, decomposing and static, but shifting and malleable.

Much as he wanted to leave the small entryway—this foyer into the realm of the damned—Rector didn't know where to go. The sap was dissolving in his system, losing its power and making him less confident of the impulsive decisions he'd made earlier that morning. He was remembering that he was hungry, and it was nearly breakfast time; and recalling that he had no great plan beyond "Find Zeke's body"—and even that plan was riddled with confusion.

Where had Zeke entered the city? That part was easy: He'd entered through the old water runoff tunnel, the one that had collapsed during the last earthquake. But where did that tunnel emerge? Nowhere near King Street Station. It'd be the other direction, in the northern end of the wall's elongated oval of territory.

He should go left.

But to the right there were people, right? People who dealt and traded in sap—people who wouldn't give him any guff about using or selling.

It'd be easier, maybe . . . simpler by far, now that Rector was a grown man and everything, and more *useful,* to waltz into the Station and announce that he'd like a job, and they could pay him in sap and that'd be all right. Someone was bound to take him on. Harry's man, if nobody else. He could learn how to distill and produce the stuff, rather than just smoke it and distribute it. That'd be practically like learning a trade, wouldn't it?

It wasn't the dumbest thing he could do. Go looking for his own kind: the outcasts, the chemists, the thugs and bullies, and makers of brain-killing venom for sale by the ounce. Even if they didn't embrace him warmly, he'd know how to work with them. Bartering bits of his soul was a skill Rector had learned years ago—so many years ago, it was a wonder he had any soul left.

No. Come for me, or I will come for you.

But no. Zeke's insistent shade would not be banished long, by the sap or anything else. Rector had lost too much sleep, been too frightened and too guilty for too long to let go of the One Sure Thing he had to do now. So he turned away from the Station path in one jerky motion that made the whole platform vibrate, and he held out his foot to feel for the top step.

Immediately, his boot slipped on a slick piece of jutting stone. He didn't slip far, and not too badly . . . at least, not so wildly that he went careening down forty-odd feet to the street level below, to whatever terrible things prowled down there. He couldn't see the street itself. Forty feet of Blight and early morning shadow obscured the bottom, which made looking down easier. He saw nothing he could crash-land on, nothing but wispy, filmy clouds that would surely be softer than pillows.

Rector felt for the wall and fought across the mildew and slime until he found a big enough crack to anchor himself. Carefully, using every remaining bit of his brainpower to balance himself and his bag, he inched forward from the first step to the next, and then to the step beyond it.

Some of them shook. Some of them wobbled and splintered, sending tiny shards of wood or rock down to the streets below.

When he stood as still as a statue, catching his breath and feeling the dampness of the stones bleed through his clothing, he heard soft moans and groans coming from somewhere not half so far away as he would've liked. He'd never seen a rotter, not up close and personal, and he'd like to keep it that way. But it was hard not to be curious when he was well out of their reach. Maybe the gassy fog would part and he'd catch a glimpse of the shambling dead.

They wouldn't see him—not all the way up there. Would they?

Rector kept moving, swinging one foot in front of the other, using the wall itself as a brace for his shoulder, his bag, and his hips.

While he climbed, he struggled to recall where he was headed. What was it called again? The place where the tunnel that Zeke took would've emerged? Surely he wouldn't have survived an hour beyond that.

If Rector had ever even known the name, he couldn't remember it now.

But *north* felt like a good enough direction, so he'd stick to that. There was always a chance, he mused, that the Doornails weren't as bad as all that. He might be able to ask around, find out if anyone had spotted the body of a boy about his own age, some newcomer who hadn't made it far. Somebody might know. For all he knew, they might have a place where they put bodies. The dead have to go somewhere, don't they?

Yes. They come here.

He steadied himself and kept moving until the path dropped away in front of him.

With a gasp, he jerked himself back against the wall, pushing like he could shove himself right through it and back to the Outskirts. Maybe this was all an awful idea. His breath froze in his throat and for a few seconds he couldn't breathe at all—or didn't dare to try.

Then he noticed a ladder continuing his path downward.

It wasn't the usual kind of ladder—rungs and sides and whatnot—and it wasn't a rope ladder like the one he'd climbed to the platform. This ladder was made of iron, and bolted to the side of the wall.

Rector crouched and reached for the top rung. His bare hands were already warm and reddening with a rash brought on by the Blight, but he ignored the discomfort and tried to give the bar a good, solid grip.

Gripping was trickier than it sounded. The metal had been coated with . . . tar? Pitch? Glue? He didn't know, but it was thick and mucky, and probably intended to work against the corrosive power of the tainted air. And indeed, he could see how some of the bolts without this protective goop were rusting with alarming vigor.

The metal groaned under Rector's boot. He pivoted so that he faced the wall, then brushed the side of the ladder with his free hand until he could reach, and lean, and get a good hold.

With his back to the ruined city, his arms and legs shaking with effort and fear and the unfamiliar posture of the forced vertical . . . he began to descend.

As he dropped himself one rung at a time, not knowing what was at the bottom—or how far away that bottom might be—he watched the rusting bolts scroll past his visor. He winced and squeezed tighter as the iron's covering made his hands gummy; he flinched as the fixtures wobbled in their settings, puffing soft red dust into the yellow air. Finally, after what felt like forever, the ladder came to a stop—giving Rector another fresh infusion of terror when he realized that the rungs had run out, and nothing but open air awaited his dangling foot.

Now it was time to look down. He did, and he gave a wheezing bark of relief: Below him, just a short hop away . . . he saw a flat surface.

With something akin to joy he released his grip on the nasty ladder and spun, dropping himself down. It was farther than it looked, enough to throw off his balance when he hit, landing oddly on one set of toes and the back of his other heel. He stumbled, swore, and recovered—then stood up straight and proud, feeling accomplished for the first time in recent memory. He'd made it to the roof.

"Now what?" he asked himself, and the words echoed wetly around in his mask. "Got to sort myself out, that's all. Got to find which way's north."

Rector had spent several years trafficking in maps, and he knew what the city ought to look like. There'd been a big Sanborn survey right before the Boneshaker happened, and the resulting charts told him where all the roads went and what they were called. But those black-and-white diagrams weren't a whole lot of help when he couldn't see the streets.

He thought hard. He could do this.

All the downtown corners had their intersection names cut into the stone curbs, but Rector concluded, with no small amount of irritation, that he'd have to be sitting right on top of one to see it, much less read it. Still, the wall was at his back. Given where he entered, that meant he was facing east. If he wanted to go north, toward the spot where the old water runoff tunnels came out, he'd have to go left, up the hill and along the wall.

He walked around the roof in small semicircles, taking in his surroundings and making sure that nothing horrible lurked in any of the corners or shadows. He saw only bits of trash—newspapers wadded and soaked, broken bottles, discarded rags, and a stray shoe.

He also found a doorway that no doubt led down inside whatever building this was—not that he wanted to go down into the darkness, because he didn't. But he had a plan again, and it was easier to stick with one plan than figure out a second plan. He opened his tied-up blanket-bag and retrieved a box of matches plus one of the taller candle stubs he'd pilfered on his way out of the orphanage.

The little candle struggled, flared, and settled into a steady flame that gave him another few feet of sight. It told him that yes, he was right—and no, there was nothing else on the rooftop with him.

He didn't really believe in God, but he thanked Him anyway on the off chance it'd do him good to be polite.

You never know. You might find out, soon enough.

"Stop it," Rector hissed at the wispy forms that came and went, billowing and eddying between the roof's raised corners, and against the wall behind him. "You're not really there."

You're getting closer. You'd better keep your promise.

"I'm working on it, ain't I?" he asked almost frantically, searching the swirling air for some sign of the familiar phantom, and seeing nothing. Except there, perhaps . . . at the edge of . . . something. The edge of the roof. His vision. His sanity.

He shook his head some more, for all the good it did him. He told the ghost, "I'm coming, as soon as I can find you. Why don't you make yourself useful, and tell me where you are?"

When he received no answer, he sniffed. The candle danced. "That's what I thought. Just like a useless kid. Making demands and refusing to help. Hey Zeke, you dummy—think about this, will you? If I die before I reach you, then neither one of us gets any grave except this miserable city."

He stepped with defiance toward the doorway, which was raised up out of the roof, and he gave the knob a stern, confident tug.

It came off in his hand.

He stood there stupidly, holding the rotted old piece of cheap metal. Then he looked at the hole it'd left and tried to reinsert the thing, in case such a simple act could magically repair it.

No such luck.

"Fine," he said. Maybe that wasn't the way he was supposed to go anyway.

Rector set the candle down and gave the door a solid kick, then a second one. His foot connected a third time, and each percussion was louder—the beating of a forlorn drum, banging out a low echo that drove the curdling gas away in fleeing puffs.

Nothing budged. *All right. Time to look for something else.* People didn't come and go from that ladder just to die on the rooftop, now did they? No. No bodies, no bones, no rotters. There was some other way down.

Methodically, he began a survey of the roof. Pools of water collected and gelled nastily in the places where the surface sagged, but Rector avoided those because he didn't want his already-filthy socks to suck up anything worse than what they'd already gathered. Every step felt like sneaking through something that was on the very verge of collapse.

He dragged his free hand along the edge overlooking the street. *Ah. There. Yes.*

His hand stopped against a plank covered in splinters—no, only partly covered in splinters, and partly covered in peeling, chipping paint that sloughed away at his touch. He held the candle up over this newfound object and discovered that it was affixed horizontally to a space immediately below the edge, where it could be easily seen from the roof.

"One of them fellows might've mentioned this. Might've made things easier," he grumbled. As he examined the plank, he realized that, in fact, it was a collection of doors laid end to end. They'd all been lashed together, braced from underneath, and affixed with guide ropes intended to serve as rails, for all the wonderful good they'd do if this rigged-together bridge were to break. But Rector couldn't get too upset about that, because that's what it was—a bridge. A bridge that went straight into the open window of a taller building next door, perhaps thirty feet away. Not far at all. A hop, a skip, and a jump.

Easy-peasy.

He climbed onto the roof's edge and placed one foot gingerly on the creaking, cracking, splitting boards. Before he could talk himself out of it, he began to run, sending the bridge swinging in the process. He launched himself through the window with such speed that his candle blew out as he landed inside the other space.

Hands on the top of his legs, he bent forward and gasped to catch his breath in the dark of the closed-off room. The only light was what straggled in through the broken window, so he paused to relight the candle, his hands shaking so hard he could barely strike the match.

When he did, he was downright stupidly happy at what he saw.

"This might work after all," he marveled to himself—and to the ghost, in case the ghost was listening.

He'd entered some kind of storage area, or refueling station, or whatever it was you called a place in an abandoned, destroyed city where you stashed helpful items to make sure you could keep on surviving.

Lined up on pegs against the far wall, Rector found a collection of big canvas satchels with proper straps and everything. Several of them had names stenciled or written on them, but two were unmarked and one of those was empty. Rector took that one. He smushed his candle stub onto the floor and picked its wick free while the wax was still runny. He then untied his blanket and moved its contents into the satchel.

Off to his right, three good oil lamps were keeping one another company. He seized one, filled it up with oil from the bottles that lined a shelf near the satchels, and took an extra bottle for good measure. Now the satchel was so heavy it was a chore to heft it onto his back. But Rector had been too long conditioned by poverty to leave anything useful just lying around for somebody else to find, so if it meant he'd have a sore back for a few days, he'd be all right with it.

He grunted and settled the satchel as best he could. It was definitely easier to hold and carry than the blanket bundle, even as overloaded as it was.

Speaking of the blanket, he didn't want to leave *that* behind. The June Gloom would linger yet for weeks. He'd need something to keep him warm, and the blanket wasn't much, but it was better than nothing. Bending down and adjusting his center of gravity to keep the satchel from toppling him over, he folded the blanket in half and rolled it up as tight as it'd go. Then he stuffed it through the bag's straps.

If he could've reached his own back, he would've patted it.

The lamp in his hand was a rusty contraption left over from when the city was walled off, but it gave far better light than his candle stub and Rector was delighted to have it. Emboldened by the great, glowing halo of the swinging lantern, he surveyed the room and settled on the stairwell as the most obvious path out.

Into the stairwell he stomped, taking strange pleasure in the feel of ordinary stairs beneath his feet. No peculiar boards, beams, or wobbling improvisations to support him—just the regular rhythm of evenly spaced steps leading down in the usual fashion.

The jostling lantern filled the space with a bonfire glow that shook his shadow as he descended.

One story, two stories. Three.

He was on the ground level now; he sensed it before he knew it as a fact.

It wasn't merely the long hike from the roof, and it wasn't simply the wider passage or the paths in the dust swept clean by the regular intrusion of feet. It was the way the windows had all been covered. They were sealed with sheets of wood, planks, corrugated tin, and a hundred other scraps of building material that had been scavenged from the city.

Rector exited the stairwell, and held his lantern up and forward. He investigated the nearest amalgam of reinforcement, and was convinced that yes, this had all been accomplished from the inside. Big nail heads jutted from piles of sturdy trash, and braided steel cables were lashed from corner to corner.

Not keeping anything in. Keeping everything *out*.

Rector spoke quietly to himself, since there was no one else to hear him. "They shore up the first floors to keep out the rotters. I get it." So the rotters couldn't climb. It was good to know.

He couldn't tell what the building had been in its original incarnation. A hotel? A bank? A boardinghouse, or other residence? He scanned the scene for some hint but didn't see one. Every identifying piece of furniture or signage, every useful scrap had been stripped and repurposed from elsewhere.

He stood still and listened, but heard nothing except the lantern's sizzling wick and his own raspy, warm breath straining through his filters. He ducked back into the stairwell and shoved his lantern out in front of himself as if it were a sword. It led the way farther down, one more flight, and it stopped in a basement.

The basement wasn't anything more complex than a freshly excavated root cellar. The timbers that held up the weaker points looked like railroad ties, and there were tracks laid down in the mud.

The lantern wasn't strong enough to tell him how far back the tracks might go; its beams surrendered to the unnatural walls and other lines, showing nothing but a large, cleared space that could've been the bottom of any silver mine or saltworks. There, three different sets of tracks stretched out in three different directions, all disappearing within ten yards. Rector didn't hear any rolling wheels, creaking carts, or squealing brakes. If these tunnels were ever used, nobody was down there now.

He closed his eyes again and backed up to the stairwell, struggling to determine which of the tracks might head off in the general direction of north. Instinct told him it was the middle set, which curved off to the left. He let his instinct win, swung his shoulders to adjust his pack, and set off.

So *this* was the underground.

Dark, close, and eerily quiet. After twenty minutes of exploring, seeking some exit other than the way he'd come in, Rector spotted a byway tunnel. The edge of his lantern's light brushed up against something that looked promisingly like a staircase.

He adjusted his mask. If he was going to hit the great outdoors again, the seal needed to be snug. He hated the seal, he hated the snugness, and he hated the way the rubber line against his face was itching something awful—a combination of ordinary friction and the Blight's irritation. Sometimes he forgot that he shouldn't scratch the seam, and one hand would reach up mindlessly to give it a vigorous scrubbing with his fingernails. But then he'd remember that it would only make the itch worse, and he'd stop himself, and swear about it.

Resisting the urge to take the steps two at a time, he let his lantern lead the way. Up he climbed, slowly enough that his chest didn't hurt and his breath didn't fog up the mask's interior.

At the top he found a trapdoor of sorts, the kind used to cover up root cellars and basements when they need an outside entrance. These doors were doubled, and they were latched from within—just like the windows in the other building.

"They probably want to keep people out, too. Not just rotters." But he suspected the security system wasn't so great, if any dumb kid from the Outskirts could let himself inside. "Or maybe I'm just lucky."

He laughed out loud at that, and tried to rub at an itchy place on his nose, only to be reminded that the gas mask blocked any serious relief.

The door's fastener wasn't too complicated. It was just a system of levers on a crank, so when he turned a wheel, the lock slid aside and the doors would swing . . . in? No. They swung out. He lifted the right-side door and raised his head a few inches to look around.

Ah, daylight. Or what passed for daylight in Seattle, which

was good enough for Rector. But the milky white sky did nothing to warm the low-lying clouds of fog and gas; instead, it made the air look colder—as if it were the frozen, blowing breath of some preposterous monster.

He considered a strategic retreat. He thought about shutting the doors and ducking back underneath the city. It was close and dark and smelled weird (or maybe that was his mask), but there weren't any flesh-eating creatures roaming its corridors. Up here, dead things walked.

But dead things walked in his head, too.

At the far reaches of Rector's vision, the flickering, twitching shade of Zeke Wilkes gave a disapproving shake of its head.

You promised. I won't wait much longer, Wreck. I'll come for you, if you don't come for me.

"You come for me all the damn time anyway."

Outside the air was scratchy and dense. He'd known that already, but had forgotten it in the short time he'd been beneath the streets. He shuddered and climbed up to the last stair, and with all the patience he could muster, he drew the doors back down behind himself until they clicked into place.

Now. Where was he?

An alley.

Navigating half by touch and half by squinting through the thickened air, he struggled to the left . . . where he encountered a fence, so he turned around to try the other way out of the alley. Hugging the building's exterior wall, he crept to its edge.

A corner. Excellent.

The steady patter of dripping water sounded nearby, and someplace not too far away he heard a building settle on its foundations, creaking and moaning. No other sound broke the spell. No footsteps. No shuffling. Nothing to indicate that he wasn't alone . . .

For one brief, alarming instant he second-guessed whether or not people survived inside at all, Doornails or Station men or anyone else.

He dropped to his hands and knees. The sidewalk was smooth and cold under his probing fingers, but he investigated every stone, every gravel- and dirt-littered brick until he found what he was looking for.

There, a few feet out. An engraving. A name.

Commercial.

And now he finally knew where he was.

 *Six*

Rector was on Commercial Street, the street which had once run closest to the Sound and the piers. Now it ran closest to the wall, and parallel to it, all along the western edge.

Rising to his feet, he fought to find his bearings. The street ran north and south, but where had he emerged? The air was clumped and uncertain, and he was surrounded by tall shadows. He had no idea where the wall was.

But he remembered now: North went uphill. South ran downhill.

"Psst!"

Rector froze.

He swiveled his head, compensating for his reduced vision in the mask, looking from corner to corner and up above the street. He saw nothing. Only the fog, and straight lines where buildings punctured briefly through it.

"Psst! Hey, you!"

Rector unfroze and flung himself into the nearest alley. It wasn't his imagination. It wasn't a ghost. In his experience, ghosts never made spitty noises and called him "Hey you!" The ghosts all knew his name.

"Go away!" he fiercely whispered back—hoping he projected more menace than fright.

"Who are you? What are you doing here?" asked the unseen person.

It was hard to tell with such an echo bouncing off the Seattle wall and all its encompassed buildings, but Rector was pretty sure the voice came from a nearby rooftop.

The hidden speaker asked again, "Who *are* you?"

"None of your goddamn business!" Rector replied more loudly than he meant to.

The silence that followed was stifling. It pressed up against his mask and pushed against his eardrums as the whole block listened to see what damage had been done. Had anything heard him? Was anything coming?

"Don't holler like that," the distant voice responded. The words were soft, lobbed with just enough of an edge to penetrate the space between them. This was the voice of someone accustomed to speaking where speaking was dangerous.

Any sound too sharp and the floodgates would open—Rector knew that much; he'd heard all about it. But there he'd gone, babbling regardless. "Sorry," he muttered. "Go away, would you?"

Above Rector and somewhere to the right he heard the scraping push of feet. Someone scrambled, and the footsteps stopped, then came again—this time sounding against metal. The speaker was descending a ladder. Coming closer.

"Stay. Away. From me." Rector leaned on the words, wanting them to sound deadly and figuring they probably didn't.

"No," came the response.

"Why?"

"Because you'll die down here, running around like an idiot. Can't imagine how you've lived this long. Let me help you."

"I don't want any help!" Again, the words were too hard. They scratched against the relative quiet of dripping water, creaking steel, and the patter of a single set of feet.

Getting closer. A lot closer. And definitely not a ghost.

Panic crept up Rector's spine, gripped his neck, and warmed the back of his head. "I've got to get out of here," he said to himself.

The other guy heard him anyway. "Not a bad idea. Come with me."

"Like hell," Rector said, and he started to run.

Three steps into that retreat, he collided with the corner of a building, bounced off, and caught himself just before falling down. His gas mask slid—not far enough to let in any of the toxic air, but one of his lenses had cracked, rendering his left eye's view a mosaic of confusion. It was hard enough to see when everything was clear, including his head. Now he was half-blind in one eye, his ears were ringing, and he felt a warm, wet trickle of blood dripping down behind his ear.

He pulled himself together, picked a different direction, and ran that way. He bolted around the offending corner, tore to the right, stumbled on the uneven paving stones, and recovered. Then he ran forward some more, faster, up the hill . . . because that was the correct direction, wasn't it?

"Oh for Pete's sake," complained the voice behind him. The voice was still coming, moving on feet that were very light and very fast in comparison to Rector's.

He ran on anyway. The blood from his ear soaked the top of his collar and made the leather of his mask feel pulpy where the straps rubbed against the sore spot, but he ignored it. He also ignored the shuffling sounds that reached him over the pounding gong of his own heartbeat and the frantic skips and jumps of his hole-pocked shoes against the street.

He spied some stairs from the corner of his eye, swiveled on his heel, and climbed them, not knowing where they went and not caring much. All he had to do was get out of the other fellow's line of sight, far enough away to hunker down and hide.

One of the stairs cracked beneath his foot and gobbled him

up to his shin. He pulled his leg out by his knee, tugging with his hands to extract the boot and keep on climbing.

He wondered briefly why these stairs were on the outside of a building, then noticed, when the fog parted enough to let him notice anything, that these were interior stairs after all. The building had fallen away, leaving its insides exposed. Flight by flight, he passed big stretches of shattered flooring eaten up by holes. He huffed and puffed upward while hugging the rail, which rattled in his hand and surely wouldn't hold him if he were to fall. It barely gave him balance enough to keep upright.

The Seattle city wall loomed up to his left, and that didn't seem correct. He'd gotten turned around somehow.

Didn't matter. Kept running. Heard nothing behind him, but the quiet might've been an illusion brought on by his stuffy ears. He wondered when it'd be safe to stop, and then he wondered what he'd do if he reached the top and there was nowhere left to go.

He didn't wonder long.

The stairs ran out.

Rector teetered at the edge. He shook his head, trying to let the blood run out of his injured ear. It didn't work, just made the pumping of his heart throb louder behind his eyes. But he didn't hear anyone coming up behind him, so maybe this would be a safe place to stop. To catch his breath. To wait until his pursuer had gotten bored and wandered off.

His breathing was muffled and ragged inside his mask, but in time it slowed. He balanced there, not looking down and not looking back, waiting to hear that voice call out again.

It didn't.

And after a good five minutes, he took as deep a breath as he dared—there above some precipice on the other side of that last lonely step, the bottom of which he couldn't even see—and he began a slow, quivering retreat back the way he'd come.

Funny. He hadn't noticed on his frantic way up how fragile the steps felt beneath his boots. The wobble wasn't his imagination. They creaked, too. He leaned toward the rail, and to the bit of wall that remained on that side.

Don't die yet. You ain't allowed.

"Shut your mouth, Zeke."

One hand on the splintered, rickety rail, he breathed real slow and kept his eyes on his feet. One in front of the other. One step at a time.

He stopped.

What was that noise? Had the stranger caught up to him? He held still and listened.

Sounded like breathing. Low, wet, and not very healthy. Coming from something pretty big. But he didn't see anything. The air was too dense; it moved like smoke in front of his lenses, one broken and one still clear.

Someone sighed.

Or some*thing* sighed. The gas-poisoned atmosphere whispered and complained, and once again Rector choked on a big gob of fear. It swelled until he could hardly swallow, and his heart caught up with a fluttering skip.

The breathing behind him—yes, behind him . . . and not his own—grew louder. Closer. So close he imagined he could feel it, warm and dank, against the back of his neck.

Stumbling now, he picked up his pace. He could fall, he thought. He could tumble and roll, and that would be faster, in a way. It'd hurt, and it'd be loud, but it'd be quick. A quick way to reach the bottom. A quick way to die. Wouldn't it? His ankle turned, almost sprained. But didn't. The joint kept locking, unlocking, with each stair.

A throaty groan shocked him with its nearness. He spun around, flailing, expecting to hit someone square in the face, but no. There was no one behind him, no one beside him—there couldn't be. To one side was a drop-off leading nowhere; to the other, a lone wall—a final surviving shred of the old building.

Another groan, more harsh this time and, if at all possible, closer still.

"It doesn't make sense," Rector squeaked. He saw no one and nothing, heard only the breathing, the moan that came with an edge like gargling.

He ran, tripping over himself and the uneven, unstable stairs. Behind him they crumbled away; he heard them clatter, bounce, and break on their way to the ground. And he heard something else, too: a *bang* so loud that at first he didn't realize it was a foot-step. Not until a second *bang* followed behind it, then a third and a fourth, did Rector recognize the rhythm of something stomping behind him.

Not some*one*. Not this time.

For one ridiculous moment he wondered what'd become of the other guy, the one who'd come after him first. Where was he? Maybe he was evil, and maybe he was a murderer, but he'd been human—Rector was sure of that much. And whatever was behind him, this unseen foe, this was not a man. Men didn't move so heavily, dropping from foot to foot with the weight of a horse. Men didn't have such strides, longer than a half flight of stairs. Longer than . . .

A crash shattered the old building wall and ripped the rail out of the boy's hands. He gasped and staggered, falling forward and catching himself. But the catch didn't hold, and he slipped down farther, tumbling less gracefully than he might have if he'd gone down on purpose—but descending all the same, and face-first. On the way down, he whacked his chin on a step and knew it would mean more bleeding, but he couldn't worry about that right now.

He scrambled on his hands and knees, ducking almost by ac-cident, but his timing was good. As his head went down and his knees went out from under him, an enormous shadow leapfrogged him in a flash of terrible motion.

Through his one good lens Rector saw a shape that had two arms and two legs, but was in no way human. He watched it sail overhead, a lunging hop thrusting the huge, heavy thing from one turn of the stairs to the one below it, shattering the place where it landed.

It bellowed, and Rector's heart nearly stopped. He still couldn't see it well, not through the gum-thick air, but there it was, only a few feet in front of him. All he could make out was a person-shaped monster that couldn't have been a person. No person was so huge, and no person had a face shaped like that, flattened and burnished like the leather on a rich man's chair. The shape shimmered—or, no, it didn't. It wasn't an illusion, not a trick of the air or the dim, runny light. The shadow was just covered in hair.

"Not a rotter," the damp, horrified boy muttered to himself. "Something else. Oh God, oh God. Something else!" His voice pitched up at the end, and he wanted to run. But he couldn't go back up; there was nothing left but the sky. Couldn't go down, because he'd never make it past . . . whatever *that* was.

The creature rallied itself and sprang.

Rector squealed, and with all the instinct of the not-quite-suicidal, he dove out of the thing's way. Straight off the side and into the mystery below. He closed his eyes and waited for the end, wondering which breath would be his last, hoping it came quick, and it wasn't so bad that he'd remember it on the other side. Hoping he didn't stick around as a rotter.

The ground caught him.

It met him with a *whump* that stunned him, knocking out what was left of his breath. The fall hadn't been far at all, and he almost felt cheated by the need to keep running.

Rector dragged himself to his feet, shaking all the way, and spun left and right.

He'd dropped only a flight or two, and landed in the mulchy, decaying rubble of the collapsed building, its floors having pancaked years before and gone soft with time and humidity. There were worse places he could've hit, but at that moment, he had a hard time thinking of any.

He crawled off the rubble and rolled out into the street. He knew good and well he'd made too much noise, but what could he do? The thing behind him, up on the stairs, was making more noise still, so Rector hoped that any nearby rotters would seek out the bigger, more vocal meal.

Once more, with bleeding head, scraped hands, and battered knees, he shoved one foot in front of the other on the uphill slope.

"Hey!" The voice was an outright shout this time, no longer keeping low.

Rector responded, "Not you again!" even though it was a lie, and he could've cried with relief just to hear another human being.

"What was *that*?"

"I don't know!" Rector called back, his voice creeping back toward hysterical territory.

"This way!"

"Which way?" He still couldn't see, didn't know where he was, and had nothing to go on except the idea that uphill was where he wanted to be. But a rustling and roaring from the wreckage of the fallen building told him he needed to pick a direction and commit to it.

Maybe one of the alleys. Maybe if he could get off the main avenues and onto the side streets, he could lose the monster that way. He bolted to the right, zigzagging up and around, then back onto another narrow street with mushy wood sidewalks. He left the walkway shortly after setting foot on it—too squishy; slowed him down—and instead he went for the middle of the road and ran up the center as fast as his bruised legs could carry him.

"No!" hollered his invisible advisor. "Not that way! You're headed right for—"

Rector didn't hear the last part of that sentence. All he heard was the rush of air and the gasp in his throat as he flew into open space for the second time in the span of five minutes. The world crunched and shook, and he could hear the fizzling stars that swam in front of his eyes.

The white-hot sparkles swarmed, popped, and faded. He thought he might be able to see now, so he opened his eyes. Or he tried, then realized that they were already open.

Standing above him was someone just a bit smaller than him. Chinese, he thought—something about the shape of the eyes behind the other guy's visor. And about Rector's own age. But that couldn't be right, could it? Everybody knew that Seattle was no place for women or children, or even grown men who'd very recently passed the ripe old age of eighteen.

But here was a living counterexample, shaking his head. Behind him, a ponytail swayed, dusting the tops of his shoulders. It was Rector's turn to ask "Who are you?" but the words wouldn't come. His mouth wouldn't work. The outline of the other boy faded until it was something cut from a coal black shadow, backlit as he was by the mouth of something wide and white—the curved edge of the street above.

A hole. He'd fallen through a huge chuckhole in the middle of the goddamn street, Rector thought as the stars came back and everything went away except for Zeke.

Zeke, who was just saying *Well done, dummy,* when Rector passed out.

Seven

Rector dreamed, or maybe he didn't.

He heard Zeke a time or two, saying his name. But Rector was tired of talking to ghosts, so he didn't answer, even when Zeke was demanding, and even when he sounded worried. To hell with Zeke and his worries. Rector was dying, anyway; they could hang out and be ghosts together, and wouldn't that be a kick in the pants? No good deed goes unpunished, or so he thought sourly as he tossed and turned and tried to tell the difference between asleep and awake, alive and dead.

He was lying on something firm, but possibly intended to be comfortable. Maybe this meant he *wasn't* dead; but the room felt very small and close, as if he were resting in a coffin. Then his thoughts circled around to the conviction that nobody would pay for a coffin to bury his sorry corpse—and, anyway, dead people couldn't possibly hurt this much, unless they were in hell. He was pretty sure of that. Read it in the Good Book once.

And with every ounce of his aching body, his rattled consciousness, his uncertain sanity . . . he wanted sap. He imagined he could smell it nearby—the tang of its cooking, the sharp whiff of the terrible yellow substance curling into smoke on a sheet of tin.

So he asked for some, on the off chance that anyone was listening . . . and, if so, that they'd be willing to share.

No one gave him any. But sometimes people talked to him.

For a while he heard voices conversing entirely in Chinese, and then came the dim sensation of being physically moved, forcibly relocated to some distant place in a cart, or a wheelbarrow, or something else that held him sprawling and left his elbows bruised. After that, he didn't hear Chinese anymore. He heard English—mostly from men, but sometimes from women.

"Yes, that's him. A little skinnier than last I saw him, but you can't mistake that hair."

"Your boy said his name's Rector. What kind of name is that?"

"No idea. He might've made it up, for all I know—but that's what everyone called him."

His eyes opened slowly, independently of each other, one slim crack at a time. The left one stuck a little. His vision cleared enough to pick out the details of a woman. She was leaning over him, her face a little too close for his comfort.

It felt familiar.

He recognized her, and realized this wasn't the first time she'd loomed over him, wearing a similar frown. His lips parted with the same degree of difficulty as his eyelids. He tried to say her name, but only a cracking wheeze came forth.

Briar Wilkes.

Zeke's mother.

If he'd had the energy, he might've recoiled. She was *mean*—he knew it firsthand. She'd threatened his life, limbs, and soul after Zeke had gone under the city walls; and now that Zeke was dead, she had plenty of reason to follow through on those threats. He wanted to cringe away from her, to sink farther into the thin mattress (a mattress? Yes . . . it was definitely a mattress) to avoid her and her inevitable wrath.

"He's waking up."

Briar Wilkes said, "If you can call it that. Hey, Rector, can you see me? Do you know what happened? Do you know where you are?"

He tried to shake his head, but it wouldn't move. His best defense was a pitiful one. He quit the uphill fight to hold his eyelids open, and let them shut, so at least he couldn't see her.

The other woman said, "It's all that powder he's burned up. It's cooked his brain. Look at him, you can see he's been using."

"Worthless kid. Should've tossed him right back over the wall."

"He reminds me of the men in the Salvation Army hospital. I told you about that, didn't I?"

Miss Wilkes again. "How one of 'em tried to bite you?"

"That's right. This boy, he's not that bad yet. It's not too late."

"You've got more faith in him than I do."

"Well, I never met him before. Could be he'll convince me otherwise."

The second woman had a funny accent, which Rector couldn't place. As his mind drifted backwards, away from the scene, he wondered where she came from. Didn't sound local, didn't sound like one of the Chinamen. And anyway, there weren't any China-women in the city; everybody knew that.

The next time he came around enough to listen, if not to talk, the same woman was speaking. She had a nice voice, he decided. Not the worst thing he could listen to by a long shot. This time she was talking to someone else—an older man, one of the Chinese fellows. His English wasn't great, but with some struggle from both sides, he and the woman were able to make themselves understood.

"Too much yellow in his nose."

"I know. But sometimes, when people . . . it's like when people drink too heavy and they come to depend on it. It's hard for them to stop, and when they do, they get sick. This might be the same thing. He might be just fine when he wakes up proper."

"Been three days."

"His color's better. His head's healing up, too. Isn't there some medicine we could try?"

"Time. Water. Tea. Boy not sick. Boy broke himself."

"You're probably right."

The Chinaman added, "If not, you shoot him. Take off his head. Have enough rotters already."

Rector didn't stay awake long enough to hear her response. It was easier to faint dead away than to listen to any further discussion of his violent dissection.

When he came around again, no one was talking, but he knew before opening his eyes that he was not alone.

He wasn't sure how he knew this. It was a quiet, odd sensation of sensing someone else breathing nearby, or someone else's heartbeat ticking away just outside his hearing. His head felt clammy, inside and out—like someone had left his skull out in the rain. Every limb was numb, and deep within his ears he heard a persistent whistling that was not at all like ringing, except that it was equally irksome.

He opened one eye and blinked it.

The room was dim, but not completely dark, due to the two lanterns at opposite ends of the room. For the first time he saw it clearly enough to note a few details: a row of cabinets without doors stuffed with bottles, tinctures, bandages, and other assorted doctoring supplies; jars with peeling labels and contents the color of whiskey; a barrel of water with a tap and a bucket; rags, some folded and clean, others dirty and piled in a basket; a small crowd of unlit lanterns with mirrors to direct their light as necessary.

And in a chair against the wall a lean figure waited with sharp brown eyes and a long black ponytail. This figure leaned forward and said, "Good morning, Rector. Good *afternoon,* really. It's almost dinnertime. Are you hungry? Thirsty? Do you want anything? Miss Mercy said I should get you whatever you asked for, if I could."

On the one hand, Rector liked the sound of being given whatever he wanted. On the other, he was barely awake and rather confused. All he could muster in response was something like, "What?" And even that single word came out missing half its letters.

The other fellow left his chair and came to stand beside Rector's bed.

"Water? Is that what you said?"

Close enough.

Rector nodded, realizing that he *would* like some water, yes, thank you. He struggled to lift his head off the pillow, and somehow dragged his elbow up underneath himself. "Thanks," he mumbled as he took the offered mug. The water smelled awful and didn't taste much better, but that only meant that it was local. The Blight gas had to be distilled out of the water for miles around Seattle to be safe, and even then it never tasted as fresh as a mountain stream . . . or even outhouse runoff.

Rector was used to it. He drank it down and didn't complain. He'd had no idea how parched he'd become. He asked for more.

His companion obliged, and this time the young Chinaman sat on the foot of the bed while Rector drank down the tepid liquid. The Chinaman drew one leg up beneath himself and began to chatter.

"I'm Houjin, but people call me Huey. Mostly I stay over in Chinatown Underground, as Captain Cly calls it, but sometimes I stay here in the Vaults, too. Why did you come inside the wall? Usually people are running away from something, or running *to* something."

But before Rector could respond, Houjin continued. "I mean, *I* didn't run here. I came here when I was small, with my uncle. I don't have any other family."

"Orphan," Rector choked out between swallows.

"Yes, both of my parents are dead. But there's my uncle," he repeated. "I heard your parents are dead, too. That's why you lived in the home with the holy women, isn't that right?"

Holy women? Rector frowned, then said, "Oh, yeah. The nuns. I lived in the Catholic home, that's right."

Houjin cocked his head and stared at Rector in a calculating fashion. "You must have been a baby when the Blight came."

Rector cleared his throat. His voice was coming back. "Not sure. Don't remember. But they tell me I'm eighteen, so I had to leave the home and make my own way."

Nodding earnestly, Houjin said, "I'm not eighteen yet, but I make my own way."

"You have a job?"

"I work on an airship. I'm learning to navigate, and maintain the engines. I want to be an engineer. Sometimes here in the city I work with the men at the Station, and Yaozu pays me to fix things. And sometimes I translate."

Slowly, Rector propped himself more fully upright. "You mean, Chinese to English? That kind of thing?"

"There's more than one kind of Chinese, you know. I speak a couple of them, good enough to go back and forth. And my Portuguese is good—better than my Spanish, but I'm learning. And I'm interested in French, too. I went to New Orleans a few months ago. Lots of people there speak French."

"You're a regular ol' dictionary, ain't you?"

"I like to talk. I like to learn different *ways* to talk. That's all."

Rector felt it'd be polite to throw the younger boy a bone. "You're real good at it. You've hardly got a China accent at all."

"Captain Cly says I've been losing more of my accent the more time I spend on the *Naamah Darling*. And the longer I spend around Zeke."

"What's a—"

Rector almost asked what a *Naamah Darling* was, but two things stopped him. First, his addled brain caught up to the fact that it must be the airship on which Houjin served. Second, his attention tripped over the word *Zeke*. So he asked, to make sure he'd heard correctly. "Zeke?"

"Sheriff Wilkes's son. He's the only other person down here who isn't old enough to be my father. He says he knew you, in the Outskirts. He's the one who told me you'd lived in the home, with the church women."

"He told you . . . ?"

"We go exploring inside the city all the time, but he hurt his leg out on Denny Hill, and now everyone says we have to be more careful. You can come out with us, if you want, when you feel better. Some of the old houses up there still have valuable things inside. Useful things, anyway. Sometimes. Not always . . ." His voice trailed off as if he were thinking of a few things in particular, but then it picked up again. "We have to look out for rotters, and for Yaozu's men, if we get too close to the Station and we're not supposed to be there. But mostly if you're quiet, nobody bothers you. And no *thing* bothers you, either."

"Zeke," Rector said again. He wasn't sure what to add.

"He's around—do you want me to go get him? He's been looking in on you, hoping you'd wake up. I know Zeke didn't have an easy time, being Blue's son; but he said you weren't bad to him. I know you were dealing sap out there, and that you ran around with crooks, but Zeke said you're the one who told him how to get inside."

"He was . . . he was an all right kid," Rector said, his words still dragging. He didn't want to ask all the obvious questions, because the answers were obvious, too. And he didn't want to say anything stupid to this Chinaboy because even though he was just some Chinaboy, he sounded awful damn smart, and Rector had a long-standing policy of being nice to smart people, in case they could be useful to him later.

So he didn't ask any of the things he wanted to ask. And he didn't say any of the things that were swelling up inside his stomach, all the memories of ghosts and dreams of phantoms, and the horrible haunting he'd undergone at the hands of Zeke.

Well, he thought it was Zeke. But that wasn't possible, was it? *Zeke is alive. Or else this kid is crazy.*

He strongly suspected that Houjin wasn't crazy. To prove it, he told Houjin, "I'd like to see Zeke, sure. It would be nice to see a familiar face."

"Great!" he said brightly. "Maybe you'd like some food, too—does that sound good? There's a kitchen on the next floor down. Do you want to get up and come with me? If Zeke's not there, he's out at the fort."

"Hang on. Let me see." Rector hauled his legs over the edge of the bed, knees first, then unfolded them and set his feet down on the floor. The floor was rough-hewn but it didn't creak, and he didn't feel any splinters against his bare toes. "My socks. They're gone."

This observation prompted him to look down at everything else he was wearing, in order to double-check that he was wearing anything at all.

The clothes weren't his. He didn't recognize them, but he wasn't prepared to complain about them. The shirt was sewn from inexpensive blue cotton flannel, but it didn't have any holes in it. His pants were cotton canvas, too, not wool for winter but lighter for summer—such as it was. They were brown, and there was a long seam sewn tightly across the knee where they'd split and been mended.

He was better dressed now than he was when he'd come inside the wall.

"Whose clothes are these?" he asked, patting himself down. "And where's my bag? The one I brought with me?"

"The clothes came from the stash downstairs, where the clean and stitched-up things go. Most of the linens don't come from salvage inside the wall, not anymore. Blight's too hard on the fabrics, unless they're treated with rubber or wax. So people down here—they barter, or trade. They collect." He shrugged, and Rector got the distinct impression that Houjin was talking his way around the fact that he didn't really know.

"And my things? All my worldly possessions? Did somebody make off with them?"

"Nobody made off with anything, except for you," Houjin said. The faint tone of accusation wasn't strong enough to mean anything to Rector until he added, "The satchel you took from the stopover room on Commercial is under the bed. Mr. Swak-hammer says you can have it, for now. It's one of his, but he's got others."

"Mr. Swakhammer?"

"Miss Mercy's father," Houjin said, which didn't add much to the store of what Rector knew. "He watches the underground. Him and a few other men down here, and Miss Lucy sometimes. And Sheriff Wilkes, but you already know about her."

"Didn't know she was a sheriff. Never heard of a lady sheriff."

"She took over the position from her father."

"Her father's been dead since the wall went up."

"Yes, but some of the people he freed from jail when the Blight came helped set up the underground. Half the people down here are outlaws, and the other half are outcasts; they like the idea of a lawman who was fair to everyone. And now, Miss Briar is Sheriff Wilkes." He changed the subject on a dime. "So, do you feel up to coming upstairs? I can always go get Zeke and bring him back, or bring you food if you're still too weak to manage."

"I'm not too weak to manage anything," Rector insisted, though his knees threatened to argue with him. He pushed against them, attempting to leverage himself upright. The first attempt failed. He sat back down and covered for the foible by reaching under the bed to grab his bag. His next effort to rise successfully propelled him into a wobbly, but upright, stance.

"Do you want a cane or a crutch? Something to lean on?"

"Goddamn, you're helpful. Are you always like this?"

Houjin smiled. It was a peculiar smile. It told Rector that he'd said too much. "I can get you food and water, but only if you can't get it yourself," he said carefully.

Rector's vision spun. He reached out for the headboard and steadied himself.

"Don't pretend."

"Don't pretend what?" Rector asked crossly.

"Don't pretend you're sicker than you really are. And don't pretend you're any *less* sick, either. If Miss Mercy sees you, she'll know. She'll either send you back to bed, or kick you right out of it."

"I'm not pretending anything, I'm just getting my feet underneath me. Give me a second, would you? Your Miss Mercy sounds like a holy terror."

Houjin shook his head. "No, she's just hard to fool. And while I'm thinking about it, I'll definitely get you a cane. We have some left over from when Mr. Swakhammer was hurt last year." He went to one of the cabinets, opened it, and rummaged through several apparatuses that Rector couldn't identify. Before long, he retrieved a sturdy, polished staff of reddish wood. He almost tossed it toward Rector, who was still teetering, but changed his mind at the last moment and handed it over instead.

"Jesus, Swakhammer must be huge. This thing could hold up a horse."

"Mr. Swakhammer is a big man. Everyone who lives here is either big and strong, or small and fast. Try the cane. See how it feels."

"It's fine," Rector said, testing his weight against the stick and finding that it could easily hold up three or four of him. "A little heavy." He took a few steps and his legs quivered slightly, but he liked the feeling of being upright. "Let me ask you, Huey—it was Huey, right?"

"Or Houjin."

"Huey, got it. Tell me, is there a chamber pot?"

"There's a pot, but there's also an inside-outhouse down the hall—or, that's what Miss Lucy calls it. This way." He pointed out the door and to the right. "It's not far. There's a basin in there, too, if you want to clean up a bit." Houjin said it like a hint.

Rector took it like one. "All right, that sounds fine. Could I talk you into getting me one more cup of water while I'm down there?"

"I'll dip one out."

"Thanks," Rector said over his shoulder. The trip down the hall was slower than he'd have liked, but every step felt like an accomplishment. When he'd finished in the inside-outhouse he returned to what he'd started thinking of as the "sickroom," and drank one last draught of water before following Houjin in the other direction.

"Where are we going, again?" he wanted to know.

"Kitchen."

"But we're underground, ain't we?"

Houjin nodded, then paused to let Rector catch up. He walked as fast as he talked, unless he remembered not to. "The kitchen has vents up to the topside, and we have a stove or two for cooking, but people don't use them often. Sometimes Miss Lucy does, and brings food down to Maynard's for her customers. But usually meals are cold, unless people want to go to Chinatown. We cook there all the time."

"Never had any China food."

"You wouldn't want to walk there, not in your shape. And the carts running between them . . . they're mostly for supplies, not people. I have an idea about that, though . . ." he said. He almost picked up his pace, as if his bright idea were fuel that moved him even more swiftly, but remembered Rector in time to keep from launching down the corridor like a firecracker. "I think we should use pump cars down here, like they do on the railroads above. We have a few, but not enough to keep a regular set of routes."

"I've seen those. I know what you mean."

"Or maybe streetcars. Not diesel ones like Texas makes—there isn't anywhere for the exhaust to go; it'd make everyone sick. But maybe something crank powered. The neighborhoods aren't very far apart, but if you're injured or carrying something, it's a hard hike. And we can't have horses and carts down here, obviously."

"Obviously," Rector echoed. Then he wondered aloud, "Wait, why not? Any special reason, other than that horses don't like living underground?"

Houjin paused and considered this. "Horses don't do stairs very well. And no one wants to clean up all the shit, and it's hard enough to feed people, let alone horses. Anyway, the Blight is funny, what it does to animals."

"It kills them, don't it? Same as people?"

If a good idea was fuel to make Houjin run, then a good question served as the brakes. He stood stock-still, and Rector could almost see the gears turning between his ears. "That's hard to say. I don't think anyone's ever studied it, like a scientist counting birds or drawing plants. But it's definitely different. Take the birds, for example."

"The birds?"

"The crows. We have hundreds, maybe thousands, inside the walls. Their eyes turned a funny color—a weird shade of orange, kind of like your hair. But other than that, they seem all right. And the rats . . . we used to have rats, but the Blight kept them from making baby rats, or that's what Dr. Minnericht said. So after a couple of years, there were no more rats."

"Weird," Rector observed.

The hike down to the kitchen was hard, but Rector made it

without too much wheezing—then realized upon arrival that he was so appallingly hungry that he could scarcely eat anything at all. It was an unusual sensation for someone who'd spent his life leaning against the edge of hunger, and he wondered if this wasn't a case of simply being too tired to eat.

He ate anyway.

In the large, carefully lit kitchen he gnawed on salmon jerky while Houjin rifled through the drawers, cabinets, and boxes for foods which would be good for somebody on the road to recovery. A great deal of dried fruit was on the menu—mostly apples and berries—but there were also cloth-wrapped hunks of bread, and a knifeful of fresh butter that tasted so good it made his eyes water. And he found his jar of pickles too, already opened but mostly full.

As he nibbled, he listened to Houjin natter on about the comings and goings of the underground, and the Doornails, and the residents of Chinatown, and Yaozu's men, who clustered around the old King Street Station. Rector knew he would only retain fragments of what he heard, but he didn't mind; it was nice to have an excuse to be quiet and think about things he dare not say aloud.

First and foremost: Zeke was alive. So had there ever *been* a ghost?

He narrowed his eyes and chewed thoughtfully, pretending to listen. Now that he thought about it, he hadn't seen or heard from the ghost since waking up. Granted, that was less than an hour of ghost-free awake-time, but still, it felt significant.

A brief, spontaneous thought flew out of his mouth, interrupting whatever anecdote Houjin was passing along. "Hey, how long was I out cold?"

Houjin paused mid-sentence, calculated, and said, "It's been four days since you fell down the chuckhole."

"Four days," he mused. Four days without sap. It was the longest he'd been sober in ages, and he wanted some now, but not with the same god-awful fervor as before. It felt more like a routine he wanted to indulge, or a habit he merely missed. It didn't feel like a gaping hole that ate his chest and his brain like a flame chewing through paper. Rector wasn't the very picture of health, that was for damn sure, but he had to admit there was a certain feeble glimmer of clarity—a candle's worth of awareness—that was catching hold, and his thoughts were lining up more easily, more cleanly.

By the light of this new and unfamiliar awareness, he recalled something else that made him shudder. He blurted out another question. "When I fell down the chuckhole, I was running away from something, wasn't I? Something was chasing me."

Houjin carefully masked his emotions so that Rector could barely see his uncertainty while he thought about his response. He sure did a lot of that: thinking before talking. Given how much talking he did, it made you wonder how fast his brain worked.

"You were running, yes. And I saw . . . *something.*"

"Oh, don't give me that. You saw it, plain as I did," Rector asserted, despite the fact that he hadn't seen anything plainly. He'd heard it, and sensed it, and even smelled it—or he fancied he did, despite the gas mask. When that foul, dank breath had come so close to his skin he thought he'd die from fright, the odor had oozed like wet dog and moldering pine needles. Like dirty feet and sour water.

Houjin hemmed and hawed. "Well, you have to understand . . . there are many dangers inside the wall. Many things that will chase you, and try to hurt you."

"Rotters. I've heard about them, and I heard some scraping around. Never actually *saw* any. But this wasn't a rotter, what I was running from."

"No, it *must've* been a rotter."

"*Couldn't* have been," Rector argued. "Rotters were people once, weren't they? And they don't grow, after they've gone all dead and rotty." Or so he assumed.

"No, they don't grow. And yes, they were people first."

"That thing that chased me was bigger than a person."

This gave Houjin an idea. He brightened. "Not necessarily. Captain Cly, he's much bigger than a regular man."

"You think your Captain Cly chased me and tried to kill me? Because I don't, and I haven't even met the guy. Whatever it was, it wasn't human. And it wasn't *ever* human," he said with certainty. "You saw it, too. You already admitted you did, so don't go taking it back, now."

"But there's the fog, and the Blight—it's so hard to see anything that isn't right in front of your face. All I saw was a shadow, coming up behind you. And yes, it was big, but . . ."

"What was big?"

Both boys jumped as if they'd been shocked. They turned to see a slender female figure in the doorway. Her hair was almost solid silver, and she wore it long down her back, but tied in a leather thong. She was Indian, Rector could see that at a glance, and he guessed she must be old enough to be somebody's grandmother, but she didn't look ready for a rocking chair. Everything about her was efficient and tough, from the fit of her clothes, which he guessed had once belonged to a man, to the rifle slung over her back.

Tough or no, she greeted Houjin with a toss of her head and a grin, saying, "Hey there, boy. Found yourself some company, I see. Where's your usual shadow?"

"His mother wanted him over at the fort. I don't know what for. This is Rector," Houjin declared. "Rector, this is Miss Angeline."

"Ma'am," he acknowledged.

"Huey pulled you out of the chuckhole, didn't he?"

"Yes, ma'am, that was me."

She laughed. "Those damn holes. Half of them are older than the wall. Hit your head up good, I heard."

"Yes, ma'am." When in doubt, stay polite; that was Rector's policy.

Miss Angeline came into the kitchen and helped herself to some of the salmon jerky, then pulled a bag off her shoulders and dumped its contents on the counter. "Picked up some cherries down south a bit, past where the Blight makes them taste funny. I ate some on the way here, but you kids are welcome to whatever's left."

"Thank you, Miss Angeline!" Houjin jumped off his stool and helped himself to a handful. He offered a few to Rector, who accepted, then told the native woman, "It's funny, right before you got here we were talking about just that—the chuckhole, and how Rector got there."

"Running through the dark in the Blight, I gotta assume."

"Yes, but running from something *strange*," he replied, every word dripping with conspiracy. "Tell her, Rector. Tell her what you saw."

"Neither one of us saw it too good. As you were saying."

"Rotters?" she guessed.

Rector shook his head. "No, not rotters. Something bigger, and something that still had some brains in its head. It didn't just chase me, Miss Angeline." Rector relayed the rest quickly, and with a shiver he hadn't expected. "It *stalked* me."

Silence fell between the three of them. Rector gazed nervously at Miss Angeline, trying to figure out if she thought there was any truth to his story. She was thinking about it, which he appreciated. In his experience, ninety-nine people out of a hundred would dismiss any given claim out of hand when it came from someone like him.

She asked, "You said it still had some brains. How could you tell?"

It'd been an impression, really. An understanding he'd reached at some point, but when? Oh, yes, now he remembered. "It figured out which way I was running, and it got ahead of me."

She nodded. "Might've been thinking. Then again, maybe it was too big to follow the way you were headed. How big was it?"

"Big," Rector said passionately, if uselessly. He attempted to clarify. "Bigger than a person, but smaller than . . . than . . . smaller than an elk."

"Is an elk the biggest thing you ever set eyes on?"

"Yes, ma'am."

"Huh. Mind you, bigger than a man and smaller than an elk—that could be Captain Cly."

Houjin grinned. "That's what I said, too."

"Not that I think he'd come after you," she was quick to add. "Huey, you saw this thing, too?"

Houjin replied around a mouthful of blush-colored cherries. "Saw it about as good as *he* did, through the fog, and the Blight. I don't know what it was."

"But you don't think it was a rotter."

"No," he said. Then, with more confidence, "No, it wasn't a rotter. It was shaped different. Arms were longer, and legs were shorter. It . . . it's hard to describe. Do you believe us?"

"Do I believe you? A bit, mostly because the thing you described reminds me of something. Not something very likely, so don't get your hopes up, but let me look into it. We can talk about it later."

"Yes, ma'am," Rector said, more disappointed than he cared to admit. It was nice that she hadn't called him a liar outright, but it would've been nicer if she'd simply said, *Oh sure—that's something I know all about, and you're not a loony case or anything.*

After Angeline left, Houjin and Rector munched quietly on the cherries, each lost in his own set of thoughts. Finally, there was nothing left between them but a pile of pits and stems, which Houjin swept away with his palm.

"You want to go find Zeke?" he asked, spitting the last pit into his hand, then tossing it over his shoulder.

"Sure," Rector said. But the more he thought about it, the less sure he was.

 *Eight*

The meal made Rector feel almost human again, which was good, because Houjin intended to show him every single sight in the underground at top speed. Rector tried to keep up, and he tried to respond when a response was called for; but the underground was full of stairs. Dozens of them. Hundreds of them. Surely thousands of them, maybe just in the Vaults alone. And since people don't just *fall* their way underground, unless they're being chased by long-armed monsters and happen to land in a chuck-hole, the residents put in stairs. That was fine—even sensible—but Rector would've given anything to stumble upon one of the "elevators" Houjin mentioned in passing. Apparently there had been hydraulic lifts installed in King Street Station. They sounded wonderful.

"So where are we going, again?" Rector asked, trying to keep the gasping out of his voice as he followed behind Houjin, his cane adding an extra beat to the rhythm of his pace.

Houjin, thereby reminded of his slower companion, dragged his footsteps back to a more followable level and replied, "Fort Decatur. Zeke's supposed to be helping Captain Cly, but he's more likely getting in the way. Given his druthers—did I say that right? That's how people say it, isn't it, *druthers*?—he'd be off with Miss Mercy making the rounds, but his mother said he had to give that poor woman a break from his company, so he's off to the fort."

"Miss Mercy . . . the nurse, right?"

"Right. She's twenty-four, and Sheriff Wilkes says that's too old for Zeke, but Zeke follows her around anyway, pretending to have an interest in medicine."

"Pretending?"

"As long as he makes himself useful, Miss Mercy doesn't mind him. But it's pretty obvious," Houjin declared, reaching up for a large lever beside a big round door, "that she doesn't like him half so much as he likes her. Hey, put your gas mask on."

"Are we almost outside?"

"Almost. You're all right running around under the city, most places. But not topside."

Houjin pulled the lever and heaved his full weight onto the huge round door, shoving it outward. It slipped on perfectly quiet hinges that moved without a squeak. The door looked far too large to be moved by someone so small, but something about the angles let it swing open despite the imbalance.

"Follow me," the kid prompted, taking a mask out of some pocket Rector hadn't noticed.

Rector fished his own mask out of his satchel, then mumbled, "Hey, this isn't mine. Mine got all busted up."

"I know. That's one of mine. Put it on."

"Like I've got a choice."

"Everyone has a choice."

As Rector climbed up the last set of stairs (he hoped), he watched the other boy slip the mask over his face with the practiced ease of someone who did this a dozen times a day, every day. With somewhat more difficulty, Rector put his on, then went over the threshold, joining Houjin outside the vaults.

The scenery wasn't terribly interesting—there was just a dark roof made of earth and reinforced timbers where the sky ought to be. Basement walls and building foundations disappeared upward like ordinary building fronts without windows, and the streets between them were packed and damp. The walkways were littered with barrels and buckets, stones, brooms, tracks, bricks, ladders, bird skeletons, rusting junk, and handwritten signs that advertised directions or left messages.

Houjin scanned those messages, some of which were written in Chinese, and shrugged to indicate that none of them were directed at him. "Let's go," he urged, his voice muffled by the filters.

Already, Rector hated the masks. They were uncomfortable and tight, and they made it hard to see and breathe.

Houjin used his foot to shove the door closed once more, locking it with a loud, low *clank* and *pop*. He explained, "It's easier to shut it than push it open. Are you ready?"

"Why wouldn't I be?" He might've been grinning behind that mask, but Rector didn't like it.

"Your first trip into the city didn't go so great, that's all."

"The second time's a charm."

"I thought that was the *third* time."

Rector sniffed, and caught a whiff of a sour mixture of charcoal, sweat, and mildewing leather. "Once in a while I get a second chance. I'm never lucky enough for a third."

Down short, meandering paths and around crumbling corners, he stuck close to Houjin, who knew his way around as if he had a map burned into his brain. Rector tried hard to pay attention, to note his surroundings and let his internal map keep track of them. Sometimes he thought he had a handle on it, but other times he was sure he couldn't have found his way back to the Vaults without a native scout and a fistful of cash.

"This place is a rabbit warren," he complained, holding his side. "Hey, can we slow it down a little?"

"Sure. Sorry. We're almost to the top, anyway. Catch your breath."

"We're near the fort?"

Houjin said, "Practically under it. I didn't want to take you the overhead way. You were griping about the stairs, so I thought this would be easier. One more set, and then a ladder. But that's all for now, I promise."

"I'll hold you to that."

Rector wondered why they'd worn their masks underground all this way, but then he noticed the tumbled walls and sunken places in the ceiling. The city was settling around them, on top of them. Slowly, he assumed—but surely. Inevitably. But for now, that dim, worrying thought was mostly tamped down or drowned out by another dim, worrying thought: Zeke was alive. And he was nearby.

Rector found himself stalling without really knowing why.

"Tell me about this fort," he started to request, but Houjin had already gone ahead.

"Right up here. Come on!" He made a show of climbing the stairs slowly, to let Rector catch up. At the same time, it was clear that the Chinese boy was impatient. He was probably always impatient with people who were slower than him. If that was the case, Rector thought the kid must spend a great deal of time frustrated out of his gourd.

One more door waited—a double-wide portal that slid sideways on a track. Long, loose flaps of rubber were fastened around its edges, and these retreated stickily. "They're seals," Houjin explained. "We need new ones on this door, but the rest of the block needs some maintenance before new seals will do any good."

So that answered one question: why the extra caution was in order.

Now to answer another one. The big one.

Now to confirm for himself that he *hadn't* been haunted by some scrappy kid he'd once known, because that kid wasn't dead.

He did his best to hide his creeping, almost choking reluctance. He didn't want Houjin to know how badly he feared confirming the truth—that his own mind had been toying with him all this time. So he did his best to scramble up in the other boy's wake, making a fumbling mess of it, but getting up to the surface all the same.

Houjin indicated a ladder that had been nailed, braced, and repeatedly affixed to a wall that didn't seem overly inclined to hold it. "The captain says we're putting in stairs here, soon. But for now, this is all we have. After you." He gestured grandly.

"Naw, you can . . ." Rector began, then caught himself and felt a stab of self-hatred. This was stupid, wasn't it? Nothing to be afraid of, except for the possibility that his mind was betraying him, caving in on itself like the city inside the wall. He shook it off. "All right, I'll go first."

The rungs were rough yet slippery under his bare hands. He wished he'd thought about gloves, but it was too late for that, and now he'd have to deal with it. His heels skidded but caught behind him. He pushed on against exhaustion and weakness, fumbling with his cane up the ladder and into a small, square room.

A watery glow soaked in through the windows, none of which had any glass in them. Along with the light came a faint sense of the world being discolored. The air was yellowed like old paper; it was a sepia substance, one Rector thought he could reach out and touch.

Houjin popped up, stepped off the ladder, and sighed. "Oh look—the sun's out," he announced.

The Northwest had many days when the sun rose but nobody saw it, courtesy of the cloud layer. The compressed fog of the Blight exaggerated this gloom, filtering every scrap of light and turning it to murk.

"And I think it's warming up."

"I think you're right," Rector agreed. It definitely wasn't freezing, and Rector was only a little cool without a coat. That was the best he could say of it.

Houjin began a monologue of copious explanations which

Rector half listened to and half ignored. "This is Fort Decatur. It's one of the oldest parts of the city, where all the white people holed up when there was trouble with the native people."

Rector thought of Angeline, who'd clearly made herself at home. "I guess they don't have trouble with them anymore."

"Why would they? The Duwamish all left, except for Angeline. But here we are. These days, Captain Cly is using the fort to start off a proper set of docks."

"As opposed to an improper set?"

"You know what I mean: someplace regular ships can come and go, not just sap-runners or pirates that can hover around or drop down air vents. The captain says that when he's done, we'll get mail and everything."

"You can't get mail right now?"

Houjin flashed him a look which, even through his visor, evidenced concern that Rector might've bruised his brain worse than previously feared. "Do you see a post office?"

"I do not," Rector admitted, resenting the look and its implications.

"Anyway, come on outside. I'll introduce you around."

"Outside" was achieved by stepping through a doorframe that had no more door than the windows had glass. Beyond this exit the air was brighter and the milky gray sun was more pronounced. For the first time since falling down the chuckhole, Rector didn't feel like he needed a lantern.

He blinked against this new light, weak though it was, and surveyed the scene with his usual measured uncertainty.

He saw no way out of the fort except the hole from whence he'd emerged. This was worth remarking on because the fort was— as far as he could see through the chalky gloom—ringed entirely with enormous tree trunks braced side by side and sealed with chinking.

The fort was not precisely rectangular. One wall was curved, and a second one had an indentation like it'd been built around something, but he couldn't see what that might've been. And in the center of this ungeometric, courtyard-style space, two dirigibles were docked. Neither one looked like it belonged to any official nation, army, or custom, which told Rector that they were pirate ships. Both were fixed to a totem pole that must've been carved from a tree bigger than any he'd ever laid eyes on. Pieces of the pole were rotting off, dissolving to squishy mulch around the edges, but enough of the impressive log remained intact to keep the two airships bobbing gently a few feet off the earth.

Houjin saw him observing the operation, and said, "That pole won't last, but it doesn't have to. See?" He pointed at the nearest corner, where a great knot of right angles took shape through the fog. "Pipework docks, almost finished."

"Almost," said someone behind them.

Rector swiveled with surprise, but Houjin just bobbed his head to acknowledge the newcomer. Without looking, he said, "That's Kirby Troost. He's the *Naamah Darling*'s engineer." Then he turned to Troost and asked, "Is Zeke up here?"

"Yeah, he's over by the Chinatown entrance."

Rector and Kirby Troost sized up one another from a cautious distance. Troost was a smallish man, shorter than Rector by several inches, and he was wearing a mask, so there wasn't much else to be said about him. But there was a posture to him, a forced casualness that Rector recognized and immediately mistrusted. He knew that posture, and often wore it himself. It was the posture of someone who's up to something.

Troost said, "You must be the kid who went down the chuckhole."

"That's me."

Neither one of them moved, or even blinked.

Houjin looked back and forth between them, sensing that something was afoot and he wasn't a part of it. Rector could've told him, if he'd had the vocabulary to do so, that this is what happens when two shysters recognize each other.

But he didn't have the words, and couldn't have explained it even though he knew it somewhere deep in his core. So rather than bring it up, he said to Houjin, "Let's go find Zeke, huh?"

"See you later, Troost!" Houjin declared over his shoulder, for he'd already taken off toward the corner the engineer had indicated.

Troost and Rector exchanged a wary nod, then Rector stepped back into Houjin's familiar wake.

As he tagged along through the greasy-feeling fog, more details of the fort became clear. Along one wall was an overhang with boxes beneath it, sheltered from the damp overhead, if not the damp that pervaded the air. Beside the small room above the ladder, Rector spied a stack of cleanly split lumber coated with lacquer to keep it from disintegrating in the toxic air. Here and there, machines and machine parts were stored or stopped mid-process, though what they were for, Rector didn't know.

He used these things, these little distractions, to keep himself from hyperventilating inside his mask. He focused on the improvements large and small; and the canvas, and pitch, and lined-up hammers and boxes of nails; and the mention of the Chinatown entrance, because that meant there was another way out of this fort—a place which suddenly felt very small and very close, even though it was so large that he couldn't see the farthest walls and edges.

And then, a few yards ahead, Houjin drew up short in front of an elongated lean-to. "Hey Zeke, guess who's up?" he said. The rustling, clinking noise inside the lean-to came to a halt.

"Really?" The voice was amazingly familiar for having said so little.

"He's beat-up and slow, but he'll live. Rector, you coming?"

"Right behind you."

He took a deep breath. It stung, and it filled his throat with the taste of rubber and powdery black filters. He exhaled the breath and used it to whisper, "No ghosts." The words echoed around inside the mask, and his warm, dank breath made the visor briefly foggy.

Ezekiel Wilkes climbed out from the interior of the lean-to.

He struggled over a stack of crates and stepped into the open with a wrench in his hand. There was a gas mask covering most of his face, just like everybody else, but Rector would've known him anywhere. Still skinnier than he ought to be, and still wearing a shock of ratty brown hair that would never lie down, Zeke might've been a smidge taller than the last time Rector had seen him, but maybe not. His eyes were the same, crinkled around the corners from too much defensive laughter. The Outskirts hadn't been kind to this kid, the son of the man who'd destroyed the city. Rector hoped the Underground liked him better.

Zeke's eyes lit up at the sight of a familiar face. "Rector! Hot damn, I never thought I'd see *you* inside here."

He scrambled the rest of the way out of the lean-to, a structure which was deeper and more cluttered than it appeared at first glance. Zeke jabbed the wrench into his belt and hesitated. Finally he thrust out a hand and seized Rector's, pumping it up and down like he'd found a long-lost brother.

Much to Rector's surprise, his supernatural unease about this meeting evaporated, only to be replaced with something equally bad: a deep-seated sense of embarrassment that he would've been hard-pressed to explain. He didn't deserve this welcome, not from a kid he'd sent off to die. Not from a kid he'd never treated well, even if others had treated him worse. Not from a kid he'd never even liked that much, and had mostly tolerated out of a dull sense of pity.

"Zeke," he responded awkwardly, trying to infuse the greeting with a fraction of the other boy's enthusiasm. "It's been a while.

Between you and me, I can't believe you're still alive." It was all he could think of to say, and he had no intention of ever telling Zeke how profoundly true it was. As it was, the words stumbled over one another, and came out with a stutter.

Zeke didn't notice Rector's discomfort. He laughed. "You and me both. So I guess Houjin's been showing you the ropes, huh? He knows this place better than I do. Probably better than anybody."

"Yeah, he's showed me . . . uh . . . everything between here and the Vaults."

"Did he get you something to eat?"

"Yep. Met that Angeline woman, too."

"The princess? She's a real character, ain't she?" Then someone called out Zeke's name and he responded. "Yes, Captain?"

From further back through the blurry banks of clotted air, someone hollered. "You got that wrench for me yet, or do I have to come get it myself?"

"No sir, I've got it. I'm coming." To Rector, he said, "You can meet Captain Cly, and Fang, and Troost—"

"Already met that one."

"Then you can meet the other two. Huey, thanks for bringing him up! I'm real glad to see him."

Houjin said, "I thought you might be!" brightly, though he was looking off behind Zeke's shoulder. "How's it holding up?"

Zeke followed his gaze, and understood. "So far, so good." Then he explained, "The Chinatown entrance is a little weak right now. The day before yesterday, we had a cave-in. It didn't do much damage, except that it let in some Blight. I don't think anybody got sick from it, though. Anyways, come on, Rector. Huey, you coming, too?"

"Might as well!"

Together the three of them—led by Houjin, who was fastest on his feet—went plowing through the thick air, back toward the docked dirigibles and behind them. There, hidden by the ships and the miasma of Blight, Rector spied Kirby Troost with another man. This other man was lying on his back on top of a wooden bench, reaching under one of the dirigible's back engines.

"Is this the one you wanted?" Zeke asked as he handed over the wrench.

The prone man reached up with one astoundingly long arm and accepted the wrench. He didn't look at it, but he grasped it with his hand and felt its contours. "This is it, thanks."

"Fourth try's what did it," Troost said under his breath.

Zeke overheard, and objected. "It's not like they're marked or anything."

From under the dirigible the big man said, "Let him alone, Troost."

"Captain Cly, if you've got a minute, you should come out and meet my friend Rector. I knew him in the Outskirts, and he's all right."

The captain slid down off the brace, which turned out to be the back half of a church pew.

And to think, in Zeke's hand that wrench had looked *big*.

Even seated on the ground, Captain Cly was nearly as tall as those who surrounded him. He was long-waisted and nearly bald, with buzzed-short hair that was a darkish shade of blond. He didn't require any further description. Rector would never have mistaken a man that size for anybody else. No wonder he'd been Houjin and Angeline's first point of reference when Rector had told them about the monster at the chuckhole—but no. Not a chance it was him.

"So you're Rector, huh?" the captain asked, looking him up and down the same as Troost had, minutes before. "Quite a head of hair you've got."

"Yes sir, that's what they tell me."

"I hear you were dealing sap on the Outskirts. Is that why you came inside the wall, for better access to business?"

Rector may have been burned out in the brain, but he wasn't completely stupid. "No sir, I'm leaving those ways behind me," he said, wondering if he was lying. "I came inside the wall because I'm eighteen now, and the orphan's home threw me out to seek my fortune."

"Not a lot of fortune to be found around here, son."

"I don't need a *lot* of fortune. I just need a roof over my head and some supper once in a while."

The captain didn't say anything, only held his steady stare. Rector gave it back, mostly because he was too tired to be flustered, not because he was feeling particularly brave. Eventually, Cly sighed. "Zeke says you were good to him in the Outskirts, and that's worth something. But he also told us you're the one who gave him the maps that led him in here. I'm not sure how good a friend that makes you."

"I was trying to help."

"Maybe you're young enough to believe that, and maybe you know better. But if Zeke likes you, I guess . . ." If he had more to say about the value of Zeke's endorsement, he changed his mind. "Anyway, welcome to Seattle. If you want to hang out around the Doornails, stay out from underfoot and find ways to make yourself useful. Otherwise, maybe you'll find that minimal fortune you seek out at the Station."

His closing words were spoken in a friendly tone. Somehow, they still sounded like a threat.

The captain gave the boys a tiny salute, barely a dip of his head, and went back underneath the dirigible. From under there, he added, "Zeke, if you want to run off and show this kid whatever Houjin hasn't showed him, that's fine with me. Houjin, I might require your assistance here in a few minutes."

"Yes sir," Houjin said, sounding only slightly disappointed. Then he perked up. "Are you almost done with the engine up-grades?"

"Yes."

"Can we move on to the hydrogen setup next?"

"Yes."

"Did you get all the parts you needed from Portland?"

"Yes."

"Even the thruster you weren't sure you could find?"

"Got one that'll do in a pinch."

"Can I have the old one?"

"I suppose."

"Do you care if I take it apart?"

Wearily, the captain said, "No, I don't care if you take it apart. Hey, Huey? Never mind what I said just now; how about you run off with those two for the afternoon? We can get started on the hydrogen tanks tomorrow. I think I'd rather take my time on the engine than have you rushing me."

"Didn't mean to rush you, sir!" he chirped, then grabbed Zeke and Rector by one elbow each. As he hauled them away from the craft, he whispered, "Quick, before he changes his mind."

Once they were out of earshot, back by the Chinatown entrance—a black, gaping hole in the ground that could've gone anywhere, for all Rector knew—Zeke used that same elbow to jab Houjin in the ribs. "You did that on purpose."

"I'd rather work on the tanks than the engine. But I knew he wasn't going to start on the hydrogen until tomorrow."

"I wish I had your knack for driving him crazy so he'd send me away."

Houjin grinned inside his mask. "Apparently you *do*."

"Not on *purpose*." He sighed. "I'm no good at ship work, and I don't like it. I don't know why he insists on trying to teach me."

"Yes, you *do*," Houjin argued.

Rector asked, "Why?"

Zeke preempted him. "Shut up, Huey."

Before Rector could press for details, a voice drifted up from the Chinatown entrance, and something at the edge of his vision *moved*. At first it looked so much like a ghost it almost stopped his heart. It was barely a flicker, and then it was something larger and fuller. It moved with purpose. The shadow was person-sized and it was masked.

Rector took a step back just as Houjin dropped to his knees. "Hello?" Houjin called down the hole. Then, clearly seeing someone he recognized, he lapsed into Chinese.

Rector and Zeke looked at each other, and Zeke shrugged. "I don't know any of that Chinese talk. Huey tried to teach me, but I didn't pick it up worth a damn."

"I don't get how anybody understands it."

"Me either, but he says there are millions of people who speak it just fine, so it works for somebody, someplace."

The flash of motion down below swished again, and with it came the shape of a man wearing loose-fitting black from head to toe, though the edges of his garments had white hems that made him appear outlined—if horribly insubstantial—in the dark. He rose up the stairs (always, more stairs) with a smoothness that once again knocked up against Rector's fear of ghosts and the way they hovered as they approached.

His masked head emerged, just high enough so he didn't have to yell when he spoke to Houjin. Whatever they discussed, it involved Rector. He knew it easily, same as he knew Kirby Troost was to be watched and worried about, by instinct or suspicion. Houjin kept peeking at him, and his mood became precise: polite, but reluctantly so. He was arguing, and losing.

Finally he stood up, and the speaker disappeared back down below.

"What was that about?" asked Zeke. Rector would've asked himself, except that he didn't think he wanted to know.

Houjin said, "Rector, we have to go down to the Station. Yaozu wants to see you."

"Yaozu?"

"He's the man who runs the Station. And everything that happens down there."

Rector swallowed, hoping the mask hid his nervousness. "I know who he is. I've heard all about him."

"Have you heard it ain't a good idea to tell him no?" Zeke asked.

"I heard that much, yeah. I still don't want to go visit the Station."

Zeke took a stab at reassuring him. He slapped a hand on Rector's back and told him, "I'm sure it's no big deal. Sometimes he wants a word with people who are new here, that's all. Maybe he heard about you selling in the Outskirts. Could be, he wants to talk business. Maybe he wants to offer you a job."

"Zeke, you're full of shit."

"No. I'm not. There are rules down here, is all."

Houjin cleared his throat and suggested, "Let's go across the bridges. It's faster that way, and we'd have to wear masks underground anyway, thanks to that cave-in."

"Right!" Zeke said more brightly. "We can take in some scenery."

"I'm not sure I'm up to more stairs yet, fellows." Rector waggled the cane for emphasis.

Zeke slapped his arm again. "Get up to it, Rector. Yaozu isn't a teacher, or one of them nuns at the orphan's home. And no matter how big you talk, he won't excuse you with a sick note."

 *Nine*

Rector very badly wanted some water, but he knew better than to ask for it, because since they'd left the serious, sturdy confines of Fort Decatur there'd been nothing to drink but the thick, smoky air. Nobody would remove a mask in this permanent state of terrible weather, and even if there'd been a spot to do so, there was no water topside that didn't run yellow.

"I don't know," he whined. He hated himself for sounding so weak, but there it was. "This is tougher than I'm ready for. I can't do this, not so fast."

"We'll slow down when we get to the third-level bridges," Houjin promised. "For now, we're still within grabbing distance."

"Grabbing distance?"

"Rotters. You know," Zeke told him, urging him forward, around a corner, and up a ledge—even being so kind as to give him a boost. "Sometimes they pile up on top of each other, and they can get higher than you think. Anything within the first floor is grabbing distance."

"Still haven't seen one." Rector clutched his side, where he felt a sharp, stinging stitch from all the exertion. "I only seen or heard one thing, and Huey tells me it wasn't a rotter."

"Come to think of it"—Zeke scratched at the spot where his mask strap wrapped behind his head—"I haven't seen too many of them myself—not lately. But we're underground a lot," he considered, "and we go out of our way to avoid 'em. Come on up, Wreck. We're almost high enough to dodge 'em."

Rector took Zeke's outstretched hand and let himself be hauled atop a carefully placed stack of debris. At the pinnacle, Houjin rummaged under an old fire escape and turned up a hook on a rope. He threw this hook up into the air—once, twice, a third time, before it caught—and it snagged a metal rung. As Houjin coiled the rope around his arm, the rung slid down and brought a rigged set of painted iron stairs with it.

"It's on a spring," he explained. "Hold it down, would you, Zeke?"

"Got it. Rector, you go on ahead. We're right behind you. Hold the rail if you feel the need. Ain't no shame in it, 'cause these things are slippery sometimes."

Rector cringed, but stepped up onto the bottom stair and gripped the skinny metal rail. Under his bare hands, it felt coated in slime. "Wish I had some gloves."

"Aw, shit. I didn't notice," Zeke said, climbing onto the structure and following Rector. "We'll get you some back in the Vaults, or maybe we can beg some off Yaozu if we ask real nice. You can't run around like that—the air will burn you if you let it go too long. There's a lot to learn about living down here. Not everybody's up to it."

"I'm up to living here, or anywhere else," Rector boasted, but the squeak of exhaustion in his voice undid his claim.

"Ten minutes ago, you weren't up to *stairs*," Houjin pointed out.

Rector grumbled, "Hush up." But he kept climbing, clinging to the rail and hauling himself forward, upward, and onto a platform big enough to hold all three of them.

They stood there shivering as Houjin flipped another latch on a door that looked no hardier than wet paper. "Inside, and we're safe," he promised. "I'll pull the stairs up behind us."

Again, Rector went first.

He let himself inside through a doorframe that was actually a large window frame. The darkness within this new space reminded him of the orphan's home, except that most of the windows were broken. This was a dingy place occupied by dust, trash, and left-over scraps of nothing useful.

Rector leaned forward, resting his hands on the tops of his legs and hanging his head down low. He desperately wanted to shut his eyes. More desperately than that he wanted to lie down, and more desperately still, he wanted to sleep for another four days.

"We have to keep moving, Wreck," Zeke nudged him. "Yao-zu's men will have the message back to him by now, saying you're coming."

Rector snapped, "Give me a minute," without raising his head.

Houjin shook his head. "You're not used to breathing in these masks. It's hard at first, but you'll learn."

"It's not the *mask*. I hurt all over. It's been a rough week." But now that he'd denied it, he realized Huey might be right. In addition to the aches radiating from the bruises on his back, arms, and legs, he felt a cramping tightness in his chest with every breath he drew. "How much farther, anyway? And will there be more stairs?"

Houjin speculated, "Maybe half a mile. But from here on out, all the stairs go *down*."

"Half a mile, I don't like. All downstairs, I can live with."

"Then keep moving," Zeke said.

"Stop being so goddamn pushy."

"I'm trying to help."

"Well, *don't*." Rector straightened himself up and prayed for a nice soft feather bed, but told God he'd settle for enough energy to make it to this crazy train station. "Let's go, if we're going."

Houjin crouched and used his hand to push down a loose

floorboard. A trapdoor lid came aside, and under it were lanterns. "All right, but take one of these. You probably won't need one, but you never know."

Zeke agreed. "Always better to have one, just in case."

"You two carry them. I can barely carry myself."

"Have it your way," Houjin said, missing a measure of his usual levity. "I don't know how long you plan to survive down here. We do look after our own, but like Miss Lucy says, the Lord helps those who help themselves."

Rector sniffed. "I'll help myself just as soon as I can breathe without hurting and walk without fainting, thank you very much. Four days," he reminded them both. "I spent four days down on my back. Give me half that to get myself back up."

Zeke said, "That sounds fair."

"You're easier on him than you ought to be." Houjin handed Zeke a lantern and took one for himself. He fished a box of matches out of his pocket and tried to strike one. "Yaozu isn't so generous."

"You act like this fellow is some kind of bogeyman."

Houjin stopped fiddling with the match and squinted through his visor. "What's a bogeyman?"

Zeke said, "A monster, sort of. Something that comes for you at night after you go to bed."

Houjin gave this some consideration, and told him, "Maybe that was it—the monster that chased you into the chuckhole. Maybe it was a bogeyman."

"It wasn't a bogeyman," Rector mumbled unhappily, now wishing he hadn't said anything at all about the thing he'd run from, or mentioned the bogeyman, either, since Houjin was obviously testing out this new English word and having fun with it. "There ain't no such thing."

"Something chased you into the chuckhole? Was it a rotter?"

"No."

And in this way, Rector found himself telling the story to Zeke, just like he'd already told it to Houjin and to Angeline. He relayed it haltingly, stopping often to catch his breath as they went deeper into the building's interior; and he continued telling it as they took a ladder up one last story to the roof (it was a ladder, not stairs, as Huey was fast to point out). He was finished with the highlights by the time they stood on the roof, testing out the long, narrow bridge that spanned the distance to the third floor of a hotel across the alley below.

Zeke put a foot on the bridge and shoved. It creaked, but didn't sag.

"Are you sure it'll hold us?"

"Pretty sure," Houjin confirmed. "It held Mr. Swakhammer the other day, and he weighs as much as all three of us together."

"Maybe he weakened it up for us."

"Maybe you're a chicken," Houjin offered.

"Calling other fellows chicken is a good way to get your nose socked in."

Houjin didn't look too worried. He said, "I'll remember that. And *you* remember that all these things—the lanterns, the bridges, and the stairs—are here for a reason. You can use them, or you can die within a day or two."

"What happened to that cheerful son of a bitch who woke me up?" Rector said, rhetorically.

"Guys, knock it off," Zeke pleaded. "Rector, tell me more about the monster you saw at the chuckhole."

"I already told you the whole story. This guy," he said, cocking a thumb at Houjin, "has heard it three times now, and I bet he's sick of it."

Houjin nudged the bridge with his toes. Unless Rector's eyes deceived him, it was made of more doors fitted together end to end, buttressed with planks. "At least it's interesting. The monster, I mean. More interesting than listening to you complain."

"You believe him?" Zeke asked.

"I saw it, too. And Miss Angeline believed him, I think."

Zeke seemed surprised. "Really?"

Houjin nodded. "She knows a lot about what happens outside the walls. Maybe something lives out there, something we never saw inside here."

"Like what?" Zeke asked.

"Like . . . an animal?"

Rector disagreed. "Never saw an animal like that before. Just like I still ain't seen no rotters."

Both Houjin and Zeke went to the roof's edge, where there was nothing but a low wall between them and the streets below. They leaned out over the abyss, squinting as far as they could through the thickened air.

Rector joined them, albeit a bit more carefully.

Zeke said, "It's weird, ain't it? Up here, we don't need to worry about getting their attention. They can't touch us. Or they *couldn't,* if they were hanging around. These blocks should be . . . there should be *dozens* . . . hundreds of the things by now. We haven't been real quiet." He sounded almost disappointed, like he'd wanted to show Rector this bizarre, interesting thing about his new hometown, but he'd been thwarted.

Rector didn't mind the silence and its utter lack of rotters. Exhaustion had settled on him like a cast-iron coat and dampened everything else—his nervousness, his faint, morbid eagerness and dread about seeing the undead, and even his irritation at Houjin.

He said, "It's all right with me. Like the nuns always say, we should count our blessings. Let's go see ol' what's-his-name and get this over with."

Over the rickety bridge they went, single file, without even the frail handrail they'd had on the fire escapes. Rector used the cane to help himself balance, but he didn't look down. There was nothing to see, he told himself. No hordes of rotters; not even a single shambler. Nothing but fuzzy tinted air, looking deceptively like a plush yellow cushion that might catch him if he fell.

Into the next building they went, through another door that used to be a window. The lanterns were still useful inside the old hotel, for the interior was all boarded up. Houjin had to visibly restrain himself from gloating about the lanterns, but what could you expect from a kid like that? If he gloated every time he was right, no one would ever put up with him.

Zeke got excited and led the way down a set of stairs (more stairs, yes, but going down) to the second floor. He knew how to get through this set of blocks, and took it as a point of pride that he didn't have to rely on Houjin to traverse the next two structures.

As they trekked toward the Station, they discussed the Chuckhole Monster, as they'd come to call it. They agreed to trust one another's stories and assume that something new and unseen was stalking the streets of the poisoned city, and they likewise agreed that it might be worth their time to go hunting for it.

Carefully.

Rector was just thinking that they'd surely gone more than half a mile when he started hearing things that implied they weren't completely alone in the walled city. Up to that point it'd been downright spooky, with nothing but their own scuffling, scrambling, and chatter to break the quiet. Now he detected the distant churn of big machines huffing in a low rhythm.

"Are we almost there?" he inquired.

"Not much farther," Houjin assured him, though he'd been saying that for what felt like hours. This time, he added, "See that big tower, through the fog?"

He thought he detected something very tall, standing as pallid as a phantom. Not more than a couple of blocks away, but it was so hard to see—even with the pale white glow of the sun still struggling down through the atmosphere. "I see it."

"We're going inside, and down underground again. The Station's on the other side."

"That's good to hear." Rector sighed. Not that he was enthused about the prospect of hiking all the way back to the Vaults, but he was taking this one step at a time. His feet were tired. His legs hurt. His chest felt as if a bear were using it for a footstool. And now he had to go chat with a bogeyman.

"What's that sound?" he asked.

Zeke answered, "See those tubes? Sticking up through the air, and up over the Blight layer?"

"I think so."

"They're air tubes, leading down to pump stations. Chinamen work the air rooms, mostly—they use coal and big engines to suck the clean air down, so we can breathe it when we're underneath."

"Except when the ceiling caves in."

"Except for that, yeah."

Rector might've asked more questions, but somewhere nearby a moan rose up—forlorn and raspy and wet around the edges.

The boys all froze. Their eyes jerked back and forth, exchanging silent questions and answers. Houjin said, "You wanted to see a rotter, didn't you, Rector?"

"I never said I wanted to. I just said I *hadn't*."

Another deep, sad groan called out. This one received an answer.

"That's them," Zeke whispered. "Down below. Don't worry too hard. All these buildings are sealed on the ground floor. They can't get inside."

"You sound pretty sure of that."

Houjin said, "He's right. These buildings get checked all the time, the ones with the bridges and seals. Yaozu doesn't want leaks any more than the Doornails do—and he's got more men working for him. He maintains the place."

Zeke went to the nearest window and hung out of it, turning his neck this way and that to get the best view through his visor. "I don't see them, but they sound pretty close."

"Not too close, I hope." Rector scratched at the back of his hand, but that only made it itch more. He scratched harder, every draw of his dirty fingernails ecstasy and misery.

Zeke looked back over his shoulder and saw him. "Stop doing that. You'll make it worse."

"I already figured that out."

"Then why are you still doing it?"

"I can't stop."

Houjin sighed. "We have to get you some gloves."

"Can you tell where it's coming from? Listen . . ." Zeke said, and they all stopped talking.

At first, the only sounds they heard were the filtered hiss of their own breathing and the scraping of Rector's nails against his skin.

But outside, the mournful, sickly, wordless cries continued.

"Let's go see if we can find them," Zeke suggested.

"Do we have to?"

Houjin said, "If we don't know where they are, we can't avoid them."

"I thought we weren't going down within grabbing distance."

Zeke hemmed and hawed as he went to the other corner window. "We have to get down and cross one street. There aren't any bridges into the tower—it's too far away from the nearest buildings."

"You two can really try a man's patience, you know that? You tell me no more stairs, and then there are ladders. You tell me we're staying out of reach, and then you admit we're headed into the road where rotters can chase us all they like."

"Goddamn, Wreck. I don't know when you got so fussy, but it don't look good on you."

"Catch me sometime when I haven't been in bed sick for a week."

"You were in bed *hurt,* for four days," Houjin corrected.

Rector would've spit if he hadn't been wearing that miserable mask. He fumed instead. "Neither one of you is worth a damn as a guide."

"Getting around inside the wall ain't like walking across the Outskirts, Wreck. And I still don't see the rotters," Zeke said. "Maybe we should—" He stopped. And he whispered, "Do you hear that?"

"The rotters?" Rector asked.

Zeke shushed them, then held out his hands to imply that Houjin and Rector ought to do likewise.

Houjin came up beside Zeke and pressed his back against the wall. He peered out the window, then told Rector, "Yaozu's guys. You want to avoid them."

"But Yaozu invited me."

"Yes," Zeke nodded. "But those fellows are trouble, some of them. Maybe they'll believe us if we say we're on a mission from their boss, or maybe they'll think we're dumb kids who're up to no good. We'll tell Yaozu we ran into some rotters and had to take the long way around. He keeps an eye on where they cluster, so as long as we're telling the truth, he won't get too mad about it."

Rector didn't like any of this, but he could hardly object, so he followed Zeke's lead. He settled down on his hands and knees in case someone his height could be spotted through that big broken window.

All three boys hid, but peeked over the edge of the sill down at the street below.

To the west of their hiding spot was the empty shell of a building without a roof. Or, to be more precise, the roof had fallen down inside it and now served as a very uneven, none-too-attractive floor. This floor had a large hole at one end, though where this hole disappeared to was anybody's guess.

Houjin kept his voice low. "That place used to be called McKinnen's; it was a dry goods store. It was too far gone to shore up and save. Not enough structure to seal it or make it useful."

"*Someone* thinks it's useful," Rector muttered back.

"Looks like it," Zeke said, almost too loudly. "What's going on down there?"

They craned their necks, still trying to keep from being seen. Their shoulders knocked together and their knees jockeyed for position. Fragments of ancient broken glass scattered under their grasping, brushing fingers.

In the ruins of McKinnen's, no more than thirty yards away, two men were backing up toward the hole in the former roof. Each man held a rectangular metal shield that looked as though it had been pounded out of tin. With these shields, the men pushed, knocked, and otherwise pressed four staggering, unsteady men away from themselves and the hole.

"Rotters!" Zeke said in a voice too high pitched to call a whisper, and not loud enough to call an exclamation.

"Fresh ones!" Houjin said back. His eyebrows crowded close together behind the visor. "*Real* fresh."

"What are those two guys doing?" Rector asked. "The ones with those . . . shields, or whatever they are."

Houjin breathed, "I don't know . . ." as if it were something he didn't often say. "It's like they're . . . they're herding those rotters away from that hole. You know what, I bet you it goes down to the underground. They're just trying to get away from the rotters. I think that's all."

Rector adjusted his position so he could scratch at his hands some more. "Why don't they shoot them?"

It was a good question. Neither of the boys had an answer.

Zeke smacked Rector's fingers away from one another in a

vain attempt to keep him from scratching, then said, "The fellows with the metal plates have masks on. The other guys don't, but they haven't been rotters more than an hour. Look at 'em—their clothes ain't even torn yet. Maybe they had some kind of accident."

With worry dripping from every word, Houjin said, "The cavein. It must've been worse than we thought. They were poisoned by the air downstairs."

Rector said, "That don't explain what they're doing in the middle of that old shop."

One rotter fell out of the ruins and into the street, and another was kicked away by the shield bearers. One at a time, the two masked men backed down into the hole—using their metal plates to hold the new rotters at bay—and disappeared. With a loud, fumbling clank and crash, a door was slammed into place from somewhere below.

The hole vanished, and the rotters were left to mill about, groaning and griping.

They wandered away in a small, sad pack, and were gone.

Rector, Houjin, and Zeke stared after them until the shambling men could no longer be seen through the fog, then they waited a little longer, until they could no longer hear the things, either. When the coast was clear, Zeke let out a nervous laugh and pulled himself to his feet. "That's just about the damnedest thing I ever seen!"

Houjin shook his head in disbelief, not disagreement, but Rector didn't get it. "What was weird about it? Rotters are weird, sure. But I thought people down here . . . got used to them. Those two fellows in masks, they were used to them."

Zeke said, "People who are used to 'em don't shove them around with big metal plates. They shoot them in the head and call it a day."

"It's true," Houjin assured Rector. "That . . . that was . . . exactly what you said. Weird." Then he fell silent.

Zeke didn't seem to notice, and Rector didn't want to push. He'd gotten enough bad news already, and there was still a bogey-man to meet. "Weird or not, we've got an appointment, don't we? Get me down to see this guy."

"Right," Houjin said firmly. He looked glad to be given a new train of thought. "Not much farther."

"You keep saying that."

"It keeps being true. Down some more stairs, across the street, and into the Smith Tower."

Zeke chimed in, "And then it's a straight shot to the Station."

This time, Rector's guides were as good as their word, though the truth of the matter didn't make crossing the street any less nerve-racking given the blind corners, the soup-thick fog, and the fresh knowledge of rotters in the area. But everyone stayed quiet and all heads were kept down, and soon they were back under-ground beneath the tall, white tower.

In the meantime, Rector concentrated on putting one foot in front of the other. It took more focus than it should have, but Rector wasn't merely tired, and he wasn't merely battered. He was also dogged by the old yearning tugs of sap, and it made him cranky. Now that he was up and around, just thinking about it made his head ache and swell. He felt the exaggerated sensation of his cheeks inflating, stretching the gas-mask straps and squeez-ing his skull. He tasted that peculiar yellow stink in the back of his throat, down past his tongue. He experienced the ghost-pains of his simmering blood, wanting to be seared like lightning.

Visiting Yaozu might be a good thing. Yaozu had plenty of sap.

As Rector followed Zeke and Houjin down streets that felt like mining tunnels, across tracks for carts, and around the more heav-ily populated corners of the Station, he began to plot. He could try negotiation. Barter. Begging. All the usual tricks. Sap couldn't be that hard to come by, there at the source.

Houjin announced, "We're here! This is the lift."

"And this will take us into the Station?"

"Yep." Zeke hesitated, looking embarrassed—even behind the mask. "But you know how it goes, Huey: This is where I turn around. Momma will kill me if I go any deeper."

Rector snorted. "Still obeying your momma? At your age?"

"You've met her. 'Sides, Yaozu wants to see *you*, not me. He don't have no use for me—he's told me so himself."

"Lucky you."

Zeke shrugged. "You might get lucky, too. Huey, I'll see you when you come back around, huh?"

"Sure. I'll bring him back. Let him go to bed, if that's what he wants."

Rector didn't like being talked about as if he wasn't there, but all he said was, "Later, Zeke. Give my regards to your momma."

"You don't mean it, so I won't bother."

"Suit yourself."

On that note, Zeke turned back the way he'd come. Houjin unhooked a retracting metal gate and slid it aside. "After you," he said.

Once Rector was on board, Huey joined him inside. He closed the gate again, pulled a lever, and together they swayed slightly as the lift jerked, then started its descent.

While they dropped—a bit too fast for Rector's liking, but at least it wasn't stairs—Houjin peeled his gas mask off and drew a deep breath. He let it out, then said, "You can take yours off, too, now. It used to be that you could go from the Vaults to the Station without wearing one, but we've had so many problems lately . . . it's just not safe."

"Nothing's safe down here. That's what it looks like to me."

"Looks aren't everything."

"They're *something*."

Houjin closed his mouth and left his hand on the lever as he stuffed his mask into the back of his pants. Likewise, Rector removed his own. It came off his face with a sucking noise that made him want to retch.

He tossed his head back and forth and combed his fingers through his hair. It was wet with sweat where the straps had held the mask steady, and everything felt like it needed to be washed. That damn Blight gas made everything slick and dirty; there was no getting away from it.

He glanced at his hands and grimaced. They bled at the knuckles and along their backs where he'd rubbed them against his pants in a desperate and futile effort to relieve the itching.

"You think that nurse in the Vaults will have some cream for this?"

The lift stopped with a bump and a clatter. Houjin opened the gate and held it for Rector, who exited into a shockingly ornate corridor.

"Maybe."

Long red runners followed the length of a marble-tiled hall, and gold brocade paper covered the walls in a fuzzy, lustrous pattern. Gas-lamp sconces hung in pairs, but they weren't hooked up to gas. Even a technological know-nothing like Rector could see that they'd been refitted for electric lights, and these glass bulbs burned hot, sparking and fizzing almost like the candles or lanterns they'd been designed to replace.

"Wow. Get a gander at this place!" Rector exclaimed.

"I've seen it before." Houjin closed the gate to the lift and started off down the hall to the right, but Rector didn't follow him. Not immediately.

"Hey, what's up with you, anyway?" he asked. "Why'd you get so quiet on me?"

"I'm thinking."

"Is that the only time you're quiet? Because this is the first time you've shut up since I woke up."

Houjin stopped and turned around. "Why do you care? You haven't been listening."

"I've been listening *some*. But now you're mad, and it's making me squirrelly."

"I'm not . . . *mad*," he argued, calculating the worth of the word, and discarding it. "I'm worried."

"About me?"

"Hell no. Something else. I'll tell you later."

Rector said, "Fine," and this time when Houjin continued down the hall, Rector followed him. He caught up and found himself worrying, too, but not knowing why. There were so many goddamn things to worry about in this place, it was hard to tell them all apart.

Houjin reached a pair of huge metal doors, painted with a mural that looked fresh from a museum, with seals, orcas, and eagles presented in shimmering pastels. He would've stopped to stare, but Houjin pushed against the doors and they split down the middle, cutting the scene in two.

"Yaozu's quarters are this way. They used to be Minnericht's, but Yaozu moved in when Minnericht died."

"Took over the guy's home and business both, did he?"

"Look at this place. Wouldn't *you*?"

The floor was marble, peppered with lush rugs in a variety of bright colors. Rector wasn't sure if he should step on them or not; they looked foreign and expensive. Then again, if you were going to put something on the floor, you had to expect people to walk on it, didn't you?

Guided by this rationale, he quit avoiding the rugs and started watching his surroundings. He noticed for the first time how high the ceilings were, and how they were covered with ornate tin tiles. "This place," he observed, "is too pretty to be underground."

"Underground people don't deserve pretty things?"

"I didn't say that. I meant it's unusual. Don't get your dander up."

"I don't know what that means," Houjin admitted.

"It means don't take no offense, 'cause I didn't intend any."

"All right, I won't. And . . . we're here."

They entered a large room with a fireplace and a table that might've been used for dining if it hadn't been covered with books and candles. A pair of reading spectacles were folded neatly atop a stack of papers.

"We're *where?*"

Houjin answered vaguely. "This is where he takes visitors. I'll be waiting in the lobby."

"The lobby? Where's that?" Rector didn't like the soft tremor of panic in his words, but there was nothing to be done about it now.

"It's where people would've waited for the trains, if the trains had ever come. There are benches, and ticket counters, and things like that." Now Houjin was the one who sounded weary, though Rector preferred to think that the boy was only thinking. That's what he'd told him, after all.

"You're just going to leave me here?"

Before Houjin could answer, a faint padding of footsteps echoed from the corridor.

Both boys looked to the entryway and were soon rewarded by the sight of a Chinese man wearing white. The newcomer was an inch or two taller than Rector; somehow his clothes both fit him well and flowed around him like a pale and dancing shadow.

Rector tried not to stare. "Yaozu?" He immediately felt dumb for putting a question mark on the end.

"Ah, yes. Rector Sherman. There you are. Thank you for coming."

"Um . . . you're welcome?"

Yaozu's English sounded better than Houjin's, which was saying something. He spoke Chinese to Houjin, who nodded and flashed Rector a half smile that Rector couldn't return, no matter how hard he tried: it battled his mood, and came out as a grimace instead.

"See you later," Houjin promised.

And then he bowed a hasty departure that left Rector and Yaozu alone together in the big meeting room, which suddenly felt rather warm.

 *Ten*

Rector stood there shifting from foot to foot while Yaozu appraised him. The boy was tired of being appraised. It made him feel like somebody's horse. Under different circumstances, he might've opened his mouth about it, but not here, and not now. Not to this fellow, who folded his arms and pursed his lips like he was considering what he wanted, and what to ask, and how to proceed.

To start, Yaozu suggested, "Why don't we sit down? Join me at the table, and we'll have a conversation."

"About what?"

"You. Coming here. What you want, what you expect. What use you can be."

"To you?"

As if he were mildly surprised, Yaozu said, "To the *city*, of course. Think of it that way. If you aren't any use to the city, then you aren't any use to *me*."

"I heard Zeke isn't any use to you."

"That's true, he's not. It's strange, really. Given his parentage, you'd think he'd show more . . . potential. However, given that his mother is so popular with the Doornails, there's no sense in throwing the lad back over the wall."

Rector squirmed. "Aw, Zeke's not so bad."

"If I thought he was, I'd have done something about it.

But you're not here to talk about Zeke. You're here to tell me what you're doing inside my city. So far as a land of opportunity goes, you could've picked greener pastures."

Rector shrugged. He did his best to hold eye contact, but it was hard. Yaozu had a stare that could pierce granite. "I . . . I turned eighteen, and got thrown out of the orphan's home. Didn't know what to do, or where to go," he said, repeating the line he'd been feeding to others.

Yaozu steepled his fingers, and leaned back in the chair. After a few seconds of uncomfortable silence, he said, "I believe . . . *most* of that."

Rector fidgeted in his seat, a hard-backed wooden thing that hadn't been designed for comfort. He tapped his foot against the nearest table leg, then stopped himself and asked, "What part don't you buy?"

"The part you aren't selling. Did you come here because of Zeke, or because of the sap market? I know you were selling it, in the Outskirts. Big Pete Holloway said one of his boys supplied you, and that you did a fair amount of business with Harry, the chemist from Vancouver who set up shop in the Outskirts."

"I did better than *fair*," Rector argued, on the off chance this was some kind of job interview.

"No, let's leave it there. If you hadn't smoked up most of your profits, we could perhaps call it *good*."

Rector swallowed. He couldn't think of a reply, so he didn't give one.

"It's written all over your body," Yaozu continued. "Your skin—the color's changing, very slightly, around your eyes and mouth. Your gums are receding. Your hair, it's very *exuberant*. But it's been falling out, hasn't it?"

"Maybe."

"Maybe," Yaozu echoed with something perilously close to disgust. "You're a user, Rector. A longtime user with heavy appe-

tites and, I'd wager, a rather serious addiction. Addicts aren't any use to me, Rector. Do you understand? I can't trust addicts. Their minds are too far gone for detail-oriented production work, and they steal too much when they sell."

"I never stole anything."

"You skimmed. Extensively. Please don't insult me by lying about it."

Rector didn't like the way Yaozu said *please*. It didn't sound like a request. It sounded like a bullet. "All right, I smoked and I sold. You want me to pay it back? I don't even know how much I took over the last few years."

Yaozu shook his head. He squeezed the spot between his eyebrows and sighed. Rector got the distinct impression he was giving this man a headache, and that headaches and Yaozu were probably a bad combination.

He continued, "I can work it off, if there's debt you're worried about. I'm an excellent salesman."

"I bet you are. But since you're now officially a grown man, with a troublesome birthday behind you, perhaps we can wipe the slate clean. Just this once. Consider it a birthday present."

"What? Really?"

"It's no great risk for me to make the offer. If you persist in being trouble, or *making* trouble, then I daresay the slate won't stay clean for long. But should you feel inclined to turn over a new leaf, then there's no time like the present. Tell me, Rector. Are you interested in a new leaf?"

"Yes sir. Very much, sir." He'd never called a Chinaman "sir" before, but, like this whole leaf-turning thing, there was no time like the present to start.

He nodded slowly. "Well, that's something. You still have the self-preservation to lie on the fly, so you're not as far gone as I'd feared."

"You . . . you'd feared?"

"I'd heard stories. About you."

"From who?"

"Customers. Suppliers. For such a young man, Rector, you've developed quite a reputation. And lest you take that as a compliment, let me assure you it *isn't*—it's only an observation, and one that leaves me compelled to observe you further, in case your clean slate gets too dirty, too quickly. Let me put it this way: You appear inconvenient to me, Rector. And I am giving you the opportunity to prove otherwise. Now, under different circumstances, this would be the part where we talk about job prospects."

"Different circumstances?"

"Different from these, yes."

Rector swallowed again, anxiety welling up in his throat and making his mouth feel unaccountably wet. "And what are *these* circumstances?"

"Finally, an actual question. It bothers me when you repeat what I've said and make it sound like a query. Stop doing that. It's the kind of thing people do when they're only pretending to pay attention."

"Yes sir. I'll stop it, sir."

"Let me ask you something, Rector. When you decided to enter this city, how did you choose your method? After all, there's more than one way inside."

Whatever he'd been expecting, this wasn't it. Caught off guard, he tried to answer. "I . . . I don't know. I heard the water runoff tunnels caved in during that quake last year. And I didn't know any of the airmen well enough to hitch a ride—"

Yaozu interrupted. "You know several well enough to ask, but you owe them money, don't you?"

"Well, there's that. Anyway, I heard you were building a doorway in the wall, something so people could come and go easier, but not too easy. So you can keep track of who comes and goes,

I mean. Like me," he added the obvious. And then, still searching for a comparison, he said, "Like a toll bridge. Or a toll door."

"A toll door?" Yaozu's eyebrows lifted very slightly. "A toll door . . . On the one hand, we couldn't charge too much, or people would take the more dangerous ways around the wall. On the other hand, it could help offset some of the repairs I'm making out of my own pocket," he grumbled. "If we wanted to get ambitious about it, we could call it a tax, not a toll."

Rector frowned. "Could you do that? Tax, I mean? This ain't a real city."

Yaozu squinted unhappily, and Rector realized too late that he'd talked out of turn.

"Seattle is absolutely a 'real city.' We have real neighborhoods and shops, restaurants and facilities. We have a sheriff—I believe you've met her. She comes from a long line of them. Or a short line, perhaps; I can't vouch for her lineage beyond Maynard, come to think of it. I've even been accused of being an informal mayor—which I find quite funny, and not altogether incorrect. Think of it, Rector: a woman sheriff and a Chinese mayor. The world would either laugh or cry."

Rector thought the world might indeed laugh, but something told him it wouldn't laugh long.

Yaozu continued. "Soon, we will have a real airship dock. The Doornails are absolutely *giddy* at the prospect of sending and receiving mail like civilized people. All these things are happening, Rector. Seattle is not dead. It is stirring, and we will bring it back around."

Rector thought, but had the good sense not to say aloud, *Under your control, I bet.* "You're right. I didn't mean anything by it. You've got a lot of people down here, that's for sure."

"I wouldn't say a *lot,*" Yaozu mused. "That's rather the problem, really—and it relates to why you're here in my office."

"It does?"

"Yes. Seattle's population hasn't exactly *boomed* since the Bone-shaker turned the Blight loose and the wall went up. We've always had more dead men than living ones here on the inside, but lately we're running low on both." He paused and pointed a finger between Rector's eyes like a dagger. "That's why you're getting the clean slate, young man. If I could afford to be pickier, I would choose someone with a better reputation for usefulness."

"But . . . isn't that good? Being low on dead men? On the way here, I was talking with Zeke and Huey about how we hadn't seen so many as we expected."

"There *are* fewer rotters these days, and the reasons are varied, but obvious. First, they are running out of fuel. Even dead things need energy to move, and after all these years, the oldest rotters are slowing down. Second, something is killing them. Whatever this something is, I've heard only rumors, but the men down here have started calling it *the inexplicable.* I don't know where they even heard that word, but whatever makes them happy, I suppose. Third—and most alarmingly, in my opinion—some of the rotters have recently escaped."

"Escaped?" Rector's mind boggled.

"Escaped, yes. A good number of them. And here's where your usefulness will be tested, Rector Sherman."

Utterly aghast, Rector couldn't keep the horror out of his voice. "You want me to round them up and bring them *back*?"

Yaozu sighed heavily. "I don't want you to bring them *back* . . . though that would be nice, wouldn't it? No, I want you to tell me how they got out."

"How they got out? Of the wall?"

"Very good, yes. Tell me how they got past the wall. Over it, under it, through it—I have no idea, but they've been trickling steadily into the forest and Outskirts, and we're down to a skeleton crew of the damn things. No pun intended."

"Wait," Rector said again. "You *want* the rotters here?"

Yaozu sighed again, as if he were second-guessing his decision and wishing he had someone smarter immediately at hand. He spoke slowly, enunciating so carefully that if Rector had closed his eyes, he might've imagined it was a white man speaking. "Yes, Rector. I *want* the rotters here. They're disgusting, they're ravenous, they're violent, and they keep the city safe from outsiders."

"They do?"

"Even more than the gas, they prevent people from coming and going. The gas can be managed with a mask and a handful of filters. The walking dead are something else entirely—not just a physical threat, but a psychological one, too. No one wants to become a rotter, Rector. People chop off their body parts to keep from becoming rotters. They shoot their friends in the head to prevent the fate from befalling others."

"No, you're right, I understand. But still . . . why keep them around?"

"You aren't paying attention, or you aren't thinking. I do hope your brainpower improves once you've had another day or two of rest. At this rate, I'm not sure you'll survive a week." Yaozu retrieved his wire-rimmed spectacles from the stack of paper, then unfolded them and put them on. He picked up the topmost sheets and shuffled through them. When he found what he wanted, he pushed the glasses up onto his forehead.

"Rector, do you have any idea how much money comes and goes from Seattle in any given year?"

"No sir, I don't."

"Millions. And this next year, if things hold together long enough, it might be closer to a billion. Can you imagine that kind of money?"

He could. He could calculate it in sap, and it made his head spin. But he lied. "No sir, I can't."

"It's more money than you could spend in a lifetime of trying. However, at the moment, the city is spending it almost as fast as we can earn it. You came here from the Vaults, yes? Well, you must've seen the place. It's a wreck, from top to bottom. The hoses that keep our air breathable"—he waved a hand to indicate even what was in the room, right at that moment—"are in desperate need of maintenance and repair. Likewise, the ceilings are caving in at the spots where water collects and the land is damp, and foundations are settling all throughout the walled-off blocks."

"What are you saying?"

"I'm saying Seattle is falling apart, and I am rebuilding it from the basements up. I can't do it all at once, and I can't do it cheaply—not like Minnericht did, when he carved out his hasty little empire a decade ago. But here's what *really* frightens everyone: The threat of structural collapse *isn't* my most pressing problem."

Yaozu's face had settled into some very serious lines. Behind that mask of professional concern, Rector imagined he could see a nervous sparkle of something else. Not fear, exactly. Something lesser, but sharp.

"Then . . . then what is? Your most pressing problem?" Rector asked.

Yaozu leaned forward, wriggling yellow lights from the fireplace glinting off his spectacles. "Other people. People like you, Rector—though not you, personally. I'm prepared to believe that you're a young man at loose ends, hunting for a place to belong. I might be wrong, but right now, we're all operating under good faith, are we not?"

"Yes sir, we absolutely are."

"Excellent. Now, when I say 'other people,' I mean sellers, dealers, vendors, chemists, and pharmacists who want a piece of the sap money. They know Minnericht is dead, and if there's one thing I must grant the man, it's that his reputation was more solid than his city. Since he's gone, word has gotten around. At best, people sense a vacancy at the top of the power chain, and they wish to fill it. At worst, they wish to come plunder what's left of his empire, and leave the city to rot."

"And you don't want either of them things to happen."

Yaozu sat up straight and smiled indulgently, like Rector had learned a new trick. "Yes! That's precisely it. I don't want either one of those things. And your new friends don't either. Now, as for me . . . am I well-beloved beneath the streets? No, not at all. In fact, a fair number of people down here would be happy to set me on fire. But the smart ones understand that I'm doing them a favor. I'm spending my own money—"

"Minnericht's money," Rector blurted out, then cringed. It'd flown out of his mouth before he could stop it.

Yaozu let it slide. "Minnericht's money, if you prefer. Regardless, I am restoring the city. This place is an investment. I want it to survive." He settled back in his seat again, slumping slightly as if this whole business wore him out, but it was all fully, miserably necessary.

Rector cleared his throat and said, "Well then, I hope you stick around."

"Me, too," Yaozu said, and the words were weighted down with cynicism. Without brightening, and without unslumping, Yaozu continued to speak in a low, firm voice. "The dead are our watchdogs, Rector Sherman. We cannot afford to let them fade into myth or memory. I need to know how they're getting out, and although I have other men assigned to this task, you are in a unique position to be of service, and I hope you will seize this opportunity to prove yourself. The Doornails will talk to you; they will let you come and go, and ask questions. Your two friends Ezekiel and Houjin can be of great assistance, insomuch as Captain Cly or Briar Wilkes will let either of them out on a long enough leash."

He hesitated, then went on. "And then there is the native

woman, Angeline Sealth. She would as soon push me off a cliff as tell me the time of day, but she's a *remarkably* useful woman in her way. It's entirely possible that she knows the streets better than anyone else alive. I am in no position to ask for her help, but *you* are."

"I already talked to her," Rector said. "Met her in the Vaults. She gave me some cherries."

"How kind of her," Yazou said, drolly. Then he rose to his feet and removed his spectacles, folding them again and setting them atop a book. "You're a salesman, Rector. You know how to talk to people—in fact, that might be the *only* thing you know how to do. So that's what I want you to do. I want you to explore. And one week from today, I want a full report of what you've learned."

 **Eleven**

Rector did not like the idea of homework, but he was happy for the clean slate and the chance to earn favor with the most frightening man in the Sound, so there was that to keep him warm at night. Unfortunately, he was too tired to feel much of anything beyond exhaustion, except the nagging need for sap—and the aggravating proximity of sap, which he was absolutely not allowed to have. At this time.

He wandered in the direction he thought the lobby might be in, but turned out to be wrong. He tried another hallway and learned he'd made another incorrect choice, and soon it became woefully apparent that he was lost.

He was not alone, though.

Men came and went around him, past him, and sometimes bumped right into him. Rector was absolutely not interested in a fight, but conversation might get him somewhere—so he looked for someone who might be friendly . . . or at least not actively hostile.

With no idea where Houjin was or if the kid had even stuck around, he was short on allies—but eventually he found an oversized room at the back of the Station line.

More like a hangar than anything else, the vast, open space was filled with balloons. They weren't flying balloons, and they weren't the sort that worked with an airship: They were collection balloons, stuffed fat and round with Blight. The balloons stretched and rolled, the seams of their treated canvas straining and squeaking as men bundled them up like bales, then stacked, shoved, and pushed them into a holding corner. They lumbered together like barrels, ready for processing.

At one end of the room, a small clot of workers wearing oversized gas masks moved swiftly and smoothly, driven by the confidence of long habit, despite the dangers of the substance they managed.

Rector fiddled with his gas mask, but didn't put it on yet, in case he didn't have to. He didn't draw any closer than was necessary to call out, "Hey fellows . . . ?"

Three of the five men turned to look at him. One of those failed to show any further interest and went back to his task, but the other two kept staring at him, so he went ahead and asked the rest of his question.

"Where can I find James Bishop?"

One of the masked workers nodded and said, "Next hallway down. Try the second door on the right." He gestured with one thickly gloved hand, then turned back to the valves at his station. He drew one of the bulbous bags into position and located its release stem before hooking it onto a set of pipes.

Rector was fascinated. If he'd had any more energy, he might've stuck around to ask questions. These were the source sacks, their contents almost certainly collected from the deepest Blighthole, down by the old financial district. Every pathetic little powder-runner knew that much. Rector also knew there was some system, or apparatus, or device . . . something that concentrated that soup-thick air down to something thicker still, until it could be poured like water.

Raw, unrefined Blight.

He'd never seen it before, and a lingering curiosity made him want to. But no, the exhaustion wouldn't let him. He struggled to recall the directions he'd been given mere seconds ago and re-membered enough to find that other hall, and the second door on the right. There wasn't really a door there at all, which was fine by Rector, who knocked on the wall beside it to announce himself.

A dark-skinned man looked up from a desk covered in small glass vials and pots, many of which were bubbling effervescently. The lower half of his face was covered with a blue cotton ban-danna, but even with this treacherous work, he didn't bother to put on a gas mask.

"Hey there, Bishop. You look like you're ready to take up train robbing."

James Bishop pulled down the bandanna so it sat around his neck. He pushed his chair back and viewed Rector with no small measure of surprise. "Wreck, what are you doing inside the wall?"

Rector grinned, and hoped it didn't look forced. "Working. For Yaozu."

"Really." Bishop said. It was a counter, not a question. "Yaozu."

"That's right, the man himself. I'm on a mission, but that mis-sion don't start until morning, and I'm not sure where I'm sup-posed to go tonight, or what I'm supposed to do. And the truth is, I'm god-awful tired."

"Not to mention a bit banged up, by the look of you." He pointed at Rector's leg.

"Yeah, I had a hard time getting inside. Fell down a chuck-hole."

"Brilliant."

Rector was determined not to take offense. "Well, it was dark and all. Anyhow, here I am. I thought maybe I'd look you up, see if I could bother you for a little favor."

Bishop scratched at a spot behind his ear where the goggles he often wore had rubbed a track in his curly black hair. "I just bet you did."

"It ain't no big favor, I promise."

"They never are."

Exasperated, Rector threw his hands up and limped into the room uninvited but unopposed. He found an empty chair and flung himself into it. "Man, I don't know why you've got to be like that. I'm tired, and I need a place to bed down for the night, and I don't know hardly anybody down here."

Bishop's eyes narrowed. The grooves in his forehead dropped to a very pronounced *V*, suggesting he was not convinced. Through this sharpened gaze he paused to stare at Rector, which Rector did not like at all. But what was he going to do about it? Nothing, that's what.

In his own sweet time, Bishop spoke. "You've been in the city a few days now, haven't you? Those scratches aren't fresh, and that rash you're getting on your hands . . . looks like you've been running around without any gloves like a right moron, I must say."

"So?"

"So, you're new to wearing masks, but not that new. I see the creases on your jaw, and around your neck. They're turning red, but they'll callus up in time."

"What are you getting at?"

Bishop folded his hands across his knees. "I'm getting at where you've been, and what you've been up to. You haven't been in the Station, or I'd have heard about it. So you're staying out at the Vaults, aren't you?"

"Ain't nobody's business if I am," he said stubbornly. "They're the ones who brought me inside in the first place," he said, whether or not it was the truth. "And they've been feeding me, and fixing me up. What do you care?"

"I don't, much. But then, I don't know much about the Doornails either, and these days we've got to pay real close attention to who comes and goes, and how. And why. But since you're here, and since Yaozu has already given you the welcome chat . . . let me ask you something: You seen or heard about Isaac West anytime lately?"

"Westie?" He wracked his brain. "Skinny guy from Tacoma?"

"Right. Rumor has it he's keen to get inside the wall and look around. And that's not a rumor I like very much. The sharks are circling, Wreck. So if you hear of anybody from the outside getting any ambitions about coming inside, I want you to speak up. It'll be best for you if you do—and best if you tell it to the Station before you say anything to those other guys."

Rector's nose felt like it was running. He wiped it with the back of his shirtsleeve, and tried not to notice the dump, yellowish stain that streaked the fabric. "Funny, you bringing that up. Harry did the same, when I stopped by his place the other day."

"I'm not surprised. We're worried, and we're watching. One way or another, they're coming for us. And it's not like we don't have enough problems down here, with the gas and all."

"And all?" Rector asked, trying to sound innocent, and failing with great aplomb.

Bishop shook his head. "There's talk about something bad walking the northern blocks. More than one something, we think; they've been spotted up on the walls, too. Not sure if they're men, or animals, or what, but they're big."

"Do they . . . do they chase people? Kill 'em?" Rector gulped. "Eat 'em?"

Bishop lowered his voice to reply, enough that Rector almost thought that the chemist was playing with his head. "We've lost four guys in the last two weeks. Found nothing left of them but pieces, like they'd been yanked limb from limb."

Rector's mouth was too dry to swallow again. "Limb . . . from limb?"

"So keep an eye on yourself, if you're going to be hanging around them Doornails. We don't mind them keeping to themselves, but maybe they're not alone. And maybe they've got ideas, and won't keep to themselves forever. Don't be a trusting fool about their company."

"Jesus, Bishop. I can take care of myself."

"That remains to be seen. However, you haven't made a grab for the sap that's not six inches from your hand, and you're looking . . . I don't know, *clearer*. You look more *clear* than last time I saw you. Maybe you'll pull yourself together yet."

"I do appreciate your confidence. So are you going to help me out, or do I have to find that crazy Chinese kid and get him to take me all the way back to where I came from? Because I sure as shit can't find it on my own." He left off what he thought about saying next, that he didn't have the energy to make the trip anyway.

Bishop rose to his feet. He wasn't a tall man, or a heavy one, either, and he wore a big brown leather apron over his clothes stained the same yellow as Rector's sleeve, and pocked with burn marks. Bishop reached for a row of round knobs, and as he turned them one by one, a soft hiss of gas fussed out through the pipes. The cooking flames lowered, and the glass containers settled down to a simmer.

"All right, Wreck. If all you need's a place to put your head, I can stick you someplace quiet."

Rector laughed with relief. When he stood up again, he nearly collapsed, but caught himself. "Thanks, Bishop. Thanks a whole bunch, man. I want you to know I appreciate it."

And as Bishop gathered up a satchel and a handful of tools, he said, "And I want *you* to know I expect you to keep an eye on those Doornails for us. You're not their kind, kid. You're ours. And you'd better remember it."

 *Twelve*

After spending the night in a clean, if sparsely fitted railroad car, Rector awoke to Houjin's insistent knock on the door.

Once Rector was awake enough to get his boots on, he let Huey take him back to the Vaults, where he slept for almost another full day on the same bed in the sickroom where he'd first awakened. No one had given him anyplace else to sleep, so he went back to the spot he knew, and he took it.

He awoke to an empty room.

If anyone had come or gone since Houjin left him there, he had no way of knowing it, and he was alone now. But he remembered the way to the washroom, and he remembered the way to the kitchen. Since an empty bladder and a full stomach were his most pressing needs, he didn't mind the privacy. He didn't mind the peace and quiet, either, considering that both of the guys he knew down there were chatterboxes from the word *go*. But the longer he was by himself, the more he had time to think.

Thinking wasn't his favorite thing to do, and it wasn't his strong suit, though he didn't consider himself a dummy by any means. No, mostly he didn't want to think because he didn't trust his thinking engine.

He knew he'd done bad things to his head, using all that sap over all those years. His whole life, it felt like. Well, not his *whole* life. The sap had a way of burning up old memories, as if it consumed them for fuel. He wanted some now, just short of desperately.

And here he'd been hoping it'd get easier as time distanced him from his last use of the stuff.

How long had it been? About a week, plenty of which was spent unconscious. Did unconscious time count, when it came to breaking a habit? A second thought came on the heels of that one: Could he find his way back to the Station unaided?

They'd have some there, obviously. He'd seen it right there, in Bishop's workshop. Bishop hadn't moved the packet, even after pointing out it was there and noting that Rector hadn't made a dive for it. Maybe it'd be there still tomorrow, or whenever he could reach it next. For one awful flare of a moment, even the specter of Yaozu's unhappy face couldn't temper the awful need.

No. He couldn't have any sap. He had a job to do, and Yaozu had no use for addicts.

Knowing this, remembering this, and *clinging* to this still didn't take the edge off how badly he wanted the drug. But it steeled his resolve enough to keep him from setting off for King Street Station right that instant on a lark.

Barely.

Instead, he resolved his way down to the kitchen, without the cane this time. He was disappointed to learn that the cherry supply had not been replenished, but he was able to scavenge enough odds and ends, bits and pieces, and stray scraps of perfectly serviceable food from inside the cabinets and barrels to fill his stomach.

It was pleasant, this sense of being full. Over the years, he'd lost track of what it felt like. The sensation was quite different from his old way of managing his hunger, which was to load himself up on drugs until he simply forgot that he hadn't eaten enough in a long time.

But even once he was content, he didn't want to stop at "full."

A lifetime of paranoia about his next meal made him want to grab everything and hoard it, but he stopped himself from filling his mostly empty satchel with whatever he could carry from the kitchen. He'd left most of the bag's contents under the sickroom bed since no one seemed inclined to take them away from him, except the pickles and he didn't need any of the foodstuffs right at that moment. He'd kept the lighting supplies and added the mask he'd been using, plus extra filters and other small sundries—including a little pot of foul-smelling cream he'd found on the table beside his bed next to a note that read simply, in blocky print, "Fer your hands. And stop scratchin at them."

Gloves still eluded him, but they were next on his list. He needed a pair if he planned to run around up top, and he had a mission—a real-live bona fide job, given to him by someone who nobody argued with.

The more he thought about it, the more he liked it.

He moved with the authority of the city's "mayor." So long as he stayed in his good graces, no harm would come to him. He mused on this pleasant fact while he chewed, eating so thoughtfully that he almost didn't hear the odd thumping noise that came from down the hall. When it did penetrate his thoughts, he concluded that it moved with the rhythm of footsteps—and when the stepper appeared, Rector froze like a small wild animal.

All his smug, hypothetical confidence evaporated on contact with the man who stood in the kitchen doorway, because he nearly filled it. He wasn't as tall as Captain Cly—and who *was,* really?—but he looked like a man Cly's length who had been squashed down to merely average height. He had a wide, flat face and arms as thick as railroad ties. In his hand, he held a cane sturdy enough to support a moose.

"Hello," Rector peeped.

The man said hello back, with only a faint note of a question. Then he said, "You're Rector, aren't you?"

"I am."

"Been out cold for the last day or so, haven't you?"

"I have."

"Huh," he said, and approached the same cabinets that Rector had so freshly raided. "I heard about your hair. Hard to miss a boy like you."

"So I'm told."

"I'm Jeremiah, but half the folks down here just call me Swakhammer," he informed Rector, not looking at him. He was too busy rummaging, hunting for something in particular. Still face-down in the storage, he added, "The nurse who's been looking after you—that's my daughter."

Rector said, "Ah. Yes. She seems to have done a bang-up job."

"She always does. So, what about you?" Swakhammer turned around with a paper-wrapped piece of something smelly in his hands. Peeling the old newsprint aside, he revealed a slab of smoked salmon that Rector wished to God he'd seen first, because it'd be camped out in his stomach by now if he had.

"What about me?"

"Are you roaming around in the Vaults all by your lonesome?"

"For the moment," Rector confirmed. "I've only been up a little while. I don't guess you know where Huey or Zeke might be, do you?"

"Both of them are up at the fort, I think. Huey flies with the *Naamah Darling* more often than not, and Zeke is trying to learn something from the captain—or trying to keep from learning anything, I can't tell which." He bit off a hunk of fish, and held the rest by its wrapping. As he chewed, he leaned back against the counter and spoke around the mouthful. "You want me to take you up there? Or do you know the way?"

Somewhat relaxed by Swakhammer's attitude, if not his appearance, Rector said, "That'd be fine, if you don't mind showing me. I've only been there once, and I wasn't half awake yet."

"All right, then. Hey, that's a real nice satchel you got there."

Oh yes. Huey had said something about it being one of Swakhammer's. "I understand it's one of yours," he said—might as well play it straight, for there was no arguing now. "I appreciate you letting me hang on to it. Or . . . Huey said you wouldn't mind."

"Yeah, I don't care. Got a bunch of them. Scavenged them out of an old army post years ago. Can't say enough for the Union's craftsmanship; they sure do make good bags. I think those things would survive . . . well, shit. They survive in here, don't they? That's a recommendation for 'em. They ought to advertise it. They'd sell 'em by the pound. Come on, I'll take you back to the fort."

Rector hoped that the man with a cane would take an easier path than the nimble Houjin, and he was glad to see that Swakhammer did indeed skip the stairs when possible. "We're going to go the easy way. I don't feel like stomping over every hill and through every holler. Got myself tore up last year, and sometimes I think this leg will never heal all the way."

"Sorry to hear that."

"Wasn't your fault. Anyhow, put on your mask, and I'll put on mine. I say that to warn you: Mine is a real humdinger."

As Rector extracted his own gear, he watched Swakhammer pull a huge contraption off a sling over his shoulder. It looked too big to be a mask, but wasn't; and it didn't look like a mask at first glance, but it *was*.

"Humdinger," Rector echoed with a whistle. "Where'd you get that thing?"

Swakhammer shrugged himself into the mask. The contraption fell over his head, and its edges settled on his shoulders. With the adjustment of a few straps and buckles it was affixed firmly, if weirdly.

"How do I look?" he asked. Every word sounded like it came through a tin can on a string.

"Like . . ." Rector struggled for words. "Like a horse that some-one put in a suit of armor. Sort of."

Swakhammer laughed, which was also rendered into a metal-lic sound that came from far away.

"Good enough. I've heard 'clockwork warthog' more than once, but 'horse' is a first. This thing was made by Minnericht, rest his soul . . . or don't, I don't care. But I keep it around because I can breathe real good in it. Masks run small on a man with a neck like mine."

Privately, Rector thought that Swakhammer had no neck at all. It was as if he'd been carved from a brick, all one set of lines.

"I wish we didn't have to wear them down under here. Didn't used to. But since the cave-ins, we've gotta do it just to be safe."

As they walked together, Rector thought this might be a good time to put his salesman skills to work. Or were they detecting skills? He liked the idea of being a detective better. He wasn't talking people into buying anything; he was asking for informa-tion, not money. And in his limited experience, people parted with information a whole lot easier.

"Mr. Swakhammer," he broached. "How long do you think it'll be until the underground's safe for breathing again?"

"That partly depends on Yaozu and his men at the Station, and the Chinamen, too. I think we probably need them more than they need us, 'cause they got plenty of men and we don't. But these shor-ing rigs"—he pointed at the ceiling, which sagged ominously de-spite a set of planks that had been braced to hold it—*"they're not worth a damn. Once those engineering fellows finish up in Chinatown—they're fixing their own blocks first, you know how it goes—they'll bring the equipment up here and we can buttress our ceiling all proper-like."*

"Equipment?"

"Mostly leftovers from when the Station was built. They've got steam-powered machines they've refitted to haul, lift, and brace. We

couldn't do it with sweat and elbow grease alone—not unless we had about a thousand more of us than we've got. The Chinamen got digging machines over there, too. I don't understand it myself, but Huey was telling me that sometimes you gotta dig holes in order to fix holes. I just leave that sort of thinking to him."

"He's a smart one, that Huey."

"I didn't used to care for that kid, or any of the Chinatown folks. But after I got blown up last year, Doctor Wong put me back together. Now my daughter works with him, and she says he's all right and I have to keep an open mind. So there you go. You can tell her when you see her that I'm keeping an open mind."

Rector nodded and kept the easy pace set by the big man with the cane. They ducked beneath low-hanging boards and clumps of bricks that had once been arched, and stepped on hollow walkways made of planks where such walkways were available.

And before he could decide what to ask next, Swakhammer said almost softly—or so Rector thought, given the buzzing quality of his words—*"I hope we get it fixed up soon. I want it to be safe. For Mercy, if not for me. I mean, if she's going to be damn fool enough to stay here."*

Sensing an opening, Rector pounced. "Yaozu told me he's working on it."

Swakhammer drew up short, then continued. *"That's right, Zeke said he'd called for you, and you'd gone out to the Station. How'd that go, anyhow?"*

"Not bad. Mostly he wanted to make sure I wasn't going to make no trouble."

"You got a reputation for doing that?"

"No sir, I don't.

"Got a reputation for fibbing out loud, I bet."

"Aw, that's not called for," Rector protested weakly. "I'm a salesman, is all."

"Same thing."

"No sir, it isn't."

Swakhammer made a sound that could've been a laugh, and pointed the way up a corridor. *"Not much farther."*

Rector was glad he'd let it go. "Good. I'm still a little on the feeble side, myself. I don't suppose there's an easier way up topside . . . ?" he broached.

"Sure, if you want to get eaten by rotters." But something about the way he said it was uncertain.

"Ain't seen hardly any rotters," Rector pressed. "I heard there was scads of 'em here, but Yaozu said there aren't as many as there used to be."

Swakhammer stopped, and although nothing of his face could be seen inside that amazing mask, his posture suggested that he was thinking about this. *"There's truth to that. At first I figured it was my imagination, but now I'm not so sure. It's the order of the day, though—things disappearing. People disappearing."*

"I don't understand . . . ?"

"Mercy will tell you all about it. It's not a coincidence, not anymore." Swakhammer shook his head, as if this was a subject he'd rather not consider. So he said, *"It's not just the rotters. The population up there"*—he gestured with his hands as though he was feeling around for the right thing to say—*"It's changing. The rotters are disappearing, but there are more birds, and the rats are coming back."*

Rector shuddered. "Rotter rats and birds?"

"No, not exactly. The air's different for them, I don't know why. It makes them sick, real sick—like mad dogs. But it doesn't kill them. It doesn't leave them roaming brainless and dead." He shifted his shoulders and resumed course, waving for Rector to come along. *"I don't know how they're getting in."*

"What if they're getting *inside* the same way the rotters are getting *outside*?"

"Who said rotters were getting outside?" Swakhammer asked quickly. Even through the mask, reading between the mechanical

lines of his speech, Rector thought he sounded entirely too innocent.

"Nobody. I just thought, if there were fewer rotters, they must
be going someplace. And like you said, there's no place for them
to go. Except out."

"You're a real thinker, ain't you?"

"Not usually. I'm just new here. Still learning the ropes."

*"You listen: If you ever think there's a breach in the wall, you
speak up, all right? We can't have these things getting out. And it ain't
particularly good to have other things getting in."*

"Other things?" The shadow of a long-armed monster flicked
through his memory, and he fought the urge to hug himself. "What
other things?"

*"Like I said. Birds. Rats. Dogs. Whatever. We don't need 'em here.
Don't want 'em."*

Rector knew a white lie when he heard one, and he almost
asked about the "inexplicable." But Swakhammer didn't intend to
share anything further, that much was clear.

Before too long, they were in the tiny antechamber with the ladder that led up to the fort, and Swakhammer bid Rector good-bye,
telling him to stay out of trouble. Rector wondered why everyone
always told him that, since it never did a bit of good. Maybe they
were all just optimists.

Up the ladder he went, and back into the smoky, swirling
atmosphere.

One of the airships from his previous visit was gone, but the
one called *Naamah Darling* remained, though no one was anywhere around it that he could see. In fact, he appeared to be utterly
alone inside the fort, which unnerved him. The place was beyond
spooky with its uniform walls, all vertical, unforgiving lines
from the ramrod tree trunks. It was a difficult place to see or to
navigate—never mind that it was mostly empty space that went
unoccupied by buildings or ships. Foggy air pooled in the corners

and misted back and forth, hiding and showing things at its capricious whim. Rector's breathing was loud inside his mask. It tickled his ears, and he scratched at them, remembering as he did so that he hadn't found any gloves yet and immediately putting that back near the top of his to-do list.

Hesitantly, he called out, "Hello?" The word came back to him, bouncing off the trunks and echoing around in the moist, dark corners. He tried it again, somewhat louder. "Hello? Anybody up here?"

Nobody answered, not even the groan of a rotter or the chitter of rats. He thought he heard something overhead—the other dirigible?—no, it was the flutter of wings. So there were birds here after all, just like Swakhammer had said. He looked up and saw disturbances in the Blight, tiny eddies and whirlpools of air tangling with feathers. The birds themselves eluded him.

He gave it another shot. "Hello? Hey, anybody?"

A harsh *caw* replied, startling him out of his skin. It was very close—practically right behind him.

"No," he whispered to himself. "It's just the walls. The sound moves funny, in here."

As he listened for the uncanny birdcall to ring again, he heard something else—something softer, and more reassuring. It was the sound of tools and then, in one quick bark, the sound of swearing. Rector didn't catch it clearly enough to note the exact word used, but he knew that tone—even if he couldn't tell the voice.

It came from the *Naamah Darling,* docked against the wall's edge, still clasping the soggy, wet mess of the rotting totem pole. The craft leaned slightly, or so Rector thought; then he noticed it had been drawn up by a cable so that its bottom and rear plates were angled toward the ground. One of those plates was off, and although no one stood beneath it, faint sounds of humanity came from within the ship.

Rector loped toward it, moving swiftly but stopping short of an outright run. Running wouldn't be dignified, and it would admit by deed that he was scared to be alone in this amazing, ridiculous, unknown place that held so many questions and horrors.

He reached the *Naamah Darling*'s underside and poked around until he found the main hatch. He was about to yank it down, but then hesitated, and knocked on it like he'd knock on an ordinary door. Something about the captain's size made Rector unwilling to barge in unannounced.

"Anybody in there?" he asked, directing his question at the smooth hull and feeling silly about it.

A few seconds later, the hatch seam released with the sound of a seal giving way, and Houjin's mask-covered head appeared. "Rector!" he said. "You're up again. You want to come inside?"

"Sure, I guess."

He stood aside as the hatch opened and a set of steps toppled out. He climbed them as invited, and Houjin pulled the stairs up in his wake, sealing the hatch with a yank of his arm and a shove against a lever.

The craft's interior was larger than Rector had expected. It had a wide open bridge and two secondary areas, plus a closed door with some kind of prohibitive warning on it. The bridge had several seats bolted into the floor, one of which was quite a bit larger than the others.

He cocked a thumb at it. "Captain's chair?"

Houjin said, "He had it made special, in San Francisco. A long time ago."

"Where's Zeke?"

"Miss Mercy sent him errand running, but he'll be back any minute."

"You by yourself in here?"

He nodded. "One of the thrusters has been sticky, and we're having trouble with our sharp lefts. I thought I'd fiddle with it while Zeke was gone."

"No luck, huh?"

"No. I think the steam injector's gone bad. We'll need a new one pretty soon. Don't want to fly this thing for long if the steering isn't great." He stared off into space for a moment and said, "I bet we could order one in Tacoma."

Rector couldn't have cared less about the ship's steering, but he cared a lot about his itching hands, so he brought the subject around without any preamble. "Hey, is there any chance anybody on this ship has a pair of gloves I could borrow? My hands are all et up with this Blight stuff. They itch like hell."

Houjin looked around him, saw nothing immediately promising, and then said, "Wait here—let me see if there's anything left in the lockers."

He disappeared through the door that strictly prohibited entry and reappeared with a floppy set of thin leather gloves. "Will these work?"

"Beautifully," Rector said before he even got them on. "Thanks. You're all right."

"They're Fang's extra set. You can put them back when we're finished for the day, and then we'll ask around in the Vaults."

"That sounds good." He worked them over his fingers and found that they were almost too snug, but far better than nothing. "So, let me ask: You're not on any official business?"

"What do you mean?"

"You're not under captain's orders, or anything? There's nothing keeping you here?" Rector prodded, looking around and making a show of being unimpressed, even though he'd never been inside an airship before and was pretty impressed.

"No, not really. What about you?"

"Me? I plan to get to work."

"For Yaozu?"

"That's right," he confirmed. He stepped up into the bridge and strolled over to the large windscreen, leaning forward to see out into the dirty air that filled the foggy courtyard area within the fort. "He thinks there's a breach in the wall someplace, and he wants me to find it."

Houjin cocked his head to the side. "A breach? Is that where he thinks all the rotters are going?"

"Yeah, he said they're getting outside. People are starting to talk."

"They are?"

"I *think* so. I think that Swakhammer fellow knows, but he got all squirrelly on me when I asked him about it. Anyhow, Huey, you think there's a chance the captain would give us a lift? It'd be faster hunting if we did it from the air." He lifted his eyebrows optimistically as he looked back at Houjin, but with the mask on, Houjin didn't see it.

"No way. Especially not with the steering gone iffy. And don't even think about it."

Now one eyebrow was held aloft with virtuousness. "Think about *what*?"

"We're not going to take the ship without permission, even if we could. Captain Cly and Fang would kill us both. Kill us *all*, since you probably mean to get Zeke involved."

"Oh ye of little faith," he murmured, quoting Father Harris.

"What's that supposed to mean?"

"It means you don't trust me, do you?"

Huey shook his head. "If I thought you knew anything about flying, I'd be worried. But you don't. And I won't help you do it."

"You think you're real smart, don't you? All sorts of brains, you've got—you think you know damn well everything," Rector said crossly.

He might've added more, but the hatch hissed and popped—and this time, from inside the ship, Rector felt his ears pop with it. He abandoned his position beside the oversized captain's chair.

"Hey, Zeke!"

"Rector, you're back! I thought you were going to sleep for a week," Zeke said, hopping up into the ship's belly and waving at Houjin.

"Well, I didn't. I hear you were off chasing nurses."

"Wasn't doing no such thing," Zeke insisted. Because he was wearing a gas mask, Rector couldn't tell if he was blushing, but it was an easy guess.

"It's a shame you didn't bring her with you. I wanted to ask her something."

"Something 'bout what?" Zeke asked.

"Something her daddy said that made me wonder. He said she'd tell me all about people disappearing, and now I'm halfway worried about it."

Houjin and Zeke looked quickly at each other, and Zeke cleared his throat. "Oh, *that*. Mr. Swakhammer didn't mean that people were disappearing from around *here*. He's talking about the train."

"What train?"

"The *Dreadnought*, the train Miss Mercy rode out west. It was a big mess, and a bunch of people died. Miss Mercy was one of the survivors, but now she can't find any of the other folks who got out alive. Ask her about it sometime . . . or maybe don't. She gets this look on her face like she's scareder than she'd tell you."

Rector chewed on this new information and decided it might not be pertinent to his task after all, so he let it go. "Fine, then. I can let sleeping dogs lie. So what about you? We've got the afternoon to kill, don't we?"

Houjin interrupted before Rector could lay out his plan. "He wants to steal the *Naamah Darling* and use it to scout along the wall."

"I never said that!" he protested. "I never even wondered it out loud. Your friend here thinks he's a goddamn mind reader, don't he?"

Zeke laughed. "You *were* thinking about it, weren't you?"

"No."

"Liar. And if you think you can fly it by yourself, you're welcome to give it a shot. It'd be a real shame, though. Here you just got into town, and we'd have to dig you a grave right away."

Houjin laughed that time, but Rector scowled. "Fine, you two have your fun. And to think I was going to invite you all to come with me, hunting around the wall."

"Hunting for what?" Zeke asked. He sat on the open hatch's edge and let his feet dangle down.

"Monsters."

Houjin grunted. "You said you were hunting for holes in the wall."

"Holes, monsters, same thing. How else would monsters get inside?" he cajoled.

Zeke said, "They've had monsters inside for years. They built a wall around 'em, remember?"

"That's not what I mean, and you know it. I'm talking about the monster that came after *me*. If nobody ever saw it before, maybe it's new. People have been talking about something killing the rotters. They're calling it an *inexplicable*. That must be what jumped me. It was definitely big enough to kill rotters."

Zeke looked at Houjin as if for approval or confirmation. For the space of a moment, Rector quietly loathed them both.

Zeke said, "What does that word even mean?"

"I don't know."

Houjin knew. "It means something you can't explain. But it's bad grammar in English."

Impatient to get back to the point at hand, Rector asked, "Are you in, or not?"

Zeke replied for both of them. "Where do you want to start?"

Ah, that was more like it. Rector sniffed, folded his arms thoughtfully, and suggested, "Why don't we get as far from the Station as possible, and work our way back around? Yaozu's fellows have probably been all over King Street."

The Chinese boy nodded approvingly. "Not a bad idea. We can take the underground tracks about halfway to the north end of the wall, then climb up and go by bridge the rest of the way."

Rector liked the sound of riding for a ways rather than walking or climbing, so he gave the plan his stamp of approval on the spot. "All right! How about you two show me where we're going, and I'll lead the way!"

Zeke flashed a thumbs-up and Houjin sighed.

All three of them exited the *Naamah Darling* and Houjin sealed it behind them, saying, "Before we go too crazy with this plan, we should stop for more filters."

"Filters?"

"For your mask, Rector. I don't know how long you've been wearing that one, but I haven't seen you change it. There's a stash in the lean-to, along with some lanterns. Let's stock up before we rush into trouble."

"Sure, we can plan out the day, minute by minute. If you want to suck all the fun right out of it."

Houjin said, "Fine. I'll get extra filters and lights for me and Zeke, and you can have fun without any."

"Don't be a jerk about it."

Houjin already had his back to Rector, and was disappearing into the fog. "Don't be a dead man."

 *Thirteen*

Once the boys were ready, they headed back under the city where they were surrounded by faint, fizzing lamps that lit the underground paths like tiny beacons. They held their own lanterns close, but did not spark them yet for fear of wasting fuel. Fuel was the heaviest thing they toted, and you could never have too much—at least, that's what Zeke said, with all the fervor of a convert.

This time they walked beyond the spot where the strung lamps hung. As full darkness encroached from within the tunnels ahead, Houjin nudged Rector with his elbow. "You're tallest, so you should light your lamp and carry it up high. It'll be brighter that way."

Rector fumbled with his satchel, readied his lamp, and lit it.

"You just don't want to carry one yourself," Zeke said to Houjin.

"One of us has to steer the cart," Houjin replied. He doesn't know where he's going, and you don't know how to hold us on the track."

"I could figure it out."

"Maybe."

"You old hens quit chattering, and tell me which way we're heading," Rector commanded.

Houjin pointed. "Down this split over here."

It was very, very dark down that split over there. Rector couldn't see anything beyond the golden bubble of light that radiated from the lantern held just above his head. The light wobbled as he shifted his grip to hold the heavy old thing more comfortably. Anything at all could've waited beyond the illumination's razor-sharp edge.

He stumbled and the light shook harder, but he caught himself.

Houjin casually outpaced him, and Zeke trotted to catch up. "Come on, Rector!" he called.

"I'm coming, you. I'm wearing somebody else's shoes, all right?" He gulped, steadied his feet, and jogged stiffly forward. "You've got to remember, I've been laid up. I'm not back to myself yet."

"There ain't nothing wrong with you 'cept you're scared," Zeke argued.

"You take that back."

"I won't, because I was scared when I got here, too. Everybody is at first. Everybody who's got a lick of sense, anyway." The younger boy practically danced down the corridor, tripping along the narrow edge between the light and the dark.

Houjin added, "You'll get used to it."

"Like you did?"

"Me?" He shrugged. "I don't remember. I told you, I've been here since I was little."

Rector struggled to keep up to the pair of them, leaning and stretching his arm to hold the lantern out farther in advance of his own steps. He lunged with it, trying to keep them corralled inside the shimmering globe. "This must've been a weird place to grow up."

Houjin shrugged again. "I don't know. Every place must be."

"You should get out more."

"I *do* get out. I've been to Portland, and Tacoma, and San Francisco. And I went to New Orleans a few months ago. I've been all over."

"Ain't you special, then."

"I didn't say that; I only said I've been places, and all those places were weird in their own way. *You're* the one who should get out more." Houjin scooted forward, just outside the light—and for a moment, he was lost. "I bet you've never been farther than Bainbridge."

Rector had never even been that far, but he kept it to himself.

The lantern caught up to Houjin and brought him into clear, sharp focus. He'd stopped at the edge of a long rail, a rail that was soon revealed to be one side of a track—the sort used by miners and loggers.

"Where's the cart?" Rector asked. Surely it must have one.

"Over here," Zeke called. He gestured for Rector to follow him, so he did, around a hidden corner to where the cart awaited. Zeke kicked a lever with his foot and the cart creaked. He gave it a shove with his shoulder and it rolled forward. A dozen feet down the sideline, it clicked onto the main pathway.

The cart was long and flat, barely as deep as an oversized bucket and not quite as long as a wagon. In the middle a handle reared up, and waved gently like a seesaw as the cart clattered forward.

Houjin swatted at the handle and it bobbed heartily up and down. "It's no Pullman, but it'll get us where we're going."

"We pump that thing?"

Zeke nodded. "We pump that thing. It's not that hard, and it's a lot faster than walking. Climb in! You can put the lantern on that hook up front."

"That way you can help," Houjin added, climbing inside and assuming a ready position.

Rector relinquished the lantern and crawled up inside, testing the boards with his feet. "Doesn't seem like there's much room in here for moving things around."

"There are wagons, empty ones. You hook them up to the back, see?" Zeke indicated a set of knobs for hitching additional wheeled vehicles. "But they're heavy, and we don't need one right now. So get in, and let's go."

They shuffled their spots, and then leaned their weight into the lever—Houjin on one side with the brake, and Rector and Zeke on the other, at Rector's insistence. Still under the weather, he said. Not up to his full strength, he insisted.

The boys faced one another as they shoved the handles up and down, and the cart rattled merrily through the never-ending tunnel. Along the way, Rector saw that there were actually two sets of tracks—one for each cart, he assumed, in case anyone was coming from the other direction.

At some point, Houjin insisted they stop for a break—though Rector quickly figured out that he didn't need a rest so much as he wanted to switch seats. Thus far, Rector had been facing forward, and whoever sat opposite him was watching over his shoulders, back the way they'd come.

Houjin said, "I need to see the next two splits. We're about to change directions. A couple of times."

"Are we going uphill from here on out?" Zeke asked.

"Yes, but it's not bad."

The rest of the way Rector watched over their shoulders, eyeing the shifting, rock-sharpened shadows as they retreated behind them. The rollicking, rattling commotion of the cart rang loud throughout the passageway; it echoed in circles, surrounding them like the bobbling light—a pocket of glowing, raucous noise bumbling on the track, screeching as the path turned and the brake leaned against the round metal wheels.

After a while, Rector almost enjoyed it, despite the rising burn in his arms, as exhaustion did not so much overtake him as threaten him from a distance. He had no intention of stopping anyplace in that claustrophobic tunnel, not after that first unnerving break. The other boys weren't likely to give him his seat back, and besides—who knew? What if the cart broke, or they couldn't get it moving again? What if the track was uneven, or imperfectly maintained, and the wheels refused to run against it without their hard-earned momentum?

The rail line split, just as Houjin said it would. It veered to the right, and soon after, to the left. The grade steepened, the pump handles stiffened, and the way became harder. Sweating and grunting, the trio forced the cart forward, shoving it up the incline.

Just when Rector was dead certain he'd have to stop cranking or his arms would fall off, the darkness shifted up ahead and he could see the end reflected in the other boys' visors.

Before too long they drew up to an open area with lights bolted onto the walls. Some of these lights were lit, but most were out. Even so, it gave the space enough illumination for Rector to find it encouraging.

Houjin squeezed the brake and the wheels squealed outrageously, sparks spit from the metal-on-metal connection, and the cart came to a halt. All three of its occupants leaned, jerked, and sat up straight with their bones still rattling. They crawled out and gathered their belongings.

Zeke went behind the cart and kicked a triangle-shaped block, which dropped down against the wheel. "Keeps it from rolling when it's parked," he explained when he saw that he was being watched. " 'Cause I don't feel like chasing it down later on. Come on. Let's hit the bridges."

They came up through the basement of an old livery stable that still had decomposing leather tack hanging on the walls. The bones of horses or dogs or maybe even men and women lay scattered about like a child's game of sticks; the boys avoided them as best they were able, but every so often the room rang out with the loud, cracking *pop* of something that once was alive.

The livery was only a story and a half tall, and above street level the windows had been left unboarded, allowing a watery wash of that feeble gray sun to spill inside. Rector turned his lantern down, then off. "Won't be needing it, will I?" he asked too late, but Houjin shook his head.

"No, we'll be on the roof soon."

"Will that be high enough? I only see the loft, and the ladder. Everything else we climbed the other day . . . all of them buildings were taller than this one."

"Different part of town," Zeke said. "Trust me, though. Any roof that'll hold us will keep us out of reach. And we'll be right up against the main wall, most of the way."

Rector frowned and scratched at the straps that held his mask in place. He didn't get a lot of traction, since he was wearing Fang's gloves, but it'd only been an idle gesture anyway. "So the wall went up smack in the middle of some buildings, right?"

Houjin replied, "Right. Cut some of them in two."

"But not all the way around, I wouldn't think."

Zeke shook his head. "No, not all the way around. Why? What are you getting at?"

"Once we get out to the wall's edge, how do we investigate without getting down within . . . you know . . . *grabbing reach*?"

"We don't," Houjin said simply.

"Then how do we avoid the rotters? The ones we're technically looking for, I mean."

"We avoid them the same way we find them," he said offhandedly. "By listening."

"What do we do if we find some, and we can't climb up out of their reach?"

Zeke said, "We run like hell, that's what we do. Unless you're packing a pistol somewhere in that satchel, and I bet you're not."

"I'm not," Rector admitted, mentally adding it to his wish list. A gun of some sort seemed to be the obvious means of survival inside the walled city. "And neither of you two have one either, do you?"

"Naw. Guns are so loud, it just attracts more of them. Once we get up to the roof, you'll see what we use to take care of them." Zeke led the way up a long flight of stairs that led to a trapdoor. He flipped it open and a puff of swirling Blight gas billowed down into the livery, dousing Rector and Houjin. They wiped at their visors out of habit or reflex. It didn't help.

Houjin ran up the steps behind Zeke, and Rector came after.

On the roof, a row of storage trunks were lined up along the western edge. These trunks did not match and had never been part of a single person's luggage set, but they were large and sturdy, and Rector thought he saw Union army markings on one of them. Footlockers, then—that's what they were. Well, footlockers and a couple of steamers.

"What's all this?" he asked.

Zeke went to the farthest left one and popped the latch. Houjin did the same to the one beside him.

As Zeke rummaged through the contents, he explained, "The Doornails keep the far corners stocked in case somebody gets stranded. You never know when you'll meet rotters, or when you'll fall through something that ain't as solid as it looks," he added, and Houjin jabbed him with an elbow. "It's easy to get hurt out here, or stuck."

"That's smart," Rector said approvingly. "So what do we have here—food? Filters? Lanterns and such? If you knew this was here, why'd we bring so much fuel?"

Houjin answered that one. "In case we didn't make it this far. The whole underground works that way—everyone survives by preparing for *just in case.*"

"Sounds like a lot of trouble."

"It *is* a lot of trouble," Zeke agreed. "But look at this, would you?" He hoisted aloft a long ax that was once painted red, now more rusty than scarlet. It looked solid and dangerous. It also looked almost too heavy for Zeke to hold, much less wield.

"What's that, an old fireman's piece?"

Zeke nodded. "Probably. And it'll take a rotter's head in two, just like that—" He swung for demonstration, and Houjin deftly stepped out of the way as if he'd been part of this particular charade before. "There's more in here, axes and even some cavalry swords, but I'm not sure I'd recommend one of those."

"Why not?"

"The metal's too thin; it's getting brittle. We need to seal these trunks better," Houjin complained. "Blight gets into everything."

"So what do you recommend?" Rector asked. He stood between Zeke and Houjin and stared down into the trunks they'd opened. He saw another couple of axes; some big saws that had been refitted with longer handles (*Must be awkward,* he thought); a few clubs, some metal and some wood; an assortment of mining tools such as picks and hammers; and a handful of things that might've been smithing tools.

The boys indulged in a brief discussion of the pros and cons of each, and Rector selected an oversized miner's pick. He tossed it from palm to palm and spun it around his elbow.

"This'll work, I think."

Zeke closed his trunk. "All you need to know is, if you see a rotter, you run. Only start swinging if you can't outrun 'em. You don't want them to bite you, that's for damn sure."

"Of *course* I don't want them to bite me."

Houjin shut his trunk, too, and slung a sharpened metal bar over his shoulder. "No, you don't understand: Their bites fester. Whatever they bite, you have to cut off."

Rector was glad for the gas mask—he didn't want the other boys to see him go green around the edges. He gulped, sniffed, and coolly said, "I've heard that before, and I'll take it into consideration. Say, what's that you're carrying, Huey?"

Huey turned the bar in his hand, twirling it like a baton, but more slowly. It was over three feet long, and appeared to be cast iron. "It was for wagon wheels, I think. To pry them on and off. I like it. It's a good size and a good weight, and I can stab with it"—which he demonstrated—"or hack with it," he showed, by jerking it from side to side.

"Or just beat somebody to death," Rector observed.

"True." Again he rested it on his shoulder. "But you have better luck stopping rotters if you can smash their brains or knock their heads off. Go in through an eye socket, if you've got the aim to hit it. Or hack at their necks, if that's an easier target."

"Jesus."

"It sounds harder than it really is. Most of the rotters inside the city have been here for years, and they're starting to get mushy."

Zeke chimed in. "And most of them don't run very fast."

Rector held the pickax and looked over the side of the roof. "This is a god-awful way to get around your own neighborhood. And you two talk like it's just an everyday thing, hacking people up and putting bars through their eyeballs."

Houjin muttered, "Don't like it, don't have to stay here."

"I'll get used to it," Rector countered.

He hefted the pickax and followed him over to the roof's eastern edge, where a drawbridge was laid out flat and ready. It groaned beneath their feet, and small splinters of old paint and decaying wood went dusting down to the dangerous, deserted streets below as they crossed.

 *Fourteen*

They walked single file through more windows turned into doors, navigating along balconies and over storefronts for eight blocks until they were forced to drop to the ground and sprint across one street and down into a storm cellar. Then they went up through an empty grocer's, scaled more stairs, and emerged on another roof, only to trip lightly down another long bridge made of doors.

These makeshift devices swayed under their feet enough that more than once the boys agreed to cross one at a time, so as to not strain the walkway.

Finally they ran out of structures; there were no more roofs or bridges to hold them aloft. Without a word, they scooted down an old iron ladder that had once been part of a fire escape. Its rusted bolts creaked, and as they descended foot by foot, hand by hand, brick dust rained down onto the dead grass and cracked streets below.

When they had no choice except to speak, they whispered.

"I'll light the lantern," Rector breathed. His voice was shaking, and so were his hands.

Equally quietly, Houjin said, "No." He put a hand on Rector's arm.

Rector yanked it away. "Why not? It's getting dark."

"No, it's not," Zeke joined in. "We're coming up to the wall. We're in its shadow."

Looking up, and squinting hard—through his visor, and through the foggy air—Rector could see the great Seattle wall peeking past the thick yellow Blight. It loomed and leaned. It crowded him, all two hundred feet of it, cobbled from stone and mortar and anything solid that had been lying around when it was built.

If he'd had any breath left after riding and climbing and hiking the mile to get there, the view of the wall from here on the inside would've taken it all away.

"It's still dark," he murmured. "Still can't hardly see."

Houjin shook his head. "Wait until later. The light will only bounce off the fog. It's hard to see out here no matter what you do."

Zeke nudged Rector's shoulder and said, "Trust us. We live here," and he set off toward the wall.

Houjin followed him, calling back to Rector, "Don't just stand there—we need to stick together."

"Why's that?" he asked, but he still hurried to catch up.

His pickax was already heavy; it already slowed him down and made him want to stop walking. Everything felt dense around him: the Blight, the humidity, the oppressive silence. His breathing came harder, and although the ache in his chest had become familiar, it rose up to something sharper. He clasped one hand across his chest and wondered what it meant, this stinging difficulty with every breath.

"Hey fellows, can we slow down?"

"You getting tired?" Zeke asked.

Houjin sighed. "Should've changed his filters when I told him to."

Zeke said, "Rector, get over here by the wall. We're not up high and safe, but at least you'll have your back to something."

Rector almost said, *Whaddaya know—Zeke's got more sense than I gave him credit for,* but he restrained himself. And he did go to the wall and back up against it, leaning there partly for support, and partly to feel that big, solid thing at his back. It didn't feel safe, not exactly. Not at all. But it meant that nothing could sneak up behind him.

One side at a time, he unscrewed the filter portals on his mask and replaced the used filters with clean ones from his pack. His gloved hands fumbled with them, but he refused any help and finally got both of the round charcoal disks properly installed.

The improvement was immediate, but it wasn't vast.

His chest still hurt when he took a deep breath, and his arms were beginning to feel the stretching sting of having been worked too hard in an unfamiliar fashion, but he'd fixed something himself. "I'm all sorted out. Let's get moving. We can start off . . . *that* way." Still pressing his back against the wall, he indicated a direction to the right.

Houjin cleared his throat. "I might recommend the other direction."

"Oh, *might* you?"

"Another fifty yards that way," the Chinese boy clarified, "and there's nothing on the other side of the wall but the Puget Sound."

Grouchily, Rector argued, "Well, maybe the rotters are headed out to sea."

"But the rats and raccoons aren't coming *in* that way," he pointed out. "Your first idea—that the animals are coming inside the same way the rotters are getting outside—was a better one. If I were you, I'd stick with that theory."

"Yeah, it *was* a pretty good thought." He worked one finger under the itchiest mask strap and rubbed, figuring he could get away with it since his nails were covered by soft leather. If he felt like being honest with himself, he might've admitted that he didn't have good thoughts every minute of every day, so he ought to stick with the ones that made it through. But he didn't feel like being honest.

In the minute or two he'd kept his mouth shut thinking about it, he'd begun to hear the soft swish and roll of waves off to his right. "Rector?" Zeke asked, in exactly the same tone you'd use to talk a dog into putting down a bone.

"All right, that's fine. You two live here, like you keep telling me. We'll go your way, and see what we can find."

The fog pooled and collected like snow. It drifted and gusted against the vertically stacked stone and twisted in small eddies; it spiraled and spun in tiny tornadoes that tugged at the boys' hair and tickled the spots where their clothes didn't cover their skin. Rector, Houjin, and Zeke moved without speaking, except to double-check that they were all together. Sometimes the air was so thick that they couldn't keep track of one another unless they held hands. When they seemed to be hiking through a rich cream soup, they would spit one another's names between their teeth, calling back and forth with as little sound as possible.

Rector dragged his fingers along the hastily erected wall, feeling the contours rise and fall, dip and crumble into a dry mortar crust. He dusted his hands off against his pants and shivered— even though it wasn't as cold as it had been a few days earlier, it still wasn't warm. It was almost never warm, and the wall's imposing shadow drained the tepid sunlight of what little relief it offered. Up above, and somewhere past the boundaries of what they could see through the pallid air, even the flapping wings of the Blight-poisoned birds were sluggish and slow.

"You hear those?" Rector breathed. "Getting closer."

"I hear 'em," Zeke replied, so faintly that if Rector had been even another step away, he wouldn't have heard him.

"I don't like them."

"They're only birds," Zeke assured him. Then he faced forward and softly called, "Huey?"

"Right here."

"Thought I'd lost you for a second."

"Keep up, you two," Houjin urged.

"How much farther?" Zeke asked.

"A quarter mile?" he guessed. "Then we'll hit the next drop down into the underground."

"Are there carts?"

"Yes. Now *shhhh*."

"Don't you tell me—"

Houjin came to a sharp stop and turned around. Zeke ran into him, but bounced back. Huey held out his weapon—not to brandish it, exactly, but to make a point. "Hush! I told you, I *hear* something."

Rector was mad, and he was scared, and he didn't like having a younger kid (or anybody else) put a long metal pole in his face. He smacked the pole away with the back of his hand with a *clang*. It hurt, and it'd certainly bruise. He wished he hadn't done it. "I don't hear anything," he fussed.

"Wait," Zeke said, holding out both hands. The hand that held the big fireman's ax drooped low. "I hear it, too."

Houjin lowered his pole, pointing the sharp end at a spot barely a foot off the ground. Still in his softest voice, he said, "Coming from down *here*."

Zeke readied his ax, holding it down at a similar level and getting ready to swing. "Raccoons?" he tried.

"Could be."

Rector heard it, too. It scratched against his ears, a hoarse, hushed breathing sound coming from knee level a few yards away. He tried to take comfort from the fact that the breather didn't sound very big; whatever it was, its inhalations and exhalations came fast and short, like a dog.

But what if it was something worse? Rector braced himself against the wall, which was cold, terribly cold, and a bit damp with condensation. "Could be a little kid," he said. The words were almost a horrified gasp, squeezed out of his mask and into the open air. "A baby, or something. There are kid rotters, aren't there? That's what I heard."

Neither of his companions responded.

"Where is it?" he asked. His friends didn't answer that, either.

The question answered itself when the low-lying clouds thinned and stretched, revealing a pair of glimmering gold eyes. The eyes did not glow, but they flashed, flickering like a cat's, or like any nighttime thing that roams and stalks.

Houjin stayed steadiest. He kept the point of his sharpened bar aimed at the thing's face. Zeke took up a defensive position at Huey's shoulder, prepared to swing the huge ax at anything that came close enough to hit, assuming he could lift it off his shoulder.

Rector plastered himself against the slimy wall, his pickax hanging from one hand. It knocked against his thigh. He clutched the weapon higher, up against his chest.

The bright-eyed thing came forward in a slinking crouch. It snarled and slathered as it crept, its joints stiff and its ears flattened. It approached them unhappily, nervously, curiously.

Hungrily.

"Mad dog," Rector wheezed.

Houjin disagreed. "No. A *fox*. It's a Blight-poisoned fox."

"Never seen one of them before," Zeke marveled, still arched and primed for battle.

Rector asked, "Is it dead? A rotter fox?"

Zeke shook the ax. "Go on, you. Get out of here."

Huey said, "Not dead. Real sick, though. The birds fight off the Blight—they live with it. Four-footed things don't handle it so good."

The ragged creature paced forward slowly and stopped within a few feet, as if considering what to do. Three people to one small, ill animal . . . it weighed the odds, and weighed its own hunger. It growled, yipped, and shook its head, but did not retreat.

"You see." Houjin planted his feet apart, ready to strike if he had to. "It's *thinking*. Or it's trying to. Rotters don't think."

Zeke swung the ax in the fox's general direction. "Get along, you dumb thing. Get out of here. Don't bother us, and we won't bother you."

His ax went wobbly, due to its weight. He drew it back up and held it with both hands.

The fox quivered and hopped back half a step. It snapped its jaws, spraying yellow-tinged spittle in every direction. Then it made up its mind, turned sharply, and dashed away. It disappeared through the fog in an instant, and the sound of its small feet—its little claws clicking against pebbles—lingered only a moment longer.

All three boys exhaled hard and let their weapons fall to their sides.

"I'm glad we didn't have to kill it," Zeke confessed.

Houjin said, "I don't know. It isn't happy being alive in here."

This time, Rector agreed with Houjin. "Should've just smashed its head in. Would've done it a kindness."

But Zeke still sagged, looking unhappy behind his visor. "I feel sorry for it. I wish we could've caught it, maybe let it go outside the wall."

"So it could go bite other foxes, and make them sick, too?" Houjin swung his bar up over his shoulder so it rested against his neck.

Zeke did likewise with his ax, and sighed. "Maybe if it got some fresh air, some regular air, it'd get better."

They still whispered, though their caution evaporated somewhat in the wake of the fox's disappearance. Rector still brought up the rear, watching backwards to make sure no one followed them, and praying that Houjin and Zeke would see anyone up ahead. It was odd, feeling so alone but knowing that they weren't—that the city crawled with sick and dying things, and dead things that hunted regardless.

Rector surveyed the wall, too, but it stayed firm and showed no signs of holes, or even cracks. There were no breaches big enough to let anything person-sized (or even fox-sized, or rat-sized) in or out. He clung to it, oddly comforted by its epic reliability.

He said, "I thought maybe that fox was a good sign."

Houjin looked back at him. His face was a masked shadow. "Why?"

"You saw it. It hadn't been inside for very long. Makes me wonder if we're close to the entrance, or exit."

"But you saw it run off," Zeke said. "Those things move pretty fast. It could've run pretty far."

Huey paused, and the two boys who followed him paused, too. "What if we're going about this the wrong way?"

"Everything feels like the wrong way, down here," Rector said. He was getting thirsty, and he was also getting the very smothered feeling of spending too long in a gas mask. He wanted to get inside, someplace where the air was clean. He was running out of patience, and he didn't want to admit it. It grieved him to think that the wall held several square miles of space, which meant that there was still a whole lot of territory to check before he could report to Yaozu that he'd done his job.

"That's not what I mean. What if the hole isn't in the wall—what if the hole is underground? Say one of the tunnels collapsed and left a spot that stretched beyond the wall, to someplace outside. What if things are getting inside that way?"

Rector snorted with exasperation. "Or what if they're dropping from the sky, hitching rides on crows or dirigibles?"

"Don't be like that," Houjin groused back at him.

"Look, Yaozu told me to check the *wall*. He didn't tell me to dig through every underground tunnel, pit, shaft, or cave. One thing at a time, all right? Let's rule out the wall, and then move on to other ideas."

Huey conceded, "That's not the most unreasonable thing you've ever said."

"God forbid you admit I had another good idea."

"It's not a *good* idea. It's a plan someone else gave you, and you're sticking to it because it's the easiest thing to do."

Zeke rolled his eyes and started walking along the wall. "Can't you two get along for ten whole minutes? I don't know what your problem is."

"This guy, *he's* the problem," Rector said.

Huey retorted with a "Shut up."

This once, Rector did so—but not because of the command. It was his turn to hear something, out in the fog. "Guys? What's that?"

From back in the fog somewhere in front of them, a voice called back. "Silly boys. You're making enough noise to wake the dead. Or call 'em to supper."

Princess Angeline stepped forward out of the filthy mist, a close-fitting mask covering her face—though her eyes showed, and her silver hair was left to flop around her shoulders. She wore a pair of canvas pants, and a jacket that was buttoned all the way to the top, stopping just under her throat. Slung around her chest was a bandolier that held a row of small throwing knives.

Houjin perked up immediately. "Miss Angeline!"

"Hey there, fellows. You're a little far from home, ain't you?"

Zeke said, "Yes, ma'am, but we're on a mission."

"What kind of mission?"

Rector stepped in, since the mission belonged to him. "We're checking the wall for holes. We think the rotters are getting out, and animals are getting in. We know the men out at King Street have been watching their end of the wall, so we thought we'd start at this end."

"That's either brave of you, or dumber than homemade sin."

"A little of both?" Zeke tried. "We were getting ready to head back to the Vaults. We're thirsty and hungry, and we haven't seen anything except for one sick fox."

"Aw, a fox? That's a shame. You saw it wandering around up here?"

Houjin said, "Yes, ma'am. We chased it off."

Angeline put her hands on her hips and cocked her head thoughtfully. "It's not a bad idea. Not the bit about the fox, but the bit about a hole in the wall. Should've thought of it myself, but I've been in and out of town a lot. My grandson is getting married out in Tacoma, so I haven't been around so much."

"Didn't know you had a grandson," Zeke said with a touch of awe.

"I do. But that's beside the point. You think we have a hole?"

Rector wasn't stupid enough to mention that it was Yaozu's theory, and the other two boys kept that particular piece of information quiet as well. He'd been warned that the princess hated the powerful Chinese man who ran most of the Station. And even if Rector hadn't liked her, he didn't want to anger a woman who wore that many sharp things attached to her clothes.

So all he said was, "A hole, a crack . . . *something* that lets things out, and lets things in."

Houjin added, "There must be someplace where people see Blight-sick animals more often. Now that I think about it, we really should've followed that fox."

Rubbing at her chin under her mask, Angeline said, "You'd never have caught him. There's plenty of strange goings-on here in the wall these days, boys, I tell you what—it gets weirder by the day."

Intrigued, Rector asked, "Why do you say that?" But he did so in a normal speaking voice, and everyone else shushed him. "Sorry! Sorry," he said much more softly.

"That's right, boy. Don't ever forget where you are." She came in close to the three of them, gathering them around her as if she meant to shield them. "Always keep your voice down low. *Always*. We can talk between us, but keep it quiet."

"Yes, ma'am," Zeke and Houjin said.

Rector nodded, then he said, "I was trying to ask: Did you ever hear of something called an *inexplicable*?"

She frowned. "Nope. What's that word mean?"

Houjin told her, and she said, "All right, I'll remember that. And let me answer your other question, Red," she said, perhaps misremembering his name, or just having decided to call him that. "Actually, how about I show you, rather than tell you."

He hemmed and hawed. "Aw, we were just heading back down to the Vaults, like we said."

"Yes, and I heard you. You're heading over to the Sizemore House?" she asked Houjin, who bobbed his head.

"Down through the basement, and back to the Fifth Street tracks."

"Good plan, good plan. I'll come with you, and on the way, I'll show you what I mean. It's only a quick detour."

"Give us a hint?" asked Zeke.

"Hard to hint, dear boy. Except to say, I'm not sure the rotters are all escaping. Between us . . . I think something's killing them."

Rector did not say that she might be right, and that she'd just hit on part two of Yaozu's theory.

Duly hushed and thoughtful, the boys followed the princess around the wall another few dozen yards, then marked their place with a small cairn of bricks and rocks. "To remember where we left off," Houjin said. "We can start here next time." And then they left the sturdy familiarity of the Seattle wall, venturing once again into the Blight-ravaged blocks of what was once the city proper.

Rector trudged after the princess, and after Zeke and Houjin, in what was becoming a regular lineup.

Bringing up the rear, that was how he preferred it. Let *them* walk headlong into whatever trouble waited. Let them stir up the monsters, or wake up the ghosts. It'd buy him time to run, if running was called for.

But run to *where*? He didn't know what the Sizemore House was, or where it was, or how to find it. Nor could he have found his way back the way he'd come. He hadn't counted the steps around the wall, or the building fragments falling down to block their paths. He hadn't counted anything. He'd only counted on Houjin and Zeke knowing what they were doing. That had been a mistake.

They moved in a nervous pack, pausing only to light a lantern when Angeline suggested they ought to. She was right. The wall's shadow was stretching to catch them, and the setting sun behind it left them straining to see.

Only one light burned, and Angeline carried it. Rector thought about objecting, but then he thought about rotters pouring out of the derelict shops and abandoned houses, and he thought they would surely go for the source of light first and foremost. Fine, let someone else carry it.

Angeline brought them to an alley between two great houses that had once belonged to wealthy men. The houses reared up out of the fog like monsters, like things in Rector's daymares. They were all peaks and gingerbread and rotting bits of unpleasant paint peeling in sheets as big as his hands. Once they might've been some bright color, but the gas and the years had bleached whatever hue they'd originally held, and now they were cumbersome corpses, decomposing where they stood.

"I'm giving you boys some credit, you understand," the princess told them, her voice low and her eyes grave behind the shield of her visor. "What I mean to show you ain't pretty. But it might be important."

She stepped aside and held out the lantern, which cast a wimpy bulge of brightened air down into the alley.

"Go on. Take a look."

"At what?" Rector asked, peering as hard as he could into that impenetrable haze.

She corrected him. "Not up there; not like that. Look down on the ground, boy. Tell me what you see."

He stepped forward in order to stand beside Houjin and Zeke and he followed Angeline's pointing finger. Where the light pooled and puddled, he saw strange forms, or pieces of forms, scattered on the ground. He couldn't imagine what these crooked shapes and splintered parts had once been part of, or where they'd once belonged.

Rector crouched down and his knees popped. He winced, rubbed at his joints, and asked, "Could you bring the light down, Miss Angeline?"

She obliged, and the unidentifiable lumps came into focus.

There, at Rector's feet, was a disembodied hand.

He jumped and toppled backwards, but caught himself on one palm.

"I *did* warn you."

He leaned forward, and Huey and Zeke came closer, too.

Houjin used the edge of his iron rod to poke at the hand. It didn't move. It didn't respond in any fashion, except to shed one finger. The digit flaked away, and the small bones that once held it together drooped pitifully—kept in place by habit and a strand or two of old skin.

Angeline took her lantern, stepped deeper into the alley, and told them, "Lads, that's just the start of it. Come have a look, won't you?" And as she went between the houses, the light seemed brighter than before—bouncing off the walls, since it had nowhere to go except back into the fog.

"Miss Angeline," Huey breathed. He was the only one who could speak.

Zeke and Rector remained silent, transfixed and horrified.

At Angeline's feet, they saw legs, arms, and half a dozen heads lying motionless and scattered. And behind her, creeping into a gruesome drift as high as her waist, a pile of dismembered undead oozed, dripped, and settled into a heap of viscous mulch.

Zeke gasped, creeping closer, though why he'd want a better look, Rector couldn't fathom. Rector just wanted away from the damn things—away from the pile, away from the alley and everything in it.

He swung his arm up over his nose, shielding his filters further with his sleeve. It didn't make a difference. "That's disgusting! Where'd they all come from?"

"I couldn't tell you," the princess shook her head. "I counted about forty before I made myself sick, being so close. Red, don't worry about covering your nose. I know you *think* you smell these things, but you don't."

But it wasn't the imagined smell that made him recoil. He withdrew from the details.

One long arm lay mere inches from his toes, and he nudged it with his boot. The curled, dead fingers splayed and collapsed. All their nails were broken. They would've been bloody if there'd been blood left; but around the edges, even on the gray, dead skin, Rector could see the crusty tint of yellow. His own nails were starting to turn that color. He'd noticed it months ago.

And over there, the nearest skull with any skin left to remark . . . its eyes were sunken and a gritty gold crust spilled from its nostrils and ears. Big, gruesome sores ate the flesh around its mouth. Rector had once had a sore like that. He'd occasionally picked a similar grit out of his own ears, and he'd sneezed it out of his nose once or twice.

The sap craving twitched between his ears and in his lungs, just like old times, but just for an instant before it was quashed by a wave of nausea. For that same instant, he thought of the Station, and about the men who considered him one of their own in some vague, proprietary way.

Then the nausea washed that away, too. Was this all they expected of him?

Houjin, always bravest—the simple result of having lived there the longest, or so Rector guessed—sidled forward and jabbed at the pile with his weapon. Just like the lone, stray hand, the corpse fragments settled and flattened, but did not squirm or show any hint of continued animation. "Look at the breaks," he said, now using the rod to point. "They're torn. All of them. Not cut, not hacked."

"They were ripped apart," Zeke said, with no small measure of awe.

"But what could do something like that?" Huey asked. "And some of these men . . . they weren't gone yet when the thing took them. Look, that one still had a mask on. I think he's one of Yaozu's men. And there's a hand over there that hardly looks rotty at all. Some of these fellows are *fresh.*"

Rector gulped. "Four of the Station men got tore up. Maybe more. What could tear forty rotters and a bunch of men to bits?"

Angeline turned pointedly to Rector and said, "I can't say for sure, but I have an idea."

"Ma'am?" Rector asked, guiltily confident that he was being accused of something.

"What you saw, when you first came into the city—you said it was a monster?"

"It *was* a monster. It chased me. It stalked me," he said, and it sounded like an echo. He remembered saying it once before, and he shivered, despite his best efforts.

"It was big, and it had long arms," she reminded him.

"That's right." He nodded violently.

Houjin backed him up. "I saw it, too. Whatever was after him, he's right. It was *really* big."

"Let me ask you this," Angeline proposed to the pair of them. "Do you think it might've been covered in hair?"

"Hair?" Rector frowned and cocked his head. "I don't know . . . I guess it might've been?"

"Long hair. Brown hair, with a little bit of red in it—not half so red as yours, I don't suppose. But like this . . ." She pulled a swatch of something stringy and russet colored out of her pocket and held it up to the lantern so the boys could get a gander at it. "I found this nearby. Lots of it, not just this little lock. It's scattered around the scene. I don't mind telling you, I took my time here. It's nasty as can be, but it got me thinking."

Houjin's eyes narrowed. "You know what did this, don't you, Miss Angeline? You don't know the word *inexplicable,* but you know what did this."

"I have an idea, and it's a strange one—but it's the only one I've got that makes any sense. Come along, boys. I think you've seen enough. Let's go to the Sizemore House and down someplace safer, and then I'll tell you about my thoughts."

 *Fifteen*

They skulked together, guided by their lone lantern. They needed it more and more, and Houjin would've struck up another if Angeline hadn't insisted they shouldn't. Instead, she recommended that the boys take hold of one another's shirts, and told Houjin to grasp her hair.

"Don't tug it—I'm trusting you, Huey. But we need to stay close," she said in her commanding, quiet voice. "And we should use as little light as we can get away with. Night's falling. We don't want to fall with it."

All in a row, Rector feeling immensely undignified, they escaped the last few blocks of the rich men's houses and ripped-apart rotters. Angeline knew precisely where she was going, and she brought them to the Sizemore House before the sun was altogether gone behind the wall. The house loomed big and dilapidated, empty and waiting. The front porch sagged, and the roof sagged, too. It looked like a balloon without enough air in it.

"Will it fall down on us?" he asked Zeke, because he was staring at the back of Zeke's head.

"No."

"Who was Sizemore?" he asked. He liked the sound of their voices; the darkness made him lonely.

"I don't know," Zeke told him. "And shush. We'll be downstairs in a minute."

By downstairs, Zeke meant the root cellar. Around the back and through a pair of giant wood doors set into the ground, the quartet descended into a space even darker than the one they were leaving—but the tunnels weren't choked with Blight, they were only tainted with it. The lantern did good work as soon as those doors were shut overhead. The nervous explorers sighed with relief, but they couldn't take off the masks.

"It looks clear down here," Rector protested. "I don't see any gas."

Angeline smacked him in the back of the head—harder than was strictly necessary to make her point, in Rector's opinion. "You don't have to see it to die from it, you silly boy. If I had any polarized glass, I could tell you true if it was safe to breathe. But I don't."

"We've got some back at the Vaults," Zeke noted.

"Next time, bring some. I expect that'll be the next step in the repair process, sending folks down through the tunnels with the lenses, seeing what's still safe and what's not safe anymore. After they fix up those cave-ins, I mean."

Rector almost said, *Yaozu will probably add that to his to-do list,* but remembered in time not to say the Chinaman's name.

He caught Zeke and Houjin looking at him, and he shrugged. If they were worried he'd blabber about his employer, they shouldn't be. Despite the recent smack, he liked the princess in that idle way that required no actual investment on his part. And he also believed the one other thing Yaozu had told him about her: She was useful. *Very* useful.

"Where are these carts you promised me?" Rector asked, looking around and seeing nothing but the same excavated, unfinished tunnels he'd seen so much of already.

"This way," Houjin said, lighting his lamp and leading with it.

Angeline looked behind them, glancing at the freshly locked and sealed doors above. It seemed to Rector that she didn't trust them, as though she wanted to climb up and give them a yank to remind herself they were secure. Instead, she rejoined the small group, this time falling into line behind Rector.

As they walked through the dank, squishy tunnel with its square beam braces, no one talked. It was as if the habit of whispering or staying quiet was sticking with them, even there beneath the city where there were no rotters to lure.

Finally they reached a bend in the tunnel that revealed a set of carts, as promised. Just like the one that had taken them up the hill and under the city, these two were parked off on a short, dead-end side track. Rector said, "Hey, look! We get to ride back home."

Zeke told him, "Most of the way. And pumping's easier, going downhill."

"And we've got four of us this time." He nodded at the princess. "Now it won't be uneven, side to side."

Angeline laughed and slapped him on the back. "I think I like you just fine, Red. Half the men in this city would be god-awful horrified at the thought of a woman working alongside 'em, much less a woman of my years. But you didn't even think twice about it—just assumed I was along for the working. I like that."

Huey sighed. "He's not noble. He's lazy."

"Lazy, noble, I don't care. Me and him will sit on this side and crank, and you two younger fellows can take the other. Between us, we'll be back in the Vaults in no time, won't we?" She kicked away the nearest cart's brake block and shoved it along its rails until it reached the main track a few feet away. "Hop on board, boys. Let's get you home, and get these masks off. Then we can have ourselves a chat."

When they'd finally reached the Vaults and the big round door had spun and sealed shut behind them, all the masks came off. Everyone stood there panting, feeling the air on their faces. It wasn't fresh air, and it wasn't particularly sweet-smelling, but Rector was sure it was the best damn air he'd ever felt, and he'd fight to the death anyone who tried to tell him otherwise. Or at least he'd argue like hell until he felt like stopping.

"Boys, I've got a thought." Miss Angeline told them. "Let's go the back way down to Chinatown and eat there. I want something hot. None of the men down here have taken to cookery, and I don't smell anything to suggest Mercy or your momma"—she said with a nod at Zeke—"is downstairs experimenting. I might want some assistance from you tomorrow, so I suppose buying you supper is about the least I can do."

"Assistance? From us?" Zeke positively pranced at the notion.

Rector didn't roll his eyes, only because without the mask everyone could see him too clearly. That damn kid, so desperate for approval all the damn time. It was downright embarrassing.

She replied, "Walk with me, and I'll tell you all about it. But first, we're stopping by the storeroom and picking up a set of spectacles. I don't know about you three, but I'm sick to death of wearing that damn mask. Let's see if we can't air out our faces a little on the way."

The storeroom was stacked from floor to ceiling with crates, barrels, boxes, shelves, and drawers. Some were labeled, and Rector picked up the highlights even with his limited reading skills. Coffee, gunpowder, socks, leather scraps, single shoes (to be mixed and matched), stray pieces of paper (printed and blank, retrieved from books and book endpapers), maps, fragments of material for patches, copper wire, assorted metal bits (one drawer for lead, one for steel, one for iron), gas masks and filters, a variety of oils and other lubricants for industrial use, hand tools, electrical tools, strips of waxed canvas to repair the great tubes that brought fresh air to the city below the streets . . .

. . . and that was only the beginning.

Angeline hunted until she found the cabinet she wanted, from which she retrieved a set of small spectacles. The lenses didn't match—one was round, one more rectangular—and the frames had clearly been bent together without regard for aesthetics from whatever sturdy wire had been most readily available at the time.

"These'll do!" she declared, sticking them on her face. She tweaked the bends around her ears and adjusted the fit until they looked like they'd stay on. "It's funny, looking through 'em. But they'll tell us where there's gas, and that's the important bit. How do I look?"

Zeke laughed, and Houjin gave her a solemn nod that just barely hid a smile.

Rector answered, "Like a million bucks!"

"A million bucks! I don't have that much, even if I look it. But I've got enough to feed us, so let's head down the back tunnels and see if they're stable enough to let us breathe like civilized people."

The lenses in the makeshift spectacles were made from polarized glass, so they cast oddly shaped rainbows around the tunnels when the lantern light hit them just right. Angeline occasionally held her hands out in front of herself, sometimes purely to look at them. She announced, "It sure is strange, how putting glass up to your face makes the whole world look like magic."

"Like magic? Really?" Zeke asked, visibly restraining himself from asking for a chance to wear them himself.

"The world wobbles a bit, and when I walk, I feel like I'm stepping forward into a big hole."

Houjin stepped around an eddy of fallen rocks, holding out a lantern to light the way ahead. Somewhere not too far away, machinery hummed to life and the dull, resonant buzz of a mechanical crank rose to a roar. Close behind this noise came a gust of air; it billowed down the tunnel, pulling at tousled hair and unrolled sleeves. It flapped and swelled like the breath of some leviathan deep in the earth's bowels.

Rector shivered. "Miss Angeline?" He touched her arm.

She stared straight ahead, through the light of Houjin's lantern and into the darkness beyond, as if she could see the wind itself, and judge it.

After a moment of concentration, she patted his hand and said, "Don't worry. The glass isn't showing me anything. This air's clean." She gave him a smile big enough to show she was missing one tooth, so far back in her mouth that he hadn't seen it before. "Of course, it *ought* to be clean. You hear that sound?"

"Yes, ma'am, I do."

"That's the nearest pump room, starting up its engines. Must be coming up on suppertime. You can set your watch by the pumps in Chinatown, and I know because I've done it before."

When they arrived at their subterranean destination, Angeline whipped off her gas-detecting glasses and stuffed them into a pocket. "Here we are, boys. Mind your manners, would you? Can't have you getting up to any mischief on my watch."

Rector heard men shouting back and forth, and the regular percussion of hammers augmented with the dragging, scraping whine of saws. At the end of the tunnel a hint of light came in several colors. When they all emerged into an underground street, he saw that the way was strung with lanterns that were shaded with colored paper. A handful of men sat before a storefront that offered bagged rice and samples of unknown herbs for sale, stacked and sorted in the open, glassless window. They looked up curiously at the newcomers, but smiled and nodded to see Angeline, who smiled and nodded back.

Here in Chinatown, the streets were wider and—in Rector's private opinion—better kept, with proper curbs and wooden sidewalks lifting the walkways off the perpetually dampened dirt. Rather than having one large structure full of apartments like the Vaults, many individual homes were installed between the tiny businesses and in otherwise unsettled spaces. Laundry was strung and cooking fires dotted the thoroughfares with warmth, feeding their smoke and ash up through great metal tubes that disappeared into the ceiling.

"What are those?" Rector asked, pointing like a tourist.

Houjin said, "Vents. They all join up in the level above. Sometimes when you're topside, you can see the exit pipes smoking like chimneys."

"Oh. There sure are a lot of people down here," he observed as another group of men passed them, and a few individuals looked out of windows or stepped into doorways to get a gander at the outsiders.

Zeke smiled and waved like he was leading a parade and everyone there had come out to see him. He told Rector, "There are a lot more Chinamen than Doornails, that's for sure."

Huey said, "About four Chinese to every white person."

"And even fewer of us natives," Angeline added. "Most of my kin had better sense than to stick around. They've gone up north, or out to the islands."

"Then why'd you stay?" Rector asked.

She was silent for a few seconds. She looked at Zeke and Huey, who clearly knew something about this story that Rector didn't. Then she said, "This city was named for my father. After he was gone, I stayed here. I was raised by these folks, more than not. We may not look it on the skin, but I consider them family. And I had other family here who died, same as the rest of you lot. I even had a daughter once."

"Did she die in the gas?"

She cleared her throat. "She died before that. Bad husband, bad marriage. Either he killed her, or he drove her to do it herself. Either way, it was a bad time for me, and for my grandson, too. He was only a tiny boy when his momma passed, so I took him on. His daddy didn't want him, anyway. So my no-good son-in-law stuck around like nothing had happened."

Rector frowned. "And no one ever punished him?"

"No, that didn't happen. He had two things about him what made him more important than my daughter so far as the law was concerned. One, he was a man. Two, he was white. And my daughter wasn't neither of them things."

They walked down the Chinatown streets, among men who looked at Rector as if he'd just come visiting from the moon. Angeline ignored the small crowd and curious stares, reached over to Zeke, and ruffled his hair with one gloved hand.

Angeline said, "This boy here, his granddaddy was the sheriff back then. I'm sure you've heard of him."

Rector nodded. "Maynard."

"Right. I told him what'd happened, and he came out to my daughter's home one night. We hunted for some kind of proof that Joe had been the one to do her in, but we never turned up nothing between us." She sighed and stuffed her hands into her pockets. "And I knew Maynard was right. He couldn't bring charges against Joe just on account of I said he was bad. It was my word against . . . against everybody's."

She paused. "Still, I appreciated the sheriff taking the time. He didn't have to, and don't I know it."

"So . . . what happened to . . ."—Rector picked up on the name—". . . Joe? Nothing?"

"A couple of years after the Blight, my no-good son-in-law picked a different name and came to live down here. He hired a right-hand man, a Chinese fellow named Yaozu—you must know of him. Yaozu tried to stop me from killing him, but he couldn't. He stabbed me, though, and left me a bad scar. Between 'em, Joe and Yaozu wreaked a lot of havoc, as Miss Lucy might say." She finished up fast, then changed the subject. Oh look, there's Ruby's," she said, indicating an open door flanked by two open windows—glassless, like all the rest. From inside the establishment came a rush of steam, bearing with it the odors of unfamiliar food sizzling on a grill.

Rector said, "I thought there weren't any women in Chinatown. Who's Ruby?" but no one answered him.

Angeline went to order their food. When she returned, she sat on the bench and leaned forward over the table, her knees splayed and her fingers folded together. "Boys," she began in a conspiratorial tone, "I want to run something past you, and I don't want you to spread it around. Understand?"

Huey and Zeke nodded vigorously, but in Rector's case, it was more tentative. After all, it depended on what she was going to tell them. There was always the chance he'd need to share it with his boss. Unless he didn't go back to the Station . . . although he had a good idea that that wasn't an option. Well. He'd see what he could do about that.

"Good, good. You're good boys, I'm quite certain," she said, flicking only a hint of a glance at Rector. "But other people might think it's a little nuts. And by 'other people' I mean the Doornails and the rest of the white folks. Huey, I can't say about you and yours." She unfolded her fingers and placed her hands flat on the table before them. "Rector, Huey, I think you saw something that ain't human. Something that weren't never human. Something *inexplicable,* to use the word the Station men are throwing about. A monster, but *not* a monster."

Rector said, "I don't get it."

She fished around for the right words, and upon finding them, she laid them out carefully.

"Imagine that none of you boys had ever seen a bear before. Now, if I told you there are bigger bears than the ones we got here—up in Alaska they have 'em twice the size of an outhouse—you'd believe me, maybe. Wouldn't you?"

"Kodiaks!" Houjin exclaimed. "I've heard about them."

"So imagine you didn't know what a bear was, but you were out in Alaska, looking for gold or some fool adventure. And say a Kodiak popped up out of the woods, stood up on his back feet, and came right for you. If you didn't know what a bear was before-hand, and if you survived the meeting, you'd run home and tell people you'd seen a monster, wouldn't you?"

Solemnly, Zeke said, "Yes, ma'am, I believe I would."

She continued. "But a Kodiak isn't a monster—it's nothing but a big ol' bear, as natural as the sun rising in the morning. But no one sees Kodiaks much, because there's never been too many of them. And the same applies here. My own people have been in this land for more years than you folks have been keeping history, and even we—"

Houjin interrupted, pointing at Rector and Zeke. "Longer than *their* history, maybe."

"Oh, all right—I don't know how long they've been writing books in China. But *my* people have been here an awful long time, and we barely know a thing about these creatures. But when we talk about them, they're called 'the elder big brothers.'"

"Elder . . . big brothers?" Rector repeated slowly.

"Yes, yes. Elder big brothers. That's what their name means in Duwamish. Sometimes they're called 'sasquatch' for short. The sasquatch are shaped something like you and me, but they're covered toes-to-top in hair, just like the hair I picked up back in the alley, and they're an awful lot bigger than men tend to grow."

Houjin peeked over at the counter, but didn't see their food yet. He chewed on his bottom lip. "That's why you call them big brothers. They look like us, but they've been here longer than we have."

"Right. Now, I think a sasquatch has gotten inside the wall, same as those foxes and raccoons. That's what we're looking for. And finding him won't be easy."

Before she could add anything else, Houjin's spine stiffened, and one of his fingers shot into the air. "You know what this reminds me of?"

Rector was dumbfounded. "It *reminds* you of something?"

"In China, there is something like it that lives in the mountains. It's called the *Kang Admi*. The Snow Man."

Rector sniffed. "She didn't say anything about snow."

"They call him that because he lives in the mountains. I've heard him called 'yeti,' but it's like you said, Miss Angeline . . . no one ever sees him. I don't know how many people believe, and how many people pass it around because they like a good story."

"Yeti, huh?" she mused. "We've sure enough got mountains here, don't we? Not so much snow this far down against the ocean, but still. Same principle—a big hairy thing shaped like a person, living in high rocks."

Zeke picked at what was left of the paint on the table. It peeled away in chips, lodging under his fingernails. "Maybe it's the same thing," he suggested. "Or maybe they're cousins, of a kind."

Someone called out from the counter and Houjin leaped up. "Food!" he announced, and before anyone could offer to help, he darted off to collect it.

When everything had been brought over, he dove in with a pair of sticks the size and shape of pencils. When he noticed Rector looking at him with utter bafflement on his face, he said, through a mouthful of noodles, "What? I brought forks for you people." He used one stick to point down at the table, where three battered metal forks were wrapped together in a cloth.

Angeline retrieved a fork and flicked one toward Rector, who picked it up and used it to poke at the contents of his plate.

"Eat it," Zeke urged him. "It's good, and it's hot. Hot food doesn't come easy in the Vaults. We don't have vents there—at least, none as good as the ones they got here."

Rector wanted to believe him. It'd been a long time since he'd had a plate of hot food in front of him, and it'd be a shame to

waste it. He scooped up a bite, held it under his nose, and shov-
eled it into his mouth. Chewing slowly, he tasted something sharp
and salty—and something green, a vegetable he didn't recognize.
The second bite had more of the same, plus at least two other
unfamiliar sources of crunchiness, and by the third bite he didn't
care anymore. He just ate.

Houjin ate more slowly (he could eat faster, Rector thought, if
he'd put down those stupid sticks), and continued to grill Angeline about the sasquatch. "What will we do if we find it? Should
we bring guns? Should we bring one of the men from the Vaults,
or someone from Chinatown?"

Rector thought Huey might've been contemplating a suggestion
Angeline wouldn't have liked—that is, bring in someone from the
Station—but he didn't say so, and the princess shook her head,
anyway. "No, we shouldn't bring no guns. We don't want to hurt
this thing."

"We don't?" Rector paused mid-bite, his mouth hanging open.
"Because I tell you what, it definitely wanted to hurt *me.*"

"Did it?" she asked. "Or was it confused, and sick, and scared?
It *followed* you, and that's all we can say for sure," she said stubbornly. "Fellows, the sasquatch are few and far between. We can't
kill one. We have to try and save it."

It was Houjin's turn to be appalled. "Save it? We can't save
anything that breathes the Blight."

"Why not? Just because no *people* have ever survived it, that
don't mean nothing else can recover."

Zeke smiled optimistically at the princess. "Like that fox? You
think we could save the other things that get inside, too?"

"Maybe," she told him. "I sure would like to think so."

Rector had concerns. He finished his next big mouthful and
said, "I thought that if you get bitten by anything that's Blight-
sick, you have to cut off whatever it was they chomped on. Even if
we had some way to save the sasquatch, and even if we let it

loose . . . wouldn't it go running 'round the woods biting other sasquatches?"

Angeline shrugged and looked down at her plate. "I don't have any idea, but I'd like to give it a chance. We know the rotters can't be saved or fixed, but we also know the crows do just fine, and the foxes and raccoons get mean, but they don't die. We should try to catch something small; a rat, or even a fox like the one you saw. We could put it in one of the empty rooms in the Vaults. Give it some clean air and clean food. See if it gets any better."

Houjin remained dubious. "That's a better idea than mounting an expedition to save the sasquatch."

"If it works, there's some chance the sasquatch could get better, too." She put down her fork beside her mostly empty plate and put her elbows on the table. "I hate to think it can't be saved."

"Is it worth saving?" Rector asked, likewise putting down his fork.

She nodded firmly. "It's not *bad.* It's just sick. Tomorrow, let's go back out there, back where I caught up to you today. Let's finish working around the wall—around that back part, anyhow—and see if we can find the hole."

"How does that help us help the sasquatch?" Zeke asked.

"Maybe we can lure it out. It followed Red; maybe it'll follow us if we look nice and harmless."

Zeke winced. "I don't want to look nice and harmless, not with a sasquatch out there, sick and hunting people."

Angeline laughed, fast and too loud. "I didn't say we'd *be* nice and harmless. I just said we'd *look* it."

 *Sixteen*

Rector awakened to a firm shove to his shoulder. It startled him upright in a tangle of covers, fueled by the alarm of someone who hasn't awakened in a bed enough times to remember where, precisely, he's been sleeping.

"What? Who? What?"

Beside his bed stood a sturdy-looking woman with dark blond hair. "Three questions in a row, and you're sitting up already. You're easier to get moving than Zeke is."

Her voice was odd to him—the vowels rolled strangely and he couldn't place their origin—but he'd heard this voice before, in that half-dream state he'd occupied for his first few days in the underground.

"You . . . you . . ." His breath caught up to him at last, and his brain kicked reluctantly into gear. "You must be Miss Mercy."

"Very good. You're even alert at such an hour, which is one small thing to recommend you. I have to admit, I wasn't entirely sure you were going to pull through and dry out, but here you are—and you're looking well, I might add. Better than before by a long shot." Her eyes moved over him in quick, efficient snaps.

"Thank you," he mumbled, scanning the dim room for his jacket and seeing it hanging on the bedpost. He reached for it, missed it once, and snagged it the second time.

She left his bed and went to her shelves, where she drew down a large lantern and lit it. The whole room went white, and Rector shielded his eyes. "Damn, lady! Warn a guy, would you?"

"Sorry," she said. She didn't sound sorry. "Let me get a look at you."

"Do I have any choice?"

"No. Sit there, hold still, and don't bite me."

"Why would I bite you?" he asked, rubbing his eyes and finally putting his hands down atop the blanket.

She murmured, "I surely hope you have no reason to," and brought the blinding white lantern (what powered that thing, anyway?) up close. She hung it on a hook Rector hadn't noticed before, which held the light over his bed. He felt like he was on stage, standing in a curiously cold pool of light.

"I'm feeling a whole lot better," he assured her, but when he tried to jam his arms into the jacket, she took it away from him and tossed it back onto the bedpost.

"Don't go covering up just yet. Let me see you."

She took his face in her hands and tilted it up to face the brilliant light. He squinted against it, but held his eyes open when she told him to. He swallowed when she told him to do that, too, and opened his mouth and stuck out his tongue—and he felt silly about every single second of it.

Satisfied that her patient wouldn't die right there on the spot, Mercy Lynch sat down on the edge of the bed and said, "You young fellows are made of rubber. You can bounce back from almost anything."

"I'm . . . I'm eighteen," he told her. "I mean, nineteen."

She smirked. "That old, eh?"

"At least. But between you and me, I'm not real sure." Now that he appeared to be permitted to do so, he retrieved his jacket and slipped his arms inside it. He pulled it shut across his chest and noticed he'd lost a button.

"I heard you were brought up in an orphanage."

"That's right. I was sent there after the Blight. I was only a little thing, so I don't know my right age. Don't know my birthday. Don't know much."

"You know plenty about sap," she said bluntly.

He had the overwhelming feeling that he'd get roughly as far arguing with Mercy as he would with Zeke's mother. Or with the princess, for that matter. He supposed it took a certain kind of woman to survive down here, underneath the walled city. That was all right with him, but he didn't really want to talk about sap.

So all he said was, "I know about it, yeah."

"How long were you using it?"

He avoided her eyes and pretended to fiddle with the empty buttonhole on his jacket. "Not sure."

"A while, I'd say. You've got the first marks on you—the marks of somebody who's bound to *turn* one of these days, if he ain't careful." She took his jaw in her hands again. She met his eyes by force, and he decided that she was really kind of pretty. Not too pretty, but nicer than plain. A smattering of light brown freckles dusted her nose and the tops of her cheeks. Her freckles were less obtrusive than his vivid orange ones. He liked hers better.

"I'm careful," he told her in his oldest-sounding voice. "I was always careful."

"Yeah, and I'm your mother. Let me make some guesses, and you tell me how close I get."

He shrugged, trying to make it look easy, as though he didn't care. He folded his hands behind his head and leaned back against the headboard. "Shoot."

"You started a long time ago, probably four or five years. But back then you were just a boy, and you had a hard time getting your hands on it, so you didn't do it much. Then you got bigger, and I'll guess you took the most likely work you could find and started selling it. Once you were selling, you had it in your hands all the time—and then, maybe a year or two ago, you were doing it so regular you probably never went a day without it. How am I doing?"

One nostril twitched involuntarily. "Not bad."

"See, I can tell it from your skin, how it's going that funny color around your eyes. Almost like you're god-awful tired all the time and just don't sleep enough. But those aren't regular circles under your lids like we tired old people get; those are pockets of sap residue, collecting there and staining your skin from underneath."

His chilly attitude slipped. "It can do that?"

"It builds up in your body, and some of it stays," she confirmed.

"How long?"

"I don't know. Years? Forever, maybe. I haven't had a chance to watch anybody use it that long. Heavy smokers don't live to a ripe old age, in my experience. That's why I'm watching every user I can, trying to learn more."

"You . . . you want to watch people use sap?"

"Do I *want* to?" She stood up again, and smoothed her skirts with her hands. "No. I don't want to watch anybody use it, least of all a young man like yourself. But it teaches me, when I can see what it does to people. Look, I don't read or write real well, but I'm taking notes as best I can, for doctors here and back East. I'm trying to learn how this stuff works, and how long it takes to kill."

"Were you taking notes on me?"

"I take notes on everybody who gets poisoned or bit. It doesn't happen too often down here, 'cause most everybody knows the rules about surviving. But once in a while a gas mask slips, or somebody gets surprised and loses a finger, and then a hand. And then, yes, I watch 'em."

She took the lantern off its hook but left it bright, and set it down on a cabinet across the room. The swish of her dress was loud in his ears, and the sway of her apron clinked as the tools in her pockets chimed together.

"Did you think I was gonna die?"

"I thought you might," she confessed. "Aside from you taking that tumble, you spent a few days waking up from the sap, and that's no easy thing. Either one could've killed you, if you'd been weaker or smaller, or maybe less lucky."

"I've always been lucky."

"Same as you've always been careful, I'm sure. But I do want to be clear . . ." she told him as she began riffling through one of the drawers.

"About what?" he asked, no longer caring much. She'd already told him he'd live. From pure muscle memory, he reached his feet over the edge of the bed before remembering that his boots weren't right there. He'd kicked them off before turning in the night before. One had slid underneath the mattress, and one was immediately to his right.

"You pick up the sap again, and it won't be too much longer. There's a point with every user, with every victim . . . and beyond that point, there's no saving them. Nothing at all to be done except put a bullet in their head so they can't hurt anyone else."

She said it so casually that it made him shiver, but he hid it. He pretended to adjust his jacket, and fished around with his feet to retrieve his shoes. "I don't plan to use it anymore."

"Oh?" She looked over her shoulder, and fixed him to the wall with one pointed eyebrow. "You don't *plan* to? I'm sure you haven't even been thinking about it, all this time, this whole week you've been here. I'm sure you haven't been imagining how good it feels, and now nice it tastes—or how bad it tastes, I don't know—and I'm sure there's no reason at all you'd go looking for it the moment your friends turn their backs."

"No, no, and no. To all of that."

"Stay away from it, Rector Sherman. Don't make me put you down like a dog." She approached his bed again, but did not sit. She merely loomed. "Because *I'll do it.*"

He steadied himself and his voice before replying, "I believe you." He shoved one foot into one shoe and wrestled with the other one. The laces didn't want to work. He struggled to make them meet and tie.

"I'm not saying that to be mean to you," she said. "Around here, folks mostly see what the gas does. But I've seen what the *drug* does. So I want you to know: I know what it looks like, when a man is using it, and I know how bad it can get. Take this as a promise: I won't let it happen to you."

The other shoe finally cooperated. "Right. I'll keep that in mind."

"Before you leave," she said, suddenly, like she'd meant to say something earlier but she'd forgotten. "I came in here to get you up because Angeline asked me to. She's waiting for you down in the kitchen area."

"Thanks."

"And another thing."

"Jesus," he swore. "Really?"

"Yes, one more thing. Get my daddy or Briar Wilkes or someone to set you up with a room of your own. You can't stay in here. This is the closest thing to a hospital we got, and I only have the one bed. Nobody needs it right this moment, but that could change at any second. I want you out."

"But—"

"But what? We've done established you're healthy as a horse, and ready to run around the city with your friends. That means you're healthy enough to have your own space, and get the hell out of mine."

"Well, ain't you a sweet thing."

"I sure as shit am," she told him as she ushered him out the door, pushing his shoulders.

He dragged his feet. "I still got things in here! Possessions!"

"You can come back and claim 'em anytime."

The woman had a reach like an octopus.

He fought her just enough to keep one foot in the room, saying, "Let me get my bag, would you?"

She threw her hands in the air and said, "Fine. Get your bag. Just *go*. I've got notes to write up."

"Notes about me?"

"*Notes*. And I write slow."

She slammed the door behind him, which Rector thought was unnecessary. How many people came and went from this hospital room that was so inhospitable? He knew it wouldn't be *his* first choice, but then, it probably wasn't anybody's first choice. He reckoned it was the only choice.

As he hiked down the halls he wriggled his feet to better fit in the shoes, then stopped by the washroom. Then it was down to the kitchen, where Angeline waited. Zeke and Houjin were already there, chewing on raisins and drinking weak, odd-smelling coffee.

"Good God, boy—you rise and shine slower than any night owl I ever did see."

Confused by the comparison and too tired to argue with her, Rector waved and went to join the other two. He helped himself to a fistful of dried grapes and sat down heavily on the nearest stool. "What time is it?" he asked, in case the answer would absolve him.

"Eight o'clock. It's ridiculous, being in bed at this hour. The sun's up, and we're heading out while the light is good. I've got extra filters, my seeing-glasses, and I've made these two bring a canteen apiece and a bit of food for lunch, so take whatever you find over there and stock yourself up, too. Water's in the barrel by the door. We'll find a sealed-off stopping point someplace along the way, and if we don't, we'll come on back."

Following Angeline's lead was the easiest thing Rector had ever done. She called the shots, and since she knew where she was going and what she was doing, he sat back and let her be in charge. It took the pressure off him to lead the crew, and it meant he didn't have to follow Houjin around at all, if he didn't want to.

He pointed down at her feet. "What's that?"

"That? That's a cage," she said. "I'll set this over by the wall, near where you saw that fox. Maybe we'll catch him, maybe we won't. Maybe we'll catch something else."

"Won't catch no sasquatch with it," Zeke grinned.

"Maybe a sasquatch foot," she agreed. "We'll need something bigger for him."

Houjin asked, "A bigger cage? Do they make cages big enough?"

"Actually, I was thinking we might have to stick 'im in jail. That's a cage just about big enough, wouldn't you say?" She spun off the stool upon which she'd been sitting. "The old jail. You know, the famous one."

"But the jail . . ." Rector fought to remember the old stories, hunting for a detail he'd never heard, or must've lost. "It was above-ground, wasn't it?"

"Sure it was. But the basement opens up to the underground. It didn't used to, but it does now—and the first floor is all sealed up from rotters, if not from the air. Downstairs there are a few more cells. The air will be much cleaner there, if not perfectly clear. Our experiment might have its flaws, but it'll give us an idea of what to expect."

Houjin thoughtfully stuffed some dried cherries and nuts into a small canvas bag. "It's not a bad idea. If cleaner air improves the sasquatch at all, then *really* clean air might make him all better."

"Or it might not," Rector argued.

Zeke tried to have it both ways. "Maybe it'll help, and maybe it won't. But we should probably get it off the street nohow, don't you think?"

Houjin remained dubious. "But how do we get it to the jail, even if we catch it?"

"We'll start with a net. *This* one." She indicated a large lump that bulged out of the oversized satchel she'd left on the table. "It's a fishing net, but it's clean and mended. It can hold a few thousand pounds of salmon, so it'll hold a few hundred pounds of sasquatch."

He was not yet convinced. "We're going to tie it up in a net?"

"No, we're going to *catch* it in a net, then we're going to tie it up with regular old rope, which is also in that bag. I'm not a dummy, Houjin," she said, almost crossly. "I'm not out to get any of us killed."

Rector sighed. "So that's all we're bringing? A net, some rope, and . . ." He looked at her torso, strung with the two bandoliers of very sharp blades. "And your knives?"

"Guns make too much noise. We don't want to attract rotters, and we don't want to kill the creature, so we're not bringing guns. But you boys keep the axes and clubs you picked up. I want you able to defend yourself, should the worst occur."

Rector complained, "A gun would defend us better."

And she retorted, "Spoken like someone who hasn't fired one very often, or fired one down *here*. If I thought any one of you boys was a Texian sharpshooter, that'd be one thing. But I won't have no amateur gunslingers shooting willy-nilly; you'll hit each other as likely as anything else. Now make sure you've got everything you're likely to need, and let's head out while the sun's up. We're burning daylight, boys! And the weather's not even half bad up there. I hesitate to suggest it, but I do think we're starting to warm up for summer."

All the way over to the carts, and on the ride up the hill, Rector worked hard to keep from thinking about Miss Mercy and the things she'd told him with that stern, almost-pretty face of hers. He fought against everything she'd said, even as some wretched, insistent little spot in the back of his head whispered that she was right.

It was the same little spot that used to hold Zeke's ghost; it was the place where phantoms rested and waited, even without the sap to fuel them. As Rector rode in the rattling cart, pumping the lever up and down without thinking about it anymore, he wondered what else lived in that awkward, cobwebby corner. Zeke's ghost was gone. Zeke himself sweated, puffed, and pumped like a champ directly across from him on the repurposed mining car; and that meant he'd never been dead, and had never haunted Rector or anybody else.

Sometimes he had to remind himself of this. And sometimes he wasn't sure how he felt about it.

Oh, in a general sense he was glad Zeke was alive. It sure took the edge off all that guilt he'd worn around his neck. But all the same, and for all he'd been afraid of the specter . . . it had been one reliable presence in his life when there weren't many others.

And now he couldn't rely on that, either.

The trip up the hill felt faster this time, partly because Angeline was wearing the awkward polarized glasses, so they could keep their masks off most of the way. This prompted Rector to poke Houjin about how come, if he was so damn smart, he hadn't thought to bring the glasses in the first place—to which Houjin responded that he didn't spend all his free time riffling around through the storage rooms in the Vaults, so he hadn't known about them. Then Miss Angeline had threatened to box them both on the ears if they couldn't get along.

Close to the end of their trip, she abruptly pulled the brake, and a fierce, hissing spit of white fire and sparks kicked up from the track. When the cart came to a full stop, she ushered everyone into masks on the double. "It was free and clear up until a few minutes ago. Then I started catching hints of it in the glass. Maybe it'll be all right for a while, maybe it won't. I don't want to take the chance."

Once again, Rector reluctantly crammed his face into a gas mask. The rest of the way indeed felt longer, even though they'd nearly reached the Sizemore House. He hated those damn masks, but when he griped about them, Angeline told him, "If they bother you that much, maybe you've picked the wrong place to live. Or work. You could always go hang out at the Station, if you want."

Carefully, he asked, "Why would I want to do that?"

"Because you're a boy who's been known to move sap, and that's where it comes from, mostly. And besides, I heard tale you'd already been down there and seen it."

"So . . . you heard about that."

"I hear about everything." With calculated casualness, she continued. "I know who you're working for, don't I?"

He thought about being contrite, and opted instead to be direct. "I expect you do."

She nodded, and unloaded the cart, making sure everyone's supplies were bundled up good and tight (including her own), and saw to it that the boys retrieved their weapons.

While she checked and refolded the fishing net, she was silent. But when she'd finished, she said, "It's no surprise. These other two"—she motioned at Zeke and Houjin, who remained concertedly quiet—"know how I feel about Yaozu. Wouldn't spit on him if he were on fire. He spent too many years propping up my murdering son-in-law down here. I can forgive it for my own peace of mind—but I won't forget it."

Rector didn't believe for a moment that she'd forgiven anyone for anything.

"That being said"—she chose her words carefully, speaking more slowly than usual—"Yaozu is not an inventor, and he's not some kind of scientist—but he understands how to run a city, or a business, or people . . . better than Joe ever did. So with that in mind, I will be as gracious as I can muster, and tell you that I don't think Yaozu is the worst thing that could've happened to Seattle. I just hope he's strong enough to hold it together against the sorts of men who are always trying to weasel their way inside these walls. If he isn't, someone will take the city away from him, one of these days."

"And better the devil you know, eh?" he said, more lightly than he meant to.

She donned her bag and started for the stairs that led up out of the cellar. "That's one way to put it. He's smarter than Joe, and that's either good or terrible, depending on how the cards fall. I'm hoping for good, because I care about this place and I want it to hold together—even if he's the glue. But I'm worried about the bad, because if he put his mind to it, he could do a lot more damage than Joe did. This city is worth saving. It's worth fixing, however we have to go about it. But it shouldn't be saved at the cost of making that drug, and all the people it kills. And that's all I've got to say about *that*."

The cellar doors parted with a shove of her shoulder.

Rector reflexively held his breath—the Blight looked like smoke, and his body rebelled against the idea of inhaling it—but he beat the instinct down.

Back into the curdled air they climbed, adjusting their gear and their garments to cover all the skin they could. Rector had hung onto Fang's gloves, and now he felt prepared to poke around inside the dead city, whether or not he enjoyed it.

"Which way's the wall?" he asked.

"That way," Houjin answered, pointing.

Rector faced in that direction and waited for Angeline to take the lead. She paused to turn around and remind them, in a soft but penetrating voice, "From here on out, we whisper. And unless it's real important, don't even do *that*. Just keep your mouths shut. We'll work our way along the wall, same as you were doing yesterday, and if the sasquatch comes out to watch us, so much the better. If it doesn't, then we'll keep looking for holes."

She left the trap near their starting point, baiting it with a piece of horseflesh she unwrapped from a packet of paper. The meat wasn't terribly fresh, and Rector was glad he was wearing a mask so he couldn't smell it. They covered the whole setup with some dead, brittle brush, but kept the camouflage light. The odds weren't great that any creature inside the wall would know a trap when it saw one, or that it'd necessarily care.

And from there, they returned their attention to the wall.

Seventeen

The farther up the hill they explored, the harder it became to hug the Seattle wall.

When it was built seventeen years previously, it had been thrown up as hastily as possible, using whatever was at hand and cutting through anything in its decided path. Houses were severed; trees were knocked over; buildings torn down and left in pieces, their exposed foundations jutting out from the wall's base. Whereas before Rector had grazed the structure with his fingers to keep tabs on it, now he could keep to it only so closely without falling into an open cellar or climbing over a crumbling old home.

Rector tried to contain his revulsion at the dank, sick press of the air. He kept hoping he'd grow accustomed to it, but familiarity bred only more contempt. He didn't like the darkness, the constant shroud that hung over everything. He loathed the revolting fog that dripped off every branch of every dead tree, like tattered ghosts or decaying moss. He would have preferred anything else to this, even the muddy tunnel beneath the root cellar. At least he could scratch his nose in the root cellar.

But onward they climbed, and upward, because Angeline told them, "I've heard a lot of animal noise and whatnot a little ways from here, at the northeast edge of the wall. Maybe we'll find our breach there, maybe we won't. But it's worth looking."

Beyond simply breathing in the masks, they also worked against the steep angles of Denny Hill. It was easy to keep from talking. No one had the stamina for it.

And everywhere they went—foot by foot, yard by yard—the wall was intact and imposing. It disappeared up into the fog, its top lines reaching well beyond their field of vision. Occasionally it jutted out through the toxic air, its silhouette a shadow shaped like castle ramparts; usually it wore its halo of fog as thickly as a winter cap, and nothing but a dim suggestion of its shape could be seen.

When they paused to rest they huddled furtively, watching the ever-shifting screen of Blight conceal and reveal the city's details at its capricious leisure. Once or twice they thought they were being followed, but nothing appeared from the alleys. Nothing leaped forth from the empty homes or shuttered businesses. Nothing joined or harassed them.

They listened, because it took less effort than speaking.

They pulled forward in a nearly vertical crawl, using their hands to hold the streets, which were eroded badly from years of rain and neglect.

For a while they heard the *whoosh, drag,* and *suck* of the farthest northern pump room, and they saw its great yellow tube poking up into the sky to reach the clearer air. The dull rumble of machinery somewhere beneath them felt like tremors under their feet. But this comforting, rollicking noise faded, and they couldn't hear it even if they ignored the sound of their own lungs hauling air back and forth.

And when that steady, reassuring sound was gone, it was replaced by something else.

Rector grasped at Angeline's sleeve.

"I hear . . ." She slowed, and stopped. The boys stopped with her. *"Something."*

"Reminds me of the noise in Chinatown," Zeke said quietly. "The men fixing the vents and the ceilings. It's the noise of men building things."

Rector made a valiant effort to peer through the fog, but failed to see anything of substance. He leaned forward to make himself heard. "I thought Yaozu was working to fix the city, shore it up, and all that malarkey."

Houjin's eyes were grave when he responded. "Not here. The north end of the wall . . . nobody lives out here. It's no-man's-land. It's too far away from anything useful."

Zeke added, "No Chinese, no Doornails. No men from the Station."

"Or there *shouldn't* be." Angeline followed Rector's lead and tried to peer through the fog by sheer willpower. She turned to the boys and said, "I think you fellows ought to head back. Let me go take a look at this. It could be dangerous."

"No way." Zeke shook his head hard enough to make the buckles on his mask rattle.

Houjin echoed the sentiment. "We're coming, too."

"I don't know . . ."

Rector pushed back as well. "It could be dangerous. You shouldn't go by yourself."

She laughed before she could stop herself, then cleared her throat and looked serious again. "There's nothing in this city that'll take a swing or a shot at me, Red. Ain't that right?" she asked Houjin and Zeke.

They nodded their support, but their eyes were anxious. Zeke said, "Even the pirates keep their promises to Miss Angeline."

She said, "And one person is quieter than four people. That's not my opinion, that's *math*."

Still the boys stood firm, so she relented. But before they resumed their hike, the princess extracted a promise from them. "If things get bad, I want you boys to run, you hear me? Don't stick around and try to be heroes. I've talked and cut my way out of tight situations before, and I'll do it again. If it all goes to hell, I want you to head back to the Vaults and tell Zeke's momma."

Rector let out a small snort. "Why? What's *she* going to do?"

Zeke turned to him. "More than you think, and she won't do it alone. She'll bring Cly, and maybe Mr. Swakhammer. And both of them have friends. Big friends, the kind who don't mind making a mess."

"Promise me you'll go?"

Collectively, they sighed, promised, and continued up the hill.

It might've been Rector's imagination, but he could've sworn that the higher they went, the thinner the Blight and fog were. He'd heard it was heavy stuff, and it pooled like liquid, or maybe the light just got better as their altitude rose. One thing that wasn't his imagination: These had been some expensive houses, once upon a time. They were huge and ornate, and even with crumbling gingerbreads and drooping porches he could see that they must have cost a fortune. They'd all agreed to maintain their silence, so he didn't ask if this was the neighborhood they'd called Millionaire's Row, but he expected it probably was. You'd *have* to be a millionaire to own one of those places, even seventeen years ago.

The higher they went, the lighter it got, and the louder the noise of busy men grew.

Angeline led in a crouch and the boys mimicked her, staying low and keeping behind cover—going out of their way to hide behind derelict wagons, carts, and outhouses rather than venture into the open. They left the edge of the wall, but not by much. They didn't need to: The noise came from nearby, close enough that they could still follow the lines of the barrier even though they weren't right up against it anymore.

They heard loud voices, voices that hadn't been asked, ordered, and reminded to stay hushed. A conversation took place that was loud enough to understand, quite clearly, at a distance—each word fired off like a gunshot in the misty, ghostly ruins.

"How much longer?"

"Hard to say."

Two men. They stopped moving within ten yards of the princess and the boys, who immediately ducked and hid.

"The chief was right, so I guess I'll shut up about it."

"You'd better. We'll be ready to get under way within a week, from what Scotty said."

"If he can be believed."

A pause, and then Rector heard two streams of liquid splash against the ground.

"Eh . . . he's got a better idea than anybody. And it's *his* money we're burning, so if he's wrong, it's no skin off our noses."

"Right. Gotta admit, I hate taking a leak out here. Goddamn gas makes my pecker itch."

"*Sure*, it's the *gas* what makes it itch."

"Shut your mouth."

"Make me."

"Can't be bothered."

"That's up to you, then."

Trousers were subsequently adjusted, and the idle conversation continued, leaving a trail of sound for Angeline and the boys to track. The two men weren't moving fast or carefully; they obviously thought they were alone. And much to Rector's personal relief, they weren't going far.

"Shit, I hate that hill."

"Learn to piss closer to where you work."

"I wanted to stretch my legs. Tired of being cooped up in there."

"Well, your legs are stretched now, ain't they? Next time just go for a walk down the street like a civilized lazy man."

"I'll consider it."

"Anyway, we'll have plenty of action soon enough."

"Don't remind me."

"If you weren't up for a fight, you shouldn't have signed on."

"I'm up for it," he insisted, though he did not come across as fully convinced.

"You heard stories, huh? About the Chinaman from Hell?"

"I heard plenty about him, and I don't think this'll be as easy as the chief expects."

"Maybe you're right."

"I hope I'm not."

All the way, Angeline and her companions followed half a block behind, staying close enough to keep their quarry but far enough away that they shouldn't be noticed or caught. Rector was dying to ask where they were going, and what was going on, and did anybody know those two fellows, and where had the men been cooped up? But there was no talking, only sneaking.

Zeke stumbled and caught himself before he made too much noise. Rector hoisted him by the underarms to keep him upright.

The wall was dark and flat behind them, framing the whole world with its bulk.

Or that's what Rector assumed, until Angeline smacked each boy's arm quietly—directing their attention up, and away, and back. She jabbed her finger hard into the air, pointing at something difficult to see and uncertain in shape.

Rector wiped his arm across his visor, still nurturing the ridiculous notion that maybe it'd clear his vision just a little bit. But it didn't, so he had to squint through the fog.

It took him a few seconds to understand why the princess was all riled up. The air fought him, and the fussy gray atmosphere didn't give him much to work with. But as he stared, he realized that something about the wall itself wasn't quite right. Its angles didn't meet up like they ought to; its authoritative shadow didn't spread seamlessly along Seattle's northeastern border.

It hit him like a train: The wall was gone.

Eighteen

The wall was not a small bit broken, but badly so—missing enough of its volume that the vague afternoon sun spilled inside the U-shaped gouge, as if a great jet of water had been turned against the wall, washing away its stones like a gully cut down the side of a mountain.

Zeke put his hand over his mouth, and Rector was willing to bet that inside Houjin's mask, his trap was hanging open, too.

The chatting men wandered off. Rector thought the plan was to follow them, but Angeline held him back. When there was enough distance between the two parties, she drew their heads close together and spoke so softly she could scarcely be heard.

"Let 'em go. We found our hole in the wall."

Zeke objected. "But they're getting away!"

"It doesn't matter. We know how they got in, and we can guess what they're up to."

Zeke frowned. "We can?"

Rector elbowed him in the ribs. "Yeah, we can. The Chinaman from Hell—you *know* that's Yaozu. They're here to hassle him, just like he said they would . . . just like he, and Harry, and Bishop all said. They're here to take the Station away from him."

"But now what?" the Houjin pushed. "If you're right, what do we do? Do we tell Yaozu? Tell the Doornails?"

Angeline said to Rector, "I expect *you'll* go running to your boss with the news, whatever we say. Perhaps he *should* know, but let's get our facts straight first. Let's go see what they're doing before we run off telling tales."

Reluctantly, Houjin agreed. "Right now, all we know is that new people are inside."

The princess corrected him. "Oh, we know more than that. We know they're up to no good, or else they'd have come inside the same way as everybody else. They picked an out-of-the-way spot where no one's likely to run across 'em, so they don't want anyone knowing they're here. And furthermore, they're bastards."

Huey cocked his head. "Bastards?"

"They broke the wall. If they did it on purpose, they don't give a damn about who gets sick, or how sick they get. They're poisoning the woods, everything in 'em, and anybody who passes through 'em. And they don't give a damn."

"*And* they let the rotters out," Zeke noted.

"Did that on purpose, too, I expect." Angeline rose out of her crouch and urged them to do the same, then led a careful march toward the jagged hole. As the boys followed, she added under her breath, "Probably thought it'd be easier if they only had to fight Yaozu—and not every dead thing in the city, while they're at it."

Rector cleared his throat. "Yaozu said we need the rotters."

As if this was precisely the prompt he'd been waiting for, Houjin immediately blurted out, "He needs them so bad, he's making them!"

Everyone stopped and turned to stare at him. Angeline asked, "What did you just say?"

"He's making them," he repeated, and it sounded like a plea for something. Understanding? Reassurance? "When we first went to the Station," he said, thrusting a thumb at Rector, "Yaozu's men locked some other men outside without masks. They were brand-new rotters. You saw it, didn't you?"

"We didn't see anybody lock anybody outside," Rector said carefully.

"You weren't paying attention, or you weren't thinking about it. Those men were unarmed, unmasked, and just barely dead. They hadn't been exposed for more than a few minutes before we got there. They'd been put out—as some kind of punishment, or Yaozu didn't like them, or whatever reason. It was obvious."

If Angeline was surprised, she could've fooled Rector. "I wouldn't put it past him. He wants the rotters to keep him company for exactly this reason." She flapped a hand toward the hole in the wall, and whoever had made it. "They're guard dogs, is what they are. And when they disappear, that leaves nobody but his hired hands watching the place. A man who's been bought and paid for can change his mind. Yaozu trusts the rotters more than his own people."

Zeke had been silent, soaking it all in. But then he said, "I know you don't like him, Miss Angeline, but the devil you know wouldn't put a hole in the wall."

Grudgingly, she replied, "You're not wrong, but let's not call him the cavalry yet. Let's go get ourselves a gander at the breach. It might tell us something."

After another ten minutes of hushed hiking and breathless silence, their masks were not clogged yet, but clogging. They wouldn't be comfortable outside for very much longer without taking a break to adjust their filters, and everyone knew it, but this was too big to ignore. And it was urgent enough to investigate despite the creeping peril of equipment that could not keep them safe forever.

For the wall was not merely cracked, and not merely burrowed through.

It was shattered—split in an untidy slash from top to bottom, its rubble scattered in every direction. Blocks had been smashed into houses, lodged in the tops of brittle trees, and tumbled across what was left of the streets.

Zeke whistled quietly, a short note of awe. "What could *do* something like that?" he asked. "Did . . . did a ship crash into it, or something?"

Houjin shook his head. "Dynamite. I bet you anything."

Zeke asked, "But wouldn't we have heard it?"

They all stood in silence gaping up at the fissure when two thoughts clicked together in Rector's head. "That storm, a couple of weeks ago. There was thunder, remember? Everybody talked about it, since we don't ever get none, hardly."

Angeline pondered this. "We might've heard dynamite, and mistook it for weather. Not bad, Red. That's as good a guess as any."

"If he's right, it's been like this for weeks," Houjin mused. "That's plenty of time for animals to get inside and get sick."

"Plenty of time for man-shaped animals to get inside, too," the princess said.

"Look over there . . ." Zeke said, peering off to the north.

Rector followed his lead and saw a swath of hazy yellow burning weakly through the fog. "Is that . . . light? I thought we were practically at the end of the wall."

"There ain't much wall at this northeastern side, that's for sure," Angeline confirmed. "But it goes around farther to the north, then back to the east. As for over there . . ."

Then Houjin said slowly, "It's the old park, isn't it? Up near the big houses, where the rich people used to live."

"This whole hill is where the rich people used to live," Zeke told them. "My momma's place was back down the hill a few blocks, over to the south."

"Yeah, but I mean the *really* rich people. The men who owned the mills, and the logging company. They lived along Fourteenth

Street, and the road stopped at the top of the hill, where they were going to put a park."

The princess nodded. "They started building it not too long before the Boneshaker came. They put down a cemetery, too, on the other side"—she waved her hand to suggest a distant location—"and they filled it up with people who'd been dead for years and years and buried downtown once already."

"Why didn't they just wait for new dead people?" Rector asked.

"They were moving the old boneyard, making way for businesses and such. I even planned for a plot at the new place, thinking I'd be here forever. And my girl's there, so I figured I'd stay with her. But the wall cuts through that new cemetery full of old folks—slices it right in half." She fell silent for a moment, then said, "She's just outside the city, now."

"But there's a park?" Zeke prodded her.

"Oh, sure. It was supposed to be a real nice one, if they ever got it finished. But the fellow who was working on it also had work in New York City, so he took his own sweet time dealing with us. I don't know if the place was finished by the time the wall went up . . . but *most* of it . . ." She took a few steps and peered at the wall from another angle, then assessed it from a third position. "Most of it ought to be inside the wall here, and real close by. Huey, you said the park was at Fourteenth Street?"

"Yes, ma'am. I saw it on a map once."

"We just passed Twelfth Street, so we ain't got far to go. You boys think you can handle another two blocks?"

Without hesitation, they each said, "Yes, ma'am!"

"All right, then, let's look. And same rules apply, you hear? We hit trouble, you three run like the devil knows your name."

"Yes, ma'am," they agreed with somewhat less enthusiasm.

"So long as we're clear on that. I think we'll have the best luck if we dodge the rubble this way, and go around—"

She stopped, and in the sudden silence the boys heard the tumbling, rattling, and pinging of falling rocks.

Everyone stood still, and no one breathed.

The rocks were small and they spilled down like a stream, just a trickle for the moment. Rector's voice shook as he said, "It's the wall. It's going to come down on our heads, ain't it?"

But Angeline put a hand on his shoulder and said, "Wait," in her quietest whisper. She was looking up—they were all looking up—but her eyes were tracking something Rector couldn't see. He tried to chase her gaze, but saw nothing except for the cornstarch-colored air.

When the pebbles started falling again, Angeline's eyes darted to their source, narrowing as they did. "Boys . . ." she said, and how she fit so much warning into four letters, Rector would never know.

"I see it," Houjin told her. He retreated a few feet and kept his face aimed skyward. "It's moving, back and forth."

"Where?" Zeke asked.

Rector echoed him. "Yeah, where? I don't see anything." But he could *hear* something, and it worried him. The scuttling patter of sliding rocks came with a structure, a rhythm. A pace, like uncertain footsteps. His chest clenched with fear, and without meaning to, he drew himself up closer to Angeline. "Is it the monster?"

"Not a monster," she reminded him gently.

He fought the urge to press his back against hers, and he struggled against the impulse to run for cover. He couldn't see the thing, but he could sense it. Did it remember him? Would it come for him again?

He didn't want to look; he couldn't help but look. So when a gust of high wind stretched and broke the stringy yellow air, he gasped, pointed, and stumbled backwards.

"Settle yourself, Red."

Zeke gasped, too, only just now joining them. "It's . . . it's . . . that's not a person!" he squeaked.

Angeline's words were level and calm. "No, not a person."

"Not a person," Rector repeated, saying it like a mantra. "Not a person." He hadn't been nuts. It hadn't been a person who'd scared him half out of his skin and chased him into the chuckhole. "Not a person; never a person. And, oh God . . ." His stomach sank, tying itself into a complicated sailor's knot. "It's right on top of us!"

But the princess said, "No," and squeezed the back of his neck.

Her strength astonished him, though it shouldn't have. He'd been climbing through the city with her for two days, after all; it shouldn't be a surprise that her grip was as firm as the nuns at the orphanage. He wanted to turn and run, but her hand was steady, and he had a feeling that it'd yank him back like a dog on a leash if he tried.

The creature up on top of the wall moved slowly from side to side, pacing back and forth. It maneuvered deftly along the blast-loosened bricks. And as the fog parted and congealed, the elongated, person-shaped creature watched them.

"She sees us," Angeline declared softly.

Zeke's eyes crinkled into a frown. "She?"

"I believe so." The princess turned to Rector and said, "I think I know what's happening here. She ain't sick, you see? She ain't coming down inside. She's smarter than that. She knows what's here."

"Then what's she doing up *there*?" Rector wanted to know.

"She's looking for the thing that jumped on you, Red. Dollars to dice, he's her mate."

Rector watched hard as the long-limbed, hair-covered creature up above—which looked almost tiny, all the way up there—came and went, out of focus. Moments later, as the fog twisted into a knot, it vanished.

More rocks and dried mortar came skittering down; and when the low-lying cloud cleared again, the wall was unoccupied. No leggy, shaggy thing glared down, and no more debris rained down, either.

Whatever it was, it was gone.

Rector let out his breath in a long, shaky shudder. He hadn't even noticed he'd been holding it.

The princess released her grip on the back of his neck and patted him there, as if to reassure him. "She's headed back to the woods for now, I expect. I don't know if we can help her or not, but at least now we know what we're up against."

Zeke kicked at a fallen rock. It tumbled into a pile of bricks and was still. "I got a fairly good look at her, and I *still* don't know what we're up against."

"Oh, you silly things. Right now, she's not the worst of our problems. Let's swing by the park before we call it a day. I'd hate to get so close and not even see our biggest one."

Nineteen

The boys agreed to stop by the park, and after a brief pause to change their gas-mask filters, they followed Angeline farther up the hill. All the way along the edge of Seattle the fractured wall kept them company, looming off to their left and casting a mighty black shadow. The rest of the way, it was as solid as ever.

Houjin breathed hoarsely into his mask and muttered, "It could be worse. I only see the one hole."

"Yeah, but it's a *big* one," Zeke said, and in the muffled silence Rector heard how worried he was.

The princess said, "It's fixable."

"How can you be so sure?" Rector asked.

"Because the wall was buildable in the first place. Now hush up, all of you. We're here."

A long row of tattered hedges reared up before them, skeletal and sad. What few leaves remained were withered and brown. No doubt they'd once been cut into tremendous blocks and lovingly pruned to keep their shape. Now they were as ghastly and lifeless as an ironwork fence gone to rust. But they marked a boundary, and Rector made a note of it.

Angeline led the way, pushing through the brittle flora, which crunched in pitiful snaps. The twigs were as light as dust, and they fluttered to the ground to join the nasty mulch where everything else had fallen.

And on the other side they saw more dead things—larger dead things. Trees that had once been mighty were now reduced to crumbling trunks, and the odd monument or piece of statuary had gone streaked and pitted from prolonged exposure to the gas. To the left they saw curving walkways with seams that had succumbed to rubble, and a large round pond with nothing inside it but a yellow-black muck. They noticed signs that had gone unreadable, the paint blistered to illegibility and the colors bleached to an ugly gold. Running through all this wreckage were paths that were once graceful, veering prettily between patches of manicured lawns and gardens, and were now uniform in their unkempt ugliness—though they retained their expensive, precise shapes. Nothing could grow in the Blight gas, and therefore nothing became overgrown. It could only rot where once it had thrived.

In the center of all this cheerless, colorless misery, a tremendous structure jutted from the center of a circular path. At first glance it blended into the wall, which ran a few yards behind it. "What's that?" Zeke asked.

He was too loud, and Angeline shushed him. But she answered as she gathered them to her like a mother hen. "This way, boys. Stay close to the wall. Zeke, that's the old water tower they was building when the Blight came. It'd look bigger if it weren't standing in front of the wall."

The tower looked plenty big enough. Perhaps half the wall's height, the water tower was a cylindrical, very tall turret made of bricks and capped with a metal roof like a boy's hat. The roof was rusting, and red-rimmed holes both large and small were eating their way through the original material, but Rector could see that someone had tied flaps of canvas down over one pitted segment. Another large sheet hung loose, having lost its moorings. It flapped against the building like a ghost clapping slowly.

From within the smooth brick tower came the noises of men at work.

Rector picked out snippets of conversation and the occasional hoot of laughter. He heard heavy things being lugged and lighter things being thrown, or hit. He detected metal on metal, and the scrape and whine of wooden crates being shoved about and pried open, their nails squeaking against the wood that held them.

Spiraling up the tower ran a series of tall windows, too narrow for a man to crawl through but big enough to let light inside. Now they let light *out,* and beneath the rust-ragged cone that topped the structure, the brilliant electric buzz of man-made bulbs and high-powered lanterns made the top floor glow.

At the tower's base, a white-painted gate had been left unfastened.

Rector watched Angeline out of the corner of his visor. She was eyeing that gate, and he knew she was probably calculating the value versus the trouble of pulling it open and investigating.

She caught him watching her and she winked. "Don't worry. I won't go for a climb without you."

"Stairs?" Houjin asked, keeping his chatter to a minimum for once.

"Stairs. Spirals of them, bottom to top. There's two ways in, I believe. The one you see right in front of us, and one on the other side." She was still thinking about it. Rector knew the look of someone weighing a bad idea, and knowing it was a bad idea, and thinking maybe it wasn't the worst idea in the world—all evidence to the contrary.

But she was as good as her wink and her word. Maintaining their best efforts at utter quiet, the four of them edged back behind the tower, between it and the wall.

There, the shadows were thicker than the fog, and it felt like night.

Rector shivered, but hid it by adjusting his satchel. "Now what do we do?" he asked. In truth, he wanted to go back to the Vaults. Badly. He itched all over, gloves and long sleeves and tall socks be damned; and his ribs were on fire from the stress of breathing so hard through such sturdy filters as the ones he now kept in his mask.

"I just want to watch. Just a few minutes," she told them.

From their new vantage point, they could see both entrances. They were closer to the "front," but it'd be difficult for anyone to leave the tower via the other door without walking past them, so Rector felt like they had everything covered. Apparently Miss Angeline did, too. She crouched down and urged them all to do likewise, squatting behind the detritus of old gardening equipment and the rubble of decorative benches that had never been assembled.

Soon the clang of footsteps on metal echoed through the tower and oozed out with the fog-diffused light. Then they heard a crunch and a loud stream of profanity, followed by, "We need to fix these goddamn stairs!"

"What do you expect? They're metal. The gas is hard on metal."

"So we should replace 'em, or repair 'em."

"Or you should be more careful."

"Go to hell."

"This isn't it?"

The front gate slammed open, ricocheting against the tower and kicking up a puff of dust that might have been brick and might've been rust. A man emerged, stomping and waving his right leg as though it was hurt and he was trying to shake off the pain. The gate's metal bars cracked and creaked on their hinges, and as the portal slowly rocked shut, a second man pushed it open again.

"You all right?"

"I'll survive. Went straight through the stairs, did you see that?"

"You did it right in front of me."

"Stop being so all-fired smart, would you?" He patted down his leg, and Rector saw that his pants were torn and there was a smear of blood above his ankle. The man was not badly injured, and he knew it, but nobody liked to have an open cut outdoors where the Blight could get to it. He planted the hurt foot down on the ground and stood up straight, looking around.

The four voyeurs all ducked down lower, not that it mattered. What their position didn't hide, the wall's shadow obscured well enough.

"Where's Otis? Ain't he supposed to be here by now?"

"What time is it?"

"Don't know. My watch stopped working yesterday. The gas seeped inside it and rotted out the innards."

"Son of a bitch, this place is miserable. Can't believe anybody lives here—I don't care how much money there is to be made."

The man with the bloodied pants leg snorted. "If you really didn't care, you wouldn't be here."

"I don't plan to move inside and set up a homestead. I'm not a goddamn fool. And I don't know if Otis's late or not, but he might be. Maybe he got lost."

"It ain't six blocks from the hole to the tower. If he got lost, he ain't got the sense God gave a speckled pup."

"It's hard to see," the other fellow insisted. "If you ain't used to running around in a mask, it can mess you up. Gets you all turned around. Maybe we should go down the hill and look for him."

"Maybe you should kiss my ass. See if Jay and Martin will go."

"They just got back from pissing down by the side of Denny Hill. Nobody wants to climb that thing twice."

"Fine, then *you* go."

"Not by myself."

"Well, I ain't going with you."

While they bickered, Rector cringed. He took Angeline's elbow with one hand and Zeke's with the other, drawing them back closer against the wall—farther into the shade, and farther out of earshot.

"But I want to see them," the princess hissed.

"Trust me. *Please*," he begged.

Houjin gave him a glare that said *Not a chance*, but he followed him a few yards back and joined the huddle. "What is it? And why are we supposed to trust you, again?"

Rector held up his hands for quiet because it was his turn to talk—and for once, he had something true and important to say. He leaned forward, and when all their heads were practically touching, he told them what he knew.

"I don't recognize the one fellow who hurt his leg, on account of it's hard to see when people are wearing masks. But the other one's name is Isaac West—I'd know his voice anyplace. He's a chemist from Tacoma who's been moving sap under his own brand, calling it *ambrosia*. I heard Yaozu didn't like it much, and I also heard West wasn't planning to change his behavior any. And that Otis fellow they're looking for—I bet it's Otis Caplan."

"Who's that?" Zeke asked, bonking his forehead against Houjin's mask.

"Used to be in the army. The Union, I mean. He was a scientist. He invented some kind of gun that everybody liked, and it made him a mint. Then he switched from dealing arms to dealing sap a year or two ago, and now he's making another mint. Bought a big house in San Francisco, but he comes up here pretty regular."

"What about the other two, the ones we followed up here?" Angeline asked.

Houjin said, "One of these guys called them Jay and Martin."

"I don't know. I don't know everybody. Give me a break."

Zeke's voice was low with awe. "I heard of Otis, back before I came in here. Every time there was a rumor going 'round that Minnericht was dead, or missing, or gonna retire, or anything, people used to say Otis Caplan was coming to take over the operation."

"I don't think he ever discussed it with Minnericht," Angeline said wryly. "And anyway, Yaozu beat him to it. Do I even want to know why you know of these men, Red?"

"Probably not, ma'am."

Zeke sat back on his heels and asked, "I think my filters are stuffing up."

The princess sighed, and looked at the boys one at a time. Seeing the same thing on each face, she relented. "I think we've done enough mischief for now. My mask is starting to chafe me, too. Let's turn around," she started . . . but whatever she'd planned to add was drowned out by the sputter of something loud, and coming closer.

Everyone tensed and retreated, and soon all four backs were pressed up against the wall—as close as they could get, as if they could melt right into the rocks that formed it.

The rumbling, roaring sound grew louder, approaching from behind them, back the way they'd come. Rector desperately shuffled through his moth-eaten memories, hunting for some idea of what the noisemaker might be. The closest he could come was the steam-powered works at the old sawmill, but that wasn't quite right. The volume was correct, and the mechanical rhythm of it was absolutely right, but the timbre and tone were all wrong. This was something smaller but still impossibly heavy. The close-pressed air made the rattling feel like an assault, and the vibrations were a personal insult as they butted and shoved. The ground beneath his feet quivered like it wanted to fall.

"What *is* that?" asked Zeke.

Houjin replied, "It reminds me of something I saw in New Orleans." And he might've elaborated, except that the persistent clank drowned out every other sound, and everyone had the good sense not to shout, in case it suddenly stopped. Instead they covered their ears and watched as a machine came crawling up the hill and into view.

It rumbled and rolled, a war carriage without a war horse, riding on enormous wheels that were spiked with great nubs for the sake of traction. The rear of the carriage was covered with canvas in an old-fashioned wagon style, but the front was sealed up with glass to create a compartment for the driver. The driver himself was a wide-set man sporting glasses and a bow tie. He was not wearing a mask, a fact that Houjin called attention to by pointing at the one he wore and gesturing back at the transport machine.

Angeline nodded, and everyone frowned. The machine's cabin must have air filters, or carry its own air supply for clean breathing. Rector could see the wheels in Houjin's head turning, calculating how on earth it could've been done . . . and wondering how he might be able to repeat it.

Rector tapped Angeline's arm and drew her closer. Right into her ear, he said, "That's Otis. I never seen him before, but I heard he was a tall fat man who's always dressed nicer than he ought to be. They say you can't mistake him for anybody else."

"Not a lot of fat men around these parts."

"Not a lot of bow ties, either," Zeke observed. "Nobody dresses up like they're going someplace fancy."

"Yaozu does," Houjin muttered, and Rector realized it might be true. He didn't know what a Chinaman wore to dress up and go out someplace fancy, so it was hard for him to say one way or the other, but it made sense to him that rich men ought to dress like rich men, and act like rich men, too. How else would anybody know they had any money?

And in Rector's experience, people didn't often take orders from men without money.

"I wonder what's inside that wagon," Angeline said. Rector barely heard her—the noise of the machine's engine made everything sound shaky and faint.

"Supplies for making sap?" he guessed.

The engine cut off, and the mayhem of its clatter died down. It settled into near-silence, except for a few pings and whistles as the motor cooled.

Caplan reached down to the seat beside him and picked up a mask, then put it on and opened the door to let himself out. He stepped down to the ground and slapped the door shut again, then stomped forward to shake hands with Isaac West and his companion.

"It's about time," West greeted him. "What do you think of the place?"

"I think it's a shithole if I ever saw one," Caplan said disdainfully, and if he weren't wearing a mask, Rector thought he might've spit on the ground for emphasis. "But if Yaozu can make it work, we can, too. I won't be outdone by no goddamn yellow Chinaman who thinks he's better than everyone else."

Angeline snorted quietly. The snort spoke volumes, so Rector was unsurprised to hear her mumble, "This one dresses real nice, but he talks real trashy. Says everything I need to know about him, don't it?"

"I expect it does," he agreed.

Otis Caplan said, "Anyone else around, or just you two?"

"Jay and Martin are upstairs."

"Go get 'em. These things are heavy, and I can't leave them sitting in the back. That part ain't sealed, and the air will corrode them 'til they're useless."

Isaac West ordered the man with the scraped-up leg upstairs with a bob of his head. He sighed, but didn't argue—not in front of Otis Caplan. Instead, he slowly turned and went through the white gate. Just out of sight, Rector heard a door open and shut with a soft scraping noise. It made him think of the seals on some of the underground doors. This impression was confirmed as he eavesdropped further and Caplan asked, "How's the tower coming?"

"We got the interior drained, cleaned, and closed up. It's practically a fortress in there, and it goes down to a basement level we didn't know about. We got that dried out, too, and we're checking its integrity now."

"But is it airtight?"

"Not yet, but we're working on it. Up top, we almost got it sorted—all we need is a little more glass and some better sealant. Then, of course, we gotta find a way to pump the bad air out, and pump good air in. We can get it as tight as we like it, but that won't do us no good if we can't breathe what we've trapped."

"The people who live here have got something figured out."

West nodded. "They got pumps, coal-fired or steam-powered. They send these big waxed tubes up above the Blight line and pump down fresh air that way."

Otis Caplan struck a pose for pondering, with his hands on his hips and his head cocked to the side. If he could've reached his beard, he might've stroked it in a villainous fashion. "Could we swipe one of those tubes?"

"I doubt it. They're awful big to make off with. Besides, the tube's no good without the pump."

"Could we steal a pump?"

"No idea," West told him.

Angeline said to Rector, "Now *that's* a man who's lying. He's just afraid of telling his boss no too many times in a row. Any damn fool knows you can't steal a pump. They're as big as a whole room."

Rector said, "Otis ain't never seen a pump. For all he knows, one might fit in a wheelbarrow."

From within the tower came the sounds of footsteps and grumbling, descending the spiral within—and using more caution on this trip than they'd shown before. Rector heard, "Watch out for that step. It's broke," as the creak of decaying metal made a straining sound that squealed all the way out into the park.

"Here they come. Help me unload," Caplan ordered West. Together they went to the wagon's rear, and Otis released a latch that dropped the back end open. "I've got the glass you asked for, and the closest thing to a sealant I could find, which is tar. I hear nothing works better against this gas, but it won't be pretty. As for the rest of the stuff, I brought enough to start a war."

He reached into the cargo area and withdrew a crate. It scratched across the floor until he had it in his arms, then, with some help from West, he put it on the ground. Isaac West said, "Too bad we ain't got an army. You can bring us all the guns you want, but without anybody to shoot 'em, they don't do us much good."

"It ain't all guns, West—though if it matters to you, I've got more fellows coming tomorrow night. We don't need an army to bring this place down to the ground. Or . . . farther into the ground. I don't know, I guess we can send it straight to the devil with what I brought." Caplan pulled a pry bar out from the wagon and gave it a twirl, then jabbed it into the top of the crate. "Get a gander at that, would you?" he suggested proudly.

Angeline, Rector, Houjin, and Zeke all craned their necks.

"Hot damn, Mr. Caplan. That's a lot of dynamite, ain't it?"

"This? This is only *some* dynamite. I've got a *lot* of dynamite packed up in the back along with the guns. I'd like to think of the guns as a last resort, really. It'll be less trouble if we can just plug up the holes, cave in the tunnels . . . less work for us, and nobody on our end gets hurt."

West turned his attention to whatever else was inside the wagon, shrugged, and said, "Sounds like a plan to me."

The gate swung open. Jay and Martin exited the tower, joined by the man who'd fetched them.

"Over here, boys." West waved them out to the carriage.

Angeline sat back on her heels and everyone else slumped over as well. Rector saw naked horror in Zeke's eyes, and something he couldn't quite pinpoint in Houjin's. At a glance it looked like anger, but it might've been fear.

The princess said, "Back to the Vaults now. All of us. We wouldn't have time left on these filters to do those men any damage—even if we weren't outmanned and outgunned."

"We need to tell my mother," Zeke said tightly.

"Your mother, and Mr. Swakhammer, and anybody else who might be helpful."

Houjin said, "I'll tell Captain Cly."

Angeline looked hard at Rector and told him, "And you'll take the news to Yaozu, because I'm not going to do it. Come on, back around this way." She led them around the rear of the tower, leading them in the hard, dark places between the bricks of the water reservoir and the stones of the wall.

"But we need to go downhill, not up!" Rector objected.

"I know, but we'll avoid 'em better over here. The wall heads farther north, see? Cuts across the cemetery, like I said. And I know a secret or two inside that cemetery."

When they were far enough to move without drawing attention, they ran as best they could—huffing and puffing through the struggle of their filters and stumbling along in the wall's shadow, where they could scarcely see the ground in front of them.

Once they were out of earshot, Houjin began asking questions. "Is there an underground entrance near here?"

The princess confirmed this without turning around or looking over her shoulder.

"Is it inside a mausoleum?"

"That's a real big word," she said. "What's it mean?"

"It's like a house for dead people. They had them in—"

"New Orleans," she cut him off. "You saw a lot down in Louisiana, didn't you?"

"Yes, ma'am. And a mausoleum is for burying dead people when you can't put them in the ground."

"A house? For dead people?" She shook her head. "Sounds like a waste of time and trouble to me. No, we aren't going to no house of the dead."

Instead, they were headed for the keeper's shack—or that's what Rector thought it must be. A tiny outbuilding at the edge of the cemetery gates, it was boarded up tight, but Angeline went around behind the thing and lifted a panel, then ushered all three boys through it. They scooted on their hands and knees, and just when Rector thought there was no way they'd all fit, he noticed the ladder.

He also noticed he was mere inches from bypassing the ladder altogether and toppling down to whatever unlit space waited below, so when Zeke crowded into him, urging him to make room, Rector socked him on the shoulder and said, "Watch it! I can't go no farther."

"You can if you head down that ladder," Angeline said from outside. "Go on, move it."

"But there's no light!"

"There's a light at the bottom, and I know where it is. Just stand by the ladder and don't wander off. You'll be fine."

She was right, he was sure, but that didn't make it any easier to descend an unknown depth into an unknown space, navigating by the feel of the rungs under his hands and feet.

When he reached the bottom, there was almost no illumination at all. Even the square overhead told him nothing, except that Huey and Zeke were leaning over to see how he was doing.

"You two get down here, would you?" he griped. "Don't leave me all by myself. I can't see a goddamn thing."

Two minutes later, they were beside him—shivering and pretending they were cold, when they were only scared silly. They clung to the ladder and waited for Angeline, who joined them as fast as she could. She dropped down beside them, skipping the last four rungs. She struck a match, and within moments, had located not a lantern, but a stash of candles.

"Sorry. I'm not out at this end often. Nobody is. Seemed like a waste to leave a perfectly good lantern here where it'd wind up going to rust before anyone had a chance to use it." She passed the stubs around and said, "These'll do for now. We'll pick up lanterns when we get back to the tracks."

Half an hour later they were back at the Sizemore House. All of them were relieved to see the familiar spot, even though it meant they still had a ways to go before the Vaults. Even Rector's recently changed filters were more clogged than he would've confessed—he was having real trouble breathing, his chest ached badly, and his heart hurt with every breath he drew. He switched them out again when they paused to reset the carts for the track, knowing they could take off their masks twenty minutes after that.

And they did, letting the rushing air of the pump cart's progress dry their sweat-and-breath dampened faces, and breathing deeply without strain for the first time all afternoon.

Fifteen minutes more and they were back in the underground Rector recognized, and soon they'd reached the huge, round door to the Vaults.

Houjin leaped up to it and flipped the lever to let the door swing out and open. Like Rector and Zeke, Huey was impatient to get inside—to get someplace sealed and safe. But Angeline said, "You all go ahead. Huey, Zeke—you know your way around best. Comb through the Vaults and see who you can find, who you can tell. Red, you see about paying Yaozu a visit. We need to call a meeting."

"But I don't know the way," Rector objected.

Zeke backed him up. "He's only been out there once or twice. One of us'll have to show him."

The princess thought about it, then said, "Then skip it. Houjin, you rustle up a message and run it to the Station; you'll do it faster anyway. Tell him what you heard up at the tower. Can you do that for me?"

"Yes, ma'am," Houjin said, with a firm nod.

"And when you got that taken care of, see if there's anyone in Chinatown you think should be informed. I got to admit, I don't know too much about who runs the show down there. I know you've got Doctor Wong, and he seems like a reasonable man. If you got anybody else who acts like a leader, bring him up to join us."

"Join us where?" he asked.

"Maynard's—where else? Zeke, you know what to do while Huey's gone?"

"Yes, ma'am. I'll take Rector and round up everyone useful, and tell 'em to meet us at Maynard's."

Angeline turned on her heel and dashed off down a corridor marked by a hand-painted sign that read COMMERCIAL STREET and pointed the way with an arrow. After she vanished, the boys looked at each other. Then Houjin drew the big door open and said, "You heard the lady. Go on down without me. I know a quicker way to Chinatown than this." From his back pocket, he pulled out his gas mask and put it back on with a sigh. "I'll catch up in an hour or two."

And then he, too, was gone.

 *Twenty*

If you'd asked Rector how deep the Vaults went, he would've shrugged and said, *A couple of floors?* However, the answer was *Five.* And this meant quite a lot of stairs. Before long, he was tired and his head hurt. And he still wanted sap. A lot. But no one would give him any, not even Yaozu, the man who ran the entire goddamn business. Rather than run back to the Station on a sap raid that would surely be more suicide mission than solace, Rector ran along behind Zeke, who acted like all these stairs were nothing at all. Then again, Zeke lived there, and he took the stairs all the time. Rector figured that anybody could get used to anything, given enough time to adjust. Maybe, in time, he'd adjust to life without the sap. Maybe he'd adjust to different people, and different air. Maybe not.

One floor held regular rooms, some of which were stuffed to overflowing with so much junk that you couldn't climb inside them if your life depended on it. One of these rooms—which didn't have a door to cover it—showed off a couple of old bed frames stacked on boxes, accompanied by what looked like a horse team's tack set, a counter for an apothecary's shop, and enough wagon wheels to outfit three or four carts.

But the next held three men, all wearing gloves up to their elbows and aprons to cover whatever clothes they didn't want dirtied. The room smelled pungent to the point of making Rector sick. Inside there were slabs of sliced fish lying out to dry, being set out for salting in a row of barrels.

"Frank, Willard. And Ed?" Zeke said. He seemed unsure of the third man's name. "You fellows think you can wrap it up down here and come up to Maynard's? Miss Angeline's calling a meeting, and it's real important."

Frank, if Rector had gauged the greetings correctly, jabbed the point of a long, thin knife into the wooden countertop. "Real important, you say?"

"No, that's what the *princess* says," Zeke grinned. "So it's up to you whether you come or not. But if I was you, I'd be there."

Zeke then passed the message to two fellows named Mackie and Tim. Rector let the younger boy do all the talking since he knew all these people—and anyway, it was like getting a guided tour of the Vaults. He'd rather pay attention to which way the corridors went, and where the exits were, and how to get to the indoor-outhouses, should he require one later.

These things were important.

On the next floor down, they found more people, and Rector finally met Miss Lucy. Lucy O'Gunning was old enough to be Rector's mother and then some, and she only had one arm, which was made of metal and the fingers of which clicked like a typewriter's keys when they opened and closed. She had a big smile upon meeting him, which was something that didn't happen every day. He liked it. He smiled back and shook the mechanical hand when she offered it to him, and did his best not to flinch or act as though it was odd.

She said, "It's good to meet you, Rector. I'd be happy to stand here and get acquainted, but I have to get back to the bar. It's all closed up since I've been down in the store levels stocking up, but if the princess wants everyone to come together, I'd better get moving and open it."

After she was gone, Rector asked Zeke, "What's wrong with her . . . arm?"

"She's only got one."

"I can see that, but it's a machine. That means she ain't got *no* arms, don't it?"

Zeke nodded. "Sort of. One she lost in an accident, and one she lost to a rotter bite." Then he continued down the hall to the sick-room, where Mercy Lynch was writing at the medical counter. She was concentrating hard and writing slowly, but there were stacks of paper beside her, in testament to her determination.

"Miss Mercy." Zeke announced their presence.

She looked up and took note of both boys, then said, "Hello Zeke . . . and Rector. Still haven't died on us?"

Rector said. "Not yet, ma'am. Not planning on it anytime soon."

"You and your *plans*."

Zeke repeated his edict, then added, "We've got intruders in-side the city," to give it some extra spice. "They've got bad ideas for the lot of us, and I think Miss Angeline has a plan."

"Intruders? Who would want to intrude . . ." she stopped her-self. "Ah. Men who want to make money on the sap trade."

Tired of remaining silent, Rector fleshed out the story with a flourish. "We saw them. They're here to raise hell, Miss Mercy—but we ain't gonna let 'em."

"I'm sure I'll sleep better at night for knowing that. All right, I'll be there soon. Go up to the main floor, and I'll swing down to the other end of this one and get my daddy—unless you saw him already."

Rector said, "Nope. Haven't seen him."

"All right. Then you two keep spreading the word, and we'll be up at Maynard's as soon as we can."

On the main floor they found Joe Burns, Jay Arvidson, and someone else whose name Rector barely heard and didn't remember. Like a great broom, the two boys patrolled the Vaults and swept everyone they found upstairs.

When the place had been scoured to Zeke's satisfaction, he and Rector went down to the main-level storage room and switched out the filters on their masks. "Time to visit Fort Decatur," Zeke said, screwing a clean carbon disk into place and twisting hard to make sure it was secured.

Rector nodded agreeably and fiddled more slowly with his own filters. This wasn't old hat to him yet, and he was still getting the hang of making sure every seal was fixed as though his life depended on it. Because his life *did* depend on it, and that thought made him twitchy. His whole life, hanging upon a small black filter that could clog or fail at any time . . . but probably wouldn't, if he set it up just right.

No pressure.

"Hey Zeke, I've been wondering," he said as they made for the exit. "Why's it called Maynard's? Is that after your grandpa?"

"Sure is," he answered proudly. "Miss Mercy says the Doornails treat him like he was their patron saint. But I only know what a patron saint is because of you and the orphan home."

It wasn't a bad comparison. "Yeah, that's right."

He thought about the small cards the nuns passed out, each one with the image of a saint and a short biography on the back. Maynard's would depict him in his hat, with his badge, buckle, and rifle. He'd be wearing a halo of gold-colored gas, and all the poor sinners would venerate him on bended knee with eyes averted out of respect. Maynard Wilkes: lawman and folk hero. A man who obeyed the spirit of the law if not the letter. He braved the Blight without a mask, back in the days before anybody knew what it was, or how it worked—only that it killed. He fought his own officers, his fellow lawmen, and the remaining civil authorities one and all . . . and he ran to the city jail to set the prisoners free. Gave 'em a fighting chance. And his famous last words, according to people who professed to be in the know, were, "None of those men were condemned. It'd be murder to let 'em die."

It was a great story, and at least some of it was true.

If there was one thing Rector had learned in Sunday school, it was that people liked stories. People *needed* stories, same as they needed heroes. Dead heroes were the best kind, really. You couldn't argue with them, and mostly, you only remembered the best things they'd ever done—while forgetting about the worst.

Once or twice, when he'd been too sublimely bored to think straight, Rector had opened up one of the Bibles lying around the orphanage. The words inside had been arranged funny, like they were spoken by someone in a play, but he got the stories anyway— and he learned about how a man after God's own heart had lied, cheated, killed, and schemed . . . but went down in history as a great king all the same, all because of a lucky shot that knocked down a giant.

Maybe Maynard Wilkes had arrested half the people inside that prison. Maybe on another day, the occupants would just as soon have shot him as name a saloon in his honor. But it was those big stories people remembered, in the end.

And now the job of sheriff belonged to Maynard's daughter. She wasn't half the hero Maynard was, in Rector's somewhat bi-ased opinion; but if anybody had to call the shots, it might as well be her. Just like it might as well be Yaozu running the Station and the sap, and it might as well be Captain Cly turning away from pirating and setting up the docks inside the city.

How much did they choose—and how much was chosen for them by coincidence and lore?

Rector shrugged off the question. How much had *he* chosen, when he'd come inside the wall? And how much had he only been driven to?

Out through the huge round Vault door and under the streets

the two boys dashed. They paused to spread the word to everyone they met, an assortment of men whose names Rector forgot as soon as he heard them. Along the damp corridors and muddy halls braced by mining timbers and railroad ties, the boys continued until they reached the ladder that would take them up inside the fort. Rector realized he almost could've found it on his own, a fact which surprised and pleased him, and made him wonder if his brain hadn't cooked up like a boiled egg quite as bad as he'd thought. He was still capable of learning his way around, and that was something.

Up the rungs they went, and into the gloomy yellow-gray air.

Zeke headed directly to the main yard with its half-built docks at the east end and called out for Captain Cly or anybody from the *Naamah Darling.* No one answered. At first Rector thought the fort was a dud, but then a man stepped out of the fog. He was wearing a mask with a hole cut in the back for his ponytail, similar to the way Houjin wore his. This newcomer dressed halfway between a Chinese man and an airman, so Rector knew it must be somebody from the *Naamah Darling,* but he couldn't recall anybody's name except for Cly and Troost.

Zeke called out, "Fang! I know you don't mean to sneak up on people, but *goddamn.*" Then, to Rector, he said, "Fang ain't got no tongue, so he don't talk. He's the first mate on the *Naamah Darling.*" Turning back to the first mate, he said, "Princess Angeline is calling an underground meeting, down over at Maynard's."

Fang nodded, then mimed looking at a pocket watch.

Zeke understood. "When? Now, pretty much. I think. Hey, you seen my mom around? Or the captain? Anybody you want to tell, tell 'em right away. After we spread the word around the fort, we're heading down to the saloon ourselves."

Fang began to sign with his hands, but changed his mind and instead held up a finger, asking the boys to wait. He walked over to the lean-to. When he returned, he had a pencil and a piece of paper. Upon it, he wrote, *I'll tell Kirby. Your mother is inside the ship. Knock first. Loudly,* and handed the paper to Zeke.

"Knock first? Well, all right. Come on, Rector—one more message to pass along, and then I'll show you Maynard's. You'll like it, I think."

Rector had a feeling that unless the saloon sold sap by the pound, he could take it or leave it . . . but Zeke's enthusiasm was such that he sat back and let the kid run with it, all the way over to the big, bobbing hull of the *Naamah Darling,* which was tethered to the old totem pole.

Forgetting Fang's note, Zeke rushed up to the ship and seized the hatch that would let him inside.

Rector, getting an inkling of what Fang's note meant, reminded him. "Hey, you saw what Fang . . . said. Maybe you should—"

"Knock, oh yeah—that's right." He struggled with the hatch, which didn't want to release. "Ain't I making enough racket, though? What's wrong with this thing, anyhow?" He gave the hatch a whack with the back of his hand, then scanned the ground for something heartier to hit it with. Not seeing anything, he made a fist and punched at the hatch while hollering, "Mother, Fang said you're in there. I need to talk to you real quick. It's important! Mother?"

And the hatch dropped violently open. It was all but flung to the ground, snapping back against the underside of the ship with a clang before settling into the usual position. But it wasn't Briar Wilkes scowling down from the ship's interior.

Captain Cly did not look happy.

"Important?" he said, his voice carefully controlled within his mask.

"Well, yeah . . ." Zeke said. "Took you long enough to answer the door. Were you in the back?"

Rector put his palm to his forehead.

"Fang said Momma's in there. I'm looking for her, and you, too," Zeke continued, clueless as could be.

Rector heard a door open with the sticky suck of seals being broken, and Briar saying, "Ezekiel Anderson Wilkes?" . . . which couldn't be good. If Rector knew one thing about other people's parents, it was that hearing all three of your given names called in one breath was a sign of bad things to come.

"Mother! There you are. We've got to get down into the underground. Everybody has to go to Maynard's."

"And why is that?" she asked, sitting down beside the crouching captain. Her feet dangled out through the hatch, and Rector saw that her boots were not tied.

"Because Miss Angeline says so. We saw something real awful today, up by the north edge of the wall. We know how the rotters are getting out, and the animals are getting inside. Long story short, we've got *intruders.*"

Captain Cly and Briar Wilkes exchanged a worried glance. The captain scratched at the side of his head, where the mask seal was rubbing against his temple. "What were you kids doing out at the north end, anyway? I suppose Houjin was with you," he muttered.

"Sure, he was with us—but so was the princess. We wouldn't've gone out there alone, of course," Zeke lied through his teeth.

"Angeline went with you?" Briar Wilkes reached down to tie her boots, and added, "That makes it a little better, I guess—I trust her to keep you out of . . . Come to think of it, I'm not so sure. She gets into plenty of trouble on her own, without you three tagging along."

The captain made a feeble effort to reassure her. "Oh, she'll keep 'em out of the worst of it, I expect. And they're standing here in one piece now, aren't they? Two of 'em, at any rate. Where's Huey?"

Zeke answered. "The princess sent him down to Chinatown to spread the same news we're telling you. There's trouble cooking out at the north end of the wall, and the whole city needs to hear about it."

 *Twenty-one*

Maynard's Saloon was packed to the gills. Even Zeke admitted, with no small measure of awe, that he'd never seen so many people crammed inside it—and, for that matter, he wouldn't have figured this many people would *fit*. But everyone had come. There were a number of men from Chinatown, and a smattering of people Rector didn't recognize at all. He didn't know where they'd come from, but a couple of them looked like airmen, maybe—and a couple others might've been miners or loggers from outside the walls.

The establishment itself was amazingly normal looking, so far as Rector could tell from peeking between the crowd. It had a big wooden bar with a mirrored backdrop, and brass fixtures that appeared to get a regular polishing. A tall player piano sat in a corner, its padded seat occupied by two thin men who stood precariously upon it in order to see over the crowds. Likewise, there were people standing on the wooden chairs that ordinarily went around the card tables.

The lights were a combination of electric and gas, and they glimmered brightly from wall to wall, flickering in the mirrored portions of the serving area and glinting off the metal trim. Maynard's looked warmer than it felt.

Everyone who pushed, stretched, and strained on tippytoes to see was facing the mirror. Miss Lucy was there, right at home stationed behind the bar, and beside her Angeline Sealth sat on the bar proper, waiting for the room to fill up to her satisfaction.

The boys elbowed through the crowd.

Rector saw the crew of the *Naamah Darling,* including the captain, Fang, and Kirby Troost; he saw Frank and Willard, who still smelled like the smoke room; and he noted Mercy Lynch standing between her father and a wizened Chinese man whose eyes were very bright and sharp behind a pair of spectacles. "Doctor Wong?" he asked Zeke.

"That's him. Hey, look—we can climb up on the piano."

"Will it hold us?"

Zeke shrugged. "I don't see why not."

They squeezed over to the instrument and shut the cover over the keys, then scaled the tall player all the way to the top. They could barely do so without knocking their heads on the ceiling, but they were pleased with themselves all the same.

Now they could see everything, and everyone.

Houjin slipped inside the door and looked around, scanning the room. He spied Zeke and Rector quickly and waved at them, but he opted not to wrestle through the crowd to join them, or further test the integrity of the piano lid. Instead, he stuck close to Captain Cly.

Briar Wilkes hovered close to the bar's edge. She wore her full regalia, as Rector had come to think of it—her father's old badge and hat, and a belt buckle with the zigzag initials MW.

The muttering in the room rose and fell in a curious wave.

Angeline monitored it, and watched the door. When she was confident that everyone important was in attendance, she glanced at Lucy O'Gunning, who nodded. The princess took this as permission to climb to her feet on the bar, high enough above the population that she could be seen and heard by everyone.

"Ladies, gentlemen, and other assorted persons whose quality I am not prepared to judge . . ." she began. She delivered this line with a smile, but it didn't reach her eyes—and it brought only a smattering of nervous laughter. "We have a problem."

Several of the Chinese men turned to one another and whispered. Angeline saw them and got an idea. "Huey? Where are you, sweetheart? I don't see you."

He raised his hand.

"Good, good. Would you help me out? Come on up and translate for me. I might be talking too fast, and English isn't my first tongue anyway."

Houjin did as she asked and came to sit beside her on the bar, urging the Chinese men to come closer so he wouldn't have to shout.

Thusly reconfigured, Angeline went on, with Houjin's translation trailing along behind her. "As some of you have heard . . . we've got a hole in the wall, and it's letting things out. It's letting things in, too. Neither of them things is any good. Worse yet, the hole didn't just happen: Somebody made it, on purpose."

She paused to let Houjin catch up, and took a breath to start again.

It caught in her throat as the door to Maynard's opened and Yaozu stepped inside, calm as you please. He held a mask in one hand and a lantern in the other. He set both beside the door, and stepped aside to close the door. He did not interrupt or do anything alarming, just folded his arms and turned his attention to Angeline.

The moment froze in place. Rector thought you could've heard a feather fall in the silence.

Angeline broke the spell by clearing her throat, looking away from Yaozu, and returning her attention to the rest of the room.

"Up at the north end of the city, at the edge of the park near the hill's natural peak, the wall's been broken open. Everything about it looks like dynamite. And we've seen the men what done it. Red, where you at?" she asked, scanning the room and seeing him atop the piano.

Rector gestured at his own chest. "Me?"

"Everybody clear a path. I want him to come here and testify."

Rector could feel himself blushing, and felt dumb for it—which only made him blush harder. He descended the piano and weaved through the crowd, stopping at Angeline's feet.

"Well? Get up here, why don't you?"

She extended a hand and pulled him up. He felt highly conspicuous, standing there beside her. Everyone in the room was looking at him now, and he didn't like it. Many of the people in the room hadn't set eyes on Rector yet, and a murmur rose up, trickled around the room, and died under Miss Angeline's glare.

She patted Rector on the shoulder and introduced him. "Folks, this here is Rector Sherman. Young Rector joined us a week ago, and he had a hard time of it at first."

From somewhere in the audience, someone asked, "Is that the kid who fell down the chuckhole?"

"Yes, this is the kid who fell down the chuckhole."

Rector's freckles were on fire.

"He was *chased* down that chuckhole, though—and if you don't believe *him,* and you don't believe *me,* you can believe Houjin over here. He saw the whole thing, and he'll vouch for it. But that's not what we're here to discuss. Not exactly, though I'll likely come back around to it." She nodded down at Huey, who caught up in his translating duties, then nodded back.

"All right, then. Earlier today, me and the three boys—Red, Huey, and Zeke over there—went looking around topside, up toward the north edges of the city. We did this because we knew there was a leak someplace. So we headed out, and we found the hole—and it's a big hole, I'm afraid to tell you. The only reason nobody outside knows about it yet is that it doesn't face anything but woods and wilderness. Now, Red, why don't you tell 'em who you saw today—who you recognized."

Rector hemmed, hawed, and coughed, then said, slowly, "It's

like she says: me and her, and them"—he waved vaguely at Zeke and Houjin—"we went looking. And when we got up toward the park, we ran into a couple of men talking. All right, so one of 'em was pissing down the hill, but you know what I mean." He laughed awkwardly, and when no one joined him, he continued. "I didn't know either of them, since they had masks on. But we followed them back to the tower—there's a big tower up there; I guess you know the one I mean . . ."

But Angeline shook her head. "Not everybody knows." Then she said to the assembly, "It's a water tower, built right before the Blight came. It's brick, it's big, and it was supposed to serve the rich folks on Millionaire's Row." She nudged him. "Go on, then."

"Yes, ma'am. Um . . . we followed them, and it looked like the men were setting up shop inside the tower. They're sealing it up—so they can work there without masks, I expect."

He paused and licked his lips. He didn't much care for this speaking-in-public thing, but with Angeline beside him, urging him on, he figured he could finish up and sit down, and people would quit looking at him all the sooner. "While we was up there, a big machine came up the hill, through the hole in the wall. It was driven by a guy I know of, a man named Otis Caplan . . ."

Yaozu began to fashion a sneer, but suppressed it before it was fully formed. It lingered on his face as a slight hint of bitterness.

"Otis is a sap-slinger from California, and he's talked real big for a while now about how he wants to make more money off his operation. He's been working with chemists on the Outskirts, cooking up his own varieties. And he wasn't the only sign of trouble out there—I also saw Isaac West, who's a chemist I know from Tacoma. He's been making the ambrosia strain of sap. You may . . ."—he surveyed the room, but didn't see any recognition from anyone but Yaozu, who raised an eyebrow, then put it down again—". . . or may not have heard of it. It's a kind of sap that's just a little different. Tastes different. Has a different . . ." He gave up trying to explain.

"What I mean is, he's offering a different product, and he makes it by stealing gas and bullying chemists. He ain't a nice fellow, and seeing him teamed up with Caplan makes me worry."

Angeline patted his shoulder again, approvingly this time. "You can sit down now, honey. I'll take it from here."

Relieved, Rector did just that—slinking off the counter and skulking back to the piano lid.

When he got there, Zeke punched him gently on the arm. "Stop shaking. You did fine."

Angeline continued without him. "I believe that these men are bringing dynamite into the city, and they don't just want it for the wall. They want to put all of you down like groundhogs, blowing up your tunnels and letting you choke on the gas." A hum of voices rose around her as the assembled men grew worried and turned to one another. But Angeline talked over them until they quieted down. "But we have the advantage here. For one thing, they don't know we're on to them."

Uncertain nods went around the room.

"And for another thing, we know the place better than they do. At best, they might have old maps from when the place was whole—but those don't amount to much. For yet *another* thing, they know about the men at the Station"—she slipped a glance at Yaozu, who didn't acknowledge it—"but they don't know about the rest of us. Likely as not, they know there are some Chinese here—that rumor's gone around enough. But they don't know how *many,* and they don't know how many friends they've got."

More affirmative nods and murmurs rose and fell.

"Personally, I think we should rout the bastards before they're able to dig in hard at the tower. But," Angeline added with a raised finger, "it's hard enough to get a handful of people—like me and the boys—out to the north end of the city. It'd be even harder to move enough men and arms for a fight."

"I have some thoughts on this matter."

It was Yaozu. All the chatter, and all the rising pretense of excitement, went as stone quiet as if it'd been shot dead.

For the first time Rector could recall, Angeline looked uncertain. She didn't respond except to stare at him tensely from the edge of the bar.

Yaozu stepped forward as much as he was able. "I do not want these men inside this city any more than the rest of you do. I am here to be of assistance." He was vastly outnumbered by the Doornails, and was widely known as the man who'd stabbed the princess last year—so even people who hadn't been sure about him before that hadn't cared much for him since. But he said "Pardon me," and he came forward. Rector thought there might be ill to be said of the man, but he wasn't a coward.

The crowd parted, men leaning backwards to clear a path as if they were afraid to touch him. When he reached Angeline's feet, he stared up and her and asked, "May I say a few words?"

The room held its breath, and Angeline took a deep one. Then she said, "If they're helpful words, then you should probably share them." Then she hopped down off the bar to linger at its end with Lucy O'Gunning and Briar Wilkes, retreating to the little knot of femininity that accounted for every woman Rector knew of in the underground save for Mercy Lynch, over by her daddy.

"I'll take that as a yes," Yaozu murmured. He turned around and jumped backwards onto the bar with a quick little leap that left him sitting on its edge. He climbed to a standing position and assumed Angeline's spot at the center of everyone's gaze.

"All the way here from King Street Station, I considered this problem—and I considered what we know. We know the broad strokes of their plan, yes. But we need more information before we begin countermeasures. First we should spy on the newcomers and make sure we know their strength and their resources."

Someone complained aloud, "But they're going to blow us

up!" and immediately shrank in upon himself, as if he wished he hadn't said anything.

"A valid concern, yes," Yaozu conceded. "However, the strategic use of dynamite is more complicated than throwing the sticks down a hole and lighting a match. I know of this man, Otis Caplan. He isn't an idiot, and he'll want to use his explosives wisely. He'll survey his intended targets and take his time selecting them."

Andan Cly asked, "How much time, do you think?"

"Houjin said they had no plans before tomorrow night, when their reinforcements arrive, so we can assume we have another day or two. Perhaps forty-eight hours. And when they do make their move, they'll attack the Station, not the Vaults. It's their primary goal, and the only firmly occupied place they're aware of."

A reluctant but positive hum considered this, and accepted it.

"This is not to say that we should dawdle. We need men—or women"—he quickly amended—"who are familiar with danger and prepared to come very close to it. We need people who can move quietly, and who know the area with great precision."

Doctor Wong frowned. "But the north side," he said in heavily accented English. He switched to Chinese to ask the rest of his question, and Yaozu replied in kind. Then, to everyone else, Yaozu said, "It's true that the area is a wasteland—that's why our enemies chose it. If they'd been smart enough to fix the hole in the wall, even with a flawed, temporary barrier, we might not have noticed their presence so soon. But their carelessness is our good fortune.

"So that leaves the question: How many of you know the north wall area well enough to monitor it, and the men who've settled in there?"

Angeline let out a little cough.

"Obviously Princess Angeline is familiar with the terrain. Anyone else?"

Houjin's translation provided a soft echo.

A burly man with a fluffy beard put up his hand. "I knew the spot, years ago. I knew it well. I worked at the sawmill, before it burned. My boss had a home up there."

Intrigued, Yaozu asked, "And you regularly visited your employer's home?"

He shrugged. "I was a foreman. I delivered messages and supplies to Mr. Yesler. I saw the tower while they were building it. The park layout's pretty straightforward," he assured the room at large. "Several streets, all running alongside one another. They dead-end . . . well, at the wall, I suppose. But they used to dead-end at the park, right around the tower."

Angeline added, "And the wall runs right behind that tower, over the cemetery. Cuts it in two."

The lumber man said, "All right, I can imagine that."

"What's your name?" Yaozu asked.

"Terrence Miller. By coincidence."

"Excellent. Anyone else? We have Princess Angeline, and Mr. Miller."

Captain Cly was elbowing Houjin, who finally gave in and said, "I remember everywhere we went, and could find my way around. I'm good with directions."

"That you are," Yaozu said approvingly. "You've only been there once?"

"Just the once."

"Your recent visit probably makes you as good a guide as Mr. Miller, who hasn't been in years, if I judge his implication correctly. Between the three of you, could you make a map? Something we could pass out to those who might join you?"

Angeline told him, "We could. We will."

"Good, good. We'll need to educate a few chosen people about the terrain."

"Only a few people?" Lucy O'Gunning asked.

"For now, only a few. And if possible, we should send out a party this afternoon. We can't waste time."

"But then what?" Lucy pressed.

He paused. "It depends on what we learn. If we can take a few days to gather ourselves and ready our defense, so much the better. If we can't, then we rush our plans and hope for the best."

"So you *do* have a plan?" Houjin sounded positively hopeful.

Yaozu gave him a chilly smile. "Yes. But it's not a plan I can enact alone. I'll need the whole underground to assist. And that's only fair, isn't it? Since it's the whole underground we mean to save. They'll come for the Station first, yes, but they'll come for the rest of you eventually. Or the Vaults will collapse upon themselves without my people—and my finances—to restore them."

Grudgingly, Briar Wilkes said, "That's true."

"Thank you, Sheriff Wilkes," Yaozu said with carefully presented deference. "We all must agree to work together, and we must understand that the solution will not be clean, tidy, or peaceful."

Kirby Troost, one of the men from the *Naamah Darling,* said, "I think we've got that part figured out. I, for one, am tickled pink at the prospect of dirty, untidy, and violent. So what do you intend for us to do, anyhow?"

Cly nudged the little man gently, as if he was concerned that too much had been said. But Troost stood his ground, and stared levelly at the Chinese man on the bar.

"Mr. Troost. You're an engineer, aren't you?"

"Close enough."

"I'll want a word with you later. You, too, Houjin. I have a team of my own at the Station, but I'll need all the mechanical heads I can put together." Then he concluded, "Between us, I believe that we can best them. *Entirely.*"

Twenty-two

The city mobilized. Houjin was carted off with Yaozu—he didn't leave with Cly's permission, exactly, but the captain didn't attempt to stop him. Angeline disappeared out the back of Maynard's as soon as Yaozu had finished speaking, as if she'd forgotten something and only just remembered it, but Rector suspected that she was trying to avoid the man altogether.

The remaining crew of the *Naamah Darling* went up to Fort Decatur to prepare the ship for launch and reconnaissance—and a potential supply run as well, if it could be made quickly enough. Zeke vanished with the captain, as if the boy could replace Houjin (a thought that made even Rector laugh), and Briar Wilkes left right behind them. Lucy O'Gunning began cleaning the bar, Swakhammer and his daughter went out the back door chatting, and there was nobody else left who Rector knew well enough to ask, *What should I do? Where should I go?*

Everyone ignored him, so he went back to the Vaults. It was either that or the Station, and he didn't know anyone there except for Bishop and Yaozu, and neither one of them seemed too likely to take him under their wing. Or even give him the time of day, without duress.

But the Vaults were easy, and not very far away. He'd figured out the path by now, and while he'd been jaunting through the facilities with Zeke he'd spied a room that nobody seemed to be using. Since he doubted that Mercy Lynch would beat him back, he let himself into the sickroom, gathered his belongings, and relocated to the other space on the next floor down.

This new room was dark, but all the rooms were dark. It was scantily furnished, but again, none of the rooms were poshly appointed as far as he knew—except maybe out at the Station, where Yaozu had enough money to appoint whatever he pleased.

Rector wondered if he ought to find his way out to the Station, after all.

The Doornails had been pretty nice to him, so far as nice went. Except maybe the nurse, who hadn't been nice, but she'd saved his life. And maybe Cly or Briar Wilkes, who'd been none too welcoming—but hadn't chased him out of the fort, either. But Zeke was all right, same as ever. And Houjin was tolerable, once you figured him out. And Angeline was fine by him, if you ignore the fact that he'd never expected to call a woman old enough to be his grandmother some kind of friend.

As he sat on the edge of the dry, uncomfortable bed, he asked himself what he *really* wanted and found no answer except a dull pang of hunger for sap, which he'd effectively concluded that he couldn't have anymore, regardless of how much he wanted it.

(Something about the dismembered pile of bones and meat. Something about the moaning, lonely grunts and wails of the rotters. Something about being so close to it all, and Yaozu running an operation with no use for users, now or ever.)

All right then. No more sap. Not for now.

He considered sharing this unhappy conclusion with Zeke or Houjin, or even Mercy Lynch—since she was so keen to hear all about sap and its effects—but he wasn't certain he could stick with the resolution, if in fact this was a resolution at all. He didn't know. He'd never made one before.

All he knew was that he'd gone a stretch without sap and he was thinking clearer than he had in a very long time, and feeling better than when he'd been on the outside—persistent Blight gas be damned. He was hungry more often than not, but he'd always been hungry outside—and now he knew where to find food, and no one would swat him with a belt if they caught him taking any. He was tired, but he'd often been tired before, and now he had a place to sleep that he didn't share with anyone else. Maybe it didn't lock, and maybe it didn't belong to him in any concrete way apart from possession being so much of the law down here, but it was his and no one was fighting him for it.

If he were to try his luck at the Station, he might find the population less accommodating, or more competitive, which was his true worry. Bishop had suggested that the Station would be filled with men more like himself, inclined to crime, drug use, and cheating behavior, and that sounded tricky. It was easier, he suspected, to be the only person of his sort. Better a big fish in a small pond.

But when he looked around the tiny, dingy, dark, and utilitarian room . . . it did not feel much different from the orphanage. It felt like a lateral move, and not a step up. Even if it was his, and his alone.

He was mulling this over when he heard a violent clatter and a keening, simpering sound that made his ears want to close up. He hopped to his feet and poked his head out into the hall, and there he saw Angeline wrestling with something that was too large for her to easily carry.

When she saw him, she smiled and set her burden down with a grunt. "Red!" she exclaimed, panting roughly as she caught her breath. "Come give me a hand with this, would you?"

"What . . . what is it?" he asked, coming closer only because she was so unafraid—and it wouldn't do for him to cringe away like a coward.

"Silly boy—it's the cage we set out the other day. And inside it . . ." She drew aside a moth-eaten blanket that'd been covering the cage. "I've got Zeke's fox."

The creature snapped and hissed, crawling in a circle as if trying to create a smaller and smaller ball of fox—something tiny enough to fit through the mesh and escape. Angeline dropped the blanket again, and the persistent fuss of the animal's crying tapered off.

"Why is it Zeke's fox?" Rector asked.

"Because he's the one who wanted to save it. Him and me, I guess, but I don't plan to look after it, and I expect he will. Help me carry this," she directed.

Rector did so, but he made sure to grab a good handful of blanket before putting his fingers anywhere within potential biting distance.

He needn't have worried. The fox cowered away from both of them.

"Where are we taking it?" he asked as he lumbered beside her, walking sideways to keep from dropping the cage and fox both.

"I thought one of these extra rooms down here might do the trick. Same as you, I expect," she said. "You picked one out? Is that what you're doing down here?" She sidled as they walked, the cage held between them.

"Yes, ma'am," he admitted. "Miss Mercy threw me out of the sickroom."

"You ain't sick no more."

"Sure, but I didn't have noplace else to go."

She stopped beside a half-open door. "Here—this room over here ought to be fine for the fox, for now. You didn't see anybody else around? Not that I think anyone'd need the space, but you never know."

"No, I think I'm the only one down here. But we can always shut the door and . . . um . . . and put a sign on it."

"Not sure how much good that'd do." She pushed the door open with her hip and backed into the room, drawing the cage and Rector along behind her. "Half the folks down here can't read. But if the idea of a snarling fox who's all sick with Blight doesn't keep 'em out, they deserve to get bit. I'll pass the word around upstairs."

Rector accompanied her to the far wall, where they deposited the fox.

Angeline drew the blanket back all the way, and the light from the corridor cast a wide shaft into the room. She scared up a lantern, lit it, and drew it close enough to the animal so she could get a better look.

Rector said, "That's about the most pitiful thing I ever saw."

"I have to agree with you there," she nodded.

The fox's ribs stuck out through its patchy fur, and its eyes were glassy and gold. They had an odd orange tinge to them—something unnatural and unhealthy, like the crows . . . except the fox did not appear otherwise well. Its tongue lolled, its eyes bugged, and its ears drooped sadly.

The princess put her hands on her hips. "First things first, then. I'll get it some water and some food, and we'll see if it don't improve."

In half an hour they'd managed all of these things, and even arranged the old blanket into something like a bed. It'd be more comfortable than the metal mesh, at any rate, and when the door was closed the room was dark and quiet. Once the fox was as comfortable as its human handlers could make it, Rector turned to Angeline and asked, "If it *does* get better, how long do you think that'll take?"

"Don't know. But Zeke'll be pretty patient with it. That boy's still finding his way. He's trying to decide who to be, and how to become it, and that's a difficult thing for anybody . . . but he's got a kind heart in him, and that's more than a lot of people start with."

Rector scratched at his wrists, which still smarted dully from the Blight burns. "Well, he got picked on a lot, on the outside. It might've made him a little soft."

"That's not always how it works, you know. Or maybe you and I have a different idea of what soft means. Soft don't always mean weak; the trees that bend are the ones that weather the storm, after all. You're a boy from the Sound. You ought to know that. Now come on—let's leave this little fellow alone and hope for the best. Maybe he'll take that food and water, and maybe the air down here will clear him out."

"It don't work on people."

"That fox ain't people." She ushered Rector out of the room and shut the door behind them both. "Peace and quiet, that's all we can do for it."

As if on cue, Houjin came bounding down the corridor, shouting. "Rector, are you down here? Rector?"

"Shh!" Angeline hissed.

Houjin drew up short and stopped himself with a skid. "Sorry, ma'am. I was looking for Rector."

"So I gathered. What do you want with him?"

"It's not me, ma'am . . . it's Yaozu. He wants him for outside work. Since he knows some of the people out at the tower, and all. Besides, he says he'd rather give Rector a job than wonder what he's up to."

Angeline laughed, which surprised both boys. "I never said the man was a dummy, did I? You two run along and make yourselves useful."

As the two boys ran down the hall to the stairs, Houjin asked, "What was all that about? What were you doing down here?"

"Setting up a room for myself," Rector said. "And while I was at it, I ran into Miss Angeline, carrying that cage we put out. She caught the fox. We gave it some food and water, and left it in that empty room with the door shut."

Houjin shook his head and reached for the stair rail. Up he climbed, and he said, "Waste of time. But it's nice of her to try—

and Zeke'll be glad she caught it. It can be his project, when he gets finished up at Decatur."

"Why aren't you up there? Why'd you leave with Yaozu? Is that air captain boss of yours scared of him, or what?"

"Cly's not scared of him," Houjin snapped. "The captain's trying to do what's best for the underground. Zeke can carry things and move things up at the fort as easy as I can; but he can't *make* things like I can."

"What are you making?" Rector asked, partly because he was curious, and partly because he didn't feel like managing Houjin and his bad mood.

His small question worked. A smile spread out over Huey's face. "Yaozu had a great idea, but he didn't know how to make it happen. So I figured it out—it was easy as pie."

"Well, what *is* this great idea?" They reached the first floor, and Houjin was nearly at a run, so it *must* be something good.

"We're going to take their dynamite, and use it against them."

Houjin stopped and faced him, and held out his hands like he could make his point better if he could gesture. "How much do you know about dynamite?" he asked.

"It blows things up."

"Right. It blows things up, but you don't want it to blow things up while you're standing there holding it. You want to be a *long way away* when it goes off," he said patiently. He'd lapsed into teacher mode.

Rector didn't care for being talked down to by somebody younger than him, but he was the one who'd asked, and now he had to take the explanation however he could get it. With a minimum amount of disdain, he said, "Obviously."

"Obviously, yes. You obviously knew that."

"Just tell me, would you?"

"Fine. In order to control it, you have a couple of choices: You can either give it a very long fuse, and light it, or you can take a very long wire, and use that wire to send the dynamite an electric spark. It's usually generated by one of those pump boxes: You shove the plunger down, it makes a spark, the spark goes down the line, and boom! But we don't want to use wire, and we don't want to use a fuse."

Rector tried to look like he was following, but he was lost. "Then what would you use?"

Houjin beamed, with a tiny, unnerving edge of mischief that was made sharper by Rector's irritation. "Time!" He took off again, Rector trailing behind him.

"Time?"

"You heard me! Don't ask me to explain yet, 'cause it'll be easier to show you. But for now, you're on dynamite duty with me—and you have to listen. I'll show you how to take care of it without blasting yourself to pieces."

Since this qualified as a noble goal so far as Rector was concerned, he listened hard and promised to do what he was told. Ordinarily he'd make no such vows, but the prospect of blowing himself to Kingdom Come made him infinitely more responsive to instruction.

"But why are we in such a rush?" he asked, and asked it quickly, when Houjin paused to take a breath.

"Because we're going to the tower."

"You told me that already. Why are we going back there, when all the action's at the Station?"

Houjin pushed all his weight into moving the big Vault door, then stepped outside into the main body of the underground. "Because, like you said—all the action's at the Station. Yaozu just gave the word: His spies are watching the Station and all its entrances, keeping track of the men who are planting the explosives."

"They ain't stopping them?"

"No, just watching for now," he said. From out of his pocket he pulled two scraps of glass the size and shape of spectacle lenses. "Take one of these. They're polarized. I don't want to wear those glasses—they look crazy, and they're too small for me. So I went back down to storage and picked up a different set."

"Good idea."

"Thank you."

Slipping the scrap of glass into his pocket, Rector asked, "Why the tower, though? What are we supposed to do there?"

"Get inside, get a look around, and steal as much dynamite as we can carry. But no more than that," he added. "We want to leave plenty inside."

"But why *me*?"

"Why *you*?" Huey stopped and turned around, as had become his habit when he wanted to make sure Rector was paying attention. "Because if you get caught, there's a good chance you can talk your way out of it. You know some of these men, and they know you—they might assume you were sent along by Otis Caplan or one of his people. If I were you, that's what I'd tell them, anyway. If we get caught, that is."

"And what would I tell them about you?"

"Tell them . . ." He thought about it. "Tell them I don't speak English, but I hate Yaozu and I'm here to kill him. Or something like that."

"You think they'll believe it?"

Houjin shrugged and resumed his trek up the underground version of Commercial Street. "Why not? Plenty of people hate Yaozu and want to kill him. Plenty of Chinese, even, because of how he helped Minnericht be so bad to them those first few years he was inside the wall. But we won't have to worry about it . . . as long as we don't get caught."

 *Twenty-three*

Out in the city proper, Rector and Houjin struggled against the gloomy, curling, coiling air. Rector found that it gave him headaches if he stared too long, his eyes straining to catch every shape, every scrap of light or shadow that made it past the Blight. He grew tired from the stress of being so persistently alert. Then again, how long had it been since he'd had any sap? He'd count the days, if he could only remember them.

Houjin waved a hand in front of his own face. Behind his mask's visor, his eyes crinkled into a frown. "It's not always this bad," he said.

"I know. It wasn't this bad the other day."

"I'm not sure what makes the difference. Maybe it's the temperature, or how much rain we've gotten—or haven't gotten. Or maybe it's related to the air currents. We know Blight behaves differently from plain old air."

"I really couldn't tell you," Rector muttered.

They stood on a street corner that wasn't marked, but since Houjin seemed confident of his location, Rector didn't worry about it. Not very much, anyway. He made a point to stick close, that was all—especially in the dismal not-daylight there in the too-quiet outer blocks. Sticking close was common sense, it wasn't chicken.

Thoughtfully, Houjin said, "Maybe I should study it."

"Do it on your own time, buddy. Which way's the tower again? I can't see for shit."

"This way."

"I don't see it."

Houjin's voice took on the tone of someone who is trying, in a calculated fashion, to keep from yelling. "I know you can't see it, but *I* know where it is. Trust me, and be quiet."

Rector didn't like being told to be quiet, but he knew it was a good idea, so with a mighty *harrumph* he managed to keep his mouth shut for another five minutes. At no point during those five minutes did he grab for the back of Houjin's jacket, strong though the temptation became.

When he feared he was falling behind, he said, "A guy could disappear in this stuff, and nobody'd ever find him," assuming that Houjin would either stop walking or reply.

Softly, Houjin said, "That's why people come here, as often as not. To disappear."

Rector hustled to catch up to the other boy's voice as it trailed through the gas. "Like that nurse?"

Huey paused, and Rector came up beside him, trying not to wheeze, but glad for the brief break. "What? Miss Mercy? I don't understand."

"You and Zeke said something about a train, and everybody disappearing."

"But all those other people didn't disappear inside here. They just . . . disappeared. Except for her. She's been trying to find them, trying to figure out what happened to everybody."

"Why?"

"Because there were rotters. Outside Seattle."

"Rotters on a train?"

Houjin's words took on that tense, impatient quality again.

"No, not rotters on a train. But rotters outside the city—all the way out in the Utah Territory, up in the mountains. Miss Mercy thinks they were made when an airship crashed down in Texas."

Rector had no idea how far away Texas was from Utah, or how far Utah was from Seattle. Quite a ways, he suspected, but he didn't want to sound dumb, so he didn't ask.

Houjin resumed walking. Rector kept pace this time, since the way was wide enough to accommodate them both. The streets were not clean, but they lacked the usual thick, wind-heaped detritus of the busier blocks, so the boys' boots made less noise than their chatter as they crept up the hill.

"How does that work?" Rector asked. "How does an airship in Texas make rotters in Utah?" He was almost proud of himself for how un-dumb that sounded.

"The airship was carrying Blight concentrate for processing down in Mexico. It crashed right on top of people, and turned them. Just like that. Just like the sap does, if you use it too long . . ."

"Hey!"

"What? I'm not accusing you of anything—only pointing out the connection. The sap kills people the same way as the gas, but it takes a lot longer. And Miss Mercy's seen lots of drug users at the end of their lives, on the battlefields and in the hospitals. She probably knows more about it, from more angles, than anyone in the world. But when she tried to reach the people from the *Dreadnought* . . . it was like they'd never existed."

Rector didn't like the sound of that, and he wasn't entirely sure why. "Or like someone took them away?"

"That's one theory. That's *her* theory, anyway. She thinks somebody important wants to keep the sap running, and keep the soldiers stocked up."

"Why the hell would anybody want to do that?"

Houjin shrugged. "It usually comes down to money."

"Money," Rector echoed thoughtfully.

His companion drew up to a sudden stop, smacking him across the chest with his arm to get his attention.

A faint hum rumbled overhead. Nothing too loud, nothing too close.

Rector guessed, "Is that one of the pump rooms?"

"No, look higher. It's the *Naamah Darling,* see?"

He couldn't see a damn thing, so he grunted noncommittally.

Huey continued, "I bet they're testing out the steering repairs. That's why they're out here, so they can take the ship low without hitting anything."

"Except the wall."

"Captain Cly won't hit the wall."

"Even if Zeke's on board, getting in the way?"

With a snort, Houjin said, "Probably not even then." He might've added something else, but the noise up above changed suddenly, slightly. A loud clapping sound. An engine revving higher. A twist in the ship's direction that brought it almost immediately overhead.

"Is something happening?" Rector wanted to know, primarily because an airship falling on his head wasn't high on his wish list of afternoon activities.

"I don't . . . I don't know."

They both listened hard and wondered what was going on, without being able to see it. Everything beyond a few feet was yellow or gray, so they used their ears to track the big ship, neither of them admitting to themselves or to each other that the craft sounded distressed.

"I'm sure it's fine," Houjin lied outright as the engine noise dipped closer.

"I don't even know where we'd run to. Should we . . . look for shelter?"

The response was firm. "No. They're not crashing, they've just—"

With a whir and the hiss of hydrogen, the ship leaped upward, taking on another hundred feet in altitude—or so Rector guessed, as if he had any real idea. "You think it could've been snagged on something, then got itself free?"

"That seems unlikely."

"But that's what it sounds like."

Huey kept his voice level, but it was tighter than a drum when he said, "I'll ask when I get back to Fort Decatur. Come on, let's keep moving."

"How do you even know it was the *Naamah Dar* . . ." Rector lost track of his question, which trailed off and dissolved into the gas. "Huey?"

Before Houjin could reply, something heavy shot down from above—not a ship, and not a pump tube . . . in fact, nothing man-made. It was something screaming, something plummeting with a roar and a crash, landing against something half crumbled, and crashing through it with a symphony of splinters, cracking timbers, and toppling masonry.

And whatever it was, it kept moving.

It thrashed and writhed, climbing steadily out of the house or shop or hotel in which it'd landed. Rector started to run. Houjin grabbed him by the arm but didn't stop him; he ran with him, keeping Rector's wrist clenched tight so they didn't lose each other.

"What?" Rector squeaked, "is . . . *that*?" But Houjin was running too hard, paying too much attention to answer.

Besides, it was after them. The cracks and stomps of the big thing's scramble were surely loud enough to raise the dead or bring them running. It was finding its footing, gathering its energy, focusing its attention, and listening to the Blight just like the boys had done.

Houjin's feet stumbled and he slowed, looking over his shoulder and then forward again, quickly. One direction, then the other. Trying not to fall. A worthy goal, in Rector's estimation, but behind them something enormously tall was mumbling to itself. It sniffed the air—they could hear it, like a windstorm up two great nostrils—and picked its direction.

It tumbled out of the wreckage of its fall, and gave chase along their retreat path.

"Shit!" Houjin gasped wetly. It was the first time Rector'd ever heard him curse, but this was a fantastic time to start getting the hang of it.

Improbably heavy footsteps clomped hard against the smooth-packed streets and uncluttered avenues, making a beeline right for Houjin and Rector, who had wholly quit fighting Houjin's attempts to guide him—by force, if necessary—farther up the hill and away from the thing behind them.

In Rector's head he was going over the possibilities. Perhaps some oversized rotter dropped in from the sky . . . maybe the giant captain? He was big, he was nearby, and the ship was right up there. Huey had made such a show of pointing it out, hadn't he?

Anything but the inexplicable.

But he knew it was all wrong. The captain would've called out, certainly. He would've said their names and asked what they were doing; he wouldn't have fallen from the sky only to scare them witless. The thing behind them rumbled a thick bellow that wasn't quite a cry and wasn't quite a call. Either way, it wasn't human.

Definitely not the captain, even as Rector's racing brain tried to maintain the hypothetical option.

"No way," he wheezed. "No way."

"Hush up!"

"Where are we going?"

"I said, be quiet!"

"Huey, for Chrissake, it already hears us!"

"Underground." He coughed. "Back to the underground."

Rector's heart took a dip down to his stomach. There was no way they'd outrun the thing. They were at least three blocks from the nearest entrance he knew of . . . if, in fact, they were anywhere close to where he thought they were. This realization made him lunge all the harder to keep up with Huey, whose grip on Rector's arm seemed terribly fragile.

An unexpected curb appeared under their feet. Houjin jumped it, just barely and just in time. Rector caught it with his shin and went flying. Momentum snapped him free of Huey's grip and he rolled off to the side, up against a wall that had held up a roof a long time ago, and now served entirely to make Rector's head spin. Stars flashed and flickered before him, and he couldn't see anything.

Even his own hand, when he wobbled it forward in an effort to right himself, looked misshapen and alien. It was coated in stars and Blight like everything else, and the prospect of getting onto all fours felt insurmountable.

Houjin was feeling around with his hands and feet, whispering, "Rector!"

"Um . . ."

A moment later, a very firm hand seized Rector's ankle, pulling it out from under him. Rector's heart nearly stopped.

"Sorry; I'm sorry," Huey said. "Get up, Rector. Get up! We have to . . ." And then he stopped talking.

The thing was very close; they could feel it more than they could hear it—the nearness of something unfamiliar and large, its existence pressing against their fear like a tangible force. It shoved against their chests, and stuffed up the filters in their masks. Neither one of them could breathe anymore except in short, horrified bursts that fogged their visors and gave them scarcely enough oxygen to keep from passing out.

The inexplicable—for what else could it be?—circled them and sniffed, always that disgusting sniffing as he tried to smell something other than the Blight. He homed in on them awk-wardly, uncertainly. When he was within a few feet (ten feet? twenty?), someone shouted.

"Over here!"

The call was loud—almost as loud as the inexplicable's roar. The call was accompanied by footsteps. Big, solid, certain ones.

"Captain!" Houjin barked, though where he'd found the en-ergy or breath to holler even that one word, Rector would never know.

"Huey? And Rector, I expect," Andan Cly added. "You two— *run.*"

The inexplicable turned. They heard him pivot on his feet, seeking this new speaker.

"Captain, no—"

"Make for the Sizemore House!" he commanded.

Easier said than done, Rector said, or that's what he would've said if he could've said anything at all. So it was just as well that he was too stunned to do much more than stagger to his feet, which scarcely held him up.

A moment of silence.

Another scraping scuff of some large foot, someplace in the foggy air.

Rector looked down at his hands and saw that his borrowed gloves were pocked with holes and his knuckles were oozing red. Everything smarted, including his knees, now that he had a mo-ment to notice it.

He should've noticed the puff of the inexplicable breathing, and the sordid, sticky sound of his lungs working against the Blight as he approached. The inexplicable had made up his mind. Two small things, or one big thing. He'd take his chances with the littler opponents.

Rector knew it, but he couldn't do anything about it. He could hardly stand, and could hardly tell that Huey's grip on his forearm was now a grip on his sleeve. Huey's fingers twisted into the fabric, securing their grip, but he was tired, too. Could either of them run?

"Run!" the captain ordered again—a shout that shook even the inexplicable, who paused for a brief moment and turned back again. His long arms swam against the air. He was uncertain of Cly, but the boys were within its reach.

The Blight wavered, pushed aside or blown that way by circumstance, and Rector caught a glimpse of the thing's yellow-gold eyes surrounded by black. They flinched, squinted, and focused on Rector's vivid red hair, which no doubt showed brighter than anything around it, a patch of color searing through the washed-out city air.

The inexplicable surged forward, his leathery, hairy hand snapping out in a move so fast Rector might not have seen it in broad daylight in the Outskirts . . . and then it snapped back. It retreated violently, immediately—and without meaning to. Even in the soupy atmosphere, Rector could see that much.

Something had him by the throat. Something hauled him backwards.

Someone.

"Captain!" Huey shouted, and the big man tumbled with the inexplicable in tow, locked against him—one long arm winched around the thing's throat. The white flutter of his shirtsleeve flashed through the viscous air and Rector watched it, following the action with mute fascination.

"*Go!*" the captain replied in a muffled, frenzied grunt, but Houjin wouldn't have it.

The boy scrambled forward. Briefly Rector thought, *Jesus Christ, what's he going to do?*—a thought that Houjin caught up with just in time to keep him from getting within grabbing distance. He tripped over himself, hesitated, and leaned back to get out of range.

"You heard the man!" Rector said, reaching forward and taking Houjin by the shoulder. "Let's go!"

"Do it!" Cly ordered.

As Rector staggered up to his proper footing, he hauled Huey with him until they were both upright, but neither could take their eyes off the weird ballet that flickered through the gas.

The inexplicable's preposterous, hairy limbs swayed and stretched, grabbing for purchase. His feet turned, his body doing an uneven pirouette as he fought against the weight of the man who held him. The man was a true giant, but still not as big as this thing in the mist. He had the inexplicable by the neck, but his grip was being shaken, battered, and knocked free. Still, the lanky heft of his body held the thing back from the boys, just far enough that his hands couldn't grab them.

The inexplicable shook himself like a wet dog. Once, twice, a third time.

And the captain fell backwards with a crunching smash into something just out of sight. His feet stuck up from wherever he'd landed, but only for the briefest of moments. With a leap he was up again, and coming again—a massive, bald shape in a gas mask and suspenders. Not quite a match for the thing in front of him. Rector knew that in a heartbeat . . . the very same heartbeat that caught in his mouth when the glittering amber eyes of the sasquatch streaked from left to right, judging his attacker. They shot through the bleak, uncertain air like two small fireworks.

They flashed and were gone, and a stomping leap launched the creature somewhere else.

In the span of a few long strides of the creature's scrambling retreat, the city was quiet again, sullen and empty even of the rotter moans and bird calls that usually scratched across every stone.

Captain Andan Cly let his torso fall forward. He put his hands upon the top of his knees, hung his head a moment, and worked hard to breathe. Huey ran to his side, fretting about a bloody smear on the back of the captain's head, but Cly waved the young engineer away. "It's all right. I'm fine. It's the filters—you know how it goes. Let me . . . let me get some air."

"What happened?" Rector wanted to know. "How did you find us?"

After another ten seconds of deeply drawn gulps of air, he said. "Didn't find you. Didn't know you were here. Found *it*. We were doing low trainers, checking that new thruster. The damn thing jumped up and grabbed us." He shook his head, stretched his shoulders, and stood up straight again. "Goddamn, it must outweigh me by a hundred pounds, and I'm no slouch."

Houjin agreed, "No sir, absolutely not."

"I opened the bay door to see what we'd picked up, and there it was. There *he* was," he said, a marvel in his words. "There he was, hanging there like a kid from a tree house. I swear to God, there he *was*."

It took the *Naamah Darling* less than half an hour to find the lot of them, and a fraction of that time to return everyone to Fort Decatur, just for now. The captain wanted to visit Mercy Lynch to see about the big, hard gash in the back of his head. Houjin could scarcely contain himself for worry, and he couldn't be stopped from recounting the fight to everyone who'd sit still long enough to listen, so he came, too.

And Rector . . . well, Rector'd had enough excitement for one day.

He went back to his room, because it was his room, and he could sleep there if he wanted to.

 *Twenty-four*

The trip to the northern quadrant of the walled city was getting easier for Rector by virtue of familiarity; but the next morning it still took nearly an hour for him and Houjin to reach the gas-filled, fog-obscured blocks near Millionaire's Row on Capitol Hill.

They skulked and tiptoed, dodging the loudest of fallen branches, bricks, and roofing tiles and listening constantly for the telltale muffled groans that said rotters were approaching.

Rector also kept one eye on the wall, up to his left. He remembered all too well the second creature—the inexplicable, or sasquatch, or yeti, or whatever anybody wanted to call her—and he didn't wish to see her again.

Soon they reached the edge of the old city park, where the landscaping was no more welcoming than last time. But in the span of a day, much had happened. The giant rolling machine was parked at the tower's base and whatever crates it'd unloaded had been carried upstairs or left stacked on the curving sidewalks and sloping grade upon which the old water reservoir perched. The boys saw stacks of folded canvas, barrels of pitch, boxes marked DANGER, and boxes stamped THIS END UP. They saw sealed water jugs and boxes of ammunition, and two tanks big enough that both boys could've sat inside one of them together. Stenciled on the side was the word DIESEL.

"What's a *diesel*?" Rector whispered.

Houjin whispered back, "Fuel. It's for that machine over there. And other things, too, maybe." Behind his mask, his eyes lit up, then smoldered down to the cunning look that said he had an idea. "And it burns as easy as kerosene . . ."

Up at the top of the tower, just beneath the conical roof, the windows were covered with black iron cages. Behind them, a warm yellow glow burned in a swelling, shrinking pulse that promised nothing good to come. Down below, the boys could hear the hum of machinery and the faint whistle of windblown Blight gas curling through the neighborhood.

Houjin jabbed Rector with his elbow. "Do you think anyone's home?"

"How should I know?"

"Didn't say you ought to. I was just checking your opinion, that's all."

"Oh." Well, then. That was better. Rector made a show of thinking about it, harder than he needed to. "I don't hear anybody. Do you?"

"No."

"Me neither. There's two ways up and down that thing. Should we split up?"

"No!" Houjin said abruptly. "Why double our odds of getting caught? We pick one side, and go up together. If we pick wrong, you know the story—you're here 'cause Otis's men sent you inside, and I hate Yaozu because . . . because he poisoned my father, or whatever else you feel like saying on the fly. If we pick right, we sneak up without anybody bothering us. And we should hurry, before Caplan's people return from the Station."

"Right, right. Good point." Rector shifted his position, and his knee popped. "You got your big sharp iron thing?"

"Yes. You got that ax?"

"Yeah. I like it better than the pick."

"Then let's go do this."

And before Rector had a chance to change his mind, Houjin left their cover and made for the tower's rear entrance.

The darkness there was unnervingly deep. The sun was still up, but shadowed, and nightfall would be on its way soon enough. The boys didn't light their lanterns, but left them slung over their backs, affixed to the straps on the bags with all their supplies.

The back door looked as black as the entrance to a train tunnel. It was even curved in an intimidating arch, and was fixed with a gate—same as the one out front. But this gate had fallen away; one of its hinges had rusted through, and it leaned sharply toward the ground. Beyond it, there was nothing but midnight, and the faint suggestion that somewhere higher up, there might be a tiny bit of light to guide them.

Rector and Houjin swallowed hard as they stared into the inscrutable void.

Rector had never seen Houjin balk before, not like this. But it wouldn't be good to chicken out even worse than a younger boy, so he steeled himself and straightened his shoulders. "I'm oldest, so I'll go first."

Huey said, "Fine with *me*," like he didn't care, but he sounded relieved.

Steeling himself, teasing himself with the thought of sap waiting at the top, Rector led the way up the short hill and around the curved walkway.

And then inside.

Because he could not see, he held out his hands, still wearing the scraped-up gloves he'd gotten from Fang and had not yet replaced. He stretched his fingers as wide as they'd go and swayed his arms slowly. He was desperately afraid that he would hit something, and, likewise, desperately afraid that he wouldn't.

What did the inside of a water tower look like? He had no idea, and too much sense to strike up a light when the passage was dotted with windows that would show a lantern's progress. But what if there was a big pool of water down there? What if he fell and drowned? Wouldn't that be something—double drowning, smothering underwater inside his mask. He shuddered and scooted one foot out in front of him, patting his toes along the ground.

He hit metal.

The edge of his boot clomped dully against it, and even this faint thud cast enough echo that he and Houjin both froze, on the verge of running away. But nothing answered it; no one called down to see what was going on, or what had happened.

The boys began to breathe again.

Rector felt outward and found the metal wall that his toes had found first. He dragged his hands around it and determined that the surface was curved, and had once been painted . . . or so he deduced from the large, bubbled flakes that came off at his touch. He could find no end to this wall, but he did find a handrail to his immediate right, so he seized the rail and explored with his feet until he found the stairs.

He looked back at Houjin, who stood in the doorway. The other boy was backlit by the marginally brighter gloom outside.

Rector held out a hand and said very softly, "Here, take my hand."

Huey did, and he let Rector draw him forward.

Then Rector said, "Like Angeline had us do: hold on to the back of my satchel."

"All right."

"And watch your step."

"I can't watch my step. I can't see my feet!" Houjin whispered, and he chased the quiet joke with a laugh that shouldn't have been so loud. "Sorry!" he said. "Sorry."

"No, it's all right. That was funny," Rector assured him with too much earnestness. "Just stick close. Don't leave me by myself up here, and don't fall through the steps like that other guy did. They're half rotted out underneath us, can you tell? These stairs . . . Jesus, they make a lot of noise, don't they? If anybody was up there, they'd have surely heard us by now."

"Don't assume anything," Houjin urged.

Up ahead, one of the tall, narrow windows let a dim shaft of lighter shadow into the narrow spiral, but it didn't reveal anything important, or anything Rector hadn't already figured out. The stairs were only about as wide as a bookshelf and eaten up with rusty-edged holes that cut through the old paint job. For that matter, the handrail wasn't in the best of shape, either. It hung from the bricks in loose, dusty bolt holes that oozed bloody red corrosion.

"How much farther, you think?" Houjin asked. "Since you can see ahead farther than I can."

"Hard to say. Just keep moving. Damn, this is a lot of stairs."

"If you had your way, there'd be elevators everywhere."

"Damn right, there would be."

A hazy gray glow announced the imminent conclusion of their climb. They rose toward it like night bugs swooping to a lantern, but kept their heads down low when it came time to breach the top.

Side by side, they peeked over the edge and found themselves at eye level with the floor.

They were alone.

With big sighs, they scampered up the last half-dozen steps and walked into the open.

They stood directly beneath the roof. It rose up to a point above them, like a frozen circus tent. Its weaker spots and open holes were covered with tarps, as they'd seen from outside, which flapped idly and without any vigor.

The room itself was circular. In it, eight oversized windows with ironwork grates provided a view of the city in every direction—except for the side facing the wall, which showed nothing but a big black barrier pressing close, as if it were trying to see inside.

"Would you look at all this junk!" Rector exclaimed, keeping his voice just above a whisper.

"Shhh!"

"Oh, come on. No one can hear us out there, and we'd hear anybody coming up the stairs."

Tables of many sizes and shapes had been hauled inside, a feat that filled Rector with wonder, but not envy. (*He* sure as hell wouldn't have wanted to carry them up that winding passage.) Upon the tables and lying beside them were more crates and an ever-present coating of sawdust, which was already going soggy under their feet.

Houjin went to the nearest table, where a substance in a series of tubes and glass vials was cooking over a gas-jet flame. "This isn't junk," he observed. "This is science. And that"—he moved to another table, where a larger apparatus was simmering merrily and unattended—"is a still. Surely you've seen one before? They're using it to remove the sap residue from the gas."

"Of course I've seen a still before, but not one that big. Or one quite like it." Even Harry's oversized operation on the Outskirts paled in comparison to this beast of a thing before him.

"Maybe it's a prototype."

"What's a prototype?"

"Um . . . it means something new."

Rector said, "Then just say 'something new'; otherwise you're showing off. Hey, this over here—is this the wire they want to use to blow us up?"

Houjin joined him beside a stack of spools, each one wrapped with coiled wire that still gleamed, which meant it hadn't been inside the city very long. "Probably," he said.

"Then how about we just steal the wire? Make 'em go get more. It'd buy us time."

"Sure, we could do that. You pick up one of those spools, and let me know how it goes," Huey suggested wryly.

Rector bent over and tried to lift one.

"Heavier than they look, huh?"

"And then some," Rector muttered. "It's good wire, though. We shouldn't leave it."

"You want to throw it out a window?" Houjin offered. "That one over there—the grate's mostly off it, and it's facing the wall. If we chuck a couple of spools out, maybe we can roll them down to the mining carts." But the grate wasn't as loose as it looked, and the spools wouldn't have fit, regardless. The boys abandoned that plan. "Never mind. Let's just swipe some of the dynamite, and see if there's anything else worth taking. Anything that might slow them down."

Rector didn't know what bits of the chemistry set and distillery were more useful than others, so he contented himself with the crates of dynamite, which he opened—very carefully— using the edge of his ax. Deploying the weapon as a pry bar, he popped the lids one at a time and swiped a couple of strays from each. He stuffed them into his satchel and tried to forget that he was carrying enough explosives to launch himself to the moon.

A muffled *clank* reached his ears from down below. Rector sat up straight. "Huey, did you hear that?"

"What?"

"Shh!" he ordered.

The clanking came again, in a steady patter that implied footsteps.

Houjin abandoned whatever it was he'd been doing and dashed quickly back and forth between the two exits in the floor at opposite ends of the circular room. These exits were not offset with rails; they were nothing more than rectangular holes indicating stairs below.

"I can't tell which way he's coming!" Houjin said. His eyes were wide behind the mask, and Rector was pretty sure his own eyes matched. But they couldn't panic. "Listen hard—we'll figure it out, and pick the other way. Just one guy?"

"I think so . . . ?" The acoustics were all lies, all bounces and bangs as the metal interior cast the sounds up against the roof. "But I can't tell," Rector admitted.

"Me either."

"Shit, he's almost—"

As the man came closer to the top, the clatter of his ascent became clearer and clearer, but by the time the boys had picked a stairway, it was too late. A round, masked head popped up at the top of the stairs, swiveling back and forth as it rose.

The head stopped. The eyes within the mask saw the boys, who were frozen together, grabbing at each other in a tangle of fear.

The man came up out of the stairwell. He was an average-sized fellow, a little taller than Rector and forty pounds heavier, and he wore some kind of protective jumpsuit that zipped all the way from his crotch to his mask.

"Hey, you. What are you doing up here?" he asked. "You're not supposed to be here . . ."

He reached toward a cargo belt that swung low on his waist, and Rector's heart nearly stopped. The man was going for a gun—he was absolutely positive of it—and as soon as he had it in hand, everything would be over. He and Houjin would both be dead, both failures, both casualties of somebody else's problem.

For all his adolescent philosophies to the contrary, Rector decided at that moment that he wasn't interested in dying right now—much less at the top of a tower in a poisoned city, inside a wall, at the hands of some stranger. The whole thing felt undignified, and maybe Rector's life thus far hadn't been too big on dignity, but it'd be a shame if he died as ignobly as he'd lived.

All of this flashed through his head like a bolt of lightning. He didn't have time to reflect, and he didn't have time to second-guess anything; he only had time to *charge*.

He hollered, because that's what you do when you charge. He swung the ax at a wobbling, frenzied pitch, and within two seconds he'd crossed the open expanse of floor between him and the man at the edge of the stairs. Houjin was right behind him, waving that sharpened iron bar as though it were a sword and they were the cavalry and this were some kind of heroic last stand—though Rector hoped with all his might that it wasn't.

They ran at the stunned man, who remained stunned enough that his hand stopped at the edge of his belt and he took half a step back.

The half step either saved him or killed him, and the boys didn't know which.

Before Rector reached him, the man toppled backwards and downward. He flailed, waving his arms and desperately reaching for some sort of balance, but he didn't find it. He only found the stairwell hole behind him . . . right where he'd put his left foot.

This didn't stop Rector, who was on fire with the zeal of self-defense.

He brought the ax back and punched with it, knocking the off-kilter fellow even farther off-kilter; and when Houjin joined the fray, the weight of the Chinese boy's heavy iron stick took the right leg out from under the intruder (or were *they* the intruders? Rector didn't have time to care).

The man in the jumpsuit went tumbling backwards, down the stairs.

As he fell, he yelped and complained, accompanied by the sound of straining metal stretching, breaking, and crumbling. As they waited for him to hit bottom, Rector and Houjin were petrified—their hands over their mouths, blocking their filters—but only for a moment.

Houjin said, "We had a story!"

And Rector replied, "I forgot it!"

"Me, too!"

"Oh, Jesus, we have to go!"

They scrambled to the other exit, Rector picking up one last stick of dynamite on his way, and Houjin nabbing a smaller coil of wire, one he could carry without breaking his back. Down the stairs they stampeded, no longer worried about the sound of their passage—worried only about escape.

"Is he following us?" Houjin wheezed as he threw himself out the door and into the creeping, thickening shadow of the wall.

Rector didn't know, so he said, "No!" and kept running.

"Wait!"

"Are you crazy?"

"Wait," Houjin said again—and with a halfhearted effort to regain his quiet and composure, he gasped to catch his breath. They were still alone, with nothing but the sound of their own breathing filling their ears. "He's stuck down there, or out cold, or something. We've got a minute, I think."

"What are you doing?" Rector demanded, still ready to run headlong down the hill and right back into the Vaults without pause. He didn't want a minute. He wanted out of there.

"The diesel," he said.

"Too heavy to carry with us!" Rector insisted.

"I know! I don't want to take it all the way." Houjin knocked the nearest steel drum onto its side and gave it a shove. It rolled and sloshed, heavily lumbering over the uneven ground. "Help me with this."

"I thought we were running—"

"Just *help me*," he insisted, shoving his weapon into the back of his belt. "I have an idea. For later."

Rector joined him at the side of the drum, planting his hands on it to help with the shoving, rolling, and guiding. "If anybody sees us, we're dead! If we get caught, I'm running, and I'm leaving you here. I'm going back underground."

"We might be dead already," Houjin huffed. "If we get spotted, we drop it. All right?"

"Fine," Rector grumbled, halfway praying that someone would see them so he could resume his flight to safety.

Both of them were almost faint with fright and exertion; their air supply came too thin to support so much running and hollering. But they pressed onward and pushed harder, manhandling the metal barrel over the hill's edge and down onto one of the curved walkways, where it could roll more smoothly, so long as it followed the path.

But then Houjin pushed it off the path, along the wall's edge. The way was harder going, but they kept at it.

"Where are we going with this thing?" Rector demanded. "It's heavy as hell!"

"To the hole . . . in the wall . . ." Houjin puffed. "Trust me . . . would you?"

"Ain't got much choice right now, do I?"

"You could find your way back to Sizemore without me."

Rector said, "Maybe," and was almost surprised when he realized it was true, never mind that he'd just threatened to do exactly that. He panted back at Houjin, "But you look like . . . you need . . . a hand. And I wanna know . . . what you want to set on fire."

"The hole."

"You want to set . . . the hole . . . on *fire*?"

"Not right now . . . but later. You'll see . . . what I mean . . ."

They stashed the diesel fuel behind a stack of stones that had been blown off the wall. They hid it with a few extras, and now that they were away from the park and the tower, they rested. Houjin marked the spot with a small pyramid of rocks.

"What's that for?"

"So we can find it later, or tell other people how to find it. Come on, let's get back to the Station and hand off this dynamite. I don't think the Doornails will take too kindly to us stashing it down in their living quarters, but Yaozu has places he can keep it."

 *Twenty-five*

Rest didn't come easy for anyone that night. More than a few people stayed up and worried, or went out to the Station hunting for news. And the men who worked out at the Station—most of them known for violence and a disinclination to be friendly—chatted nervously with the Doornails and Chinamen alike about where they'd found the dynamite and how much damage it might've done, had they not unhooked it and stashed it someplace safer.

They replaced everything they found with forgeries made out of pebbles wrapped in paper. These false sticks wouldn't fool anyone on close inspection, but Yaozu didn't think the tower men were likely to double-check them. After all, he'd given the order that the lines must be left in place—and the lines were long, some running as much as four or five blocks in length.

Everyone was counting on the fact that the tower men did not intend to come any closer to the Station than necessary.

Rector's sleep in his new room was as restless as everyone else's; he tossed and turned, and dreamed badly—of rotters and inexplicable monsters, and of Zeke's ghost—but Zeke wasn't dead, and that's how he knew he was dreaming. He shook himself awake and heard the high-pitched fuss of the fox in the room down the hall . . . which wasn't much more pleasant than the dreams of things that wanted to eat him.

But he was awake, and there was nothing to be done about it.

He pulled on his boots and listened to the unhappy creature until it quieted, and its vocalizations were replaced with the soft, muttering syllables of someone speaking gently.

Rector knew it was Zeke even before he got down to the fox's room.

The door was cracked open. He pushed it, letting a little more light inside.

Zeke crouched next to the cage, his fingers precariously close to the fox's quivering, pointed nose. The boy looked up when Rector entered. "Oh, hey Rector. Just checking on the fox. Angeline told me he was down here."

"Making plenty of noise, ain't he?" Rector rubbed at his eyes, and scratched at the sweaty, itchy seams where his mask had sat against his face for too many hours.

"He's scared. And he doesn't feel good."

"He drank the water. That'll make anybody feel like shit."

Zeke nodded and said, "I brought him more, though, and he drank that, too."

"You get him to eat anything?"

"Some jerky." He held it up, and Rector saw that he'd been hand-feeding the fox through the slim wire bars.

"You got to be careful. If that fox bites you . . ."

"He's not trying to bite me, he's only trying to eat. I think he'll get better, if he gets enough grub in him." Zeke gazed at the fox as though he'd give almost anything to pet the thing's ears.

"Don't be a dummy," Rector warned. "That fox ain't nobody's dog. It'd bite you even if it weren't sick. That there's a wild animal, and if it gets better, it's going right back outside the wall, where it belongs."

"That's fine. I don't mind turning him loose; I just don't want him to be so damn sick. I feel sorry for him, is all."

Rector sat down beside Zeke and drew up his knees. "I'd feel sorry for you, if we had to cut off your hand or something."

Zeke smiled, but didn't withdraw his fingers or the jerky he offered the fox. The animal took another bite, chewed it, and then
retreated to the cage's far end. It turned in a circle and flopped
down, looking dejected . . . but maybe less dejected than it had the
day before.

"You couldn't sleep either?" Zeke asked.

"I been asleep. I just woke up."

"Everybody's riled up. All this talk of dynamite and fire . . .
the Station is going to war with the tower. Only the tower don't
know it yet."

"I *hope* they don't know it," Rector said nervously.

"What do you mean by that?"

He told Zeke about the inexplicable and Captain Cly, and
how he and Houjin had almost been caught. He added, "I can't
imagine they knew who we were, or what we were doing. They
might've noticed we opened some of the dynamite and took a bit,
but there's always the chance they'll write it off to boys being
boys."

"Ain't that just about the dumbest expression? Boys being
boys . . . what the hell else are we supposed to be?"

"Damned if I know."

"Me either."

They sat together in silence for a minute, staring at the pitiful
fox, then Zeke said, "I been thinking. Even if we catch the inexplicable and stick him in the jail, how will we give him clean air? If
Captain Cly can't take him, then the thing's too big to wrestle.
And I don't think he would understand if we held a gun to him."

"Miss Angeline seems to think we'll manage."

"I know, and she's usually right. But the spaces under the
jailhouse aren't sealed; the sasquatch wouldn't get enough clean
air like that. He's not like this little fox. We can't just put him in a
crate and stick him in a corner."

"Then what did you have in mind?"

"Well, I was thinking, see: How do *we* get clean air when we're moving around up topside?"

Rector said, "Masks. Filters. All that rigmarole."

"Right. So what if we put a mask on the monster?"

Rector leaned back thoughtfully against the wall. "How do you know he'd wear one? He could yank it off."

"Not if we tied up his hands, or something. If there are any irons left in the jail, and they aren't all rusted through, maybe we could hitch him up like a crook."

"Sounds tricky."

"Yeah, but it'd be easier than convincing him to come with us just because we're nice people who want to help him. If we can get him to the jail and get him food and water, maybe he'd settle down enough to trust us."

"That kind of thing don't happen."

"It don't?" Zeke pointed at the fox. "That fox is scared to death, but it knows I don't mean it no harm. If the inexplicables are something more like people, they must be even smarter. Even if he doesn't understand us, he might understand we're on his side."

"All that sounds real nice, but I'd be afraid to see it in action. And anyway, where would we get a mask big enough to fit him?"

"The captain has a big head, but he's got a mask to fit it. So does Mr. Swakhammer."

"You want to ask him for a loaner, to stick on a monster?"

"No, I'm just saying—there are big masks. I saw a fellow wearing one once. It was like a big glass bubble with a row of small filters and tubes instead of two big filters. I think it'd fit over the inexplicable's head."

Rector tried to imagine this mask, and failed. "I have to see this thing."

When they left the fox it was resting. They shut the door to let it sleep off whatever it could, then went hunting for the big glass bubble Zeke swore existed someplace. It took them over an hour to find it, in the very back of the second largest storeroom on the bottommost floor. When they did, Zeke held it triumphantly aloft.

Rector could hardly believe his eyes. "That's the damnedest thing I ever saw!" he exclaimed. "Who made it?"

"Doctor Minnericht. It's a good idea—a mask that you can see out of all the way around. It reminds me of something I saw in a book once, a drawing about people who go underwater and swim around without coming up for air."

Rector had never seen such a book. "People can do that?"

"I don't know. It might've just been a story."

"Let me see that thing."

Zeke handed it over. "Sure, but be careful with it. That's the only one. But you saw the monster—I mean, the inexplicable. Do you think this would fit over his head?"

Rector weighed the thing in his hands. It was heavy indeed—heavier than it looked, and big enough to hold a few gallons of water. "I think so, yeah."

"Then we should try it. Let's take it to Angeline, when she gets up and around."

"What time is it right now?"

"No idea. Maybe a smidge before dawn."

Rector yawned. "No wonder I'm so tired."

"Should've stayed in bed."

"So should you," he shot back.

"Well, neither one of us did—so let's go to the kitchen and get some breakfast. Then we'll see what Angeline has to say about the mask idea, and she can tell us if she thinks we're crazy."

 *Twenty-six*

Angeline did not think they were particularly crazy. In fact, when they caught up to her and Houjin in the Vault's main parlor area, she rather liked the idea. "It'll be easier to put a hat on 'im than haul him anyplace civilized for safekeeping, won't it? Of course, this won't make it any easier to catch him."

"No, that part will be up to us," Houjin said. He was holding the mask and examining it, no doubt thinking of ways it could be improved. "If only we knew what he wanted, we could lure him out—maybe get him to chase us."

Rector shuddered. "I hate everything about that plan."

"Food," Zeke proposed. "Water. That's all the fox wants, as far as we can tell. It ain't even trying to bite us or nothing."

"It's a start," the princess mused. "But running through the Blight carrying a bucket of water . . . that plan won't end well. Food will be easier."

"What do they eat?" Rector asked.

Houjin smirked. "He tried to eat *you*."

"I bet I'm *delicious*. But I don't want to be monster bait."

"Not a monster," she reminded them. "Call him by his name, Sasquatch. Is that so hard?"

Rector said, "No, ma'am," and Zeke shrugged.

Angeline shook her head. "I'm still thinking about food. Just about everything native to this place lives on the same diet, if it'll eat plants and animals both. Let's assume Sasquatch is that kind of creature."

Rector frowned. "Why?"

"Because it's shaped like us, and kin to us, and *we're* the sort of creatures who eat both plants and animals. Which gives me a good idea . . . You boys stay out of trouble for the morning. I'll be back in a bit."

"Wait . . . where are you going?" Houjin asked.

"Fishing!"

With that abrupt shift in plan, she took off. After she was far enough gone that there was no chance she'd overhear, Houjin leaned forward conspiratorially to ask, "Say, what are you two doing for the rest of the day?"

Rector shrugged and Zeke said, "I was going to go up to Fort Decatur in case the captain needs anything. Why? You got something fun in mind?"

A thrilled—but in Rector's opinion, unnervingly sharp—grin spread across Houjin's face. "Do you want to come with me to the Station and see what I've been doing? I'll show you what I'm making to fight the men at the tower."

"Why are you working all the way out there?" Zeke asked.

"You wouldn't want me fiddling with dynamite around here, would you? And before you say it: Yes, I know your mother doesn't want you there, Zeke. But Yaozu won't bother you if you don't bother him. He's got too much else to worry about right now." Houjin looked at Rector, using his eyebrows to ask for backup.

Rector got it and said, "Sure, and I won't rat you out. Come with us, won't you, Zeke? Let's get a gander at Houjin's toys. It beats hanging around watching the captain moon over your momma, don't it?"

He winced. "Figured that out, did you?"

Rector laughed. "I ain't dumb or half blind, you know."

"Fine, all right. I'll go with you. But if I'm going to risk getting hollered at, Huey, this had better be *good*."

Leaving the mask behind for now, they hiked together out to King Street Station, taking the underground passages rather than the overland route. Rector found that he preferred the trip to the Station over the trip elsewhere in the underground, because it was almost entirely downhill. Sure, it meant he'd be going uphill on the return trip, but as a destination, it was easier than heading up to that damn park.

Near the Station's edge, they reached a fork in the tunnels.

"This way," Houjin said. "I want to show you something."

Upon reaching a sealed door, he pulled out the lever and gave it a tug. The door squeaked, and the rubber flaps surrounding its edges protested. They dragged it along the ground with a scraping, sucking noise. On the other side of that door, a second sealed door waited.

Zeke explained, "Two doors between you and the outside air. That's the rule, if you can make it."

Rector checked the polarized glass Huey'd given him. "But the air's pretty clear, according to this."

"Yes," Houjin said as he reached for the second door's handle. "But it hasn't always been. This part collapsed about five years ago. The place we're going . . . it wasn't always underground." He drew back the second door. Its seals complained, too, but it slid along the ground and made way for the three boys to pass.

Beyond it, Rector found himself confused.

He wasn't inside a room, or underneath a floor or cellar. He was standing in a beautiful train car. Curtains covered the windows, and the plush seats were clean, plump, and ready to be sat upon. Small tables were installed between two of the rows, allowing people to face one another and chat or play cards.

Zeke pulled back one of the curtains, revealing a view of nothing at all—except, Rector realized, a wall of dirt. "It's a shame, ain't it?" the younger boy said.

"A shame, I guess. It's real nice in here. Feels like . . . like . . ."

"It's a Pullman car," Houjin supplied. "One of the fanciest they ever made. The gold leaf is real, and so are the crystals. Leaded glass, all over the place. And look at the carpet!"

Rector gazed down at his feet. His boots suddenly seemed insufficient to stand upon the rug. It was Persian in design, blue with gold vines and tiny orange flowers. Instinctively, he stepped off to the side, not wanting to rub the wet dirt of the underground into the lovely pattern.

Zeke laughed, and Rector told him to shut his mouth. But he said, "Naw, I'm not laughing at you—I'm just laughing. Everybody does that, is all. This is one of the prettiest places in the city, this little car right here, and even the rough old Station men don't want to bother it any."

"Sometimes Yaozu comes here and smokes," Houjin said quietly, like he was passing on a secret. "I heard he makes the chemists come in here and clean it, keep it all dusted and shiny."

Zeke gave Rector a nudge. "Anyway, come on. We can't work in here. Yaozu would throw a hissy fit if we smudged one of the brass fixings, or anything like that. Huey, are we headed for your workshop?"

"Yes!"

"You have a workshop?" Rector stepped back onto the carpet because he had no choice, but he tiptoed gently to keep from smushing it.

"I have a place I work when Yaozu wants something."

Rector followed behind as Houjin opened the other door at the train car's far end. Stepping out and through this door, he found himself back in an ordinary-looking tunnel, braced with the usual miner's rafters and affixed with dirty lamps to light the way. "So the captain don't mind you hanging out down here?"

"I don't think he likes it, but he doesn't try to stop me."

"Could he?" Rector pushed. Was Houjin secretly a Station man waiting to happen? It was an interesting thought.

He took one of the lanterns off its hook. Without turning around, he said, "I don't know. Maybe. If he said I couldn't fly with him anymore, I'd have to think about it. Maybe I want to live down here forever, and maybe I don't, but I like having options. And so far, any time Yaozu has asked me to do something for him, it's always something that'll help the city out, so the captain doesn't care enough to make a fuss about it."

Rector followed along in silence until he passed a fallen over-hang that had collapsed under the weight of rocks and tree roots.

Houjin saw him looking at it. "That used to be one of the waiting platforms. Part of the wall fell down on it, during a quake. And the back yards where the tracks go are mostly buried now, unless somebody cut tunnels through them."

"Like that car back there?"

Zeke said, "Yeah. But I haven't seen too much of the back lots."

"Because you're not allowed down here," Rector recalled.

"My mother doesn't *like* it when I come down here. That's not the same thing."

"Close enough. You said so yourself, the other day."

"Well I'm here now, ain't I?"

"Must be feeling mighty brave."

Zeke sniffed and stood up straighter as he tagged along be-hind them. "I just want to see what Huey's working on, that's all."

"So you've got a story all lined up for when your ma finds out you was here."

"You already said you wouldn't tell her, and I know Huey won't. So I'm thinking she won't find out."

Houjin led them deeper, down through an entrance that took them inside the train station proper—Rector knew it because he recognized the pretty marbled floors and the tiles that were set into the walls for decoration. There were runner rugs down here, too, but they looked worn and sad compared to the tapestries in the old train car.

Somewhere in the distance he could hear the *clank, clang,* and *clatter* of the elevator, but they were a long, many-doored hallway away from it when Houjin stopped and pulled out a key.

Rector tried to keep from sounding impressed when he asked, "Your workshop locks?"

"Yaozu thought it might be a good idea. This would have been one of the engineers' offices if anybody had ever used this station for traveling."

"How nice for you," he said, more crossly than he meant to. He'd never owned a key to anything, not in his entire life. Not even now that he had his own room.

Houjin unlocked the door and led everyone inside, setting his lantern on a small table beside the door. On the wall above it, there was a metal bubble with a button in the middle. Houjin pushed the button. With a sputtering series of sparks, a line of bulbs lit up overhead. They were connected on a wire, and hanging low enough that he could've touched one if he stood on his toes.

He lifted one hand almost mindlessly, reaching for the light as if it called him.

"I wouldn't, if I were you," Zeke warned him. "Them things are hot."

"Not yet. But they will be soon," Houjin confirmed. "They're electric, and it takes them a minute to warm up."

"I've never seen so many in one place." Rector withdrew his hand.

Houjin nodded and reached for a large box, which was sitting beside an even larger desk. The desk was littered with wires, coils, tools, schematics, stray parts, and scraps of paper covered in Chinese characters. The box was heavy, if Houjin's posture could be gauged. He used his elbow to clear a spot, then set the box on the desk.

He said, "Electric lights are better than torches and candles down here, because they don't leave smoke everywhere. Better than lanterns, because fuels like kerosene are heavy to carry around. And you don't have to keep refilling the bulbs. You just change them out once in a while."

"Where do they get their power from?" Rector asked.

"The pump rooms, same as the air circulation. They run on coal."

"Coal's heavy, too," he pointed out.

"True, but we're already using coal to power the air circulation. It was easy to rig up a generator and siphon off some of the energy. I'm telling you," he said as he began to unpack the box, "electricity is the future. Before long, we won't be using coal anymore, or any of the petroleum derivatives."

Houjin had just used two words in a row that Rector didn't recognize, but Rector played along like this made perfect sense to him. "I like how they don't smell like anything."

"They *do* have a smell," Houjin argued lightly. "You notice it after a while. But it isn't very strong, and that's not why I brought you down here. *This* is what I wanted to show you."

He held up a device that appeared to be made mostly out of dynamite, with a handful of other things attached.

Both Zeke and Rector jumped back.

"Shit, Huey!" Zeke said. "Warn a guy before you start flashing that around!"

"It's perfectly safe . . . for the moment," he added, bouncing it gently in his hands. "Nothing to spark it off. You wouldn't want to go playing catch with it, but it won't blow us up," he said with a grin.

Rector eyed the dynamite bundle with a mixture of horror and curiosity. "Is that . . . is that a clock you got tied to it?"

"Yes! Here," he said, placing the odd contraption on the desk, beside its box. "It has an alarm—you can set it to strike at a certain time."

"Like . . . to wake you up? I've heard of those," Rector said.

"To wake you up, to tell you to go to work . . . it doesn't matter. The point is, it *strikes*."

"And what's that thing next to it?" Zeke asked, pointing at a strange little device about the size of two thumbs pressed together.

"It's a dry cell battery."

Rector didn't have a clue what that meant, and a shared glance with Zeke told him he wasn't alone. "Why's it stuck on that board?"

The alarm clock and the battery were fastened to each other by a copper wire. A piece of brass was affixed to the clock's alarm key, and all of the pieces were mounted with screws and bolts to a board which was a bit smaller than a loaf of bread.

"I don't get it," Zeke confessed.

"It's . . . these, you see . . ." Houjin pointed at various spots on the board, settling on the two bits of brass. "These are the contact points, you understand? When the alarm rings, it sends an electrical current from the clock to the battery, just like the current in a hand-pump trigger."

Zeke eyed the clock with suspicion. "The alarm's not going to ring, is it?"

"The clock's wound down. It couldn't strike if it tried."

Rector stared at the board and its weird components, then considered the dynamite, and the clock—and he thought of the enormous grandfather clock at the orphan's home, and how it'd chime as told, every hour on the hour. And just like the spark that would jump between the connectors, the answer flickered between his ears.

He said, "This means you can tell the dynamite when to blow up."

"Yes!" Houjin exclaimed. "That's it exactly! We can tell the dynamite to explode at five o'clock, or eleven o'clock, or whenever we like—but it explodes when we're a long ways away from it. We're going to surprise those tower men out of their skins! They'll never know what hit them. If any of them survive, they'll come looking for us—but we won't be anywhere they can reach us, not by then."

"That's . . . that's *genius,*" Zeke said with naked awe.

"Thank you. I'm excited by it myself. Yaozu brought up the idea; he thought it was possible, but he didn't know how to make it happen. But that's Yaozu's kind of genius," he said as an afterthought. "He doesn't know how to do everything, but he knows who to ask."

A knock on the door made everyone jump, but it was only a Chinese man in a rounded hat. He said something to Houjin, who nodded quickly and made a brief reply. The other man left, leaving the boy to explain. "Angeline is outside waiting for us. We should go."

They backtracked through the Station, and Rector marveled again at how beautiful it all was—practically the inside of a mansion, or how he'd always imagined a mansion must look. Every surface gleamed and glowed.

Maybe that was it. Everything was made out of something that shone. Brass, glass, marble . . . it all conspired to toss the electricity and gaslight around the echoing space, making them look warm and bright without being harsh.

They didn't go all the way back to the Pullman car. Instead, they exited in a different direction, and Houjin led them straight to Angeline, who they found reclined on a bench with her hat over her face.

"Napping on the job?" Zeke greeted her with a grin.

She pulled the hat aside and whapped him with it. "Didn't

realize you three would turn up so fast. I'm old and I'm tired, and I can close my eyes if I want to."

Rector fished around in his bag for a mask, suspecting he would need it. "So what happens next? You're back, and looking for us. Did something interesting happen?"

"Yes and no, by which I mean I have an idea where the sasquatch might be hanging about. I don't know what you boys have done all morning, but I've been near the tower, keeping my ears open. It's a good way to learn things."

"And what did you learn?" Houjin prodded politely.

"I learned that them fellows don't have the faintest idea we've been snatching their dynamite," she said. Rector noticed that she'd lumped herself in with the Station men, courtesy of her word choice. "They've been coming and going, reporting back, telling their boss what they've been up to. It'd be more helpful if we didn't already know."

"Do you know when they plan to blow us up?" Houjin asked, doing the same thing, and siding with Yaozu's people.

"They're still deciding, but leaning toward tonight around dark-thirty. At some point, they'll need to coordinate better than that, but for now all I have is their general idea."

"Are we going to let them try?" Zeke asked. When everyone looked at him a little funny, he added, "Well, we have the advantage on them right now, but once they figure out their explosives didn't work, they'll know we're on to them."

Houjin pondered this a moment and replied, "The Station fellows . . . and whoever else is coming along . . . should time it as close as possible. It'll confuse the heck out of the tower men, if they try to blow us up and their tower goes up in smoke instead. We'll have more of an advantage than just surprise: We'll shock them silly."

"Let's not worry about that right now," Angeline said. "The

other thing I learned from the tower men is that they're worried about some oversized rotter, hanging around about halfway down Denny Hill."

"The sasquatch! Let's hope he stays there. Now all we have to do is track him and catch him," Rector said. When he put it out there like that, the task sounded big. It sounded frightening. It sounded like something he'd rather skip in favor of picking live dynamite out of cubbyholes.

The princess said, "I've got my net, that helmet you found, and some fresh fish. How about you boys? You got your weapons?"

They didn't, but these things were stashed at the Sizemore House tunnel entrance, so they could be retrieved easily enough. Angeline was satisfied by this, and after making sure they all had masks and the usual supplies, she led them away from King Street Station and under the city, along the hand-cart tracks, and up the incline toward Denny Hill and the Sizemore House.

They emerged ready for battle.

Twenty-seven

Everyone was masked and armed. The boys carried their usual weapons, and the princess had her knives—but, as she'd told them, she hoped they wouldn't be necessary. On the way, they'd discussed the state of Zeke's fox, and she was encouraged by the creature's progress. Not healed in a day, certainly. But any sign of improvement was cause for optimism, and perhaps it wouldn't take so much to bring the sasquatch back around.

As they began their stealthy quest, Angeline reminded them: "We're here to save him, not hurt him. Don't you forget that. But at the same time, I expect you to defend yourselves if you need to. I'd rather have the three of you alive than the sasquatch."

Rector followed along behind her, and then near her as they spread out from one another by just a few feet.

That was the rule. They were to stay within sight of one another—no exceptions, no detours, no side excursions, no matter how interesting something looked or sounded. If something off the beaten path needed investigating, you said something to the group . . . and the group decided whether or not it was worth a visit. In case of rotters, everyone knew where to access the underground, and how to hole up in a remaining building in case an entrance wasn't nearby. There were safe spots throughout all the neighborhoods, even this one, but they weren't very close together. One for every two or three blocks, no more than that.

If trouble came calling, they'd have to run.

As Zeke confessed while they walked quietly along the blocks, it was almost spookier without the rotters. He whispered, because Angeline said they could whisper. They were far enough from the tower that none of the men were likely to hear them, and they didn't want to hide from the sasquatch; they wanted to lure him out. Quiet voices were tolerated, and even encouraged.

"It's like this," he said, placing one foot carefully on the far side of a fallen stone slab, and testing his weight against it before stepping across. "When you know the rotters are here, it ain't a surprise to find them. They used to be pretty much everywhere, but you just stayed away from the spots where you knew they'd be."

He slipped on a patch of pebbles, caught himself, and continued. "But when they're just . . . when they're *gone* . . . then you don't know where they are. And they could be anyplace," he told them. "You can't stay away from anyplace if you don't know where it is. It's like trying to avoid everything—you can't do it. So you wind up scared of every place, and every sound, because any place and any sound could mean a rotter's coming to get you."

Houjin solemnly agreed, but added, "I wonder how many are left." And then, more brightly, "I wonder if we could use them against the tower men!"

Rector liked the idea. "You mean, if we could wrangle them—like a herd of cattle—and drive them up the hill? That'd be a hell of a sport."

"But there aren't enough of them, not anymore," Zeke said.

"We don't know that for sure. They sometimes bunch up in pockets," Houjin countered. "And Yaozu's making more of them—we saw that for ourselves."

Angeline shuddered. "That man, I swear. He'll go straight to hell someday and feel right at home."

They wandered and searched, ultimately creeping down along

the hill's incline because it was easier going down than up, and because the old city prison was that direction, too.

"It's another few blocks that way"—Angeline indicated east—"and lucky for us, it's no farther."

Lucky for them indeed, Rector thought, when a rhythmic bluster of faint background noise became loud enough to catch his attention. With the mask rubbing against his hair, making static sounds against his ears, it was hard to say at first, but eventually—yes—he detected the draw and puff of something breathing. And it wasn't one of his fellow party members, he was fully certain of *that*.

He stopped without noticing he'd stopped. He stood in his tracks like an animal aware of a predator, like a small thing wanting to become smaller for fear of a big thing.

Everyone looked at him.

Rector held up a finger, pointing at nothing but the gray-green sky beyond the Blight. He tried to ask if they heard the noise, too, if they knew where it was coming from, and was it close—was it as close as it felt? But when he opened his mouth, it was too dry to speak.

Angeline backed up against him, readying her net. Over her shoulder, she said to him, "I hear him, too, Red."

He pushed himself against her. Knowing that something was coming for him yet again, he felt better with her beside him.

"Stay calm," she urged. She passed her net to Houjin, who didn't quite know what to do with it except to hold it ready. She pulled a wrapped, fresh fish out of her pack. It must've weighed ten pounds, Rector thought wildly—it could've fed a family of four, or half a dozen orphans in a Catholic home outside the wall. Why hadn't they ever gone fishing to feed the kids? Did nobody in the church know how?

Frantic, disjointed thoughts scattered through his head, tumbling in all directions as his fear stirred them up and shook them.

"He wants me," he breathed.

"Red, my boy . . . he doesn't know what he wants."

The fish was still on a line as thick as a cable, with a great metal hook fastened through its mouth, jabbing through its cheek. If there'd ever been any blood, it was gone now. And Rector didn't know what fish blood looked like, anyway, or if they even *had* blood . . . and now his mind was racing so wildly that the thoughts came faster and faster, each upon the heels of the last one. He could not remember having ever thought so quickly or so clearly about nothing at all of any importance.

He wanted a hit of sap worse than he'd ever wanted anything in his life. That'd slow his mind down, wouldn't it? Sap would fix it. It'd temper his fluttering heart, drag his thoughts down, keep him calm. Keep him ready for any kind of action that required more thought than running and screaming, in case running and screaming weren't enough.

The princess thrust the heavy fish toward Zeke, who hesitated. She changed her mind, retrieved the net from Houjin, and gave the fish to him instead.

Louder and louder came the breathing, from something so huge his wheezing gasps filled the whole block. The creature was hidden in the foggy air, but he was moving; the source of the sound slipped from left to right, accompanied by heavy footsteps.

Zeke backed up against Rector, too, not for protective purposes, but from the ordinary, human need to band together for defense. Houjin joined them, and soon they were in a nervous back-to-back circle, everyone facing outward . . . everyone looking through the fog, straining to see what lurked inside it.

Angeline shifted the net in her hands, and elbowed Houjin so he'd hold up the fish.

"Hello out there," she said softly. "We know you're watching us. Are you hungry?"

Zeke tried it, too. "Hey out there, Mister Sasquatch. Miss Angeline says you don't mean us any harm."

In response, they heard a loud huff or cough. It was the chuffing sound of something with a stuffy nose, a congested torso. It was off to their left. Everyone calibrated accordingly, twisting to observe the location without leaving anyone's back undefended.

Angeline picked up the thread. "You're stuck inside here, aren't you? You're just trying to go outside, isn't that it? You've got a lady friend over there, beyond the wall. I seen her when I went fishing. She got up close to me, and didn't make a sound, but she watched from the trees."

"You saw her?" Houjin whispered.

She lowered her voice. "Sure did. She's a pretty-colored thing, smooth and brown-red, like cedar."

The big thing groaned, or roared feebly. Rector retreated as deeply as possible into the tangle of his friends, wanting nothing more than to bolt for the nearest shelter; and if he had the faintest idea where that might've been, he might've done so. But he didn't, and the only thing keeping him from being by himself in the Blight, in the wrecked city, was this knot of humanity.

His mask fogged. His eyes watered.

"He's coming," he said, and he hated himself for how much it sounded like whining.

Angeline's cadence was steady as a rock, and her words poured like honey into the fog. "That's all right. Let him come. How about this, boys—all of us, now. Let's start moving toward the jail. Let's see if he'll follow us. But don't make any fast moves, or sudden gestures. We don't mean him any trouble, and we want him to know it."

In a bunch, all four of them began a retreat. "Which way?" Rector asked.

"Follow me. Don't take your eyes off the fog."

"Couldn't if I tried."

"You know what I mean."

If the footsteps, scrapes, and ragged breaths from deep within the fog could be believed, the sasquatch trailed them. Not closely, but without much space between them, either. "How much farther to the jail?" Rector asked.

"Not so far, Red. Keep your calm. The sasquatch don't want to hurt you."

"Then why'd he try in the first place?"

"Don't know. Maybe he didn't."

There she went, harping on that again. Well, she wasn't there when it happened. Rector *was* there, and he knew when something or somebody wanted to tear off his head and play catch with it. Frankly, the sasquatch hadn't been the first to consider it.

Inch by inch, foot by foot, they clustered and sidled and ambled along, no one breaking from the group. When it seemed as though the sasquatch might be falling behind, or losing interest in armed prey that outnumbered him, Angeline reminded him of the fish. She urged Houjin to hold it up and let it sway back and forth.

"Come on, big fellow," she told him. "Don't you smell that? Don't you want to come in close, and take a big bite of it? There ain't much to eat inside the wall, I know. You must be hungry as can be."

Houjin waved the fish like a pendulum, his arms straining against its weight. "You think he can actually smell this?" he asked.

"Don't see why not."

"Because the Blight smells like rotten eggs and cat piss, that's why," Rector murmured. "If he can smell the fish through the gas, then his nose deserves a blue ribbon." You didn't have to breathe the stuff day in and day out to know the reek of it. The odor permeated everything—clothing, wood, and supplies. And of course, Rector had burned enough sap to have a much more intimate familiarity with the concentrated stink.

"He can see the fish, even if he can't smell it," Zeke tried.

"Then his eyes need a blue ribbon, too." Rector couldn't see more than a dozen feet in any direction, and sometimes not even that far.

"Boys, don't argue. The jail's just at the end of this street. Keep yourselves focused. We've almost got him."

Rector didn't recognize the street. It looked like any other neighborhood inside the swamped city: low, squat buildings that were sometimes houses, sometimes stores, and occasionally something else. The taller structures were all farther to the southwest, down nearer to the water. There weren't any hotels this far up the hill, or train stations, either.

This corner of the wall-wrapped space hadn't been developed much. Rector supposed that was why they put a prison here. And when the prison came into view, it wasn't an imposing sort of place, or a particularly cruel one in appearance. It was flat and single storied, built of stone gone slimy with the years and the gas.

"There it is," the princess said.

"That's it?" Rector asked. "Don't look like much."

Angeline said, "It ain't much. The main jail was downtown, on Third Street at Jefferson. But that one was emptied before the Blight got too bad. The people who were here . . . they were the ones left to die."

Zeke turned his head to stare at the unimpressive rectangle with the tiny barred windows. "So these were the ones my granddaddy saved. I always thought it was the big jail, the main jail down on Third Street."

She shook her head. "No. He'd have saved more than a couple dozen folks if he'd emptied that one."

"Stories get bigger in the retelling," Houjin noted.

"Doesn't matter." Zeke shifted his grip on his old fireman's ax, which he'd reclaimed from Rector. Like the fish Houjin wielded, it was almost too big for him to swing and it looked ridiculous, but Rector had gotten tired of arguing with him. "He saved them. Including Captain Cly—he was there. Him and his brother. He told me about it."

Houjin dutifully tipped the fish back and forth, even though his arms were shaking. "I'm glad he did. Saved the captain, I mean."

They reached the corner where the jailhouse stood, melting on its foundations.

Angeline said, "Zeke, I want you to do something for me, all right?"

"Yes, ma'am."

"I want you to go open that front door. If it's locked, the lock won't hold. Move as gentle as you can. Don't startle the fellow we brought along with us."

"Yes, ma'am."

He swallowed hard and left the group.

Moving with exaggerated slowness, as if to show that he was utterly harmless—never mind the ax—and that his task was wholly uninteresting to any creatures that may lurk in the fog . . . he approached the jail's door.

Rector could see the doors from his vantage point pressed against Angeline's back. Although someone had chained them years ago, the chain looked about as strong as wet twine. Eaten up with rust and moisture, it crumbled when Zeke gave it a tug and clattered to the ground, disintegrating into a puff of damp red dust and a pile of rubble.

"Sasquatch won't follow us inside," Houjin speculated.

Angeline told him, "You don't know that."

Zeke disappeared over the lockup's threshold. Angeline nudged Houjin and Rector to do likewise. Together they crept over the last of the rubble, Houjin holding forth the fish like a talisman, as if it could protect him—and Rector thought maybe it could. If Rector were a sasquatch, faced with the prospect of eating a boy or eating a fish, he believed he'd go for the fish first.

So he did what Angeline told him and stumbled backwards, forward, spinning slowly as they calibrated themselves to move together. And one by one—Rector first, then Angeline, then Houjin, who stayed at the threshold with the fish a moment longer—they stepped inside.

Darkness washed over them all, blinding them until their eyes adjusted.

"Huey, get in here. Keep showing him the fish, that's right. Keep coming. I've got your back. He won't hurt you—just bring him along. I've got my net."

"He isn't coming."

"He'll come."

But he didn't. Not at first.

He camped outside the jailhouse and—as its occupants soon realized, with no small degree of nervousness—he peeked in the windows and ran away. Then again. And a third time. A fourth. He lingered, skulked, and mulled the whole thing over. The fish. The jail. The four small things inside.

Zeke watched for a bit, but as the sasquatch contemplated his next move, the younger boy left the team and wandered back into the gloom. The bland, uniform, brown-black shadows were cut only by slats of weak sunlight, filtered too many times to be stronger than a candle in the overwhelming darkness. Zeke slowly chased them anyway, following the little rays as far as they'd take him.

While Angeline and Houjin watched the entrance and waited for company, Rector watched Zeke, then joined him.

"What are you doing?" he asked, whispering without knowing why. The place felt like a graveyard, but that wasn't right, was it? No one had died here. Even Maynard hadn't died until he got back to town, or that's how the story went.

"Just looking," Zeke murmured. "Never been here before, but I heard so much about it."

His hands trailed along cabinets and cubbyholes for mail; they dragged furrows in the dust along a solid plank desk covered with brittle scraps of curling paper. A metal stamp was on the floor. Rector found it by accident, kicking it with the edge of his boot. He retrieved it and examined it.

Zeke asked, "What's that?"

And Rector said, "Looks like something for making dates, over and over again." He placed it beside a long-dried-out ink pad. "The kind of thing you use on official papers. Like birth certificates. Or court papers," he added, thinking that it was more likely the prison processed felons than babies.

"Oh."

But Zeke's attention was already elsewhere.

He puttered over to a board on the wall, about the size of the blackboard back at the orphan's home. It was covered in rows of hooks, and each hook held an iron ring set with a single key. A small plaque beneath each key indicated which cell door it fit. Each of the keys was too corroded for anything but looking at, so Zeke didn't molest them.

And at the board's far left, a single hook was empty.

Beneath it was a grimy plaque that read, "Master set."

He touched the empty hook with one gloved finger, then tugged it as if it would grant him a wish. "This is the one," he said. "The master set. Maynard took the keys, and he went . . ." Zeke turned on his heel and disappeared down the corridor that ran between the two rows of cells. He continued. "Down here. He went down here. And one by one, he opened the cells."

It was true, the doors were open. Some of them hung sadly on their tracks, ready to fall over if anyone so much as breathed on them. But back in the past, they had indeed been unlocked—and thrown aside so the occupants could escape.

Zeke left the only footprints.

"He let them go, so they'd have a chance. Not all of them lived," he mused. "Some of them were already weak, or sick, or what have you. And nobody knows how much gas it takes to turn somebody, or how much it takes to kill. But my granddaddy'd already run a mile through the Blight, up the hill. He was already poisoned."

Unbidden, a thought rose in Rector's mind.

Nobody knows how much sap it takes, either.

He did not say this aloud. Instead, he asked, "Do you think he knew he was dying? Your granddaddy, I mean."

Zeke stood between the rows, facing Rector—and backlit by the small barred square of a window that barely let in enough light to notice. Still, it cast a funny striped halo around the kid's head; it made him look like a ghost.

"Dagnabbit," Angeline complained from the main room.

Zeke sighed, and Rector shivered free from whatever spell he'd been under.

The princess continued to blaspheme. "The damn thing is sticking to his guns."

Rector and Zeke both returned to the main room, kicking up dust and bumping into things in the dull ambient light. Rector asked, "Where is he?"

Angeline shrugged, and said, "He's staying outside. Maybe we should go back out again."

Houjin nearly agreed. He seemed fully prepared to agree, standing at the threshold same as before, holding the shimmering dead fish with a drooping arm. He began to say something to that effect—that he thought they should go back outside, and take another try—but he didn't get the chance.

He was beaten to the punch by a long, hairy arm.

It whipped inside and seized him with a snatch so slick that, for a split second afterwards, nobody moved. No one was sure what had occurred, or what ought to happen next. One moment, Houjin was standing there with the fish and looking like he felt a little silly. The next, he was simply *gone*.

Zeke snapped to attention first. He barreled past Rector, and though Angeline shouted his name, commanded him to *wait,* he dashed out into the Blight-thick air.

"Come back here, boy!" she shouted, but she followed him, her net poised and ready for throwing. And Rector went, too, right behind her, because he didn't know what else to do.

Out into the Blight they burst. Somewhere in the fog, Houjin began to holler, then abruptly stopped.

"Huey!" Zeke shouted.

"Houjin, where are you?" Angeline called.

Rector swung his head back and forth, trying to place the sound of Houjin's breathing, or the rumbling shakes of the big thing moving—carrying the boy off, or doing worse to him. "Huey?" he called.

He shut his mouth after that and listened. He brandished his miner's pick in every direction, spinning around and hunting any noise that meant the monster was at hand. He halted, sharp as a compass needle, pointing toward a thick spot in the Blight.

Zeke needed no further instructions, so he charged—but Angeline grabbed him by the shirt and yanked him back.

"Don't you just go rushing in," she ordered, and some faint memory at the back of Rector's head added *where angels fear to tread.* "I'll go—you're too worked up. Houjin?" she cried again, and nobody heard anything except soft, wet munching sounds.

Zeke tore himself out of Angeline's grasp, twisting his body to unfasten her grip, and launched himself forward once again. This time he was too fast; she missed with her second swipe, and Rector took off after him like a sheepdog herding a wayward lamb.

"Boys!" she shrieked.

But he didn't quit running, chasing after Zeke's disappearing back. Behind him, he could hear Angeline on his heels; he didn't turn around to look, and she quit wasting her breath telling the lot of them to stop.

Zeke zipped in and out of the gas, zigzagging around obstacles and pushing himself through the thick air; it moved like curtains, billowing in a storm. Zeke ran like a phantom, darting into the mist. It gave Rector flashbacks—nasty ones—but he shook them free. He shook Angeline free, too, without meaning to. Her footsteps disappeared behind him, and again, he didn't look back. He wasn't sure what he wanted to see, or why it would matter.

He had no idea where he was, no idea what Zeke was chasing, and no idea what they'd do when they caught up to the sasquatch.

Zeke wasn't much farther ahead in the planning process, and when he drew up short, Rector collided with the back of his head, nearly knocking his chin straight up into his skull. Dazed, he stumbled backward as Zeke stumbled forward. He caught himself on a splintered crate, then bounced over to a wall and held a corner of it until the stars that speckled his vision could be persuaded to die down.

The stars died down. The Blight gas thinned.

And Rector saw them.

The sasquatch was facedown in the last of the salmon, ignoring the needle-thin bones and slurping the scales, blood, and juices as if he was half-starved—which he probably was. How long had he been inside? Weeks, at least. What was there to eat within the wall? Nothing, except for rotters. And how good could they taste?

He hunkered forward, and even in that position he looked bigger than Captain Cly, heavier than three or four men put together. He was covered in hair the color of tobacco and cherry pits; his hands were long enough to play two octaves at a stretch on the piano in Maynard's. As the creature ate, his body quivered and the ratty, clumped locks of his fur trembled and swayed.

Houjin was seated against the same building that Rector held for support. He did not look hurt, but his arms were curled around his knees and he panted, trying to catch his breath inside his mask. Zeke was between Houjin and the sasquatch, his fireman's ax held up in warning. The weapon shook in his hands, too heavy by half, but he planted his feet and *dared* the creature to take a step toward his friend.

The sasquatch didn't care. Yet.

Rector kept his voice as calm as he could, and said, "Fellas, come on. While he's eating. Let's go. Zeke, put that thing down. Huey?"

Houjin turned his head to see Rector, but he didn't otherwise move.

"I'll . . . I'll help you," he said, in case Huey was too scared to move, or in case he was hurt and Rector couldn't see it. "I'm coming," he added. Still clinging to the wall's edge—purely because he believed it was stronger than the long-armed brute before him—he followed it to the stunned or injured boy and bent down to reach him.

Neither of them looked away from the sasquatch.

But Rector whispered down, "You all right?"

"Yes," Huey whispered back. "Zeke? Zeke, let him go. He doesn't want you. He doesn't want me. He just wanted the fish."

"And he's almost out of fish," Rector warned.

Zeke seemed glad for the excuse to lower the ax. It swung from his hands like a clock pendulum, until it knocked against the ground. "I don't want to hurt him, anyhow."

"I know you don't," Rector said, still afraid that one loud word would shatter the fragile moment. "Let's go, us three. Let's go back to the jail, and find Angeline. Let's leave while that thing'll let us."

But now Zeke hesitated. "Look at him. He's in real bad shape, same as the fox was."

"We're none of us in tip-top condition, kid. Let's get out of here."

"Wait," the younger boy said plaintively.

Houjin climbed to his feet, using the wall to brace his back as he scooted to an upright position. Rector held out a hand to him, and Huey took it—and it was only then that Rector saw that his shirt was torn, and his chest was covered in long scratches where the creature had seized and absconded with him. If they didn't hurt now, they'd hurt later. The Blight would see to that.

Rector pulled Houjin over, helping him step across a fallen slab of brick and drawing him back, farther away from Zeke . . . who still hadn't moved.

Huey found his voice. "Zeke, let him alone. We'll find Angeline and come back."

"You two go without me."

"Nothing doing," Rector said. "We're all three leaving."

"Be patient. Just be patient," he urged. "He didn't hurt Huey. Not bad, and not on purpose if he did. He could've hurt him, and he didn't."

The sasquatch had eaten the innards and had moved on to the fins, picking them apart and gnawing the chewy, tough flesh as if he'd consume every part of the fish—even the parts that should not be eaten. The fins were tougher than they looked, but he scraped them between his teeth, nabbing every stray sliver of nutrition.

And then he was finished. His hands were empty—licked clean, even—and there was nothing else to distract him. He turned his attention to Zeke, who was standing closest. The ax was still head down on the street, threatening no one and nothing.

The sasquatch lifted his massive head and grunted.

Zeke swallowed hard. "Your eyes," he said to the sasquatch. "They're going gold, like the crows."

"Maybe his eyes have always been gold. Zeke, I swear and be damned . . ." Rector complained.

Zeke ignored him. "We want to help you," he said to the creature. "We want to help you feel better, and go outside where your lady friend is waiting for you. You want to go back outside, don't you?"

"He don't understand you!"

"He understands what I *mean*. He knows I'm not—"

Whatever else Zeke planned to say, it was lost to a moment of terror when the sasquatch jumped smoothly to his feet. He leaped and squatted like an oversized ape, his legs shorter than its arms and his posture far top-heavier than a man's.

Zeke let out a squeak and dropped the ax handle.

It clattered to the ground.

The sasquatch put one foot forward, then another. With every step, he gained confidence and speed. Rector thought about throwing the pickax; he thought about turning and running; he thought about finding another weapon, maybe grabbing Zeke's ax and giving it a toss. But there was only time for thinking, and no time for doing.

No time to do anything but watch, and wait for the next breath and heartbeat. Wait for him to seize Zeke like he'd taken Houjin.

Except Zeke didn't have anything edible to offer. Nothing except himself.

But by now, Angeline had caught up to them, swung around them, and gotten behind the sasquatch.

When she leaped out of the fog it was a thing of beauty. She flew with her net flung out before her, and landed just behind the sasquatch, just within range to throw the net, and pull it tight.

The sasquatch staggered. He was moving too fast to stop outright, or even turn around; but he tottered and tried to hold his feet steady. He spun like a dancer, and his spine bent and shifted, struggling to hold himself steady.

Angeline reached out with one long leg and kicked as hard as she could. She caught the creature in the soft spot behind his knee, and his knee buckled. The whole beast went down, toppling with a rolling shudder and then a low cry that shook any rooftops left standing.

The princess stood above the creature with her hands straining against the pull of the net.

"Boys!" she cried. "Help me move him! Help me tie him!"

All three lunged toward her, now that the beast was down. They wrestled with the ropes and dodged the grasping fingers and groping hands of the imprisoned thing; and when Angeline told them which way and how far, they began to shove, prod, and manhandle him back toward the jail. The irons there were rusted and the bars were uncertain, but he had to go someplace, and he couldn't come downstairs. He couldn't go to the underground, and he couldn't go to the tower. He had no place of his own, not while he was as sick as the fox but a hundred times its size.

It was an hour of heavy work and terrible labor, for the sasquatch did not agree with his handling, and his four captors were working against the air, and the filters in their mask. They rolled the protesting brute when he couldn't be compelled to walk or crawl.

But at times, Rector felt that he wasn't fighting very hard. He was tired and sick. He had just had a meal for the first time in days. He didn't want to be brutalized into a jail cell, but he didn't know that that was coming. And he was still strong enough that Rector shuddered to consider how strong he must be when he hadn't been breathing poisoned air for ages.

Something that size can't help being strong, he thought. *Something that big is dangerous because he outweighs you, not because he outruns you or outthinks you.* It was almost funny, now that he looked at it. It stunned him that he'd ever been afraid of him in the first place . . . at least until a swing of one shoulder knocked him flat onto his back and took the wind right out of his chest.

"Watch yourself," Angeline said. "He's stuck, but he's tough."

Rector picked himself up. He leaned forward, bracing his hands on top of his thighs. He took a moment to catch his breath and said, "I don't think he meant that one."

"I don't think he did either. Are you hurt?"

"No, ma'am."

"Then come back to the party. We're almost there, and he's almost done fighting."

Houjin said, "That's good, right?"

"Yes and no. When he's too tired to fight, he's too tired to be bullied along. Let's get him settled before he faints away altogether. I don't know if we can carry him."

By the time they reached the old prison on the hill, the sasquatch was barely able to stand. They'd worn him out with the journey, or so Rector hoped—otherwise, he would spring to life the moment their guard was down and kill them all, that was his personal suspicion. He watched the sasquatch exhaustedly as Angeline guided him into the sturdiest-looking cell. There was still a wall loop made to anchor chains and leg irons, and when the princess gave it a hearty yank, it didn't budge. She affixed the net thereunto, tying it with careful knots.

When she was certain that the sasquatch would not leap up and murder the lot of them, she stood and put her hands on her hips, eyeing the unhappy creature with victory . . . but also pity.

"Poor thing," she said. "I hate leaving him all tied up like this, but what can we do?"

Houjin brought forward the glass mask they'd toted all the way from the underground's bottommost basement. "We can put this on his head, and see what happens."

"You think he'll just let us do that?" Rector asked incredulously.

She shook her head. "Not happily, but we need to try it. Here's what we'll do: I'll take one of my knives and cut his head loose from the net, then one of you boys can put the helmet on him and make sure it's all secure. Watch out for them teeth, though. Some of 'em are as big as my thumb."

The sasquatch was propped in a halfhearted slouch against the dirty wall.

He flinched and growled when Angeline came toward him with a small blade, so he understood more than you might expect—Rector gave him credit there. But since she didn't hurt him, he didn't lash out. Instead, he held very, very still while she trimmed away the lines necessary to fully expose his head, as if he had popped through the neck hole of a sweater.

She held his gaze for a moment, but it was inscrutable. His eyes were deep-set in a flattened face that was a mass of leathery brown-black wrinkles. Those eyes—which, yes, as Zeke had noted, were turning gold—told them nothing.

"Inexplicable," Rector breathed.

And Houjin said, "Sasquatch."

"Here he is, boys. Only a handful of folks have ever seen him, or ever will, I expect." She took the big glass helmet in her hands, and passed it toward Zeke. "You do it," she told him.

Zeke took the helmet and held it up, checking for cracks and testing its filters. The sasquatch's eyes followed the globe. He tracked the thing up into the last slivers of light, watching it catch those rays and reflect them, bowed and broken, in the curve of the glass.

Zeke lowered the helmet, putting it in front of the creature's face and letting him get a good look. "See? It's just a mask, like the ones we wear—but a little different." As he showed the sasquatch, he appeared to be genuinely curious and paying close attention. "I'm going to put this on you. It'll feel funny at first, but then you'll breathe better. You'll feel better, I think. I'm going to try it now. Let me do it, please? I don't want to fight you for it."

To Rector's frank astonishment, the brute held still, like he was kept in place with a madman's jacket and not an oversized net made of fisherman's yarn. He closed his eyes when Zeke lowered the helmet-mask, cringing when the seals settled around his neck. He stretched and leaned inside the device, gazing out at them with questions he couldn't ask and they couldn't answer.

"I know, it's a little tight. You're a lot bigger than the folks it was made for. I hope it's not too uncomfortable, though—and trust me, it'll be for the best. The seal is snug, but it's sitting against all that hair . . ." Zeke's voice trailed off apologetically.

Houjin mumbled, "I guess we'll find out." He was poking at the scrapes on his torso, doing his best not to scratch them. He realized he was being watched, so he quit worrying the minor injuries and closed his tattered shirt, then crossed his arms over his chest to hug himself. "Well, now what?"

The sasquatch stared out at them, his head filling the fishbowl-shaped object to full capacity. His chest rose and fell with a little more difficulty than before, but he did not appear to be in any pain—or even, Rector noted, serious distress.

Angeline observed this, too. "Now, we let him be. The sun's down, or close enough to it, and we have trouble waiting tonight."

Zeke frowned. "We're leaving him?"

"Only for now, sweetheart. We'll come back for him in the morning, but it's best to keep him out of the way for now. Things are going to get messy inside these walls. Better he's safe in here than roaming out in the park." She paused, and said the rest as if she feared it was a terrible omen.

"Or out at the tower."

 *Twenty-eight*

As night fell, the city grew more anxious with every stretch of every shadow.

Hanging over everything was the knowledge—the absolute certainty—that violence waited on the other side of that bleak horizon when the sun was lost and the walls held only darkness. Together, the whole underground held its breath. The men at the Station, the Chinese in their district, the Doornails in the Vaults, the former pirates up at Fort Decatur . . . everyone took the logical precautions, stocked the necessary weaponry and supplies, and waited to hear that it was time to go.

Houjin had disappeared upon returning from their adventure with the sasquatch.

Rector assumed he'd gone to lie down or find Mercy Lynch to see about some salve for those scratches; but Zeke reminded him that, no, Houjin had business back at the Station with his alarm clocks and dynamite. If he was scratched up at all, he'd see Doctor Wong or work right through it. He was tough, that's what Zeke said.

Angeline had left them to pursue some interest of her own, though she hadn't specified what. So it was only the two boys for the moment, killing time inside Maynard's with a number of other men who were likewise waiting for word.

When word came, it arrived from down below.

It came on the silent feet of messengers who slipped up from the tunnels to warn the assorted factions that *It's here, it's now. They're moving, and we must move faster.*

Packs were hoisted onto backs. Masks were checked, and clipped to suspenders and belts. Goggles and spectacles with polarized glass were jammed quickly onto faces, and warm, shuttered lanterns were readied. They needed light, but not too much light. They needed to see, but not be seen.

As the men filed out the door, Rector and Zeke fell into line behind them, joining the flow. They'd already talked it over between themselves, and with the lumberman Mr. Miller. Their plan was not to make for the Station, but to head toward the tower. There, they would serve as lookouts, manning the perimeter and helping identify the enemy should the fray become heated.

They'd been given lanterns that were different from those the other men carried. These had been designed by the late Dr. Minnericht, and Yaozu called them *spotlights.* They were gas-powered and heavy—like a larger version of the focus beams Rector had seen a time or two before—but when they were lit and aimed, they directed a brilliant, steady light for many yards. They would use these lights to blind the tower men, and single them out.

"We aren't going to kill anybody, are we?" Zeke had asked.

Rector told him, "No, that's a job for other people. We're just here to watch our own. It's us or them, Zeke. Us or them."

Now that the moment had come, Zeke was valiantly holding his composure in place—better than Rector, maybe. Rector shook beneath the load of his oversized lamp. He felt uncommonly sweaty, and his heart wouldn't stop banging around in his rib cage. He was nervous, that was all. He knew it, but that didn't make it any easier.

On their way out the door, a woman's voice called Zeke's name.

It wasn't his mother, thank God. It was Lucy O'Gunning.

"Zeke, baby."

"I'm not a baby, Mrs. O'Gunning."

"I didn't mean it like that," she said. She seemed to wrestle with some internal question. Her brows furrowed, and her mechanical arm fidgeted with the edge of her apron. "I only mean . . . your momma doesn't know you're off to join them, does she?"

"I'm old enough," he said calmly. "And Momma's up at Fort Decatur with the captain, helping with the ships and hydrogen."

The last of the men exited Maynard's, leaving just the three of them standing on its threshold. Mrs. O'Gunning was nearly too worried to speak. She spoke anyway. "You don't have guns, do you?"

"No," Rector assured her. It wasn't true. One of the Station men had let him borrow one. But he was semiconfident Zeke had nothing on him except the miner's pick.

Zeke held his ground. "We're only playing a supporting role."

"Yeah? And who told you that?" she asked, knowing as well as Rector that it wasn't the way Zeke usually talked.

"Yaozu. He wants us out of the way, but he knows we can help. We'll be real careful, Mrs. O'Gunning, and we'll be back tonight for some cider, if you'll let us have any. I think we'll all be celebrating before long."

A new voice chimed in. "I don't."

Now Zeke started stammering. "Hello . . . Miss Mercy."

"Heading out to fight, are you? Well, I don't guess anyone could stop you. But I'm not looking forward to a celebration, because I know who'll be patching up those of you who fall out of trees, or get your fingers blown off, or get shot when the tower men realize they've been had."

Lucy O'Gunning nodded sadly. "You got the rooms set up?"

"As best I can. Rector, you've moved your stuff out, ain't you?"

"Yes, ma'am."

"Good. That's one more bed, plus the six we've got on either side. I pray we don't need 'em. Miss Lucy, I was hoping I could trouble you for a few bottles of your highest-proof grain alcohol. Might want it later on."

"Sure, honey. I'll get you what I've got."

Lucy reluctantly turned away from the boys and opened the door once more, it having closed itself behind them. But Mercy Lynch lingered, and she said to them, "Best take care of yourselves. I've seen boys younger than you made heroes, and made dead."

Zeke blushed, Rector would've sworn to it. "We'll take care of ourselves."

"I hope so. You're grown men, or close enough as makes no difference to anyone but your mothers. So stay alert, keep your head down, and don't take any silly chances." She left them with that, and the last thing Rector saw as she disappeared into Maynard's was the battered Red Cross on her bag.

Rector swatted at Zeke's arm. "Don't let her put you off. We got a job. Let's go do it."

"I know, but . . ."

"But nothing. Don't let her see you going soft."

They stuck to the faster tunnels, even though it meant they had to wear their masks; and they took the hand-cranked mining carts with gusto, their fretful energy making double time on the straighter stretches, carrying them through the lines of track that took them up the hill at a steeper grade. At the tunnel's end, where the tracks all stopped and the lanterns were turned up to their brightest glow, the travelers paused briefly to let their arms rest and their backs unwind from the effort.

Then they loaded themselves back up like pack mules and struck out for the city.

Each boy allowed himself one candle stub, carried in a hurricane glass. It barely did anything except tint the darkness yellow, but it was comfort enough to keep them moving forward. Someone standing half a dozen yards away couldn't have seen them, so little light did the candles offer—and that was the idea, but it made for slow going.

The blocks were darker than dark, blacker than night's usual fall, because it fell on Seattle, where the air was thickly curdled and surrounded by the wall and its omnipresent shadow, resisting any interference from the moon and candles alike.

Upon reaching an unmarked corner, Rector asked, "Are we going the right way?"

Zeke checked the compass Houjin had given him. "Yep."

"I never thought I'd say this, but I kind of wish Huey was here."

"We'd be better off with Angeline. Not saying he's useless or anything, 'cause he sure as hell ain't. But this has never been his part of town. She knows her way around better."

"I wonder where she went."

"So do I," Zeke admitted. "Heck, she might be waiting for us. Or listening. You never know, with her. That woman's got ears all over the place, and it's a good thing, too."

"Sure is."

"We should probably be quiet."

"Probably," Rector agreed.

And they *were* quiet, for about thirty seconds. Then Rector said, "But it's god-awful dark. And so quiet that I can't hear a damn thing. Does that make sense?"

"No, but I know what you mean. Hey—what's . . . ?"

Zeke stopped abruptly, and Rector stopped in time to keep from running into him. "What is it?"

"It's the wall."

"It's *the* wall, or it's *a* wall?"

"Can't tell." Zeke patted at the stones, running his candlelight up and down it. "I think it's *the* wall."

"Did we really come that far? I thought we were supposed to turn up toward the park before we hit it."

"We were. But we didn't."

"You're shit for a navigator, Zeke."

"That's what the captain says. And Kirby Troost. And Fang."

"I thought Fang don't talk."

"He writes things down just fine, and he signs with his hands. I don't read it too good yet, but I'm learning. Anyway, I'm pretty sure this is the wall. We overshot our turnoff."

"I think maybe you could be forgiven. It's goddamn dark out here."

"We should *really* be quiet."

"I know, I know." Rector swallowed hard, and dragged his hand along the wall. "I just wish we were using lanterns. Or we could break out these stupid spotlights. They're heavy, I swear to God."

"If we had lanterns, we'd be real easy targets."

"I know," he said again. "But how far off course do you think we went?"

"Can't be that far." Zeke stepped around him and put his free hand on the wall. "The wall runs in one big circle, so it's not like we'll get lost *now*. If we follow it north and east, we'll run right into the park."

"That's not the world's most comforting thought in the world."

"At least we'll know where we are."

What Zeke didn't say, and Rector didn't bring up, was that they had no idea where along the wall they were—and they had only a few hours worth of filters in their bags. If they didn't find the breach, or the tower, or some other landmark soon, they'd be in trouble.

Both boys knew it, and they thought about it.

It was the only thing that kept them quiet for the next fifteen minutes.

Fifteen minutes was long enough. It gave them time to determine that yes, this was *the* wall, and not *a* wall belonging to some

oversized building; and it gave them time to get within earshot of
the great breach, the broken place where poisonous air oozed out
into the Washington Territory. Out near the breach the Blight
thinned, becoming less dense from the leak that spooled out into
the woods like sludge running down a drain. Their candlelight
went farther. The boys took pains to cover the glass with their
gloved hands, and then Zeke blew out his own light entirely.

At the breach, there were people talking, but it was too quiet,
too distant yet, to recognize any of the voices. "Take the tail of my
jacket," Rector whispered. "Crouch down low behind me. We
don't want to get separated."

"Are they from the tower?"

"Don't know."

They drew up closer, knowing that their allies ought to be approaching the big, ugly break in the wall as well—but not knowing if they'd arrived ahead of them, or if these were other men
coming inside from the Outskirts to reinforce the impending fray.

But then Rector saw lanterns, and heard a loud *clang* that
shook the whole block. He and Zeke stopped moving, stuck right
where they were with one foot up and half a breath drawn in.
Then they heard, "Be careful with that!" They knew the voice.

"It's Huey!" Zeke said with relief.

Huey went on to inform some unseen person, "And keep it
away from the gas lamps. Keep it away from *all* the lamps, until I
say so. We'll need to pour it in a few minutes. Mr. Harper, do you
have those pipes set up? Those hydraulics?"

"Almost," Mr. Harper grumbled back.

Rector stood up straight and said, in an almost normal speaking voice, "Hey, Huey, and whoever else you got over there . . ."

The sounds of guns snapping to attention stopped him short.

He threw his hands into the air.

"I was just going to say," he continued, "that it's only me and
Zeke. Don't anybody shoot us!"

"Hey guys!" Houjin said cheerfully. Rector still couldn't see him through the gathered murk, but when the boy's shape emerged from the blackened fog, he recognized the gait and the general shape. "Everybody put down your guns."

Someone—Mr. Harper, Rector assumed—groused something about being ordered around by a schoolyard full of boys, but none of the boys in question gave a damn.

"How much longer before it starts?" Zeke asked.

Houjin looked anxiously up at the wall, and out through the darkness toward the tower. "Not sure, but not long. You two had better get in position."

Rector said, "We're headed there now. Got sidetracked."

"Sidetracked?"

"Lost," Zeke clarified. "It's dark."

"Do you know where you're supposed to go?"

Zeke nodded. "Roof of the old governor's mansion. Climb up the back side, where the wall's done fallen away, and up top we'll find extra gas for the lights."

"Yaozu made you memorize that, huh?"

"More or less."

"All right, then go on," he told them almost reluctantly. "I've got work to do here. Be careful."

Rector slapped him on the shoulder. "You, too, Huey. Now, you want to point us toward this governor's mansion?"

"Straight up the hill, count four blocks, and it's the big white house on the right. Can't miss it."

"I could miss a city full of houses at this time of night," Zeke said ruefully. "But I can count four blocks."

Before they left, a Chinese messenger came running up to Houjin. He had a lantern in his hand, and sweat had dampened his shirt. His mask's visor was filled with condensation, and his eyes were wide. He rattled off something fast that Rector didn't understand, but Houjin made a snappy reply and then translated the highlights.

"The Station men are setting up the pump boxes now. Rector, Zeke—you'd better run!"

Faster than they should have, Rector and Zeke tripped and stumbled through the shadowed city, using only Rector's candles and their wits to maneuver around dead and fallen trees, over uneven paving stones, up and down curbs, and past the first block . . .

Second block . . .

Third block.

By the third block they had to blow out Rector's candles, too; they were too close to the tower, and they knew it. They could hear the men out there, and once they were closer to block four, they could see the glow of still fires and gas jets illuminating the top floor where the men had been working.

Rector smacked into a barrier, let out a surprised grunt, and flipped forward before Zeke could let go of his jacket. The smaller boy fell forward, too—over a low ironwork fence that snagged his pants. They tore with a ripping sound that seemed ungodly loud. But when they held their breaths and listened, no one asked where it'd come from, and the noise of workers in the tower did not change its timbre or tempo.

"A fence!" Zeke whispered.

"Yeah, I know! Get offa me!"

"Sorry."

The fence was barely hip-height and made of cast iron; it had collapsed beneath them immediately following its assault on Zeke's pants. It was hard and sharp and covered in rust, but it didn't pose any real barrier to the yard, or the enormous house within it.

The boys collected themselves and stood on the lawn. A big lawn. Once, it was no doubt lush and green and landscaped. Now it was a flat expanse of nothing, leading up to a huge white blob that turned out to be not a house, but merely a porch. The porch had columns bigger than many of the houses Rector had ever seen.

"This *has* to be it," he said.

Zeke nodded, which Rector only barely saw. "Come on. Around back, they said."

But Rector heard something coming up fast, headed right at them. He grabbed for Zeke, missed him, and instead gave him a hard shove that sent him facedown into the brittle, gruesome grass. Zeke began to protest, but Rector threw a hand over his mouth—crushing the boy's mask against his face.

"Shh!" he commanded.

Zeke came to the immediate and well-advised decision to not fight, but to lie there as still as possible. It worked out well. Not three seconds after he'd hit the dirt, a man came dashing up past them—right past the mangled fence. The man was carrying a lantern that swayed and jerked in his hands as he ran, casting dramatic spears of light up into the fog and through the skeletal tree limbs that overshadowed everything near the park.

"Caplan! Westie!" he cried out.

Rector cringed, fearing for a moment that they'd been spotted after all . . . but no.

"Something's wrong!" he shouted toward the tower. Then he added, "It's me, don't nobody shoot!" which was absolutely the wisest way to approach anybody in Seattle, these days. "Something's wrong downtown!"

From the top of the tower, somebody hollered back. "What's going on? I don't see no fire! I didn't hear no dynamite!"

"No sir, the Station's still standing!"

"What do you mean it's . . . ?" Swearing followed, and the sound of someone descending the brittle metal stairs.

"It's starting," Zeke said in a muffled grunt.

Rector pulled his hand away from Zeke's mask. "It started already. We gotta go."

They picked themselves up and took half a dozen seconds to relight their candles. Then they ran, guarding the little flames with their palms. Behind them came the rising noise and clatter of men whose plans had been thwarted.

As promised, the back of the house had fallen down altogether, exposing three stories and a convenient set of stairs that started just above ground level. The boys pulled themselves quickly along the stairs and scrambled up, up, and up that third staircase, then up another set to the wide, flat roof.

From there, the city looked strange; it looked blanketed rather than poisoned. They could even make out the moon above, and its cool, shimmering light gave them just a hint of where everything around them was located. Still, Rector kept his eyes on his candle. He moved carefully, and reached a hand back to grab Zeke's shirt. "Stay close to me now. This roof is straight, but it might not be sound."

"Might not? More like probably *ain't*. The back wall didn't hold up, did it? That doesn't bode well for the roof."

"Hang close. I don't want to pull you out of a hole."

"Like Huey pulled you—"

"Can it."

"Sorry. You're right. I don't want to fall in a hole."

Rector found the roof's edge with his eyes only inches before his feet would've found it the hard way. "Stop!" he said—a little too loud, but Zeke obeyed. "Here. The edge is right here. Let's put our stuff down and set up before things get crazy."

With relief and exhaustion, they dropped the heavy packs that contained the big gaslights and all their accoutrements. Only once had they been shown how the lights were assembled, but it wasn't as complicated as it sounded. While they worked by one small bubble of candlelight, they eavesdropped on the tower from behind a row of long-dead shrubs.

"All of them? At once?"

Rector said, "That's Otis, I think."

"It must be something with the gas, or something. Messing with the wires."

Zeke asked, "Who's that?" and Rector answered, "I don't know."

"That's one goddamn hell of a coincidence!"

The clattering of descending footsteps echoed like the banging of gongs, and Otis Caplan's lantern lit up the small windows as he passed each one. When he reached the bottom floor he kicked the gate open and stomped out into the yard, shouting for various lieutenants and henchmen. Some followed him down the tower, down the stairs—and some charged up from Millionaire's Row, coming up the wide streets with their lanterns held high and a great deal of complaining.

"What are you all doing back here?" he demanded.

"Sabotage!"

"What?"

"Someone sabotaged our sabotage! All of it! There's fighting down at the Station right now—they opened fire on us! They came right for us!"

"They were waiting for us! They knew we was coming!"

Zeke whispered to Rector, "You all ready to go?"

"Yep. How about you?"

"All I gotta do is flip the switch."

"Me, too." Then Rector asked, "How do we know when to turn 'em on?"

"Huey said we'd know."

Down in the open space, at the circle in front of the tower where all the streets met, Otis Caplan was furious. His light swung back and forth in his hand, as though he'd love for someone to come close enough to beat with it. He stalked toward the men, some of whom were bleeding and ragged, and a few of whom were wheezing like maybe their masks weren't working quite right.

"Where's everybody else?" he demanded.

"Still there. Or dead!"

"That's horseshit, and I won't hear it!"

"But, sir!"

"It's horseshit! Those damn Station monkeys and that yellow-headed, slant-eyed son of a bitch—"

Whatever else he had to say about Yaozu, he didn't get to finish it.

Behind him, a bell began to ring—the chime of a wake-up call. It jingled for two full seconds, giving everyone present just enough time to wonder what the hell was going on before the tower exploded.

It blasted outward and upward, a cascade of bricks blooming and billowing, flung from their foundations. Twisted, melted metal hurtled in 360 degrees, flattening whatever the bricks missed on their first wave and slicing trees into kindling. The bricks smashed any windows within a hundred yards, including those on the old governor's mansion; they gusted inward, a million little daggers glittering in the resulting fire.

And there was *plenty* of fire.

As the conical tower roof slapped down upon the park in peeling, shriveled pieces the size of horses, the still in the tower spread burning fuel in every direction—and everything close had sparked, and some of the sparks had caught.

Rector and Zeke looked up to see a dozen flickers of flame licking dead trees, downed walls, and the brittle shrubbery that once had decorated the manicured lawns. Only then did it occur to Rector that it hadn't rained in a week, at least. Maybe two.

He grinned. "Zeke, guess what: Summer's here."

"Must be, otherwise none of that shit would light."

"Speaking of light . . . I think this is where we come in." Rector cranked the little switch to turn on his spotlight, forgetting that the thing had been aiming straight up into his face. It came on with the brilliance of a dozen suns. He instantly dropped it—but Zeke caught it. "Jesus Christ!" Rector swore. "I can't see!"

Zeke laughed. "Me either, hardly. Give your eyes a minute, and turn that damn thing around!"

Blindly, Rector fumbled the light away from Zeke; he heard the sizzle of leather and thanked heaven for Fang's old gloves, even in their terrible condition, and he swung the light toward where the tower used to be. As his eyes adjusted, his lamp joined Zeke's beam, and the light of the two hissing, portable gas lamps with their heavy mirrors joined the glimmer of the growing fires along the trees. The ring of dead fauna spit and hissed, glowing warmly. It shined upon a scene of confusion . . . which was swiftly becoming a scene of pandemonium.

All the men who were able rose from the ground, crawling to their feet or simply crawling away. Otis Caplan was down for the count and maybe longer, but two of his men tugged at him—drawing him up and away from the smoldering rubble of the tower. They hoisted him, and he dangled—slung between them, a dead weight.

And then someone started shooting.

At the edge of the woodwork Chinese men and Station men waited, and Doornails, too. Rector and Zeke knew it, even though they couldn't see them—and it was their job to make sure the tower men didn't see them, either. The spotlights flashed and swung; the boys aimed at the tower men, blinding and revealing them as they tried to flee, or tried to mount their defense.

They had nowhere left to retreat to.

They were in the open, and there was far more light than anyone expected, though the fire was running out of fuel as it backed up to the wall. It fizzled and petered, but some of the bigger trees still burned, and gobs of brick fell from their branches, raining down on the heads of anyone unfortunate enough to hide below them.

The tower men shot back, and they struggled to rally. But there weren't enough of them left, and there weren't any places to hide except maybe . . . the big mansions. They could mount a defense from a place as huge as the governor's old place.

This dawned on Rector right around the time it dawned on a few of the brighter survivors. Rector pointed his spotlight down at those who ran toward him, and he told Zeke to do the same. "Hit them with it! Don't let them get inside!"

"These aren't guns! We can't shoot them and keep them away!" Zeke protested, even as he followed Rector's suggestion.

"Pretend they are. Hit them in the face and keep them blinded—make 'em easy to see!"

And then, he prayed, *maybe some of the Station men or the Doornails will pick them off before they reach us and kill us both.*

Three men fell to bullets before they arrived at the house's big black door. Seven more were behind them, and they missed the lights, dodged the bullets, and reached the columned front porch. Soon the boys heard the loud thunk of someone beating on a solid wood door, knocking it hard, shoving it with shoulders and kicking it with heavy boots.

"Shit!" Zeke said. "Can't hit 'em with the lights from here!"

"Not like this," Rector admitted. He stood up, balanced his spotlight on the edge, and said, "But maybe like this." And he shoved it over the side. It crashed down to the porch and through it, shattering somewhere below and showering the men with glass—but otherwise not hurting them, or so Rector thought.

Zeke followed suit, tossing his light over the side and listening for the smashing of timbers, roofing tiles, and maybe men's heads. But his didn't even break through the porch, and Rector grabbed him by the arm. "They don't know the back's fallen down. We have to get out before they get in!"

Now, with the fires and the shouting, there was plenty of light and noise to navigate by. The boys dashed back across the roof with their packs, so much lighter without those spotlights, and they half fell, half skidded down the stairs until they had dirt and dead grass beneath their feet again. At the front of the house, they heard the old door shatter.

"Where do we go now?" Zeke asked, nearly in a panic when he realized they weren't alone down there—that men were running back and forth around them, some of them friends, some of them foes. "We'll get shot!"

"We can't stay here, or we'll get shot anyway! Or burned up," Rector added, as if the second option were a better one. "Back to the crack in the wall—they know us there."

"But that's where the rest of these men are going . . ." Zeke pointed out, and it was probably true—Rector could see that now. The ones who weren't holed up shooting inside the hulking white mansion were making a beeline for the exit, a strategy that wasn't altogether idiotic, in Rector's considered opinion. So what the heck—he figured he'd join them.

"Four blocks down," he said.

"But they won't see us! They'll shoot us!"

"No, we'll go *this* way," Rector informed him as he took him by the wrist and dragged him in the opposite direction of what Zeke had clearly expected. "One block over the other way, then four blocks down. We'll have time to announce ourselves, and join the fight if there's a fight to join." It dawned on him just then that this was why armies wore uniforms, so you could tell your side's fellows from the other side's.

They dashed to the left and found the edge of the nearest block, then hunkered down long enough to light a lantern outside spotting distance of the park; but when it was lit, they didn't

take time to catch their breath. They only gathered their strength
enough to begin another dash, this time downhill—and only one
street over from the mayhem that was spilling down that same
hill, hoping to escape.

"Rector!" Zeke gasped. "Rector, do you hear that?"

Rector gasped back, "What?"

"I hear . . . I hear . . ."

And then Rector heard it, too. They weren't the only two people
who were wheezing their way along the hill. Something else was
nearby, something rather close and very sudden. It charged up out
of the fog and straight at them.

A rotter. An old one.

Zeke screamed outright, and Rector would've joined him if
he'd had the time to do so—but he didn't. Rector was out in front,
and the rotter seized him first. He shoved it back, and it pushed
forward, moaning and grunting as its jagged rows of broken teeth
snapped for Rector's face.

The dead thing struggled with strength it shouldn't have had.
A thing so skinny, so far decomposed . . . it shouldn't wield a grip
like that; it shouldn't have been able to grasp, hold, and bite with
such ferocity. It clung to Rector, pinning his arms and knocking
him to the ground where they rolled together, the rotter clamping
its jaws over and over, and Rector swinging his skull—his only
free weapon—in an attempt to headbutt the thing away from
him.

A second rotter loomed up out of the fog, revealed by the light
of the dropped lantern. Rector tried to call out and warn Zeke,
but bless the kid, he was already on it.

The pick was in his hands, its handle slung over his shoulder
like a baseball bat. Zeke shook with terror but he held his ground,
his feet planted to the spot as if he'd grown roots there—and
when the rotter came in close, running up with no idea of anything except that it was hungry, Zeke swung and hit a home run.

The pick went through the rotter's left eye and came out the back of its head. Through sheer centrifugal force, Zeke swung around and ripped out the eye, the temple, and part of the brain, which splattered against a boarded window and dribbled downward.

But there was no time to call it a victory.

Rector had leveraged his knee up between himself and the rotter. He threw the creature back, but only a bit; it snapped for his arm, almost caught it, but didn't quite. Then Zeke was on top of it, taking another swing. His second shot wasn't as clean as the first, but he clipped it heavily with the side of the pick, knocking it off balance. The rotter fell away, letting Rector climb to all fours so he could retrieve his ax . . . if he could find it. It'd been strapped to the pack he wore on his back, which had fallen off when the rotter hit him. Where was it?

There.

He seized it and threw it, almost in the same motion. From his position on the ground, Rector lacked the room and the leverage he would've liked, but this was a rotter, so when the ax caught it in the throat, it still tumbled backwards, largely without its head.

Zeke reached the twitching rotter first. He yanked the ax out of its throat, dropped it down on the thing's face once for good measure, and then handed it back to Rector. As he helped Rector up, Zeke asked, "Are you all right? It didn't bite you, did it? Is your mask still on tight?"

"Yeah, yeah. Yeah to all of that," he said, but he sounded drunk. He felt drunk. His head hurt and everything was spinning. He was reasonably certain he was going to faint.

Zeke shoved the ax back into his hands. "I hear more of them—we have to run for the Sizemore House! We'll get down in the cellar!"

"How will we . . . how will we find it?"

"We're two blocks down and one block over. I've been counting. Two more blocks, and we ought to hit it." He retrieved the lantern. "If not, we turn back for the wall and try again. You're sure you ain't bit?"

"I'm sure." He swallowed hard, resisting the urge to pat himself down. There wasn't time. He shook his head and it still hurt, but it would have to work whether it wanted to or not. "I'm fine. I'm fine, I swear. Let's go."

This time when he ran, it began as a wobble, but he picked up speed as the slope worked in his favor. One more block down, and he asked, "How much farther? Was that one block or two? I can't tell where the break is, in the dark."

As if someone on high had heard his complaint, a billowing blast of vivid orange flame erupted to his right. He could actually feel the warmth of it radiating outward in a roiling thunder of superheated air, slapping against him and rippling his clothes.

He and Zeke shielded their eyes from the wall of flame, for the amazing light burned through the fog like nothing they'd ever imagined. It was a perfect, steady flare, a pure barrier that closed off the crack in the wall so that nothing would enter, and nothing would leave. Nothing would survive the passage.

"So *that's* what Houjin wanted the diesel for," Rector mused.

"What?"

"Diesel. It's fuel. We stole some from the tower. He said it burns."

"He wasn't half kidding," Zeke agreed. He lowered his hand and squinted into the light. "They won't let any of them go, will they? All those fellows are going to die."

"One way or another. If there are any survivors, I bet you we've got new rotters in the morning. Yaozu will see to that."

"And we helped kill them."

Rector did not say that he expected that he'd helped kill more than a few people, given how long he'd been selling sap, and how many people he'd watched it kill. "It was us or them, you know."

"I know. But still. It feels . . ."

"Don't worry about how it feels, 'cause that don't matter right now. What matters is we routed 'em, and they can't touch us—or the Vaults, or the Station, or Chinatown either. Maybe it's dark and wet, and maybe it's full of hungry dead things, and maybe it smells bad and the food tastes weird and the place is falling down around our ears. But that don't matter, Zeke. It don't matter because Seattle is ours, and *they can't have it.*"

Rector sniffed and wiped a smudge of sooty sweat from under his chin.

"Now help me find the Sizemore House before any more rotters find us. Let's go home, all right?"

Twenty-nine

Come morning, everyone was battered, bruised, singed, and uninterested in getting out of bed . . . except for Zeke, who shoved at Rector's stiff, unhappy shoulders. "Get up, you. Come on, we've got to go get the inexplicable."

Into his pillow Rector mumbled, "I don't have to go do *shit*."

His head ached. His arms ached. His knee ached, and he wasn't even sure why. He had a deep-seated suspicion that if he pulled his face off the pillow, he'd see that Zeke was holding a far-too-bright lantern that would blister his eyeballs. This did not encourage any rising or shining on his part.

"Fine then, I'll just go by myself and tell everybody you were too chicken to come along."

Still facedown, Rector complained, "You wouldn't."

"I might."

Even though Rector didn't care—and he *didn't*—what Zeke did or didn't tell anybody, he rolled over. The blanket twisted around his legs; he kicked his foot free and cracked open one eye. He was right about the lantern.

It *burned*.

"Tell 'em whatever you like."

"You're already awake," Zeke noted. "Might as well get yourself up and do something useful."

He opened the other eye. "Why don't you drag Huey out to

play with the inexplicable, if it's so damn important to have company?"

"He didn't want to come. He didn't say that, but I know him well enough. It scared him, and he don't want to see it again. I can't blame him, except that I *do*." Zeke gave Rector another shove for good measure, then withdrew—holding the lantern higher and farther away, thank God.

"He's no dummy." But he sat up, rubbed at his itching eyes, and yawned.

"He's pretending he's got work to do. He's sticking close to the fort and pretending like he can't leave. But the captain's not even over there—he's off someplace with my mother. I bet."

"That must be strange."

"Yeah, but what am I going to say about it? He's all right, and even if he wasn't, he could toss me over the wall with his pinky finger."

"Ain't that the truth." Rector reached for his boots—or whoever's boots they were—and stuffed his feet inside them.

"Come on, hurry up."

"Don't rush me. I'm working on it."

He almost knew the way to the outer blocks by now. He realized this at the same time he realized that he still wasn't sure how to get back to the Station, so perhaps he'd made some kind of decision without noticing it.

Not worth wondering yet, not quite so soon.

The day was quiet after the night's cacophony of violence and light. It was an odd thing, and it felt like distance, but it wasn't, was it? The wall had a hole just a few blocks north; the city had a leak and terribly ill animals and dying people; and the tower was gone—blown to a million bricks by Huey's handiwork on the clock-bomb.

Neither Zeke nor Rector brought this up, even when they hiked through the fog-shrouded streets and sometimes kicked a gun, or noticed a nearly new gas mask lying beside a body.

Not all of the bodies became rotters. Most of them, yes. But nothing on earth is any use without its head. Few things are any use when they're cut or blown or chewed in half. Whatever the cause, no rotters reached out with rickety, grasping fingers as they slogged up the hills and between the narrow blocks of the time-blasted city. So instead of talking about it, the two boys only considered it as they walked side by side. They were careful to stick to the walls for shelter and cover, and they guided each other away from any debris that made them wonder, even in the slightest.

The prison itself was as they'd left it, quiet and squat. Missing its front door and still as clogged with Blight as ever, it was the very picture of someplace unloved and unused, and almost certainly forgotten.

Inside, Seattle's second city jail felt like the tomb it'd almost become seventeen years ago and change. Not a sound. Not a motion. Not a breath to stir the dusty beams of light that cut inside halfheartedly and none too efficiently. Not until Rector and Zeke came inside. Their filters gusted as they exhaled, and sparkling motes of yellow-brown dust eddied in the puddles of ill-formed illumination.

But then, listening and walking with exaggerated care, they heard the faint, rhythmic sounds of something large drawing steady breaths and pushing them out again. The barest hint of a filter's hiss underscored the sound, and then the slow, sad scrape of some fur-covered body part sliding along the floor.

Past the empty cells, with their leaning doors and rusting bars, they walked. Down the corridor of legend, where Maynard Wilkes had set the prisoners free and then raced to outrun the Blight.

It felt far away, same as the night before, and same as the silence after the fire.

And here was the great peacekeeper's descendant—a spindly thing, smallish and slender. A kind boy, if not the imposing man his grandfather was alleged to be. But his mother was a little woman, and come to think of it, Rector didn't know anything about Leviticus Blue. So this was what you got when you stirred up people and made families. Unexpected combinations. Unlikely weaknesses. Uncommon strengths.

Ezekiel Wilkes was not a bad sort. He'd worked so hard to save that fox, and he'd held his own on the top of the governor's mansion with the mirrors and lights. Perhaps Rector needed to rethink the things he thought.

The inexplicable was seated on the ground, wedged in the corner in his absurd glass helmet that fit too closely. But he was no longer tangled in Angeline's net. The net was discarded in pieces, shoved to the side.

Sasquatch looked up at them. His gaze sharpened. And it was probably Rector's imagination, but the creature looked . . . clearer. Not healthy, but *aware* in a way he hadn't previously.

Zeke began talking, because that's what Zeke did. "Hey there, Mister Sasquatch."

"He doesn't know his name. Angeline said so."

"I don't care," Zeke said. He didn't look back at Rector. Then, to the seated animal that was neither an animal nor a person so far as either one of the boys could tell, he added, "You're looking better. I see you looking at me, and I think your eyes are better. I know it's only been a little while, but the cleaner air will help you, if you let it."

He kept his voice level and smooth, and was careful to not make any sudden movements. It took Rector a moment to notice that he was copying Zeke's posture and methods.

"You know what you're risking," Rector breathed. "You open that door and turn that thing loose . . ."

Zeke took out a key—had he taken the key with him? Why

did everyone but Rector have keys?—and jammed it into the vintage lock with its rusty edges and squeaking mechanisms. He turned it, jerked the body, and the fastener popped and came away. The door opened. Inside Zeke stepped—still cautious, but with a curious confidence Rector wasn't sure he'd ever seen before.

(But he had. With the fox, back in the Vaults.)

And the world was full of surprises.

The inexplicable did not move except to track Zeke with his eyes, sparing a slashing look of curiosity toward Rector. But since Rector was hanging back, he kept most of his attention on the scruffy, brown-haired boy in the weird mask. His gaze drew circles on the mask, as if trying his damnedest to understand what it was, and what was underneath it. Not looking at Zeke's face, but trying to figure out if Zeke had a face.

"It's a mask," Zeke told him, as though he were reading the creature's mind. "Does the same thing as yours." He pointed at his filters, at the visor. And then he very, very slowly crept forward until he was well within grabbing distance, then crouched down just far enough to be at eye level with the sasquatch. He held up one finger, moved it slowly to the bulbous glass helmet, and gently tapped its nearest filter.

The inexplicable cringed.

Zeke didn't. "See? Same as mine. And I bet you're thirsty as can be inside that thing, but you can't take it off quite yet."

"I said, he don't understand you. Everyone says he don't understand you," Rector told him from his position of relative safety, back behind the door. He was already working out the mental ballet—the emergency measures that would surely force him to shut the door with Zeke inside, buying himself the minute and a half necessary for a head start before the creature yanked it clean out of the wall and came after him.

Zeke ignored him. "Mister Sasquatch, I'm going to take this

cuff off you now, all right? Please don't . . . please don't pull my head off, or anything. I'm only trying to help."

"You're insane."

"Here, like this. I'm taking your arm now. Don't hurt me or nothing, 'cause I'm not trying to hurt you."

The chain rattled dully in Zeke's gloved grip as he wrestled with the key and did his best to keep from hurting the manacled thing on the floor. The sasquatch studied his every move, either waiting for an opportunity or only trying to figure out what the hell was going on, Rector didn't know. When the cuff came off, it dropped with a heavy clank and kicked up a tiny cloud of angry dust.

Immediately, but slowly, the creature reached his hand up and touched the filtered helmet.

As if it hadn't occurred to him that it was a bad idea, Zeke shot his hand out and took the thing's wrist. "No!" he said quickly, then withdrew just as fast as he'd objected. Rector knew that look—it was a gesture he'd seen a hundred times on the outside, when other kids had picked on Zeke and he'd ducked back, waiting to get hit.

He didn't get hit.

"You . . . you got to leave it on, see?" Zeke did his best to explain, but confusion and discomfort was written all over the thing's puffy, dark-colored face. "You got to leave it on. But not for too much longer—because we're taking you outside."

"I think it's too soon."

Over his shoulder, Zeke said, "He'll die of thirst if we leave him here too much longer, and he can't have anything to drink while he's in the helmet. You can tell he's better. All we have to do is get him outside."

"If you say so."

"Just help me, would you?"

"How?" Rector asked.

Zeke made a frustrated little noise in response. "Stay out of the way, I guess. And if this thing kills me, run home and tell my mother so she don't wonder what happened."

"Great. I'll do that." *And she'll blame me,* he added in his head. "Did you even bring a gun?"

"No. You heard what the princess said about guns."

The whole time he talked, Zeke kept eye contact with the creature, and not Rector. He took a step back, and then another one. He held out his hands in an inviting gesture, urging the creature to stand up and follow him. "Come on, Sasquatch. Let me help you get home. Let me get you out of here."

Not wholly convinced, but game to see where this was headed, the sasquatch scooted unsteadily to his feet. He folded his legs under himself and shoved, bracing his hands on the wall, on the floor, on the window frame and the half-rusted bars that still filled it. The cuff on his other hand fell slack, its chain already dislodged from the manacle and the wall, both.

"He could've walked out of here anytime," Rector marveled.

"Maybe. I don't know. The other lock was in better shape, and he's pretty weak right now." Zeke backed away farther, to the door's edge, to the spot where Rector was stuck as if there were nails holding his feet down to the hard-packed earth floor.

The sasquatch followed him, wobbling and scratching at the seal around his neck.

"Oh . . . *boy* . . ."

"Hush up, Rector. He's doing fine."

Out through the front doorway where there wasn't any door left to close, and into the deserted streets where there wasn't any fire anymore, the inexplicable followed Zeke. Stalked him, even. His legs weren't very stable and his head looked ridiculous inside that globe, but he didn't pry the mask off, and he didn't tear Zeke's head off. Rector didn't have anything to do except look out for rotters.

Rector brought up the rear, watching the sasquatch strive to keep his head up. Sometimes he tipped and toppled, then jerked up straight again. "The mask is heavy," Rector observed. "It must be hurting his neck."

"Must be," Zeke replied, glancing backwards and around, keeping track of all the rocks and debris in his path. He avoided the clutter where he could, and climbed over it where he couldn't. All the while, he kept his arms up and out, showing he meant no harm, and asking the sasquatch to follow.

Please come with me. Please let me help.

Up the hill a few more blocks, not very far. There weren't any people there yet, but the previous night's battle was increasingly evident. Zeke shuddered when the way was blocked by a pair of mutilated corpses. (Mutilated by what? Neither of the boys looked too closely.) Walls were burned and charred pieces of clothing billowed in the Blight as it moved on its usual currents. Pieces of hair and flannel with burned-off edges rolled into the gutters in clotted clumps.

Rector thanked God he couldn't smell a damn thing.

The breach in the wall was not yet repaired, and might not be for a while yet. But it was covered, down at the base, by a great flap of burlap and wax, stitched together hastily and imperfectly and strung across the crevice like a curtain.

"Better than nothing," Rector breathed. How much better, he couldn't say.

By now, Zeke was prepared to trust that his strange ward wouldn't run away or take to violence. He turned his back and climbed the lowest rocks to reach the curtain. He fumbled with the ties that held it, and the sasquatch watched with his vivid, unblinking eyes.

Those bright eyes widened when the flap came aside, revealing a hole. It was large enough for Zeke to walk through, almost, so it'd be large enough for the sasquatch to crawl through.

Light came through on the other side. Not brilliant light, but a creamy, soft glow that was far more mist than Blight.

Through the hole, Rector saw trees, and the edge of an old building, and part of a road that nobody but the tower men had used in years. He saw the rest of the world, away from the Station and the Vaults, and out of the Blight (or it would be, when they got this hole fixed); he saw a portal to someplace else a million miles away. And it was right over there, a handful of feet on the other side of those huge, rumbling rocks.

He could've climbed through it as easily as the sasquatch.

 *Thirty*

The next day, Rector found the old jail again without too much trouble. He had a compass and a lantern, though it was daylight and he hoped he wouldn't need them. He also had his ax, some extra filters, a canteen of water, some dried cherries and pemmican, and a number of other just-in-case supplies in the pack he wore on his back. A pack kept his hands freer, and his balance was better in the event he needed to run or climb.

He was no great fan of running or climbing, but in the walled city he never knew when it might be called for. There were rotters, after all.

Not as many rotters as there once were, no. Still, their ranks had plumped overnight for reasons everyone knew but nobody talked about. He didn't like them, but he knew the city needed them, after a fashion. So he learned to take precautions and tried not to complain too much.

This was his first jaunt alone through the city since the day he'd arrived.

He didn't yet know his way around as well as he'd like, but he had one of Mr. Miller's hand-drawn maps and he'd been up and down the hill enough to know some of the landmarks. He knew where the wall was, anyway—and if you found the wall, you could find your way almost anywhere.

If you had enough filters. If you didn't die of thirst.

Every trip to the surface was a risk even once you got used to it, like most of Seattle's residents had. Even if you were ready for anything, and in tip-top physical shape, the rotters could still get you. The gas could still get you.

Rector thought maybe this was the only place in the whole world where you could die just from standing still. But he wasn't standing still. He was on his way to the old jail.

Dark, cool, and spooky, it was a relic of a place. Rector could feel it: Here was a spot where a story happened . . . a *real* story, not something made up and fed to small children so they'd sleep, or be proud, or behave.

Not every place had a story like the jail, or Maynard. Or the sasquatch.

It was brighter inside the jail today.

The sun was up above the Blight, burning clear in a vivid blue sky for the first time all year. If Rector was lucky, it'd be dry and bright for a couple of months—and even warm, for a while. If he was less lucky, better weather would come in fits and starts, without settling in until September, at which point summer would vanish one afternoon as if it'd never been there at all. Since it hadn't.

But for now, while the brilliant sky worked hard to cook off the ever-present fog, everything was kind of all right.

Dust specks and dirty air polluted what sunlight made it inside the old jail. The bits of abandonment floated smoothly, silently, stirred only by Rector's presence. His foot kicked against something that clinked.

When he looked down, he saw the jailer's key ring, cracked and crumbled almost to dust. It'd been discarded by the door and forgotten for almost as long as Rector had been alive, but it was a token. A relic more than an artifact.

He picked it up because it seemed rude to leave it. Maybe he'd give it to Zeke. Maybe he'd put it on a saint's card.

"He's gone."

Rector whirled around. He knew the voice, but it nearly stopped his heart since he'd thought he was alone. "I know the inexplicable's gone. Me and Zeke took it outside yesterday. What are you doing here, Miss Angeline?"

She leaned against a brick support post, arms folded and gas mask showing nothing but her eyes. She wore what she always wore: menswear that had been tailored down to fit her. Her silver hair was braided and coiled back, and today it was mostly covered by a scarf, except where snowy tendrils peeked out around her ears.

Rector looked back and forth between the woman and the empty cell.

"Where are Zeke and Houjin?" she asked.

"Still in bed, I expect."

"Everyone's had an exciting couple of days. Some more than others. But I'm glad you boys are all just fine. I'd have felt pretty bad if any of you'd gotten hurt. I'd feel responsible, a little bit."

"Why's that?"

"I was the one who helped you learn your way about, and roped you into helping with the sasquatch. I urged you to poke your noses around the tower. Everything worked out for the best, I reckon, but even so, you don't want anyone to get shot up over it."

Rector had been wondering something, though it only just then sprang to his mind. And since the princess was standing right there, he went ahead and asked. "Where were you that night at the tower, Miss Angeline? I didn't see you anyplace, once the fighting got started." Quickly, he amended the question to include, "I'm not accusing you of chickening out or nothing— 'cause I'm real sure you didn't. Or wouldn't. I just didn't see you, that's all."

She smiled inside the mask, her eyes crinkling up tight. "Funny thing about being an old lady . . . sometimes, it's like being invisible. I was there, honey. Trust me on that one. And I saw you and

Zeke up on the old governor's mansion. You two did a real good job."

"Thank you, ma'am." He figured he wouldn't get a straighter answer out of her, so he didn't press for one. It was easier to change the subject. "Where do you think the sasquatch went, once he got outside the wall? Do you think he'll be all right?"

"Where'd he go?" She unfolded her arms. She stepped forward and came to stand beside Rector, staring into the empty cell right along with him. "If you forced me to give you my best guess, I'd say he had a long nap and woke up feeling better—feeling clearer, and stronger. I'd say he pulled off the mask, or his lady friend pulled it off him. He'll have to eat and drink. One of 'em will take care of it."

"You think they're that smart?"

"I think instinct is an interesting thing, for all the things it can tell a body. What are your instincts telling you, these days?"

He frowned at her. "What?"

"You heard me. What do your instincts say about being here, staying here? You going to hang around the Vaults, or go to the Station? You going to stay inside Seattle, or seek your fortune someplace else?"

"I'm gonna . . ."

He thought of his small room in the Vaults, not unlike the room he'd had in the orphanage a few weeks before. He considered the Station and Yaozu and Bishop, and Zeke and Houjin, and earning an honest living or a dishonest one, but earning something, somewhere.

"It looks like you folks need a few good men around here."

"We do," she replied too solemnly to imply anything.

"The place is falling apart. Yaozu's got money, but not as many people as he needs. And those docks—the ones the captain's setting up at Decatur—he'll need people to man them. The patch job where the wall's broke—what'd they use, canvas? That won't hold anything, and it'll take a lot of fellows a few weeks to fix it, at least. Never mind all the tunnels falling down and the buildings rotting where they stand, if they still stand. There are jobs in here, that's all I'm sayin'. And there aren't any jobs out *there,* in the Outskirts. Not for someone like me, unless I want to go back to selling." He said it offhandedly, as if the thought hadn't occurred to him.

Angeline went ahead and asked. "Do you want to go back to selling?"

Why lie? "Yeah, I do. It's easy, and everyone's always happy to see me."

"But?"

"But," he paused. "I can't handle the sap anymore. That's not to say I don't want it, but I know I can't have it. It'll kill me."

Which didn't stop him from promising himself, in the back of his head, that next year, on the anniversary of leaving the orphanage, he'd treat himself. On his birthday, he was allowed; that's what he'd decided. That was the only thing that held his cravings at bay, the prospect that this lull was only temporary and it couldn't possibly last. He hoped maybe he'd be strong enough, come next birthday, to put off any indulgence until the birthday after that . . . and then the birthday after that. Each year it might get easier, or it might not.

But for now . . . for now he needed to think. He needed to figure things out. He'd resolved to survive another year, and he'd need his brain if he wanted to make that work.

So. Yes. Just for now. No more sap. Not until next year.

Next year he'd give it a shot, or he wouldn't. Next year he'd start seeing ghosts again, or they'd leave him alone. Next year, maybe he'd have a better idea of what he wanted, or where he wanted to be, and what he wanted to do.

But for *now* . . .

Epilogue

Mercy Lynch adjusted the electric lantern, propping it atop a stack of weathered, damp-swollen books. The light burned brightly across the desk in her office, in her clinic, in her city; it spilled across her hands, and it cast weird shadows across the woman who stood behind her, overseeing her progress.

Mercy frowned at the paper and tapped her pen's nib into the inkwell. "Miss Angeline, how do you spell your name? I've got the first part, but I don't know about your daddy's."

"You could just spell it 'Seattle' if you want to."

"I'd rather do it right."

Angeline smiled, and patted the younger woman's shoulder. "You don't have the letters for it, not in English. But when I write it down for white folks, I do it like this . . ." she said, taking a pencil nub and scratching *Sealth* on the nearest scrap of unused paper. "And that's close enough."

"Thank you, ma'am. That'll work just fine. And thank you for keeping an eye on that redheaded boy."

"Somebody had to do it."

"I'm glad it was you. You're a good reporter, and now that we've got all these notes between us, I'm getting a picture of what sap withdrawal looks like. After a fashion."

"You really didn't think the boy would make it, did you?"

Mercy shook her head and reached for a large envelope she'd

stitched together out of canvas and twine. "No, I didn't. I've never seen anybody that far gone come this far back. Rector's shown us the outer limits of what can be survived. Of what can be saved. He's young, and that worked in his favor; but he wasn't so healthy at the start, and that worked against him. All in all, I think he's been a real good test case."

"Poor fellow never had much of a chance. The children they pulled from the city, especially the ones as little as he was . . . not all of them lived long enough to grow up at all. And them that did didn't always grow up right." Angeline stood up straight and stretched her shoulders. She walked to the edge of the sickbed and sat down on it.

Mercy paused, then gathered her stack of papers and began to stuff them inside the makeshift envelope. When the package was full, she turned her seat around to face Angeline. "Are there any figures on that? Any numbers, about the things that went wrong with the little ones?"

"None to my knowledge, unless maybe the orphanage kept track."

"But Rector's the last of them, ain't he? The last one of that generation."

"If he's not the last, he might as well be. The rest have either growed up and moved on or died. Just like Rector would've died, without you looking after him."

The nurse shrugged this off. "All I did was let him alone, and make sure he got plenty of water. His own body did the rest. He's looking brighter now, have you noticed? The yellow under his eyes, I think it's fading. Might even go away, someday, if he keeps his nose clean."

"It might or might not. He might, or might not."

"He seems to get on good with Zeke and Huey. Maybe they'll be a good influence on him."

Angeline cocked her head, and nodded to indicate that it was possible. But then she said, "Or maybe he'll be a bad influence on them. It could go either way."

"Oh, I don't know." Mercy tied her package up with twine, being careful to leave the address clear. It was going to Sally Louisa Tompkins, care of the Robertson Hospital in Richmond, Virginia. "Huey's too smart to fool, and Zeke's such a gentle thing . . . I think they can handle their new friend all right."

"As long as he keeps his nose clean." Angeline borrowed Mercy's expression.

"Yes, well. There's that. But you didn't catch him using, or see any sign that he'd done so?" she asked for the dozenth time.

"No, dear, I didn't. And no one out at the Station would give him any—on Yaozu's orders. If that boy can keep his head on straight, and if he can stay away from the rotters, and if he can keep his mask on, and if he can make himself useful down here somehow or other . . . he might be all right."

The nurse held the package in her lap and absently ran her fingers over the address. The ink had dried, and nothing streaked. "We sure do say *might* a lot, don't we?"

"The world's an uncertain place."

"That it is," she agreed. And then, somewhat quietly, "More uncertain than either of us knows. But someone, *somewhere* knows. And someone, somewhere is keeping everyone god-awful quiet."

"You mean, how all those men disappeared? The ones you tried to reach?"

For a moment Mercy was silent. She stared down at the package. "Not the ranger, not the Union captain, not the passengers I shared the car with. Not the Mexican inspector, and not the Confederates who made it out alive. *No one,* Angeline. It's too many people to be a coincidence. Too many people lost, or silenced."

Then, as if to change directions, she said, "You know how slow I write, don't you? I'm not too good at it, and that's no secret."

"You do a real fine job, Mercy."

"No, I don't. But it's kind of you to say that. And you know that every time I send Captain Sally a stack like this, I write it out again so I have a copy. It takes me forever and a day, but sometimes I feel like I'm mailing these things to a hole in the ground, and I can't stand to see it lost."

"That Captain Sally sent you a message by the taps once, over in Tacoma."

"That's true, she did." Mercy lifted the package, squeezed it, and listened to the brittle paper rustle within. "But all it said was that my reports arrived, and I should keep sending them. And . . ." She set the package aside. "And anyone on earth could've sent that message."

"Now you're just getting yourself all worked up for nothing."

Mercy's hands fluttered, as if she wasn't sure what to do with them. She picked up a pencil stub and chewed pensively upon it. Then she removed it from her mouth and asked, with deadly seriousness, "Am I?"

Angeline shooed her worries away with a flip of her wrist. "Of *course* you are, baby. Your letters are getting through just fine, only it feels like years 'cause you're mailing through a war zone. Maybe some of your messages get lost, that's possible, sure. But no one's stealing them on the other end. No one's burying them in a hole."

"Or burning them," she murmured. "Or hiding them. Or giving them to the wrong people to read."

"Now that's just *nonsense*. What would anybody want with your notes, except a doctor wanting to treat these men?"

Mercy rose to her feet and pushed her chair back under the desk with the back of her knee. She gave her pencil stub another bite, and then came to sit beside Angeline on the edge of the low-slung bed. The lantern gave both of them a chilly glow. It wasn't warm light, and it cut the room into peculiar shadows.

Softly, the nurse said, "Sap is a terrible thing, and the world is full of men who trade in terrible things. You said it yourself: There's a war, Angeline. And wars *feed* on terrible things. The Union has plans to make this nasty powder into a weapon, and if they take too long at it, I'm sure the Confederates will try it for themselves. The notes I'm sending to help Captain Sally find a cure . . . they're notes that could help make terrible things. And that's exactly the opposite of what I want to do. But it cuts both ways. I can't say the truth and promise who will hear it, or how they'll use it."

They rested in companionable quiet, save the fizzle and pop of the electric light.

Finally Angeline tried, "You know, when the air dock's finished up at Fort Decatur, things'll be easier for your notes. First a dock, then some taps. Then you won't have to rely on people like me, or Captain Cly, or anyone else to send your messages. You could just fire off a telegram and ask if everything arrived all right."

"I do look forward to that day, Miss Angeline. And I do wish for word from . . . someone, anyone who was with me on the *Dreadnought*."

Angeline's pocket began to chime. She pulled out a watch and gave it a glare. "That's my reminder, I need to head out if I want to catch the train to Tacoma."

"Then you'd best be going."

The princess winked, then climbed to her feet. "I see how it is."

Mercy gave her a friendly swat on the leg and said, "You know good and well you're welcome here, you ol' madwoman. I swear."

"I'm just joshing you," she grinned. She made for the door, then stopped herself. "You know," she said, "you should keep trying for that Texas Ranger. I bet he's the one you're most likely to reach."

"You think?"

"Sure. He's not Union. He's not Confederate. If there's some awful conspiracy, you don't think it covers both territories and Texas, too, do you? Texians don't answer to either one, except when they feel like answering to the South."

"It's a good thought, Angeline. Thank you, I'll try him again—through the rangers office in Austin."

"Good girl. Don't you give up on it yet. Too many people know about that train for everybody to vanish at once. You'll find him," she vowed, and she tipped her hat before leaving the nurse alone.

When Angeline was gone, Mercy sat back down at her desk.

She picked up a piece of paper and pencil, but her hand hovered over the blank sheet. She changed her mind and put down the pencil, pushing away the paper and worrying about the Texas Ranger who'd been her companion on the westward journey.

Where had he gone? Where had *everybody* gone?

She murmured, "And if I hadn't disappeared into Seattle, would I have disappeared anyhow . . . just like everyone else?"